Without warning the bottom of the box burst, and cold paper-wrapped steaks scattered on the ground, leaving Zoey holding nothing but soggy cardboard. She swore softly. The box was useless; the bottom was completely gone. She threw it aside and knelt down to begin gathering the steaks. But she had only picked up three or four when the tears she had been holding back for so long caught up with her.

Zoey sat among her strewn steaks and wept, wept at the unfairness of the fire. It had taken everything from her: her home, her parents' health, her college tuition, her freedom, everything. She buried her face in her hands and cried silently in the moonlit street.

She didn't stop even when she heard footsteps. That'll be Christopher, she thought. He'll help me carry these steaks.

But it wasn't Christopher who said, "Zoey?"

It was Lucas.

Titles in the MAKING OUT series

1. Zoey fools around
2. Jake finds out
3. Nina won't tell
4. Ben's in love
5. Claire gets caught
6. What Zoey saw
7. Lucas gets hurt
8. Aisha goes wild
9. Zoey plays games
10. Nina shapes up
11. Ben takes a chance
12. Claire can't lose
13. Don't tell Zoey
14. Aaron lets go
15. Who loves Kate?
16. Lara gets even
17. Two-timing Aisha
18. Zoey speaks out
19. Kate finds love
20. Never trust Lara
21. Trouble with Aaron
22. Always loving Zoey
23. Lara gets lucky
24. Now Zoey's alone
25. Don't forget Lara
26. Zoey's broken heart

Coming soon
27. Falling for Claire
28. Zoey comes home

MAKING OUT

Zoey's broken heart

KATHERINE APPLEGATE

Pan Books

Cover photography by Jutta Klee

First published 1998 by Macmillan Children's Books
a division of Macmillan Publishers Limited
25 Eccleston Place, London SW1W 9NF
and Basingstoke

Associated companies throughout the world

ISBN 0 330 35261 X

1 3 5 7 9 8 6 4 2

A CIP catalogue record for this book is available from
the British Library.

Printed and bound in Great Britain by
Mackays of Chatham plc, Kent

To my brother, Chris,
with thanks for a lifetime of technical support

Zoey

I was in the shower when my roommate, Anika, came into the bathroom with the cordless phone and said it was Mr. Preston calling for me. I stuck my head around the edge of the shower curtain and said, "Who?" because the only Mr. Preston I know is our neighbor on Chatham Island, and I couldn't imagine why he'd be calling me in California.

So Anika said, "Mr. Preston, your neighbor," and I said, "Well, for heaven's sake, tell him I'll call back; I'm in the shower," but she just held out the phone with this worried look on her face and said, "He says it's important."

That should have worried me, but it didn't. The words didn't even sink in. I was too busy wondering if Mr. Preston knew that I was in the shower, which would mean he also knew I was naked, and how that would be pretty gross. But the second I put the phone to my ear and heard him say my name, I knew something horrible had happened, and the first words out of my mouth were, "How are my parents? Are they okay?"

Mr. Preston hesitated, and then he said, "They're

going to be," and I
didn't even hear what he
said next because I was
so relieved.

It's funny, writing that
all down. It sounds like
it happened so slowly,
but in reality it was just
a matter of seconds. It all
happened in less time
than it takes to walk from
one room to another, but
even so, I had time to
think: Now I have to go
home. Now I have to go
home and see Lucas.

Then it occurred to me
that Mr. Preston was
still talking. I had to ask,
"What?" and he said,
"There's been a fire. . . ."

Claire

I had just walked into my room when the phone began to ring. Something about that really bothered me. I guess it was the coincidence of the phone beginning to ring just as I walked into the room, as though someone knew I had just gotten home.

I guess I must've thought it was him. Sean. The stalker. Jake wasn't home, so I just shut the door behind me and let the phone ring and ring. Finally it stopped and then started again, and I thought, *Oh, this is ridiculous; what am I afraid of?* So I took a deep breath and picked up the phone.

And it was Dad, telling me that there had been a fire at the Passmores'.

"Passmores' the restaurant?" I asked.

"No, the Passmores' house," he said.

I still didn't get it. "Their garage or something?"

"No," Dad said. "The whole house. It's gone." And then he said something about survivors. . . .

Aisha

I was asleep and dreaming.
In the dream Felicia was
standing in front of me in a
beautiful red velvet gown, and
her hair was all drawn up in
this gorgeous, complicated style,
and she was about to put on
some of the perfume Christopher
had given me for my birthday.
I could see the bottle in her
hands so clearly. I told her
not to use my perfume, and we
began arguing back and forth,
and finally she said, "Oh, go on
and take it; I don't even like
it, anyway," and held out the
bottle, and just as I reached for

it I woke up and Felicia was holding out the phone and saying, "Aisha, wake up. It's Christopher, and he says it's important."

I was so sleepy that I was actually surprised that Felicia was wearing a Snoopy nightshirt and not a velvet dress. Very slowly I put the phone to my ear, and Christopher said, "Eesh, I don't know how to tell you this, but . . . there's been a fire at the Passmores'."

Right away I thought of Zoey and said, "Oh, no, not Zoey! She's not . . ."

"No, no," Christopher said. "She's in California, remember? And her parents are fine."

I was so relieved that I let out a huge breath. Christopher was still hesitating, though, and I realized that maybe he hadn't called me in the middle of the night to tell me that everything was okay. "But?" I asked.

"It's Lara," he said. "I don't know anything for sure. But it sounds . . . pretty bad."

Nina

I was at my wonderful office
job when the phone rang and The
Buzzard said, "Nina, it's for you,"
but of course she didn't give me
the phone; she sat there, holding
it and giving me her no-personal-
phone-calls lecture, and I was
saying, "Yeah, yeah," and nodding, and
so finally she gives me the phone
and it's Dad.

So I say, <u>what?</u> in this annoyed
way because I can't believe I had
to listen to The Buzzard's
lecture just for dumb Dad. But

then Dad said, "Nina . . . there was
a fire at the Passmores' house
last night. We've been trying to
reach Benjamin, but he's not
answering. Do you know where we
can find him?"

I didn't say anything, and after
a minute Dad said, "Nina, are you
there?" and I said that I was
and that I didn't know where to
reach Benjamin if he wasn't in his
room.

Dad hesitated and asked if there
were people with me, and I said
yeah, and then he said he thought
he might come by school and pick
me up in an hour if that was

okay. I said okay and thanked him for calling and we hung up.

I guess I must have looked pretty pale and freaked out because The Buzzard said, "Nina, why don't you go in the back room and fold the Wind Ensemble's concert programs?" (This is her idea of consolation.) So I went into the back room, and I had only folded a couple of programs when I looked down and saw a tear had made a big blotch on the front of one.

I suppose I had an idea of what Dad was going to tell me, but I was really crying for myself.

Because once I had been so close to Benjamin that I would have known where to find him. And I had been so close to Zoey that the call asking where Benjamin was would have come from her, and not my dad.

LUCAS

I WAS in the emergency room for exactly two hours. The doctor washed the soot off my face, cleaned my cuts with peroxide, and checked my pupils, all of which my mom could have done at home for free.

I asked the doctor if I could go to work, and he looked a little surprised. He said that I shouldn't take the boat out, but he thought I'd be okay to go work on the lighthouse.

I went behind this curtain

to get dressed, And the doctor said casually, "Lucas, how much do you remember about the fire?"

And I said, "Everything."

He said, "Tell me about it."

So I told him about finding Mr. And Mrs. Passmore near the front door And dragging them out And about the explosion And the fireball And how I could actually hear the Passmores' wallpaper crackling as it peeled off the walls, And landing on the soft cool grass.

The doctor said, "What about just before the explosion?"

And I said, "Uh-huh?"

"Did you see anyone?" the doctor asked.

And as soon as he said that, I remembered. There had been a slender form on the stairs behind Ms. Passmore—the form that disappeared after the explosion. . . .

BENJAMIN

My day started like any other normal day.
I just got up, went to class, had lunch, and
then took the bus up to Mount Sinai to see
my ophthalmologist. So I was gone basically
all day by the time I got back to my dorm.

I got straight on the elevator and stood
behind these two guys I recognized from my
floor. One of them said, "So why is that cop
hanging around? Did someone get busted?"
And the other one said, "No, he's waiting to
give someone bad news."

I thought, God, I wonder if someone's
grandparents died, although I'm not quite
sure why I thought that.

Then the first guy said, "What bad
news?" and the second guy said, "I heard
them talking about it at the front desk. His
half sister got crisped in a fire."

I was very removed during this conversation.
I was actually busy thinking that I hate the
slang everyone uses, like "shag" for "have
sex with" and "loaded" for "drunk" and
"crisped" for "killed," and how stupid it
makes us sound, because I do it, too.

Then the elevator opened and I got out
and saw the cop standing by the door to my
room, and I opened my mouth to say,
"Lara?" but all that came out was a scream.

One

Zoey waited outside Logan Airport in the twilight. Benjamin was picking her up, and he was late. She was wearing a red blouse of Anika's. It was a California blouse, thin and summery, and Zoey shivered slightly in the early evening breeze.

My blood has thinned, she thought. Then, *Don't be dumb. Blood does not thin in a matter of weeks.*

"Zoey!"

She looked up. Benjamin was waving at her from the other side of the crosswalk. Zoey was startled. He was wearing his old Ray-Ban sunglasses. For a moment it made her think of the old days, when he was blind.

But then Benjamin reached her and she was hugging him and everything felt okay again.

"Sorry I'm late," he said over her head.

"It's okay," Zoey said, still hugging him. At last she let go. "Gosh, it's good to see you."

"You too," Benjamin said, smiling down at

17

her. He picked up her suitcase and led her back to the car.

Zoey was surprised to see the old familiar van. But what else would Benjamin be driving? Their *van* hadn't burned down, just their *house*.

Benjamin unlocked the door for her and she climbed in, still marveling at how familiar everything was. Benjamin put her suitcase in the back and got in beside her. They pulled out of the parking lot, and Zoey was suddenly thankful that Benjamin had gotten his driver's license over the summer so that he could pick her up, alone. Zoey didn't feel that she could bear to talk to anyone else right then.

"When did you get home?" Zoey asked him.

"Yesterday."

"When—" She hesitated. "When is the funeral?"

His lips tightened. "Tomorrow."

Zoey rubbed her hand against her cheek. "Benjamin, I'm so sorry about Lara. I know how close you two had gotten."

"Thanks," he said.

His voice sounded distant, and Zoey thought, *I shouldn't have said that. He knows I could barely tolerate Lara. I shouldn't have pushed it.*

Suddenly Benjamin's hand closed over hers in her lap. "Thanks," he said in a warmer tone. "I'm glad you understand." He checked the rearview mirror. "Listen, are you hungry?"

"Oh, not really."

"Well, I am," Benjamin said. "Do you mind if we stop for something?"

"Of course not."

They took the next exit, and Benjamin turned into a McDonald's drive through. "What can I get you? A hamburger?"

Zoey shook her head. "I'm really not hungry."

Benjamin frowned. "You have to eat."

"I just want a Coke."

"Okay." Benjamin drove up to the intercom and ordered a Coke, Sprite, and a Big Mac. He drove to the pickup window and then pulled into the parking lot.

Zoey looked at him in surprise. "You're not going to keep driving?"

"No," Benjamin said, unwrapping his hamburger. "The Big Mac is too messy."

Zoey didn't say anything, but she wished he would keep driving. She was beginning to feel a little panicky. She wanted to see their parents and what was left of their house.

Benjamin took a bite of his hamburger and then put it on the seat between them as though it didn't interest him. He pushed the sunglasses up onto his head, and glancing at him, Zoey saw why he had worn them. His eyes were red rimmed and swollen. It looked like it would hurt to blink.

Benjamin avoided her gaze. He rested his elbow on the open window. "Zoey . . ." He sighed. "We should talk before we get home."

Zoey tensed. So that's why he had pulled in here, to break some horrible news to her. "What is it?" she asked warily.

He gestured inarticulately. "It's everything. Mom and Dad are in the hospital, and Mom, at least, is going to be there for a while."

"How long is a while?"

"Maybe eight weeks."

"Eight weeks!" Zoey repeated, horrified. "That's two months." She didn't know why it sounded worse to think of it in terms of months, but it did. "What about Dad?"

"The doctors say that Dad won't be in for quite so long, but probably several weeks."

Zoey's fingers were digging into the sodden side of her Coke cup. "Are they—burned?" she asked desperately.

Benjamin looked at her. "Yes, but not badly. Mostly they're suffering from smoke inhalation, which has messed up their lungs, apparently."

Thank God. Zoey let out a long breath. "How do they look?"

Benjamin seemed uncomfortable. "I hear they look okay," he said.

"You hear?" Zoey repeated. "Haven't you seen them?"

He shook his head. "You know how I feel about hospitals."

"But this is Mom and Dad!" Zoey said.

Benjamin didn't answer, but she saw his jaw tighten stubbornly. Zoey sighed. Well, *she* wasn't afraid of hospitals. She would go see her parents as soon as possible.

"And the house?" Zoey asked after a minute. She might as well find out just how bad things were.

Benjamin sighed. "The house is gone."

"Gone? What do you mean?"

He rolled his shoulders uncomfortably. "I mean—it's gone. There is *nothing* left. Nothing," he repeated, as if he could hardly believe it, either.

Zoey closed her eyes as pain gripped her heart. *Houses are inanimate objects,* she told herself sternly. *I will* not *cry over inanimate objects. I forbid it.*

After a moment she swallowed and opened her eyes. Benjamin was watching her. "You okay?"

She gave him a wan smile. "I will be." Then something occurred to her. "Was the house insured?" She felt naive asking that, but she honestly didn't know.

Benjamin nodded, but he looked troubled. "It was insured, but money is still going to be a big problem."

"I can imagine," Zoey said. "Who's going to run the restaurant while Mom and Dad are in the hospital?"

Benjamin ran a finger all the way around the steering wheel before he answered. "As far as I can tell, I think we are," he said finally.

"*We* are?" Zoey repeated. "But how can we? We're both going to college."

Benjamin nodded. "Yes, we're both going to college. Very, very expensive colleges."

"But you said there was insurance—"

"Zoey, there's some insurance, yes," he said. "About enough to cover the basic rebuilding and some medical expenses. But who's going to pay for furnishing the new house? Who's going to pay if Mom needs to stay in the hospital even longer? Who's going to run the restaurant? Who's going to pay *tuition?*"

"Okay," Zoey said angrily. "I get your point."

Benjamin reached over and took her hand again, gently. "I don't like it, either, but there's just no other way. We're going to have to drop out and enroll again next year."

But Anika and I are going to go skiing! Zoey thought irrationally. *I'm wearing her blouse! We're going to go to the Theta Chi party!*

A hard lump rose in her throat. She couldn't even look at Benjamin. She knew he was right. They had to come back to Chatham Island. Back to Lucas and everything she had wanted so much to leave behind.

She knew Benjamin wanted her to respond, to agree with him and start planning the future. But she could only stare out the window at the darkening landscape, jabbing her straw absently against the ice in her cup.

Finally Benjamin started the engine and put them on the road toward home again.

Two

Zoey was self-conscious as she and Benjamin walked up the aisle behind Lara's mother. The congregation was a blur, but she could still sense them all watching them, the *family members*, as the funeral director led them to the front row.

She sat down next to Benjamin with a small sigh of relief and quickly bent her head as the minister rose to deliver the eulogy.

Benjamin was stiff beside her, tall and formal in his dark suit, with his sunglasses firmly in place. Zoey didn't know if it was rude for him to wear the sunglasses indoors or if it was okay because it was a funeral. She wished her mother were here so that she wouldn't have to worry about it.

The eulogy washed over her as meaninglessly as air. Zoey couldn't concentrate. None of this seemed real. Lara—dead? Their house—gone? Their parents—hospitalized? No, none of it seemed real.

Zoey realized she was twisting her handkerchief into a knot and forced her hands to lie quietly in her lap. She looked toward the coffin at the front of the chapel—and that's when she saw Lucas.

He was in the second row on the other side, and Zoey could see him perfectly out of the corner of her eye. It took her breath away. His face. Lucas's face. She felt a sinking in her stomach as she realized that she'd been looking—hoping?—to see his face ever since she'd left Chatham Island. She had walked along campus, unconsciously scanning the crowds, searching for a pair of eyes with perfect crinkles at the corners, a mouth that smiled sardonically, longish blond hair. Now that she was actually seeing him, she could scarcely believe how wonderful he looked, how familiar and longed for and perfect. A lump rose in her throat, and she looked away.

I will not look back, she thought sternly. *I will not look at him. I will not look at him. I will not look at him.* I will not loo—

She looked.

Nina was in the same row as Lucas, and again Zoey's heart caught with a small tug. Nina's expressive mouth and large gray eyes, the brandy-colored hair—all the same. Nothing

26

had changed in the few weeks Zoey had been away.

Five, six, seven people separated Lucas and Nina on the pew, but Zoey was sure they were aware of each other's presence. Had they planned to sit together? Had they exchanged small soft smiles as they sat down with their respective family members? And when they rose to leave, would Lucas wait at the end of the pew and gently cup Nina's elbow as she stepped into the aisle?

Zoey looked away. *Don't torture yourself,* she thought.

But trying not to look at them was nearly impossible. Zoey felt as though her neck were on ball bearings; it slid so easily into the position where she could see them.

The minister's words broke into her thoughts.

"Now, I would like to ask the congregation to have a few quiet moments of prayer while the pallbearers take Lara from the chapel."

All around her heads bent obediently, but not Zoey's. She watched as Lucas rose. He was one of the pallbearers—damn Benjamin for that! Her anger made it hard to sit still. Lucas was a traitor, a coward, a liar, a cheat. He had no right to take part in this service or even to be here at all.

Zoey's chest heaved with rage, and then as Lucas passed her row she quickly lowered her head so that he couldn't make eye contact.

She pressed her handkerchief to her mouth and closed her eyes. She looked as though she were deep in prayer, but in actuality her mind was so full of an angry buzzing that she could barely hear herself think.

"I didn't know funerals had receiving lines," Christopher said softly.

Kendra nodded. "I thought that was only weddings."

"Me too," Aisha whispered.

But obviously this funeral had a receiving line, and everyone shuffled through it on their way out of the chapel, stopping to offer condolences to Zoey and Benjamin.

Aisha thought that seeing Zoey and Benjamin alone in the receiving line next to Ms. McAvoy made it seem like Mr. and Ms. Passmore were dead. But of course, they were just in the hospital. Only Lara was dead. *Only.* Aisha closed her eyes.

"You okay?" Christopher asked, concerned.

Aisha opened her eyes and smiled at him. "I'm fine," she said. She reached up and touched his face gently with the back of her hand. She still couldn't believe he was hers again.

The line moved forward, and Aisha and Christopher were at the front. Aisha shook hands with Ms. McAvoy and murmured, "I'm so sorry for your loss," hoping that it was the right thing to do. Behind her she could hear Christopher and Kendra say the same thing, so she guessed it was.

Aisha moved along the line. When she reached out to hug Benjamin, for the first time she saw the look in his eyes. His eyes were so haunted and troubled that it was painful to look at them. Aisha flinched mentally from touching him, but luckily her arms seemed to have better manners than her brain, and she hugged him easily.

"Oh, Benjamin, I'm so sorry," she whispered in his ear.

"Thank you," he said.

And then she was hugging Zoey, who thankfully looked just the same as always: tanned and delicate and pretty in a dark blue dress.

"Oh, Eesh," Zoey whispered. "Thanks for coming."

"Of course I came," Aisha whispered back. "How are you holding up?"

"Oh, okay, I guess," Zoey said. Her eyes

flickered beyond Aisha and then back. "Come outside with me?"

"Now?" Aisha said. "Don't you feel well?" Then, wondering why she was forcing Zoey to stay in the funeral receiving line if it was painful for her, Aisha added, "Come on."

Zoey linked her arm through Aisha's and turned to go out the chapel doors. Aisha gave Christopher a quick, reassuring smile over her shoulder and happened to glimpse Nina Geiger a few places back in line. *So that's why Zoey wants to leave,* she thought.

Zoey dropped her arm as soon as they were outside. "Thanks," she said a little sheepishly. "There are some things I just can't face today."

"I understand." They walked aimlessly down the chapel steps and then just stood there in the bright sunshine. Aisha and Zoey had only discussed Lucas and Nina's kiss very briefly. Zoey didn't seem to want to talk about it much, which Aisha understood. Of course, Nina had talked Aisha's ear off about how much she regretted it and missed Zoey, but Aisha had a feeling that Zoey wasn't ready to hear that just yet. *They'll work it out together,* Aisha thought. *I just hope it's sooner rather than later.*

"Benjamin looks like he's in rough shape," Aisha said.

"Yes, he—he was very close to Lara," Zoey said.

"And how about you?" Aisha asked.

Zoey sighed. "Lara dying—it doesn't seem real to me yet. I mean, I know it's all Benjamin can think about, which makes me feel even more shallow that I'm not thinking about Lara. Especially after what she did."

"Christopher told me that she led your parents out of the fire," Aisha said.

"Dragged them is more like it," Zoey said. "They were already unconscious. If she hadn't gone after them, there's no way they would have made it." She took a deep breath. "That's why I feel like I should be more honestly grieving for her. Instead of thinking about how we're going to run the restaurant, and how I'm going to get my stuff back from California and everything else."

Aisha frowned. "What are you talking about?"

Zoey glanced up. "Benjamin and I have decided to stay here and run the restaurant."

"Indefinitely?"

Zoey nodded miserably.

"Oh, Zoey." Aisha put her hand on Zoey's arm. "Isn't there some other way?"

"No. Benjamin and I stayed up all night,

trying to think of some alternative." Zoey gave a small smile. "I have an actual blister on my fingertip from punching numbers into the calculator for so long." She held up her finger for Aisha to inspect.

"Where are you going to live?" Aisha asked.

Zoey shrugged. "Right now we're staying with friends of my parents in Weymouth, but we'll probably try to find an apartment on the island. Maybe Christopher's old place or something."

"An apartment!" Aisha repeated. "That's crazy. You can stay with my folks."

"Eesh, we can't afford that—"

"I meant for free."

Zoey sighed. "I know you did, but your parents need those rooms."

"Not my room," Aisha said, calculating rapidly. "And September is kind of a slow season, so I'm sure they could find somewhere to put Benjamin, too. Let me ask them tonight."

Zoey looked relieved but doubtful. "Aisha, you can't—"

"Of course I can," Aisha said firmly. "Your parents would do it for me if the situations were reversed. We both know they would. I'll work it out tonight, and you can move in tomorrow, okay?"

"Oh, Eesh," Zoey said, hugging her. "God, I can't thank you enough."

"No problem," Aisha whispered, holding Zoey close. It felt so good to be among friends again, away from Felicia, her nightmare roommate.

Zoey pulled away, wiping at her eyes. "When are you going back to school?"

"Christopher's driving me tomorrow morning."

"Oh, then I won't see you again," Zoey said, looking crestfallen. "We want to stay near the hospital in case they let us see my parents."

"You haven't even seen them yet?" Aisha asked, surprised.

Zoey shook her head. "But the hospital says tonight or tomorrow. Hopefully by then I'll have convinced Benjamin to go with me."

"He doesn't want to go?" Aisha said. If her parents were in the hospital, she'd want to be with them every minute.

Zoey shook her head. "He says he doesn't trust hospitals. But we'll see."

"Well, call me tonight," Aisha said. "And I'll be home practically every weekend to share the room with you."

"Oh, gosh, you don't know how many problems living with your parents would solve," Zoey said. "You really are the most wonderful person in the world—oh, no, Benjamin's signaling me from the top of the steps."

"Well, he's probably a little tired of holding down the fort in there," Aisha said. "You go on back in, and I'll check with my parents."

"Oh, okay," Zoey said. "And listen, if I don't get a chance to talk to you again, be sure to thank Felicia for me."

For a weird second Aisha thought she'd heard wrong. "Felicia?" she asked.

"Yes, she wrote me the sweetest letter," Zoey said absently. She was already climbing back up the steps.

"*Felicia* wrote you a letter?" Aisha said, feeling like an idiot for having to repeat everything Zoey was saying.

Zoey turned around, looking puzzled. "A condolence letter. I just got it this morning."

"Why would Felicia write you?" she asked. "She doesn't even know you."

Zoey shrugged. "Not like you do. But we've had a couple of intense phone conversations. Listen, I have to run."

"Oh, sure, go ahead," Aisha said.

Zoey and Felicia had had intense phone conversations? About what? And when?

34

Aisha's eyebrows drew together as she thought. Obviously that could only have happened when Zoey called to speak to her, Aisha. Except that Aisha had never received a single message saying that Zoey had called. She was sure of it.

Three

Nina carried a tray of meatballs out of the Grays' kitchen and set them on the buffet table.

"Hi," Lucas said in her ear, causing her to jump. He reached past her and stabbed a meatball with a toothpick. "How's it going?"

"Terrible," Nina said in a low voice without turning around. "Lucas, we shouldn't have come."

"Why not?"

Nina turned around to look at him. He looked very handsome in a dark gray suit and pale blue tie.

"Because we're upsetting Zoey," she said.

Lucas's mouth tightened. "Yes, I can see that. But this is a funeral, Nina, not a Tupperware party."

Nina was too worried that Zoey might look over and see them to ask Lucas what Tupperware had to do with anything. She ate three meatballs rapidly in a distracted way. Then she was sorry because she had three toothpicks in her hand and didn't know what to do with them.

Lucas was looking over the rest of the food and Zoey was nowhere in sight, so Nina decided to risk talking to him for another second. "Have you ever seen *Revenge of the Cat People*?" she whispered.

"Uh-huh." Lucas popped two gherkins into his mouth.

"You know how the cat people's eyes glowed all green?" Nina asked. "Well, *Zoey's* eyes glowed like that when she saw me today."

"Nina," Lucas said with his mouth full, "Zoey's eyes did not *glow*, okay? She may be angry, but she's not possessed by the devil."

"I knew you were going to say that," Nina whispered back, "but I swear it's true. I—oh, my God, there she is."

Zoey had just entered the room, and now she stood staring at them.

And just look at us, Nina thought sickly. *With our heads together, whispering guiltily.*

For a moment she was actually *scared,* actually *afraid* of Zoey and the anger glowing out of her eyes. She decided to skip tossing Lucas an "I told you so" glance and instead abandoned him. She turned blindly, darting down a narrow hallway and through the first door she came to.

Nina closed the door quickly behind her and stood leaning against it, breathing heavily, as if Cat People really were pursuing her. After a moment, though, she calmed down and looked around. She was in a small L-shaped room that the Grays obviously used as a linen cupboard.

Nina was kind of interested despite herself. Imagine living here and being able to just walk in and choose from dozens of sheets. You could go years without ever using the same sheets or towels twice. Of course, Nina also had a sneaking suspicion that if you lived here, you probably spent a lot of time ironing and folding sheets, but still, the idea of so much choice was really appealing and—

She heard a noise.

The faint but unmistakable sound of someone sniffling. She wasn't alone in here. The sound was coming from the other arm of the L. Nina tiptoed forward and peered around the corner—and froze.

Benjamin was sitting on the floor, crying. Piles of snowy white towels rose up around him as he sat with his head bent and his face buried in his hands.

Oh, no, Nina thought. *This is terrible. He obviously wants to be alone. I'll just slip out of here and—*

At that moment Benjamin looked up and saw her. His face was tear-stained. He didn't seem surprised to see her standing there, poised for flight. He just held out his arms in the timeless gesture of children who need a hug.

Nina didn't hesitate. She went to him and knelt awkwardly among the linen, pulling his dark head onto her shoulder. "It's okay," she said softly, automatically.

Benjamin turned his head so that his wet cheek pressed against her neck. "It's not okay," he said, his voice clogged with tears. "All those—people out there. They didn't love Lara. They didn't even know her! They just came because they're friends of my parents."

"I know, I know," Nina said soothingly.

"I'm the only one who cares!" Benjamin said. "I'm the only one who cares about what she did! She saved my parents, Nina! She should be a hero! She shouldn't have a lot of people standing around, eating cake and talking about—about—"

"Shhh," Nina said gently. "I know you miss her. I know you loved her."

It was apparently the right thing to say because Benjamin's arms tightened around her and he said, "Oh, I did, I really did."

Nina drew small circles on his back with her hand, and after a little while Benjamin's shoulders stopped shaking. He didn't let go of her, though, and Nina didn't want him to.

She knew that he was only reaching out for comfort, that he could as easily be crying on the shoulders of Mrs. Gray or Aisha if they had been the ones to come in here and find him.

But as she knelt there with him among the smells of bleach and cotton, touching his soft hair and the back of his neck—how well she remembered the texture of his hair—Nina was very happy to be the one to comfort Benjamin.

Lucas was barely aware of the fact that Nina had bolted. He was too busy watching Zoey as she lifted her chin and turned away from him. She walked through the crowded room with her head held high and her back ramrod straight and marched out onto the porch, letting the door slam behind her.

Lucas followed.

Zoey was already on the porch steps by the

41

time he opened the screen door. "Zoey," he said, carefully shutting the door behind him.

He didn't really expect her to stop—why should she turn around at the sound of his voice?—but he wanted her to slow down so he could go past her and she would know it was safe to go back inside.

But Zoey not only stopped, she whirled around to face him. Her eyes were blazing. "Yes?" she asked. "What do you want, *Lucas?*"

The sarcastic way she emphasized his name got to him. She made it sound as though he were unworthy to speak to her. As though his name was unpleasant to say. As though it made her angry just to be reminded of him. His own anger mounted.

"I'll tell you what I want," he said, his voice soft but intense. "I want you to stop acting like a spoiled little brat."

Zoey's eyes widened. *Whatever she was expecting, it wasn't that,* Lucas thought.

"How dare you?" she whispered ferociously, climbing back up the steps. "How dare you talk to me like that? How could you even dare to show your face here today? You knew—"

"The reason I came had nothing to do

with you," Lucas said. "I came to show my respect for the dead, for Lara—"

"Lara! You didn't respect her any more than—"

"As of two days ago I respect Lara more than anyone I've ever met," Lucas said, so quietly and firmly that Zoey's mouth snapped shut. "I'm here because of that. And to show my respect for your dad and for Benjamin because they cared about Lara and it's important to them."

God, I sound like my father, he thought sickly. *My dad and all the other fishermen who talk about "respect" and "honor" and "the right thing to do." I'm becoming one of them.*

Zoey looked at him scornfully. "Oh, you're just so noble, aren't you?" she said. "And why did Nina come? For the same self-sacrificing reasons? Or just to torment me and—"

"Stop it," Lucas said, surprising himself with the harshness of his voice. "This is a funeral, Zoey. It's not about *you*, hard as that may be for you to believe. Your brother is walking around like a zombie, and all you can think about is yourself. Now stop acting like I've crashed your thirteenth birthday party, and get inside and start showing some

43

gratitude to all the people who cared enough to—"

Lucas broke off abruptly as he realized something.

Zoey was staring at the floor, a deep flush staining her neck and cheeks. "Anything else?" she asked in a tight voice.

"No," Lucas said weakly.

Lucas had realized he wanted to kiss her. He hated himself for it. Himself and Zoey. How could he want someone he was furious with? How could he want someone who hated the sight of him?

Zoey went past him without making eye contact. He heard the screen door open and close and the sound of Zoey's voice, sincere and sweet. "Mrs. Norton, thank you so much for coming. I know how much this means to my parents. . . ."

Lucas leaned both hands against the porch railing and took several deep breaths, wondering if he would ever want anyone but Zoey ever again.

Dear Aisha,

Boy, as soon as you left, Mom moved your dumb friend Zoey into your room, and she's even worse than you! She takes, like, hours in the bathroom, and she complains when I shoot BBs at her, even though I have the gun set on the soft setting. What a baby!

Benjamin's staying here, too, but he's cool. He's telling me all about what it was like to be blind.

School sucks. Mrs. Allison says to tell you hi. Actually what she really said was, "Your sister, Aisha, was a far more conscious student than you. Please give her my regards." So there you are.

Love,
Kalif

Dear Kalif,

I think Mrs Allison probably meant a "far more _conscientious_ student," but knowing you, "conscious" is a very real possibility.

I'm glad to hear you miss me, even if only in comparison to Zoey. I'm glad you like Benjamin, and I'm sure he wouldn't mind if you asked him _one_ or _two_ questions about what it was like to be blind.

Parents' Weekend is coming up, and I want you to come, even though I know it'll be really dumb. Do you think I want to talk to Mom and Dad the whole time?

Love,
Aisha

PS. You'd better not be using my stereo!

Four

Claire went to see *Death of a Salesman* at the student union partly because she had nothing better to do and partly because it was on the English lit syllabus and she figured if she saw the movie, she wouldn't have to read the play.

But after about half an hour she was so bored that she decided she'd rather read the Cliffs Notes or even the actual play, which would at least be faster.

She gathered up her sweater and purse and stood up. She was surprised when the guy next to her also stood up and followed her out of the darkened auditorium.

"Are you okay?" he asked. He was a little taller than Claire, with short dark hair and mischievous black eyes and very white teeth. He was wearing baggy tan shorts and a T-shirt.

"Of course I'm okay," she said coolly.

"Well, I could tell that movie upset you," the guy said.

Claire gave him her wintriest smile. "I wasn't upset; I was bored."

"Don't be embarrassed," the guy said easily. "It was an upsetting movie for someone with a sensitive nature."

"Well, I don't have a sensitive nature," Claire said, and then regretted it. It hadn't sounded like quite what she meant.

She turned and began walking toward the union doors, but the guy fell in step beside her.

"So does this happen to you a lot?" he asked. "Getting upset?"

"I'm not upset!" Claire said, so loudly that a couple of students sitting in the lobby turned to look at them.

"Of course you are," the guy said. "You're practically shouting. I'd better walk you back to your dorm."

"No," Claire said shortly.

"Oh, no trouble at all," the guy said, as though she were merely protesting out of fear that she might inconvenience him. He held open the glass door for her, and they walked out into the street.

Claire would have liked to march away and leave him standing in the gutter, but she was wearing a short yellow dress and clogs and she knew that any attempt at escape would make her look like a fleeing duck. She would just walk along icily, as though this person had nothing to do with her.

But the guy didn't give her a chance to freeze him with silence. He started chattering right away. "Okay, my name is Paolo O'Connell. I have a Spanish mother and an Irish father, in case you're wondering about the name. I'm a freshman, just like you—"

"I'm not a freshman," Claire lied.

"Sure you are," Paolo said. "Only freshmen go to movies at the union. Anyway, what else can I tell you? I'm from New Jersey, I have three sisters, and I like *The Partridge Family* better than *The Brady Bunch*."

"What does *The Brady Bunch* have to do with anything?" Claire asked, exasperated.

"Everything," Paolo said. "Because there are only two types of people in the world, those who like *The Partridge Family* better than *The Brady Bunch* and vice versa. And I thought you should know which group I belong to."

"Those are *not* the only two types of people in the world," Claire said firmly.

"Well, there are some other subdivisions," Paolo admitted as they passed under a street lamp. "Like, people who like *Jeopardy* better than *Wheel of Fortune,* and people who like *Little House on the Prairie.*"

"People who like *Little House on the Prairie* better than what?" Claire asked.

"Oh, well, just people who like *Little House on the Prairie,*" Paolo said. "They're really in a category all by themselves."

Claire shook her head. "Did you spend your entire childhood watching television?"

Paolo considered. "Yes, pretty much." He grinned. "Now, tell me about yourself, Claire."

She bristled. "How did you know my name?"

"It's on your sweater."

"Oh," she said, feeling distinctly foolish. Damn her stepmother, Sarah, for always giving her and Nina these stupid Lands' End personalized sweaters. She was happy that her dorm was in sight.

"Don't you hate it in movies when the Spanish or Italian guy refuses to call the American girl Claire or Ann and calls her 'Clara' or 'Anna' instead?" Paolo asked.

"No," said Claire, who did in fact hate it.

"Oh, well, in that case I'll call you Clara," Paolo said. "Although there's really no accounting for tastes."

Claire sighed and quickened her pace.

She walked into the lobby of her dorm, and Paolo followed her. Claire waited until they were within hearing distance of the security monitor before she turned to him.

She had her speech all prepared. She was going to tell him firmly that she didn't like people following her home from the movies, that when she said no, she meant it, and for him to leave her alone from now on.

"Hey, Marjorie!" Paolo called.

Marjorie Bingham, who, next to Claire, was probably the prettiest girl in the dorm, was walking lazily toward the cafeteria. "Oh, hi, Paolo," she said in her soft southern voice.

Paolo jogged to catch up with Marjorie, leaving Claire, who had opened her mouth to deliver her speech—well, leaving her speechless.

Five

"So what do you need to know?" Christopher asked Benjamin in the back room of the restaurant.

Everything, thought Benjamin.

"Uh, pretty much everything," he said aloud, hoping that the "pretty much" made it sound like he at least had some clue as to what was going on.

Christopher smiled encouragingly. "You probably know lots more than you think you do," he said. "You've been working here since you were a kid, right?"

Benjamin nodded weakly, since that seemed easier than explaining that he had only worked at the restaurant when he couldn't think of a way out or when he really needed the money. Probably the regular customers knew more about running Passmores' than Benjamin did.

"Okay," Christopher said, gesturing to the stacks of papers on the desk. "This is accounts receivable, this is accounts payable, payroll, supplier invoices, the bookings notebook, the supplier notebook, and, uh, I don't know what the heck this pile is, so I guess you don't have to worry about it."

Benjamin did his best not to look overwhelmed.

"Now, really, all you have to do is stay on top of accounts payable and payroll until your dad gets back," Christopher said. "We can let accounts receivable slide, and I don't think we have any special bookings coming up or anything."

Christopher glanced at Benjamin and smiled understandingly. "Look, don't worry about it. I'm going to be here every single day."

Thank God, Benjamin thought.

He looked at Christopher, at his tired eyes and his broad shoulders that could work so many hours at so many jobs.

"Thanks," Benjamin said.

"No problem," Christopher said. "Now you just—"

"No, I mean, thanks for all the work you've done since the fire," Benjamin said. "I know that you've been running the restaurant single-handedly, and Kendra's been waitressing. We would have had to close without you."

Christopher shrugged. "You would have done the same for me."

Except I don't know how, Benjamin thought. *I can't even imagine how.*

"So, anyway," Christopher was saying. "I'm going to take Aisha back to school, but I should be back in plenty of time for dinner. And Kendra's coming over in an hour to help you with lunch. You just sit here and look through this stuff, okay?"

"Okay," Benjamin said, because he couldn't think of anything else to say.

"I'll explain anything you don't understand when I get back," Christopher said.

Benjamin sat down in the chair in front of the desk. Christopher gave him a reassuring thump on the shoulder and then left.

Benjamin stared at the mounds of paper in front of him. He stared for so long that he became uncomfortably aware of the clock ticking, and just because he had to start somewhere, he picked up the notebook labeled Orders.

He was relieved to find that it was just an ordinary school notebook. The pages were filled with his mother's haphazard handwriting and Christopher's more precise one, each entry giving the date, the supplier's name, the product ordered, and the amount. Pretty straightforward—

A knock on the door interrupted him.

"Come in."

A burly redheaded man with a mustache stuck his head around the corner. He was wearing a John Deere cap and pushing a trolley with a small freezer. "Mr. Passmore around?" he asked.

"Mr. Passmore's in the hospital," Benjamin said. "Can I help you?"

"Well, who *are* you?" the man asked mildly.

Benjamin didn't want to say "Benjamin" because that would make him sound about five years old, but he also didn't want to say "Mr. Passmore" since he'd just said Mr. Passmore was in the hospital, so he said, "Mr. Benjamin, the temporary manager."

"Oh," the man said, looking pretty unimpressed. He stroked his mustache. "Well, I'm delivering an order of chicken breasts. You got authority to sign this invoice, Mr. Benjamin?"

"Sure," Benjamin said, hoping this was true. He took the invoice and initialed it.

"Where should I put this?" the man asked, gesturing at the trolley. "Just leave it in the kitchen, like usual?"

"Yes, that's fine," Benjamin said.

"You need to order anything else?"

Benjamin was suddenly very happy that he'd been studying the Orders notebook. He opened it again now and, flipping to the last page, ran his finger up the column of company names until he found the company printed on the invoice, New England Beef and Poultry. There it was in his mother's handwriting:

8/30 New Eng Beef & Pltry sirloin 300 lbs

Benjamin figured he should probably get the same again. He closed the book and turned back to the man. "Yes, I'd like three hundred pounds of sirloin," he said.

The man's sandy eyebrows waggled for a second, but he didn't say anything. He just scribbled something on his clipboard. "Okay," he said. "Thank you, Mr. Benjamin. Have a good day."

"You too," Benjamin said, leaning back in the chair and feeling kind of professional and pleased with himself.

"Christopher, have you ever called me and talked to Felicia instead?" Aisha asked.

The question surprised her. She didn't know she had intended to ask it. She didn't know she was even thinking about it.

They were in the car on the way back to Harvard. Christopher had just taken the Cambridge exit. He considered her question.

"I don't know," he said.

Aisha glanced at him in annoyance. She might have known he'd say that. And it wasn't true, because of course he *knew*. He *had* to know unless he had another personality or something. But if she pointed that out, he would just say he didn't remember and—

"Probably," Christopher said, interrupting her thoughts.

She looked at him. "What?"

"I said, probably."

Aisha narrowed her eyes. "What do you mean?"

Christopher shifted in the driver's seat as he looked for the turnoff to her dorm. "Well, I just meant probably. I mean, you both live there, and we talk pretty much every day, so the odds of Felicia answering—"

Aisha groaned. "Christopher, please please please don't get all nerdy and turn this into a story problem. It was just a question."

"Okay," he said, smiling at her as he found a parking space. "But I could work out the exact probability and send it to you."

Aisha laughed. "Send it to my dad; he'd be more interested. Although he'd probably redo it and send you his own answer."

They both got out of the car, and Christopher reached into the backseat for Aisha's suitcase. They smiled at each other.

"Want to come upstairs?" Aisha asked.

"I thought you had class," Christopher said.

"Not for an hour."

"Then sure." Christopher took her hand.

Aisha felt a shiver of apprehension. What if Felicia were there?

Well, what if she is? Aisha thought irritably. *Then you introduce Christopher, and that's it. Why get all nervous about it?*

Why, indeed? But she was. She could feel her palms sweating as they crossed the parking lot. Once they were inside the building, she dropped Christopher's hand and rubbed her palm against her pale yellow blouse. It left a damp mark.

Oh, great, she thought. *Now I'm going to look all rumpled and dirty, and Felicia will be picture-perfect as usual—God, why am I even thinking this way? I must be insane.*

Still, her face felt flushed and clammy as she put her hand on the doorknob and rattled it gently. "Felicia?"

No answer.

"She must be out," she said to Christopher, trying not to sound all happy and relieved.

She unlocked the door, and they stepped inside. For once Felicia's side of the room was neat and clean, not a piece of laundry or a dirty dish or wet towel in sight. Aisha was almost annoyed. She wanted Christopher to see what a pigsty it normally was.

Don't be so petty, she told herself.

"Doesn't look too bad," Christopher said, as though he could read her mind. He set her suitcase down by the closet and looked around. "So this is where you live."

She smiled and pushed her hair off her face. "Yup. Do you want a drink?"

"Sure."

Aisha opened their tiny fridge. "Well, you can tell that two girls live here. Do you want diet Coke or diet Snapple?"

He laughed. "Snapple, please."

She opened a diet lemonade and handed it to him.

He took a long drink and then pointed to the

Bill of Human Rights poster that hung on the closet door. "Is that Felicia's?"

Aisha nodded, opening her own can of Coke.

Christopher studied the poster for a moment and then glanced at the copy of *A Brief History of Time* that lay on Felicia's nightstand. "She seems like an interesting person," he said casually.

Aisha's throat closed, and her hands tightened on the Coke can. Did Christopher mean that? Would a guy really walk in here and look at Felicia's poster and book, both of which struck Aisha as nerdy and pretentious, and think Felicia was interesting? And not just a guy, any guy, but Christopher? *Did* Christopher think Felicia was interesting? Or did he just think she had interesting *stuff?* And what did he, or any other guy, think of *Aisha's* side of the room, and her posters and framed photos and books, which now all seemed hopelessly unsophisticated and frilly?

"I'm glad you invited me up here," Christopher said.

"You are?" Aisha asked hoarsely. "Why?"

Please don't say so that you could get a better idea of how cool Felicia is, she thought frantically.

Christopher took the Coke can out of her

hand and set it on her desk. "Because I thought you were going to make me kiss you good-bye in the parking lot," he said, putting his arms around her. "And I thought we might get arrested for indecent exposure."

For a moment Aisha felt nothing but overwhelming, giddy relief. Then she slid her arms around Christopher's neck and kissed him. She forgot all about posters and books, and interesting and uninteresting, and sides of rooms, and even her twelve o'clock class, for which she was twenty minutes late.

LUCAS

OKAY, this WAS stupid, but I wrote to the University of Maine And Asked them for A copy of their freshman literature syllAbus. I figured I could reAd on the boAt And mAke up some lost time. So I went to the librAry And gAve it A whirl.

The SCARLet LetteR
   Adultery? No, thAnks.

"The Tell-TAle HeArt"
   Guilty conscience isn't reAlly for me right now, either.

Moby Dick
  OR fishing stories.

WALt Whitman, "Song of Myself"
  CAll me CRAZy, but is
this guy tAlking About
sex?

The Awakening
  MoRe guilty Adultery.

The GReAt GAtsby
  I RefuSe to ReAd A
book About some poor slob
trying to win bACk A
girl.

EthAn FRome
  MoRe guilty Adultery.

"The Open Boat"
  No, thanks.

Robert Frost, "Stopping by
Woods on A Snowy Evening"
  Is this About Santa
Claus?

Six

Lucas was so surprised to see Nina waiting in Dr. Denby's office that for a minute he wondered if he'd wandered into the wrong office. He checked the nameplate on the door. Right office.

He and Nina bumped into each other from time to time, but she never called him anymore. Although now that he thought about it, he never called her, either. He missed her. Next to Zoey he missed her more than any of the things that had disappeared from his life.

He crossed the waiting room to where Nina sat, wearing chinos and a fuchsia tank top, nervously sucking on an unlit Lucky Strike and reading an issue of *People* in a sort of bug-eyed way.

"Hey," he said softly, causing her to jump. "Aren't you supposed to be in school?"

She blinked at him nervously. "Oh, I deliberately scheduled this during my office job."

She didn't ask him to sit down next to her,

but he did, anyway. "What are you here for?" he asked.

"Just an annual cleaning," she said. "You?"

"I have to get a cavity filled."

They were silent for a minute, and then Nina gave him a wan smile. "I can see why books and movies never take place in dentists' offices, because that has to be the single most boring conversation I've ever had."

Lucas smiled back at her, and then they both fell silent again. Lucas stretched out his legs and studied the tips of his shoes. "So," he said at last. "Have you talked to—to Zoey?"

Nina shook her head. "No. I saw her on the street once, and she actually crossed the street to avoid me. It was horrible." She tugged on one of her earrings. "Did you talk to her?"

He smiled tightly. "More of a shouting match. Well, me shouting and Zoey standing there."

"That's what I'm afraid of," Nina said. "What were you shouting about?"

He shrugged. "Her behavior at the funeral. I mean, I know I hurt Zoey and—"

"We," Nina said.

"What?"

"*We* hurt her."

"Well." He hesitated. "I know that . . . Zoey got hurt, and I'd give anything in the world to change that if I could. But she's concentrating on herself and, um, what happened so *much*."

"I don't mean to sound unsympathetic," Nina said. "But I'd concentrate on it, too."

"Even when your brother needed you?" Lucas asked. "Even when both your parents were in the hospital? When your house burned down? Zoey's going to need a lot of help if she and Benjamin are going to run that restaurant, and I'm worried that she won't get it because she's too busy trying to avoid us."

"Oh," Nina said. She studied her fingernails. "You're very noble."

Lucas smiled thinly, remembering the sarcastic way Zoey had said the same thing. "Why do you say that?"

"Because you're worried about Zoey," Nina said. "And I can only think about myself and how I wish she would come over so we could spend the whole day doing something completely unproductive, like watching a *Real World* marathon on MTV."

Her voice wavered on the last word, and Lucas realized that she was near tears.

"Hey," he whispered. "It's okay. I miss her, too."

Nina nodded but kept studying her fingernails.

"Let's talk about something else," he said desperately.

Nina sniffled. "What?"

"Um, what do you really think of Dr. Denby?"

Nina looked up at him, and he was relieved to see that her eyes were dry. She gave him a faint smile. "I hate him," she said simply.

Lucas was so happy to distract her that her severe reaction to Dr. Denby didn't even surprise him. "Why?" he asked.

Nina began ticking off the reasons on her fingers. "One, his breath always smells like onions, no matter what time of day it is. Two, he calls me Claire. Three, he hasn't changed the posters on the ceiling in about a decade. Four, when he gives me a shot, he says that his 'tin soldier is going to bite me,' which is what he says to toddlers—"

"Yeah, he says that to me, too," Lucas said, but Nina was too caught up.

"Five," she continued. "He always wants to set me up with his stupid son Matthew, who I happen to know from reading everyone's confidential records is flunking English, and I have half a mind to tell Dr. Denby that."

"How did you get your hands on Matthew Denby's confidential record?"

"Office job," Nina replied.

Lucas nodded. "Well, uh, far be it from me to tell you what to do," he said, kind of shocked by how many reasons Nina had for disliking Dr. Denby. "But I personally wouldn't tell him anything insulting until *after* he finishes doing your teeth."

Nina threw back her head and laughed. "Oh, my God, you're right," she gasped. "I—"

And then suddenly she clapped a hand over her mouth and looked stricken, as though she'd just remembered who she was talking to.

She probably just did, Lucas thought sickly.

"Nina," he said. "It's—"

He was about to say, *It's okay to be friends with me.* He didn't get the chance, however, because just then the nurse called, "Miss Geiger?" and Nina sped across the room and through the door and into the clutches of Dr. Denby as though she couldn't get away from Lucas fast enough.

* * *

Claire was in the dorm basement, sorting her laundry and wondering why she felt homesick.

She loved Boston, liked her classes, enjoyed her freedom, had fun with her new friends—so what was missing? Claire had no real longing for North Harbor. Or did she? Wouldn't it be nice to walk into the grocery store and have Mr. Harriman say, "Well, hello there, Claire"? Or Mrs. Norton hail her from across the street, calling, "Claire, how's school going?" Or to walk into her own house and have Janelle look up from whatever she was doing and say in her mild voice, "Hi, Claire, are you hungry?"

Yes, that was what she missed, Claire decided. The familiarity, the friendly informality, the day-to-day quality of her life there. Here everything was so terribly new. How many times was she going to have to go through the routine of meeting people? *Hi, I'm Claire . . . from Maine . . . climatology . . . I live on the sixth floor. . . .* When would she find someone she clicked with?

Just then someone said, "Hello, Claire," with such obvious warmth and pleasure that a smile sprang to Claire's lips, transforming her from pretty to stunning in an instant, and she looked up, her eyes sparkling.

Her smile froze.

Paolo stood in the doorway of the laundry room.

Claire quickly dropped her gaze, but it was too late. He sauntered across the room. "Hey, you actually looked happy to see me there for a minute," he said. "Have you missed me?"

She gave him a scornful look. "How can I miss you when I see you all the time?"

She did in fact see him all the time. It turned out that he was a security monitor, which meant that he spent several hours a day patrolling the dorm. He seemed to spend the rest of his time hanging out in the lobby or the cafeteria, always at a table full of pretty girls. Not that she noticed, Claire quickly corrected herself.

Paolo's lazy smile seemed to say that he knew she noticed how the girls crowded around him, but he only shrugged. "Can I keep you company, Claire—I mean, Clara?"

She rolled her eyes. He even pronounced Clara "Clahra" instead of making it rhyme with Sara. "Only if you call me Claire," she said.

He pulled himself up and sat cross-legged on the dryer next to her. "Okay," he said agreeably. He turned off his walkie-talkie.

"I hope nobody has an emergency," Claire said wryly.

"Not a chance," Paolo assured her. "There hasn't been an emergency since I started working here."

"Really?" Claire asked casually, thinking of Jake. Due to a screwup at his college Jake had nowhere to live, so Claire had taken him in. It had been lucky for both of them that she had a large single. "No girls smuggling guys into their rooms or anything?" she asked Paolo.

"Oh, well, sure, but that's not an emergency," Paolo said. "I mean, no one screaming for help. Well, except one girl, actually."

"She screamed for help?" Claire asked, concerned. "What was wrong?"

"A mouse had died facedown in her bowl of candy corn," Paolo said scornfully. "She made me come and take it away."

"Oh," Claire said. She didn't know you could call security and make them take away a dead mouse.

She suddenly realized that the whole time she had been talking to Paolo, she had also been sorting her underwear. Hastily she opened a washing machine and swept the pile of lace and cotton and snaps and elastic inside. She added soap and started the machine before she glanced at Paolo.

He was smiling, obviously not having missed anything. "I like the Super Friends pair," he said.

Claire flushed.

Paolo laughed. "It's okay. I have sisters, remember? I've seen lots of dirty underwear."

"They weren't dirty," Claire protested.

"Then why are you washing them?"

"Because I'd worn them," she said. "You know what I mean. They weren't *stained*."

His eyes danced. "What a charming conversationalist you are."

Claire opened her mouth to protest but then thought better of it. Why get in any deeper? "Why don't you go rescue some other girl from the dangers of dead mice?" she demanded crossly.

"Because I'd rather tease you," Paolo said. He was looking at Claire speculatively, and for once she didn't see that mocking light in his eyes. She only saw a guy looking at her appreciatively. "Claire," he said. "Would you like to go to a movie with me? Something less upsetting than the other night? *Bambi*?"

"*Bambi*?"

He smiled. "We can leave before the forest fire."

"No, thank you," Claire said, happy to have the upper hand. She pushed her hair away from her face.

"Okay," Paolo said with maddening indifference. He swung himself off the dryer. "I'll see you around, Clara."

"Not if I see you first," Claire said, but Paolo must have guessed she would say that because he said it at the same time, making her sound foolish.

He left the laundry room, laughing, and Claire frowned in irritation. Suddenly she decided that she would spend the evening studying at the library so she wouldn't be around to watch him flirt with countless other girls.

Dear Claire,

Just to let you know what life is like without you, last night I went to dinner and a movie with Dad. Now, is that sentence a cry for help or what? Normally I wouldn't have gone, but Sarah is on a two-day business trip (and seldom have I wished for someone to come back so much), and Dad's been all mopey and lonely, so when he asked me if I wanted to go out to dinner, I didn't have the heart to say no. He added the movie part with my permission.

Anyway, he was a complete idiot and said to our waitress, "This is my date! I'm on a date with my daughter!" Plus, plus we saw about fifty million people from school, and Lord knows what they thought. Plus, plus during the movie Dad kept asking me questions in a really loud voice, and everyone pretty much wanted to snap a muzzle on him.

It was, without exception, the most depressing night of my life.

I sure miss you.

Love,
Nina

Dear Nina,

I'm sorry to hear about your date with Dad. I took him to McDonald's with me once and he was a real dork, saying "Mcplease" and "Mcthanks" to the cashier. And we saw some guy from school who said hi to me and Dad wheeled around and shook <u>hands</u> with him and said how pleased he was to meet a friend of mine, and of course the guy wasn't a friend of mine; he was the biggest nerd in school. (In fact, he had your office job that year. I'm serious.)

Anyway, not much is going on here. If Dad gets to be too much for you, you can always come visit. I'll introduce you to this guy I know who reminds me of you for some reason. I guess because you both laugh at your own jokes. Anyway, his name is Paolo, and you'll like him more than I do.

Love,
Claire

Seven

"So you're from Chatham Island?" Tony the hairdresser said to Nina. "Why come so far to get your hair cut?"

Nina tried to give him a meaningful look. "I couldn't find anyone who didn't give me a bad haircut," she said.

"Do you always have that goatee thing?" the salon receptionist asked Jake.

"No," he said, touching his chin self-consciously. "I was up all night studying."

"Well, you should keep it," the receptionist said, smiling. "It's great."

"Would you like a little gel or mousse or something?" Carla asked Aisha.

"No, thanks," Aisha said.

"Oh, come on, just a little," Carla said.

"Show me how much you think an inch is," Claire said to the stylist.

He showed her.

Claire adjusted his fingers. "No, *that's* an inch," she said, sitting down in the chair. "Take off more than that and I'll organize a protest outside your salon."

"So, I see we're having a bad hair day," Gary said to Christopher as he sat down in the barber chair.

Christopher frowned. "What do you mean?"

"I mean the way your hair looks today," Gary said.

"It always looks like this," Christopher said.

"What do you mean, your hands are stuck in my hair?" Aisha asked, panic making her voice shrill.

"Relax," Carla said, although her own voice sounded high. She turned awkwardly to call over her shoulder. "Maxine? Maxine!"

"Oh, hi," Gary said to Zoey. "Are you here to have your roots touched up?"

"No, I'm just here to buy some shampoo," Zoey said slowly. She looked at him. "And this is my natural color."

The barber examined a clump of Benjamin's hair. "If I didn't know better," he said, "I'd say you have chicken gravy in your hair."

"I do have chicken gravy in my hair," Benjamin said.

The barber met his eyes in the mirror, and Benjamin sighed. "It's a long story."

"Voilà!" Tony said, spinning Nina around so that she could see herself in the mirror.

Nina sighed. "I guess I have to go to Portland," she said.

"Okay, okay," Maxine said contemplatively as she studied Carla's hands stuck in Aisha's hair. She picked up a pair of scissors. "Would you, um, consider something a little shorter than your current style?"

Eight

The nurse showed Zoey to a small changing room. "As soon as you change into your gown, I'll take you in to see your parents," she said cheerfully.

"Okay," Zoey said absently. "Thanks."

The nurse started to leave and then paused. "Don't you have a brother?" she said. "I could swear your dad said something about—Benjamin?"

Zoey smiled. "You have a good memory," she said. "Benjamin is covering the restaurant tonight so I could come."

"Oh, well, then I guess we'll see him tomorrow," the nurse said.

Don't count on it, Zoey thought. Benjamin had been adamant about not going to the hospital. He kept asking if Zoey didn't remember what had happened to him in the hospital when he was ten years old? He'd gone in seeing and come out blind. No, he was not going to the hospital.

Zoey sighed.

She went into the small room and began sifting through the stacks of folded green gowns. She tied on a gown and tucked her hair into a cap.

The nurse reappeared. "All set? You want to see your mom first?"

"Sure."

The nurse led Zoey down the hall to a different wing, keeping up her light steady chatter. "I know your mom's really looking forward to seeing you, Zoey. She gets tired pretty easily, but I think you can probably stay for several minutes. Here we are." She stopped in front of a door that was slightly ajar and pushed it the rest of the way open. "Darla? Zoey's here."

Zoey felt shy suddenly as she stepped timidly around the nurse. She looked expectantly toward the hospital bed.

Her mother was in an oxygen tent—a thick, intimidating plastic canopy hung around the bed and tucked under the mattress. An IV dripped into her, and tubing ran up each of her nostrils. She was very thin, too, her collarbones pushing whitely against her skin above the hospital gown.

Thank God Benjamin isn't here, Zoey thought. *I don't think he could deal with her like this.*

But Zoey forgot about the tubes and oxygen tent when she saw her mother's warm blue eyes light up at the sight of her. Zoey's own eyes filled with tears. "Hi, Mom," she said. It came out little louder than a whisper.

Her mother gestured toward her throat. "Hurts," she croaked.

"It hurts her to talk," the nurse said softly to Zoey.

Zoey nodded. "Well, then, I'll do the talking for both of us, all right?" she said, trying to smile. The nurse touched her arm and left.

Zoey moved closer and sat in an armchair next to the bed. She wished her eyes would stop watering.

Her mother's eyes were damp, too. Zoey smiled. "Don't you cry," she ordered in a mock-stern voice. "Or else I'll cry through our whole visit." She took a deep breath. "What can I tell you? Benjamin and I are fine. We're staying at the Grays', did you know that? They're the nicest people on the planet, I think."

Zoey took a tissue from a box on the night-stand and wiped her eyes gently. "And, um, Benjamin and I are running the restaurant."

Hopefully we're not running it into the ground, she added silently.

"Zoey?" She looked up. The nurse was standing in the doorway. "Your time's up, I'm afraid."

"It can't be!" Zoey said, dismayed. "I just got here."

"I'm sorry, but those are the rules," the nurse said. "Next week your mom will be out of intensive care and you can stay longer."

Zoey stood up reluctantly. Her mother's eyes were still watching her. "Bye," she said hoarsely.

"Good-bye," Zoey said awkwardly. She wished she could think of something else to say, some way to make her mother feel better. She tried to think of what her mother would say to her if the situations were reversed, and it came to her immediately. "I love you, Mom," she said, leaning forward. "Don't you worry about a thing. Just concentrate on getting better, and I'll see you soon."

She blew a quick kiss and hurried out the door the nurse was still holding open. "Good job, Zoey," the nurse whispered. "I know it's hard when people can't speak."

She led Zoey back down the hall to her father's room.

Mr. Passmore was sitting up in bed. He had a tube in his nose, too, but he looked wonderful to Zoey.

"Dad!" she cried, hugging him.

"Hello, honey," he said, stroking her hair. His voice was hoarse. "It sure is good to see you. Where's Benjamin?"

"At the restaurant," Zoey said, sitting on the edge of the bed.

"How *are* things at the restaurant?" Mr. Passmore asked. "You guys have everything under control?"

"Oh, yes," she said. "Everything's going just fine. No problems at all."

"Good," he said. "Although I was thinking about calling your cousin Adam to see if he could come out here and help us."

"I didn't even know I had a cousin Adam," Zoey said.

Mr. Passmore smiled faintly. "He's my cousin, which makes him your second cousin, once removed."

Zoey groaned. "I never understand that once removed stuff. But why would he want to come work in the restaurant?"

Mr. Passmore shrugged. "I'll talk to him," he said vaguely. "So tell me what else is going on."

Zoey told him about the Grays, about Christopher, about Kendra, and then she noticed that her father had fallen silent.

"Is something wrong, Dad?"

He shook his head. "I was just wondering . . . about Lara's funeral?"

Zoey tried not to wince. She didn't want to

talk about Lara. "What do you want to know?" she asked gently.

Mr. Passmore paused. "Was it what she wanted?" He coughed. "Would it have made her—happy?"

Zoey glanced up and saw her father watching her hopefully. What was it Lucas had said? . . . *As of two days ago I respect Lara more than anyone I've ever met. . . .*

She cleared her throat and gripped her father's hand. "It was a beautiful funeral," she said firmly. "It was fitting for—for someone as brave as Lara."

And saying that, for the first time ever Zoey felt really good about her half sister.

From Claire's Scrapbook:

The Bangor Daily News

GIRL WOUNDS INTRUDER WITH HAMMER

NORTH HARBOR, ME. Claire Geiger, an eighteen-year-old Chatham Island native, critically wounded an unidentified young man when he broke into the house of Mr. Benjamin Passmore, nineteen, a friend of Ms. Geiger's.

The intruder has been hospitalized for a severe head wound, reportedly the result of a blow by Ms. Geiger with a hammer. Weymouth Hospital lists him as in critical condition.

Police say that the intruder apparently entered the Passmore home expecting Ms. Geiger to be there. They would not speculate further on motive, although one source says that Ms. Geiger's actions were "a clear-cut case of self-defense."

Police are withholding the name of the suspect until his family can be notified.

Ms. Geiger was unavailable for comment.

The Portland Press Herald

INJURED BOY'S CONDITION IMPROVES

NORTH HARBOR, ME. Robert Sean Thompkins, the seventeen-year-old who was critically injured during an attack on a young Chatham Island woman, has been taken off the critical list at Weymouth Hospital. "We are cautiously optimistic about a full recovery," hospital officials said yesterday.

"Although there remains a possibility of permanent motor control damage."

Thompkins remained unconscious for over twenty hours. Police have questioned him but will only state that Thompkins is "still under investigation."

The Bangor Daily News

THOMPKINS ACCUSED OF "REIGN OF TERROR"
NORTH HARBOR, ME. Robert Sean Thompkins, the seventeen-year-old boy injured during an attack on Claire Geiger, eighteen, of Chatham Island, has been accused of stalking Ms. Geiger for weeks before the attack.

Neil Barker, an attorney for the Geiger family, says: "We do not wish to go public at this time with the details, but Thompkins was an acquaintance of Ms. Geiger's who became obsessed with her. He had been writing and calling for weeks leading up to the attack. He is clearly a very disturbed individual."

Police say they are investigating the charges.

The Boston Globe

"NOT OUR SON" SAY ALLEGED STALKER'S PARENTS
BOSTON, MA. "Our son could never do the things they say he did," says Mrs. Betty Thompkins of Boston. "Robert was on the honor roll. We never heard a word about this Claire Geiger. If he was so obsessed, why didn't we, his parents, know?"

The Thompkins's son, Robert "Sean," seventeen, is recovering in a Maine hospital after receiving a severe head wound during an alleged attack on Ms. Geiger, eighteen. Ms. Geiger claims Thompkins was obsessed and stalking her.

"Robert is a gentle boy," Mrs. Thompkins insists. "Loving, generous, vulnerable."

"If this stalking business is true," says Edward Thompkins, Robert's father, "why didn't she go to the police? Why are we just hearing about it?"

Neil Barker, an attorney for the Geiger family, says that "Claire did not go to the police because she knew how ineffective antistalking laws are in Maine. Instead she took measures to protect herself."

"She took the law into her own hands is more like it," Mr. Thompkins says. "She wanted to be judge, jury, and executioner for my boy."

The Bangor Daily News

THOMPKINS FIT TO STAND TRIAL

WEYMOUTH, ME. Yesterday court-appointed psychologists pronounced Robert Sean Thompkins mentally fit to stand trial and participate in his defense. Thompkins, seventeen, pled not guilty to charges of harassment and stalking. His alleged stalking victim is Claire Geiger, eighteen, who wounded Thompkins with a hammer last August in what she claims was self-defense.

Thompkins's lawyer, Hal Bowker, said yesterday that Thompkins may countersue Geiger for attempted murder. "A hammer is as much a potential murder weapon as a gun or a knife," Bowker said in a press conference yesterday.

Neil Barker, an attorney for the Geiger family, says that such a countersuit would be "ludicrous." He points out that criminal prosecutors have failed to press charges against Ms. Geiger, stating that according to letters Thompkins had written Ms. Geiger, "It was very clear he was out to get her. He meant to do her great, if not fatal, harm."

Mr. Barker confirmed that Ms. Geiger would be testifying.

A trial date has not been set.

Zoey

Sometimes I feel so angry that I think I can hear a buzz in my head, a continuous buzz. What if it never goes away? You read about things like that sometimes: migraines that last for twenty years, hiccups that continue for decades, so why not an angry buzzing?

Basically it seems that there isn't one single thing in my life that doesn't make me angry. I'm angry at Lucas for cheating on me, I'm angry at Nina for lying to me.

I'm angry at my parents for not having

better insurance or a better emergency-contingency plan. Yeah, that's right, I'm angry at my own parents as they lie in the hospital. That's me, an equal opportunity angry person.

I'm angry at the fire for destroying my house, for pulling me out of school. I'm even angry, in a way, at Anika for writing me such cheerful letters about everything I've missed.

And I'm angry at Lara for dying. That sounds strange since I'm also grateful to her for so many things. But when Lara died, she took some part of my brother with her, and I'm not sure he'll ever get it back.

Nine

Christopher woke up shortly before six and was shocked to find that he could see his breath. He jumped up to shut the window and then slid back into bed, shivering. Amazing how it was summer one minute and almost winter the next. Of course, this fog would burn off by ten, and the day would be beautiful, but not in time for Christopher's paper route.

Christopher groaned. He tried to remember why he thought getting his paper route back would be such a good idea. Oh, yes, he remembered. It was right after he got the phone bill and saw all those calls to Aisha.

But it was worth it, Christopher thought. It was worth it to hear her voice every day. *Which reminds me,* he thought, squinting at his alarm clock. *We agreed to talk at six-fifteen this morning.*

He reached for the phone. He wished that they could talk at a more reasonable hour, but he was going to be hopping from job to job all day long. He dialed.

"Hello?"

"Eesh?" Christopher said. "Did I wake you?"

"No, I was up," Aisha said, but she didn't sound like that was exactly true.

"How are you?" he asked softly. "How's organic chem?"

Aisha gave a small groan. "Don't ask," she said. "How was dinner at my parents'?"

"The usual," Christopher said. "Benjamin and Zoey were there. Your dad gave me some really boring book about the history of the American flag, Kalif tried to give me an Indian rope burn, and your mother gave me a glass of buttermilk. And we all watched television together, although I fell asleep after about ten minutes."

"Why did Mom give you buttermilk?" Aisha asked.

"Because she thinks I'm too thin and peaked," Christopher said.

"Well, you do work too hard," Aisha said. "But that's no reason to feed you *buttermilk*. Gross."

"I thought so, too."

Aisha let out a little cry. "You mean you *drank* it?"

"Well, sure," Christopher said. "I was trying to be polite."

"Polite is one thing," Aisha said. "Buttermilk is another."

"All in the name of love," Christopher said, smiling.

He waited for Aisha to respond, but she didn't. Then he could make out the sound of her talking to someone else.

"Christopher?" she said, coming back. "I think I'm going to have to cut this short. Felicia's trying to sleep."

"Oh," Christopher said, because he didn't know what else to say.

"Sorry," Aisha said. She sounded distracted. "Talk to you tomorrow?"

"Sure."

"I love you." She said this very quietly.

"I love you, too."

They hung up.

Christopher stood up and began pulling on his clothes. The phone call hadn't lifted his spirits as usual. Aisha hadn't sounded like herself, especially not there at the end when she'd meekly given in to Felicia and hung up.

Christopher frowned. What was distracting Aisha? Was it just roommate problems? Or something else?

Organic chem is distracting her, he told himself. *It would distract you, too.*

97

But Christopher was unconvinced. Schoolwork never distracted Aisha. Only something personal could do that . . . like another guy?

He shook his head to clear away the thought and headed out into the cold gray morning.

The phone woke Nina at eleven-twenty. "Hello?"

"Hi, Dida, it's Keddra."

It took Nina's sleepy brain a full minute to translate that to, "Hi, Nina, it's Kendra."

"Kendra?" she said at last. "Do you have a cold?"

"I have a *bodster* cold," Kendra said. "Add I'b callidg you because—"

"What kind of cold?" Nina asked.

"Bodster."

"Monster?"

"Yeah."

"Oh," Nina said. "Go on."

"Well, I'b callidg you because"—Kendra broke off briefly to sneeze, then Nina heard the sound of Kendra blowing her nose, and when she came back, her voice was clearer— "I'm supposed to work the lunch shift at Passmores', and, well, I know this is really short notice, but I wondered if maybe you could fill in for me?"

Nina was silent for so long that Kendra said, "Are you still there?"

"Yes, I'm here," Nina said. "And I can fill in for you. No problem. When do I start?"

"In about ten minutes," Kendra said apologetically. "If you can make it."

"Don't worry about a thing," said Nina, whose eyelids were still crusty with sleepers. She hung up with Kendra and leaped out of bed.

As she was splashing cold water on her face Nina realized that she'd never worked as a waitress before, but she brushed the thought aside. She'd eaten at plenty of restaurants, hadn't she? That ought to be just as good. She was far more worried about what Zoey would say. But Passmores' needed a waitress. Surely Zoey would see that.

She threw on a pair of plaid shorts and a clean T-shirt and practically ran over to the restaurant. Even so, she saw that she was five minutes late. Great.

The restaurant door was propped open, and as Nina entered she was relieved to see that there weren't any customers waiting yet. Only Zoey behind the cash register, frowning and preoccupied as she studied a receipt.

Zoey looked up and saw Nina, and her eyes narrowed. "What are you doing here?"

Nina suddenly realized her mouth was dry. "Um, Kendra called me," she said, "and she has a cold, so she asked me to cover her shift."

"Forget it," Zoey said shortly.

"Zoey, I just want to help—" Nina began.

"I don't want your help."

God, she is stubborn, Nina thought. *But what are her options? What's she going to do—close the restaurant?*

"I'd rather close the restaurant," Zoey said, as if reading Nina's mind. "I'd rather lose a whole day's earnings than work with you. Is that clear?"

"Zoey," Nina said desperately. "I won't bother you. I just—"

"You've never even waitressed before," Zoey said scornfully. "You'd only be in the way and make a million mistakes."

Nina's eyes stung. That wasn't fair. Maybe she didn't work in a restaurant, but she did work in an office. Right now she actually had paper cuts on her tongue from stuffing ten thousand envelopes. That's how dedicated an employee she was. And Zoey was making her sound like some spoiled brat. "Zoey—"

"Just go," Zoey said.

"But—"

"What's going on?" a voice interrupted.

Benjamin was standing in the doorway to the kitchen, wearing an apron. Nina had never been happier to see him in her life, which was saying a great deal.

"Kendra's sick," Zoey said.

"She asked me to cover for her," Nina said quickly.

Benjamin looked wary. "That would be—"

"I've already told her to leave," Zoey interrupted.

"Leave?" Benjamin repeated. "Why?"

"Because I don't want to work with her!" Zoey practically shouted. "I won't! I won't do it!"

Benjamin put his hand to his forehead as though he felt a headache coming on. "Zoey, we don't have a choice," he said softly.

"*I won't work with her,*" Zoey said again.

I can't believe they're talking about me this way, Nina thought sickly. *It sounds like they're talking about some horrible stranger, but they're not. They're talking about me.*

"Zoey, be reasonable," Benjamin was saying. "I have to be in the kitchen, and you can't handle the cash register *and* the bar *and* the tables."

"Maybe I should just go," Nina said softly, but neither Benjamin nor Zoey heard her.

"What about . . ." Benjamin was clearly thinking hard. "What about if you work the bar, Zoey? And I'll keep an eye on the cash register from the kitchen, and Nina can work the tables?"

And that way Zoey won't have to deal with me at all, Nina thought nauseously.

Zoey's mouth tightened. "Whatever," she snapped, and marched behind the bar.

Benjamin turned to Nina and smiled a smile that didn't reach his eyes. "Okay," he said too heartily. "You can wait here by the door, Nina. When people come in, just grab a menu and lead them to a table and ask them if they want a drink."

"All right," Nina said weakly.

"I'll be in the kitchen if you need anything," Benjamin said. "Don't hesitate to tell people you're new, okay?"

She nodded.

Benjamin touched her shoulder briefly and then went back into the kitchen. Zoey was rattling glasses angrily behind the bar. And Nina waited for her first customer, tears of humiliation gathering in her eyes.

Dear Mrs. Pressman,

Thank you so much for the card and flowers. They mean a great deal to my parents.

Thank you also for attending Lara's funeral. Friendship is very important to us right now.

Benjamin

Dear Mr. and Mrs. Norton,

Thank you so much for the card and flowers. My parents really enjoyed them.

Thank you also for attending the funeral. I know it would have meant a great deal to Lara.

Benjamin

Dear Mr. and Mrs. McRoyan,

Thank you so much for the card and flowers and for attending Lara's funeral. I know it would have meant a great deal to her. I'm not sure how well you knew Lara, but she was a very special person.

Benjamin

Dear Mrs. Cabral,

Thank you so much for your letter and for attending Lara's funeral. I know it would have meant a great deal to her. She thought the world of you. I'm not sure how well you knew Lara, but she was a very special person, very kind.

Benjamin

Dear Mr. and Mrs. Geiger,

Thank you so much for attending Lara's funeral. I know it would have meant a great deal to her. She thought the world of you. I'm not sure how well you knew Lara, but she was a very special person, very kind and loving, generous, sweet, giving. . . .

Burke showed the letter to Sarah. "Lara *McAvoy?*" he asked.

Ten

Claire drained the water from her Hot Pot of noodles into a bowl with a satisfying *whoosh* and billow of steam.

"Fire department," said a voice from behind her.

She looked over her shoulder. Paolo was standing in the doorway, walkie-talkie in hand.

"Oh, very funny," she said. When she turned around, Paolo was sitting at her desk. "Excuse me," Claire said, "but do you ever *work?*"

He grinned. "Not usually. What are we having for lunch?"

She rolled her eyes, but since he didn't show any signs of moving, she got another bowl out of her drawer and served him half of her ramen noodles. She pulled Jake's chair up to the desk.

Paolo smiled at her. "Our first date."

Claire shook her head. "This is *not* our first date."

"I guess you're right," Paolo said with his mouth full. "Our first date was the night I walked you home from the movie. Hey, we're practically going steady."

Claire laughed in spite of herself. "Want some Coke?"

He nodded, and as she leaned over to the tiny refrigerator he said, "This is delicious. You're a great cook."

"They're *ramen noodles!*" Claire protested.

Paolo ignored her. "You're perfect: beautiful and a good cook."

Claire set two cans of Coke on the table. "Paolo, I refuse to be complimented on ramen noodles. And I don't look very beautiful right now. I'm not wearing any makeup—"

"And you have a pimple on your chin," Paolo added.

"I do not," Claire said indignantly, wondering if it was true.

"Listen," Paolo said with maddening sincerity. "I still think you're beautiful, warts and all."

"Warts!" Claire exclaimed from the far side of the room, where she was examining her face in the mirror.

"That's just an expression," Paolo said.

"My skin is fine," Claire said, turning from side to side. And she secretly thought she did look kind of beautiful, makeup or no makeup. She'd drawn her rich dark hair back and secured it casually with a clip, and she wore the same jeans and black turtleneck that every girl in Cambridge seemed to be wearing.

She sat back down and picked up her fork. "Do you ever have normal conversations with anyone?"

Paolo's eyes lit up. "Is that what you want?"

"No, it's not what I *want*," Claire said. "I just wondered if—"

"Okay, let's go," Paolo interrupted. "Hello, how are you?"

Claire blinked. "What?"

"Okay, now you say, 'Fine, how are you?' "

"No."

"Come on," Paolo pleaded. "How are we going to have a normal conversation otherwise? Or do you want to talk about the weather? Boy, this sure is a nice brisk autumnal day—"

"Who says autumnal?" Claire asked. "I mean, in everyday conversation. You sound like an English professor."

Just then Paolo's walkie-talkie let out a squawk, and he picked it up. "Yeah?" He listened for a minute. "Right now? Well, I'm kind of busy. I'm having lunch with a beautiful girl. Although she has a pimple."

Claire gave him a sour look.

Paolo laughed into the walkie-talkie. "No,

the dark-haired one," he said. "Okay, be right there."

The dark-haired one! Claire thought furiously. *So now he thinks I'm one of his harem!*

Paolo clicked off the walkie-talkie and stood up. "I'm afraid I have to go. Someone's phone got stolen on the second floor."

Claire looked at him coolly. "Well, you know, neither rain nor sleet nor dark of night . . ."

He grinned. "When can I see you again?"

"Since when do I have a choice in the matter?" Claire asked, and Paolo laughed.

Just then Jake appeared in the doorway. "Hi," Claire said casually.

Jake looked a little apprehensive to see a security monitor in their room, so Claire hurried to introduce him. "Jake, this is Paolo O'Connell. Paolo, this is Jake McRoyan."

They shook hands, which amused Claire.

"You're a friend of Claire's?" Paolo asked.

For no reason at all Claire thought about Paolo saying *the dark-haired one,* and she answered before Jake.

"He's my boyfriend," she said, ignoring the shocked look on both their faces.

"Oh, yes, and an iced tea, please," the woman at table two said, handing her menu to Nina, who could barely keep from groaning. Because iced teas came with free refills, which meant even more running around lifting that stupid heavy pitcher and trying not to splash.

"Sure thing," Nina said weakly. She took the menus and trotted back to the kitchen to give the order to Benjamin. Her feet ached from all these trips to the kitchen and the tables. Nina tried to think if she'd ever seen an overweight waitress. She doubted it. Not with all this exercise. Besides, when did they get to eat?

Nina was really beginning to wonder when *she* would get to eat. She'd rushed out of the house without breakfast, and she'd been working three hours now. Every time she served a cheeseburger, her eyes were wide with longing. Maybe she could get Benjamin to make her a shake or—

"Miss, could I have the check, please?" the man at table three asked.

"You can get your check and pay at the register," Nina answered with a cheerfulness she was far from feeling.

"I'd like my check now so I can look it over, if you don't mind," the man said.

Nina looked at him with thinly veiled irritation. *Want to make sure I'm not overcharging you for your BLT, huh?* she thought. *Big spender.*

"Coming right up," she said aloud. She knew now why waitresses said things like "Coming right up" and "Sure thing" and "No problem." Because if they actually said what they really meant, every sentence would begin with, "Listen, you idiot . . ."

She went over to the cash register and began hastily tallying the check. Her back was beginning to ache, too. Well, at least nobody had ordered a cocktail yet, so she hadn't had to deal with Zoey. No one was sitting at the bar, either, so Zoey was totally free to hunch moodily over the counter, watching Nina make mistakes.

And Nina made so many mistakes! Who knew you were supposed to pour water out of the *side* of the pitcher so it didn't splash? Who knew you always approached customers from the left? (They weren't horses, after all.) And then there were the just plain dumb mistakes, like when she took the woman's order but not the man's and had to return, cheeks burning. Or dropping that plate of fries. Or putting a straw in a Coke with the wrapper still on. Or—

"Could I have some more iced tea?" asked table four.

"Could we have the check?" That was table one.

"I asked for pickles with this—"

"We've been waiting—"

"If it's not too much trouble—"

"I ordered the soup—"

The voices were crowding around Nina, and she looked up, bewildered. Who should she take care of first? Plates were waiting for her in the kitchen. And what about this man's check? What was she going to do? *What was she going to do?* Her eyes filled, and she was swaying on her feet.

And then suddenly a strong hand was on her elbow.

Benjamin, she thought.

But it wasn't Benjamin, it was Christopher, absently holding on to Nina and surveying the room with his sharp eyes. He brought his gaze back to her. "You okay?"

She blinked and nodded. "All right, then take this pitcher and refill all the iced teas." He thrust the pitcher into her hands, and she moved away. Behind her she heard Christopher say sharply, "Zoey, stop leaning on your elbows. Get those plates out of the kitchen and deliver them before they're cold."

Christopher himself flipped quickly through Nina's messy pile of checks, correcting her math here and there, and distributed them to the correct tables.

Within minutes twenty people were happily eating their meals instead of threatening mutiny. Nina looked at Christopher with a grateful smile that was almost blinding.

He took her by the arm again and began steering her back toward the kitchen, taking a final scan of the room as he went. "Zoey, keep an eye on things," he said.

He led Nina into the kitchen and sat her down at a little table. "Nina's on break," he announced to Benjamin. "You got anything to spare?"

Benjamin looked pretty harassed himself. "Um, yeah, a hamburger. Over there."

Christopher slapped the burger on a plate and put it in front of Nina. "Sorry, but I don't have time to make you anything else."

"No, no, I wanted a burger," Nina said. She took a bite. Heavenly. Or maybe that was just because she was sitting down.

Christopher was tying an apron around his waist. "I'll take over back here," he said to Benjamin. "You go out by the cash register—" He broke off. "Weren't you going to take this afternoon off and go see your folks?"

Benjamin bit his lip. "Well, when Kendra called in sick, I thought I'd better stick around."

But Kendra didn't call in, Nina thought. *She called me. He's lying.*

"Well, you can go now, if you like," Christopher said.

"Oh, I don't mind working the register," Benjamin said. He gave Nina a quick wink and hurried through the swinging doors.

Christopher checked the food on the grill and then began readying the plates. "You were doing a good job," he said to Nina.

She groaned. "Don't flatter me," she said. "Those people were ready to draw blood."

Christopher laughed. "You should have seen me on my first day. I actually got fired." He turned serious. "You really were trying hard. I appreciate it."

Nina warmed to the praise. It would have been nicer to hear it from Zoey, but since that didn't seem likely to happen, she would take what she could get.

Christopher set a plate of fries and a Coke in front of her. "Got to keep up your strength," he said.

Just then Benjamin came back into the kitchen, wheeling a trolley with a giant plastic foam freezer on it. "The steaks I ordered just arrived," he said, panting.

Christopher frowned. "What steaks?"

"From New England Beef," Benjamin said. "They're outside, bringing in the rest."

"The rest?" Christopher asked. "How much did you order?"

"Three hundred pounds," Benjamin said, puzzled. "That was how much my mom ordered."

Christopher hit himself on the forehead. "That was our entire fall order," he moaned. He was standing next to the freezer, and he swung open the door. "Look," he said.

Nina looked. The freezer was full of neatly wrapped white parcels. She looked at the freezer on Benjamin's trolley.

She and Christopher and Benjamin spoke at the same time, but that was okay because they all said the same thing: *Where are we going to put it?*

Eleven

The sounds of the lawn party were already boisterous outside, but Aisha still stood by her bed, wearing a towel and trying to decide what to wear. She had plenty of clothes, pretty new clothes bought with her summer earnings, and they were spread out on the bed in front of her: the raspberry-colored suede vest, the needlepoint-plaid linen shorts, the chartreuse blouse with the notched collar, the blue silk blouse with the zippered front, the lime green miniskirt with small flowers.

Such beautiful clothes, and yet Aisha didn't want to wear any of them because—because—

Because she wanted Christopher to see her in them when she wore them for the first time.

Now that is really lame, Aisha thought.

But it was also true. She wanted to wear her new clothes for the first time—the time you felt the most beautiful in them—when Christopher was around to see her.

I am not one of those girls who only comes

alive when her boyfriend is around, Aisha told herself. *After all, I'm going to go to the lawn party, I'm going to dance, I'm going to mingle. But I worked hard for these clothes, and if I want to wear them around Christopher, I guess I can do just that.*

She decided to wear a new outfit that Christopher had seen last weekend—a long purple skirt and sleeveless white blouse. She was just fastening the skirt when Felicia breezed in.

"Hey, you look nice," Felicia said.

"Thanks," Aisha said. "How was your study group?"

Felicia shrugged and threw her books on the bed. "We spent more time drinking coffee and making fun of the professor than studying."

Aisha felt a small pang. Why did it seem like Felicia had already carved a niche for herself here at Harvard, with coffee after class and study groups and a circle of friends, while Aisha still felt like such an outsider?

"Are you going to the lawn party?" Felicia asked.

"Uh-huh."

"If you wait while I take a shower, I'll go with you," Felicia said, peeling off her T-shirt.

Aisha summoned a smile. "That would be great."

Felicia slipped into her robe and disappeared down the hall. Aisha did her makeup while she waited.

Felicia was back in a few minutes, wearing a towel, her wet hair combed back, her cheeks dotted with moisture. "Okay," she said, opening a drawer. "I'll be ready in just a sec."

"No rush," Aisha said.

Felicia stepped into a black miniskirt and fastened a white lace bra. She stood in front of her closet, finger combing her damp blond hair. "God, I hate all my clothes, and I just bought them a month ago."

"I know what you mean," Aisha said.

Felicia apparently gave up looking for a shirt and crossed the room to her dresser. She picked up her hair dryer and began drying her hair, still arranging it with her fingers. "So," she said, glancing at Aisha in the mirror, "I've hardly seen you since you went home for the funeral. How was your trip?"

"Oh, all right," Aisha said. She paused. "Zoey said to thank you for the letter."

"Oh, good," Felicia said absently. "I hope you don't mind me writing to her."

Aisha was startled—maybe because she *did* in fact mind.

"No," she said slowly. "Why would I?"

Why would I mind? she thought. *Just because you run hot and cold with me? Just because you didn't even bother to mention to me that Zoey had ever called?*

Felicia shrugged, turning off the blow-dryer. "I don't know. Some people are really possessive about their friends."

"Well, I guess I'm not one of those people," Aisha said, trying to keep her voice light. "How did you get her address, just out of curiosity?"

Felicia was putting on mascara, and Aisha thought she saw the mascara wand tremble just a little. "I called directory information," Felicia said.

"Oh, right, of course," Aisha said.

You wouldn't have looked through my address book, would you? she thought. *How many of my other friends did you look up while you were at it?*

Then she suddenly thought she was being paranoid. So what if Felicia *had* looked through her address book? What did it matter? Felicia had done a nice thing for a friend of Aisha's, a friend who had appreciated the gesture, had said it helped her. Now, where was the harm in that?

I've got to try harder with Felicia, Aisha

118

thought. *I've got to learn to like her and trust her and see what everyone else sees in her.*

"Oh, boy, this is beautiful," Felicia said, interrupting her thoughts. She was touching the suede vest, which still lay on Aisha's bed. "Could I borrow it?"

Again Aisha was surprised. They had never borrowed each other's clothes before, had never even discussed it.

"Tonight?" Aisha asked, stalling for time.

"Well, yeah, if that's okay with you," Felicia said.

No, it's not okay with me! Aisha wanted to shout. *I paid almost ninety dollars for that vest, and I haven't even worn it yet myself! I don't want it to smell like smoke and sweat! I don't want to have it dry-cleaned if you spill something on it!*

But for some reason she didn't feel comfortable saying any of these things. Maybe because she'd never had sisters, she wasn't used to telling someone not to wear her clothes. Besides, hadn't she just thought that she needed to try harder with Felicia?

"I—um—sure," she said at last.

"Oh, thanks," Felicia said. She slipped on the vest and buttoned it.

Aisha looked at her and wanted to cry. The

raspberry color made Felicia's skin glow. The rich suede was a perfect foil for Felicia's corn silk hair. And worse—oh, far worse—was the way the vest fit as though it had been tailor-made for Felicia, molding softly to her small waist and generous breasts, showing just a hint of cleavage. It was practically the sexiest top Aisha had ever seen.

"Ready?" Felicia asked brightly, smiling at her reflection in the mirror.

Aisha swallowed. "Sure."

Felicia looked at her, a tiny line between her eyes. "Are you okay?"

Aisha nodded. "I'm fine," she lied.

I don't think I'll ever be able to enjoy wearing that vest myself, she thought. *But sure, I'm fine. Just fine.*

It was after eleven when Zoey closed the screen door to the restaurant kitchen behind her and tried to give Benjamin a cheerful smile.

Benjamin didn't smile back. He was leaning on the counter by the kitchen phone with a notepad and pencil in his hands. He'd been calling everyone on the island, trying to find freezer space for the excess steaks.

Zoey set three white-wrapped steaks on the

counter. "Mrs. Norton and I tried and tried, but we couldn't fit those last three in," she said. "Did you have any luck finding another freezer?"

Benjamin nodded. "Christopher has taken some over to the Pressmans', and Mrs. Gray thinks they have some room. She even said they might buy some from us."

Zoey couldn't stop herself from wincing. "Oh, Benjamin, I hate to see them do that," she said. "They've done so much for us already."

Benjamin's eyes were bleak. "I know," he said quietly. "And they couldn't really buy enough to make a difference, anyway."

"Did Christopher get through to New England Beef?" Zoey asked.

"Yeah, he finally called the manager at home," Benjamin said. "But he says that they can't take the steaks back. That's their policy, and they won't make an exception."

His voice was flat and angry—angry with himself, Zoey knew. She wished she could make him feel better. "Well, we'll just have to call a few more people," she said gently. "We'll find the freezer space, I'm sure."

"That's not the only problem, Zoey," Benjamin said. "The bill for all these steaks is just about going to wipe out the restaurant account."

"Oh, no," Zoey said.

"We're going to have to tell Mom and Dad," Benjamin said dismally. "So they can transfer money from their savings account."

"Oh, do we have to tell them?" Zoey said. "Isn't there something else we can do?"

"Not that I can think of," Benjamin said tersely.

Zoey flushed. *Don't make him feel worse than he already does,* she thought.

"Well," she said with false brightness, "why don't I take another load over to Mrs. Gray's, and then we'll see where we stand?"

Benjamin sighed. "Okay. Do you want some iced tea or anything before you go?"

"No, I'm fine," Zoey said.

Benjamin added the three steaks she'd brought back to a cardboard box he'd already packed and put the box carefully in Zoey's arms. "Is that too heavy? Do you want me to take it?"

"No, no. It's no problem," Zoey said, trying not to pant. The box *was* heavy, but she didn't want Benjamin to go over to the Grays'. She didn't want him to see the pity in anyone's face. "You make a few more calls."

Benjamin held the door open for her, and she trotted through, limping slightly because of a blister on her right heel.

"I'll be right back," Zoey said. Benjamin didn't answer.

She moved away from the restaurant slowly. The box was bulky, and the bottom was moist. The cardboard edge was soaking her shirt where the box touched her stomach.

Zoey sighed. She was hot and sticky and tired, and at this rate it looked like they might be up all night trying to place the steaks. *All I really want to do,* she thought, *is take a long hot shower and have Lucas rub my shoulders and—*

She almost stopped walking, she was so startled. Where had that thought come from? She wasn't used to random thoughts about Lucas slipping into her mind. She guarded against them by spending all her time concentrating on how much she hated him, how he had betrayed her, how he had lied to her.

So why was she suddenly fantasizing about back rubs? *I must be exhausted*, she thought. *I'll think about something else, something happy.*

But there weren't many happy things to think about. She didn't want to think about Berkeley and her friends there. She didn't want to think about Nina. She didn't want to think about the restaurant and how little money they were making. She didn't want to think about telling her parents that they needed money. She didn't—

Without warning the bottom of the box burst, and cold paper-wrapped steaks scattered on the ground, leaving Zoey holding nothing but soggy cardboard. She swore softly. The box was useless; the bottom was completely gone. She threw it aside and knelt down to begin gathering the steaks. But she had only picked up three or four when the tears she had been holding back for so long caught up with her.

Zoey sat among her strewn steaks and wept, wept at the unfairness of the fire. It had taken everything from her: her home, her parents' health, her college tuition, her freedom, everything. She buried her face in her hands and cried silently in the moonlit street.

She didn't stop even when she heard footsteps. *That'll be Christopher,* she thought. *He'll help me carry these steaks.*

But it wasn't Christopher who said, "Zoey?"

It was Lucas.

He knelt beside her. "Zoey, what is it?" He put his hand on her shoulder.

At his touch all the old anger came back, and she jerked away. "Don't touch me."

Lucas sat back on his heels and ran a hand

through his hair awkwardly. "What happened? Did your box break? Do you need some help carrying this stuff?"

Zoey glared. "I don't want your help."

Lucas sighed, as though he had known she would say that. "Well, do you at least have freezer space for all the meat yet?" he asked.

"How did you know about that?" Zoey snapped.

"Benjamin called my mom to ask if we could take some," Lucas said.

Damn Benjamin! Zoey thought. *Can't he let us handle anything without calling my ex-boyfriend for help?*

She stood up awkwardly and began picking up steaks again.

"At least let me load them onto your arms," Lucas said.

Zoey sighed. "Fine," she said ungraciously. She stood still while Lucas stacked the steaks into her outstretched arms.

"Um, something you might think about doing," he said tentatively, "would be selling the steaks to another restaurant. I do a lot of business with a place in Weymouth, and I'm sure that if you called and said you were a friend of mine—"

Anger almost made Zoey throw the steaks on the ground again. "Lucas, how many times do I have to tell you that I don't need your help? I don't need it, I don't want it, and I won't accept it. Is that clear? And as for being a friend of yours—"

"You're going to have to start taking help from somebody," Lucas said. His voice was quiet. "Otherwise the restaurant is going to overwhelm you, and you'll drown in self-pity."

"I don't feel sorry for myself!" she flared, lying.

Lucas was unruffled. "Well, I'm a little surprised to hear that, but I'm glad. I know you feel like you're making a big sacrifice for your parents, but did you ever think about the sacrifice *Lara* made for them?"

Zoey's cheeks burned, and she said nothing. God, he was right. Here she was, pining for Berkeley when Lara was—was—

"You forget that I know what you're going through," Lucas said gently. "And I mean, I know *exactly* what you're going through. I know what it's like to have college yanked away. I know what it's like to have to take the job and responsibility that used to be your parents'."

"I hadn't forgotten," Zoey mumbled. But she had. She had been so caught up in her own misery that it hadn't occurred to her that this was exactly what had happened to Lucas.

She looked at him. His blond hair was silver in the moonlight, and shadows made his face seem older. He moved with effortless ease, the result of the hard labor he did. He now had energy to spare. Watching him, Zoey felt a longing so strong, it almost made her cry out.

Oh, Lucas, she thought sorrowfully. *Why did it have to end like this between us?*

Her longing must have shown on her face because Lucas suddenly said, "Zoey?" in a way that made her heart pound. He stepped closer to her, and after a long moment he reached out and touched her face with a fingertip. She wanted to tell him not to touch her, but she couldn't seem to speak.

"Oh, Zoey," Lucas said softly. His hand moved gently against her cheek. "I've missed you so much. I can barely stay away from you. I used to dream that you would come back to the island, and now you have, and you won't let me near you."

The steaks were heavy in Zoey's arms, but she didn't move. She felt hypnotized.

Lucas's finger touched her lips. "Zoey, can't we try again?" he asked softly. "I would never—"

Zoey's paralysis broke, and she shoved him away with her pile of steaks. "No!" she said angrily. "No! We can never try again! Never! I'm sick of trying again!" Her voice wavered. She turned around so that she wouldn't have to look at him.

She heard him sigh, and then after a minute he put the last steak into her arms and Zoey lowered her head. She began walking away.

"Zoey?" Lucas called.

She turned.

"The restaurant in Weymouth is Uncle Harry's," he said softly. "Ask for Harry Nicholas."

Zoey nodded. She knew she should say something, even if it was only thanks. But even that word stuck in her throat, and in the end she said nothing at all.

27 Climbing Way
North Harbor, ME

Mr. Harvey Craven
Town Building Inspector
City Hall
103 Main Street
Weymouth, ME

Dear Mr. Craven,
    I am very interested in obtaining the original blueprints for One Camden Street in North Harbor. Do you have them on file?
    Your help is appreciated.
                        Sincerely,
                        Lucas Cabral

Town Building Inspector
City Hall
103 Main Street
Weymouth, ME

Mr. Lucas Cabral
27 Climbing Way
North Harbor, ME

Dear Mr. Cabral,
　　Unfortunately the blueprints for One Camden Street are not on file because the house was built before 1960.
　　Our records do reveal, however, that Skaa Modern Architecture applied for a building permit for that site in 1957. Perhaps they could help you.
　　Best of luck.

　　　　　　　Sincerely,
　　　　　　　Mr. Harvey Craven
　　　　　　　Weymouth Building Inspector

27 Climbing Way
North Harbor, ME

Skaa Modern Architecture
332 East Glendale
Weymouth, ME

Dear Sir or Madam,
    I am very interested in obtaining the
original blueprints for One Camden Street
in North Harbor, which I believe was built in
1957 or 1958.
    Would it be possible to obtain a copy?
    Your help is appreciated.
                        Sincerely,
                        Lucas Cabral

Skaa Modern Architecture
332 East Glendale
Weymouth, ME

Mr. Lucas Cabral
27 Climbing Way
North Harbor, ME

Dear Mr. Cabral,

    One Camden Street was designed by Mr. Skaa himself, and he took the blueprints with him when he retired.

    You may contact him at 220 Bluebird Lane in Presque Isle, Maine.

    Best of luck.

                Sincerely,
                Ms. Linda Wilkes

27 Climbing Way
North Harbor, ME

Mr. Eric Skaa
220 Bluebird Lane
Presque Isle, ME

Dear Mr. Skaa,

I am very interested in obtaining the original blueprints for One Camden Street in North Harbor, which I believe was built in 1957 or 1958.

Would it be possible to obtain a copy? I would do almost anything to get one.

Sincerely,
Lucas Cabral

Twelve

Christopher and Zoey looked up Uncle Harry's in the phone book.

"Okay," Christopher said, "here goes." He picked up the receiver.

"Don't forget to say that *you're* the friend of Lucas's," Zoey said.

Christopher nodded and rolled his eyes. *How could I forget when you keep telling me that every two seconds?* he thought.

He dialed and put the receiver to his ear. One ring, two rings. "Hello, Uncle Harry's."

Christopher turned his back to Zoey and tried to make his voice sound deeper, older. "Hello, could I speak to Harry Nicholas, please?"

"Speaking."

Christopher took a deep breath. "This is Christopher Shupe, and I'm a friend of Lucas Cabral's."

"Oh, right," Harry said, warmth filling his voice. "How's Lucas?"

"He's fine," Christopher said, hoping this was true. "The reason I'm calling is—well, I run a restaurant over here in North Harbor, Passmores'?"

"Uh-huh?"

"And, well, our assistant manager ordered a lot more sirloin than we can use, and Lucas suggested that we call you and see if you might, ah, want to take some of it off our hands."

"I could probably do that," Harry said agreeably, and it was all Christopher could do to keep from saying, *You will? You will?* "Where's the sirloin from?"

"New England Beef and Poultry," Christopher answered.

"Grade A?" Harry asked.

"Absolutely," Christopher said. *Benjamin only orders the best,* he thought crazily.

"Just how much extra you boys got?" Harry asked.

Christopher smiled wryly at the word *boys*. Apparently his deep voice wasn't fooling anyone. "About three hundred pounds," he said.

Harry didn't whistle, and Christopher was grateful. "I could probably use about a hundred pounds of that," Harry said thoughtfully.

Christopher was disappointed, but it would be good to get rid of even a third—

"And I got a friend in the restaurant business across town who'll take the rest of it," Harry added. "Let me just clear it with him, and I'll call you right back."

"That would be great," Christopher said, weak with relief.

"What's your name again?" Harry asked.

Christopher told him and gave him the number.

"Okay . . ." Christopher heard the rustling of papers. "Why don't I send a couple of boys and a truck over for it at noon? Or doesn't that damnable ferry run then?"

"Oh, we would deliver it to you, sir," Christopher said.

Harry laughed. "Christopher, you sound about Lucas's age, am I right?"

Christopher paused. "Something like that."

"Well, you're probably running the same hand-to-mouth operation, then," Harry said. "I can afford to send a couple of guys over a lot more than you can afford to take a few hours out of your workday. Trust me, it's no problem."

"That would be great," Christopher said again.

"No sweat," Harry said. "You give my best to Lucas."

Christopher thanked him again and hung up.

He turned to Zoey. "He's going to buy all of it," he said simply.

Zoey shouted and hugged him. "Oh—my—God," she said, giving three little hops. "I've never been so happy in my life."

"And he's sending some guys over to pick it up," Christopher said.

Zoey hugged her elbows and spun around in a small circle, the skirt of her ridiculous baby doll dress swirling. "What a wonderful man! Thank you, Christopher!"

"You should thank Lucas," Christopher said.

Her face closed like a door. "I don't want to talk about that," she said.

I'll bet you don't, Christopher thought, but he only shrugged and said, "Okay. But let's go over to the Grays' and borrow their golf cart. We can pick up all the steaks and have them back here before lunch."

Zoey groaned. "Why didn't we think of the golf cart last night? Come on."

They locked the restaurant and headed down the street, Zoey bouncing along happily at his side.

"So when are you going to go visit Aisha?" she asked.

"I don't know," Christopher said thoughtfully. "I've been so busy here, and Aisha's been acting a little odd."

"I've thought so, too," Zoey said.

"You have?" Christopher asked. His heart swelled with relief. So it wasn't just him.

"Yes," Zoey said. "She's been really preoccupied. I think it has something to do with Felicia."

"Her roommate?"

"Uh-huh." Zoey nodded. "I can't understand why, though. Felicia is really nice."

"You've met her?" Christopher asked, surprised.

"Oh, no," Zoey said. "But I've talked to her on the phone, and when Lara—after the fire Felicia wrote me the nicest letter, with a quote, although of course she didn't know how much I like quotes. It was Shakespeare. 'When sorrows come, they come not as single spies, but in battalions.'"

"*Hamlet*," Christopher said.

Zoey looked at him. "Is it? I didn't know which play."

Christopher wouldn't have known, either, except that he had seen it written down somewhere recently. But where? He frowned, trying to remember. It wouldn't come to him.

"Anyway," Zoey was saying. "I don't know why I found that quote comforting, but I did. Maybe because it seemed like people have been having trouble for *centuries* or something. But Aisha doesn't like her."

"I get that impression, too," Christopher said.

"There must be a good reason," Zoey concluded. She looked at Christopher. "Because I trust Aisha's judgment, don't you?"

Christopher thought for a moment. *A good question*, he decided.

Claire was happy as she slid into the booth across from Jake. It was so good to get out of the dorm, even just for lunch. She was tired of seeing the same faces in the cafeteria every day, tired of eating the industrial-tasting food.

"Pepperoni and garlic?" Jake asked.

"Sounds good." Claire smiled as she looked across at Jake while he placed their order. She couldn't decide whether she liked his goatee or not. Sometimes she thought it gave his face more character. Sometimes she could imagine Nina saying, *Excuse me, but are you aware that a mouse died on your chin?*

"What are you smiling about?" Jake asked.

"Oh, nothing." She shrugged. "I'm just happy to get away from the dorm."

"Yeah, I know what you mean," Jake replied.

"So," he said, turning back to Claire. "I don't mean to pry, but, uh, if we're boyfriend and girlfriend, shouldn't I at least *know* about it?"

Claire blushed. "I'm sorry about that," she said. "I just—I wanted Paolo to stop bothering me, and that seemed like the easiest way."

Jake shook his head. "Claire, he's not *bothering* you; he *likes* you."

"Well, I don't like him," Claire said.

"Why not?"

Claire frowned. Paolo did bother her—in more ways than one. He irritated her, and she thought about him more than she wanted to. But how could she explain to Jake that she didn't want to get involved with someone whose personality changed like quicksilver, who ducked her attempts to maneuver him, who laughed at her anger, who got under her skin as thoroughly as Paolo?

"I'm just not looking for anyone right now," she said finally.

Jake smiled. "Everyone's looking," he said. "All the time."

"Including you?" Claire asked.

"We're not talking about me," Jake said.

Unfortunately, Claire thought. "Well, let's just say that with my history, I'm not really looking to rush into another relationship."

Jake looked uncomfortable. "I'm part of your history," he said.

Claire smiled faintly. "I know, but you're not the part I'm referring to."

"Oh," he said. "Aaron?"

She nodded. "And Sean."

"Oh, God, Claire," Jake said. "I'm sorry. I'm a jerk."

She laughed. "Why? Because you forgot that I had a stalker? Don't worry. I'm glad that people *can* forget."

"But you can't," Jake said.

"It'll take me a little longer," Claire said lightly.

"Is that why you haven't been back to North Harbor yet?" Jake asked.

Claire hesitated, then nodded. "Part of it, I guess. Why haven't *you* been back?"

"I'm not sure," Jake said, considering. "I almost went back for Lara's funeral, but I felt too guilty."

"Guilty?"

He nodded. "About the way I treated Lara, and the times I yelled at her, and how I never believed anything good about her. And I should've believed because when it counted, Lara was just about as good as you can be."

"I know," Claire said. "My dad said something about a falling beam? And that investigators say she could've gone right out Zoey's window and been safe."

Jake nodded soberly. Then he smiled faintly. "Let's talk about something else," Jake said. He stroked his chin. "What do you think of my new goatee?"

A shadow fell across the table, and Claire thought, *Thank God our pizza is here, and I don't have to answer.*

But when she looked up, Paolo was standing next to their booth, smiling. "Mind if I join you?" he asked.

NATIONAL INSURANCE FIRE CLAIM FORM

Policy Number: 589912KSH

Date: September 30

Policy Holder: Jeffrey R. Passmore & Darla K. Passmore

Person Conducting Inventory: Zoey Passmore

Check destroyed in fire:

Living Room		Dining Room	
	Articles		**Articles**
✓	Books	✓	Buffet
✓	Bookcases	✓	Candelabra
✓	Chairs, occasional	✓	Centerpiece sets
✓	Chairs, upholstered	✓	Chairs
✓	Clocks	✓	Chandelier
✓	Curtains and drapes	✓	China cabinet
✓	Desk	✓	Chinaware
✓	Fireplace accessories	✓	Clocks
✓	Lamps	✓	Crystal
✓	Mirrors	✓	Curtains and drapes
✓	Pictures	✓	Glassware
✓	Stereo system	✓	Lamps

Kitchen and Pantry		Bathrooms	
	Articles		**Articles**
✓	Chairs	✓	Chairs
✓	Chinaware	✓	Clothes hamper
✓	Clocks	✓	Curtains
✓	Coffeemakers	✓	Dressing table
✓	Curtains and draperies	✓	Hair dryer, curling iron
✓	Dishwasher	✓	Medicinal supplies
✓	Pots and pans	✓	Mirrors
✓	Radio	✓	Razor, electric
✓	Refrigerator	✓	Rugs
✓	Rugs	✓	Scale
✓	Silverware	✓	Toilet articles (misc.)
✓	Stove	✓	Towels and linen
✓	Tables		Other items

Bedrooms		Miscellaneous	
	Articles		**Articles**
✓	Beds and springs	✓	200 pages of a romance novel
✓	Blankets and spreads	✓	Letters Nina wrote from camp
✓	Bureaus	✓	The corsage from my first prom
✓	Chairs	✓	My baby book
✓	Chests	✓	A photo of my mom when she was 12
✓	Clock	✓	My sense of security
✓	Clothing	✓	My happiness
✓	Desk		
✓	Dresser		
✓	Dressing table		
✓	Lamps		

Thirteen

"Nina, I'm not paying you to read those confidential reports," said the school secretary, more commonly known as The Buzzard.

"You're not paying me at *all*," Nina said, scanning another report. "Remember? You docked me two weeks' pay because you think I stole an electric pencil sharpener."

"Well, you were the last known person with access to the supply room," The Buzzard said primly.

"But what do you think I *did* with it?" Nina protested. "Do you think I spend my time away from here doing story problems or something?"

The Buzzard was unruffled. "It's been known to happen," she said.

I'll bet it has, Nina thought. *With the bunch of nerds who had this job before me, it was probably an ongoing issue.*

She languidly opened another folder.

"Nina," The Buzzard said. "The Parents' Night invitations were supposed to go in the mail on Friday. Your work is really getting very sloppy, and your attitude is—"

Nina yawned delicately.

"Nina Geiger!" The Buzzard said, shocked.

"What?"

The Buzzard pursed her lips. "That was exceptionally rude."

Nina was startled. "What was?"

"Yawning while I was talking to you."

"I was sleepy!" Nina protested.

"Well, you should have suppressed your yawn until I was finished," The Buzzard said.

"Suppressing a yawn can damage your eardrums," Nina said darkly. "We learned it in biology."

"Nonsense," The Buzzard said firmly. "Furthermore—"

Thankfully the phone rang just then, and Nina moved to answer it. The Buzzard left huffily to collect the absence slips.

"Office," Nina mumbled into the phone.

"Could I speak to Nina, please?"

"It's me, Dad."

"Oh, wow," Burke said. "You sounded so professional, I didn't recognize you."

Nina sighed. Burke's enthusiasm about her office job grated on her nerves. "What's up?" she asked, trying to sound interested.

"Oh, well, I have two spare tickets to a benefit dinner," Burke said. "It's to benefit this new violin prodigy, and after the dinner he'll give a short recital."

"Uh-huh." Nina stifled another yawn.

"Well," Burke said. "I thought perhaps you'd like to go. You could take Benjamin."

"Dad," Nina said slowly. "I know that you tend to be a little slow on the uptake, but months should be enough lag time even for you. Benjamin and I broke up."

"I know. But—"

The second line began ringing. "Hold on a sec, Dad," Nina said. She slammed the hold button and picked up the other line. "Office."

It was some woman wanting to know when the Parents' Night invitations were going to be mailed out.

"When I'm good and ready," Nina snapped. She picked up the first line again. "Dad?"

"Yes, I'm still here," he said cheerfully. He had endless patience with being put on hold because he considered it part of her professionalism. "Anyway, even though I know you broke up with Benjamin, I thought he might enjoy this. He's been through such a rough time lately."

Oh, I'm sure he'd enjoy it, Nina thought. *He just wouldn't go with me.*

"I'll keep it in mind," she said finally.

"All right," Burke said. "Let me know."

"I will."

"Okay. Bye. Have a good day."

"You too," Nina said.

She hung up and leaned her elbows against the reception counter, no longer even making a pretense of stuffing envelopes. She was too depressed. Now Burke was interfering in her social life. Was she that pathetic? Yes, she supposed she was. After all, her best friend no longer spoke to her, and her boyfriend had dropped her like a hot potato and—

"Hi, Nina."

Benjamin was standing in front of the counter.

"Benjamin!" Nina said. "What are you doing here?"

He smiled. "It's nice to see you, too."

She flushed. "I was just—"

Thinking about you, she almost said.

"I didn't expect to see you here," she said instead. She didn't look him in the eye. She wasn't sure how to act.

"I need a copy of my transcripts," Benjamin said. "I might take a couple of night classes before I go back to Columbia next year."

Nina pushed a form across the desk toward him. "Well, you can fill out a request," she said. "And maybe if The Buzzard is in a good mood and has nothing else to do, she'll get around to pulling them for you."

Benjamin laughed, too. "God, this place never changes," he said, scratching his name and address on the form. "When I was walking down the hall just now, Mr. Hemple poked his head out of the typing room and said, 'Hey, Passmore, shouldn't you be in class?' Doesn't he realize that people do eventually graduate?"

Nina laughed, but she still couldn't look directly at Benjamin.

He handed the form back to her and then hesitated. "Nina, are you uncomfortable about what happened at the funeral?"

Her cheeks went red, and she looked down at the counter. She shook her head.

"Because you shouldn't be," Benjamin said. "I'm glad you were there for me. You helped me a lot."

His voice was so gentle and unembarrassed that she raised her eyes to his face. It was the same kind face as always.

"Well, you were right," she said softly. "What

you said about Lara. She was heroic."

She could see by the glad light in Benjamin's eyes that she'd said the right thing. They smiled at each other across the counter.

"Benjamin, would you like to go to a violin recital with me?" Nina said. "It's actually a benefit for this violin—player." She'd wanted to say *prodigy*, but she couldn't remember the right word.

Benjamin smiled. "I'd like that."

"You would?" Nina said.

He laughed. "Sure."

"Okay, then," Nina said. "I'll call you about the date and time."

"Sounds good," Benjamin said.

"How are your parents?" she asked.

He looked suddenly wary. "They're fine."

"Good," Nina said. "You must miss them."

A wry look passed over Benjamin's face.

"What is it?" Nina asked.

He shook his head. "It's just that I didn't realize it until you said that."

"Realize what?"

"That I miss my mother," Benjamin said. "I miss my mom."

Just then The Buzzard bustled through the office door. "Mr. Passmore," she said sternly. "Please let Ms. Geiger get to work. Shouldn't you be in class, anyway?"

Nina and Benjamin burst out laughing, which only made The Buzzard look more disapproving. Benjamin waved to Nina and ducked out the office door.

Nina went back to stuffing envelopes, working happily and singing "Rollercoaster" with so much gusto that even when The Buzzard stuck her head out of her office and said, "Nina, please quit that racket," she couldn't stop.

"Yes, we do mind if you join us," Claire said rudely, and Jake was amazed by the physical change in her. An angry flush had colored her cheeks, and her eyes were flashing. Jake wondered if she knew that she looked even prettier when she was angry. But then, since it was Claire after all, he figured she did.

Paolo sat down next to Claire, anyway. She didn't move over, though, so he was barely on the banquette and had to balance with one leg in the aisle. Still, he looked perfectly at ease.

"It's nice to see you again, Clara," he said to Claire. "And you too, Jake."

"Clara?" Jake asked.

"It's my nickname for her," Paolo said.

"I hate it," Claire said instantly.

"She hates it," Paolo agreed amiably.

She glared at him. "Is there an echo in here?"

"I don't know. Is there?" Paolo asked. He looked up at the ceiling. "Hello? Hellooo?"

People at neighboring tables glanced at them, and Jake hid a smile. No wonder this guy drove Claire crazy.

Claire was rolling her eyes. "Will you please be quiet?"

"Hey, you asked the question. I was just trying to help you out," Paolo said. He checked his watch. "Unfortunately I can only stay a few minutes. I'm supposed to be meeting one of my students here."

Jake was puzzled. "Your students?"

"I tutor a couple of subjects," Paolo said.

"*You* tutor a subject?" Claire repeated incredulously. "Some poor unsuspecting slob signs up for a tutor, and they get you? What subjects, if I may ask?"

Paolo didn't seem offended. "Spanish, Portuguese, and microbiology."

Claire frowned. "What is your major, anyway?"

"Premed," Paolo said, looking pleased with the question.

Claire choked on her water. "You're going to be a doctor?" she asked. "Specializing in what? Teenage girls with upper leg problems?"

"I haven't decided yet," Paolo said, grinning. "But I'll keep that in mind."

"Excuse me," Claire said. "I need to get out."

Paolo stood up. "Where are you going?"

"To find a quiet place to slit my wrists," Claire said. "You'd better be gone when I come back."

Jake and Paolo both watched her cross the restaurant toward the rest rooms. She was wearing jeans and a red velour shirt. Her dark hair shone against the rich fabric.

Paolo turned to Jake and smiled his disarming smile. "Did I interrupt something?"

Jake was suddenly uncomfortable. "Uh, no," he said. "Just lunch."

Paolo studied him silently for a moment. "Are you and Claire really going out?" he asked.

Jake hesitated. "Something like that."

"Something like that?" Paolo's eyes were bright with interest.

"Well, it's, uh, complicated," Jake said.

"Complicated because you have a rocky relationship?" Paolo asked. "Or complicated because you're not really going out and Claire made that up?"

Jake sighed. He didn't want to be disloyal to Claire, but on the other hand, his life was difficult enough without having to pretend to be Claire's boyfriend. "Look, just—don't tell her I told you, okay?" he said.

Paolo nodded thoughtfully. "I didn't think so," he said. "So . . . Claire wants to discourage me."

"You might say that," Jake said.

Paolo shrugged. "I can wait," he said. "She's so—perfect. So sweet and gentle. I could wait forever."

Jake looked up. Claire was coming back from the rest room, her eyebrows drawing together ominously when she saw Paolo still sitting at their table.

Jake wondered suddenly if he and Paolo were talking about the same person.

Zoey

Pros and Cons of Running the Restaurant

Pros	Cons
	- Too much responsibility.
	- Those stupid trays are really heavy.
	- I have to talk to gross men when I work the bar.
	- I have to serve gross men when I waitress.
	- I used to like french fries.
	- The cash register has ~~never~~ balanced out.
	- Benjamin gets really bossy sometimes.
	- I have to see Nina.
- I might have to see Lucas.	- I might have to see Lucas.

Fourteen

The bus was early, but Nina knew that the driver would just sit there until it was time to go. She sighed and climbed aboard, anyway—and then cried out as her forehead crashed against something hard.

"Ouch!" she said.

"Ow!" said a simultaneous voice.

Nina opened her eyes, still rubbing her forehead. "Lucas?"

He smiled painfully, rubbing his own forehead. "Hi, Nina."

"Sorry," they said, again simultaneously, and then smiled.

"I wasn't looking where I was going," Nina said.

Lucas shrugged. "I was bending over to pick up my change."

The bus driver spoke up. "Well, now that you've both recovered, why doesn't one of you get off and the other one get on?"

Nina scowled at him. "What does it matter? We're the only two people on here."

"Don't you sass me, miss," the bus driver said, pointing a finger at her. "This isn't the school bus, you know."

Thank God it's not, Nina thought, *or he'd probably call my father or give me detention or something.*

"I'm sorry, but it seems we have to cut our conversation short," she said to Lucas. She gave the driver a haughty look as she dropped her coins into the change box and deliberately walked to the very back of the bus and sat down.

A minute later she jumped when Lucas spoke to her through the open window. "We can still talk this way, you know," he said.

Nina pressed the latches and slid the window all the way down. "I didn't even get a chance to ask you what you were doing in town."

Lucas held up a brown paper bag. "I was just getting some supplies for Guy."

"Is he the guy—I mean, the, uh, man you work for at the lighthouse?" Nina wondered whether it was all right to refer to someone named Guy as a "guy." She silently cursed his parents.

"Yeah," Lucas said. "And you? Where are you going?"

She sighed dramatically. "The library. I have to give an oral report on nuclear power."

Lucas frowned. "Do you understand that stuff?"

"Nope," Nina said. "But the report's due tomorrow, so spurred by terror, I'm learning."

"Tomorrow!" Lucas repeated. "Can you be ready by then?"

Nina leaned her elbow out the window. "Well, if worse comes to worst, I thought I might make a tape recording of my dad explaining it, and then I could claim that I interviewed an engineer or something."

Lucas burst into laughter. "Nina, that's the most hilarious thing I've ever heard."

"I'm serious, though." Nina smiled uncertainly.

"I know," Lucas said, gasping. "That's what makes it so funny." Suddenly he looked up at her, and his face grew serious. "Nina, can we go back to being friends?"

"We—we are friends," Nina lied.

"I mean, friends who do things together," Lucas said. His hands gripped the edge of the open window. "It's not just you. I haven't called you, either. It's—" He hesitated.

"The guilt?" Nina said sardonically. "Is that the word you're looking for?"

He nodded. "Nina, we're never going to let— anything happen again, so—"

Nina moaned softly. "Lucas, please, let's just not talk about it. Okay?"

"No, not okay," he said, his voice low and solemn. "I know that you'd like to pretend that what happened between us never happened, but it did. We did what we did, and now Zoey's hurt. Last night I asked her for another chance—"

"You did?" Nina asked, startled. "What did she say?"

He grimaced. "It doesn't really bear repeating," he said. "But for just a minute, just a second, I caught her looking at me, and she didn't look angry or stubborn or . . ." He shrugged.

Nina sat back, defeated. *If only Zoey could forgive Lucas*, she thought. *Then maybe she'd forgive me.*

"My point is," Lucas said, "that we might as well learn from what happened. Haven't we at least learned that it won't happen again?"

"Oh, of course it won't," Nina said. "I would never let it happen again."

"Well, neither would I," Lucas said. "So why are we avoiding each other? As punishment?"

Nina picked a piece of foam out of a tear in the seat next to her. "Maybe," she said softly.

"Then isn't it time we got over it?" Lucas asked. He cleared his throat. "I mean, couldn't we both use a friend right about now?"

Nina looked up and studied his eyes, so full of kindness and hope. She felt suddenly as though a knot inside her chest were loosening, a knot that had been painfully tight for weeks. She took a deep breath.

"Yes, Lucas," she said solemnly, although she was smiling faintly. "I could use a friend right about now."

With her hand she covered his where it gripped the window edge. They smiled at each other. "Want to come over later?" she said. "You can be—"

You can be the engineer on the tape, was what she'd been about to say, but the words dissolved on her tongue.

Over Lucas's shoulder she could see Zoey, standing in the ferry parking lot, watching them.

Aisha and Felicia had pushed their desks together to make a sort of table, and now they sat across from each other, heads bent over identical thick Shakespeare texts as they studied for the next day's exams.

The window was open to catch the evening breeze, and occasionally voices reached their room as students passed. Aisha felt strangely at peace. This was the time of day she liked best, and she liked studying. At Harvard she didn't feel like the nerdy brainiac she had sometimes felt like in high school. Studying here just felt *right*. Everybody was doing it.

Across from her Felicia sighed and stretched. She was wearing a plain green T-shirt, and her blond hair was pulled back into the kind of sloppy, artless ponytail Aisha could never manage. "Is it my imagination," she said, "or is everyone in Shakespeare named Antonio?"

Aisha smiled. "Are you ready for tomorrow?"

"Not yet," Felicia said. "You?"

Aisha shook her head ruefully. "Not even close. I liked Shakespeare in the beginning, when we were reading the tragedies. . . ." Her eyes strayed to the quote from *Hamlet* she had taped to her closet door: "When sorrows come, they come not as single spies, but in battalions." She shrugged. "But these histories are so dry."

Felicia nodded. "I know. Sometimes in the middle of *King Lear* I would think, hey, the guy could turn a phrase, but with *Richard II*, it's all I can do to keep my eyes open."

Why can't we just have nice, normal conversations like this all the time? Aisha wondered. *Why is there usually such an undercurrent of tension?*

"What are you doing for dinner?" Felicia asked.

"I'll probably work right through," Aisha said.

"Me too," Felicia said. "Do you want to order something in from the deli?"

Aisha smiled. "That would be great."

"Okay." Felicia looked at her watch. "We'll take a break in an hour and order then?"

"Sure."

Felicia looked at Aisha for a long minute. "It's funny how we never sit next to each other in class," she said thoughtfully.

Aisha tried not to roll her eyes. Felicia made it sound like they had no control over where they sat in class, like it was something random. In fact, Aisha was always acutely aware of Felicia in Shakespeare class. She always felt a twinge of rejection when Felicia hurried in— looking sleepy but elegant, a bright wool scarf around her neck and a cup of coffee in her long fingers—and sat with her friends in the front of the lecture hall.

"Maybe we should," Aisha said tentatively. "Sit together, I mean."

Felicia nodded. "If you're not sick of me after tonight's marathon," she said, smiling. "I have a history exam, too."

Aisha groaned sympathetically. "How much studying do you have to do for that?"

"Let's just say I couldn't be *less* prepared," Felicia said. "All those treaties; I can never keep them straight."

"Oh, Christopher is really good at history," Aisha said absently. "He actually reads it for fun."

"Maybe I'll have to call him for help," Felicia said casually.

Aisha glanced at her quickly, but Felicia was already reading again, her dark lashes casting sooty shadows on her cheeks. Aisha studied Felicia's high clear forehead, her straight nose and full lips. *Right,* she thought sarcastically. *You're going to call Christopher for help. Over my dead body.*

Then she lowered her own head and tried to lose herself in Shakespeare again.

Zoey

Those cowards! Those
lying, low-down, cheating,
conniving bastards!

When I think of all
their promises: I'd never
cheat on you again, Zoey.
I only love you, Zoey.
It's over between us.
There was never anything
there, not really. We both
love you. Can't we start
over? Can't we be
friends again? What crap!

And why bother to lie?
I already knew. Lara had
already told me. They had
already admitted it. Can't
they just own up to it
for once?

Oh, and when I

remember the way my heart rolled over when Lucas touched me the other night, I feel so sick and hollow, I'm afraid I might throw up.

Fifteen

Zoey washed glasses behind the bar with trembling fingers and hoped that Mr. McRoyan would decide it was time to go home after this drink. Either that or a fiery pit would open and swallow him. Or he would pass out, and she and Kendra could haul him into the back room to sleep it off. Any of those alternatives would be fine with her.

But Mr. McRoyan only raised his glass and said tersely, "Scotch on the rocks."

"Yes, sir," Zoey said weakly. She poured the drink and set it in front of him on the bar.

Mr. McRoyan didn't thank her. He just stared at her with small red eyes. He had seemed more and more restless since Jake had left for college, more aggressive and hostile, too.

He's sloshed, Zoey thought worriedly, *and I have a really bad feeling that he's going to turn mean any minute now.* She wished more than anything that Jake were home, so she could call and ask him to come get his father. But

Jake was off at college, and Zoey didn't really relish the idea of talking to Mrs. McRoyan. She wondered suddenly if her parents had ever had to deal with him in this condition. Maybe this was a common occurrence. Maybe Mr. McRoyan got crocked on a weekly basis or something.

Kendra came up to the bartender station. "I need a white wine for table four."

Zoey poured the wine, and as she handed Kendra the glass she said in a low voice, "Look at Mr. McRoyan. Don't you think he's had enough?"

Kendra glanced over at Mr. McRoyan, her nostrils still pink from her cold. "What makes you say that?" she said, looking back at Zoey. "Other than the fact that he's swaying like we're at sea and half his drink is down the front of his shirt?"

"Should I cut him off?" Zoey asked anxiously.

Kendra bit her lip. "Maybe we could get some food inside him."

"Oh, that would be wonderful," Zoey murmured gratefully.

"Mr. McRoyan?" Kendra called brightly. "Can I get you anything? A cheeseburger? A ham sandwich?"

Mr. McRoyan glared. "If I wanted food, I'd

ask for it." He snorted. "Actually, if I wanted edible food, I'd go somewhere else."

Kendra flushed and turned away. "Well, that didn't work," she said to Zoey. "We're going to have to cut him off."

"He's not going to take that very well," Zoey said.

"But we *have* to," Kendra said.

Both girls glanced at the framed copy of the liquor license that hung behind the bar. It said, plain as day, Liquor Shall Not Be Served to Any Person Who Is, or Appears to Be, Intoxicated.

Well, Mr. McRoyan certainly fits that bill, Zoey thought, watching as Mr. McRoyan waved a hand in front of his face as though he were swatting at a fly. She realized with a start that he was actually signaling her.

"Oh, God," she said to Kendra in a low voice.

"You have to cut him off, Zoey," Kendra said. "If you don't and he does something, your parents could lose their license."

Zoey nodded bleakly. *Wouldn't that be a nice surprise for them when they get out of the hospital?* she thought.

She forced herself to walk back over to Mr. McRoyan's end of the bar. "Yes?" she asked politely.

"Scotch on the rocks."

"Mr. McRoyan . . . ," Zoey said softly. "I really think you've had enough."

He stared at her stupidly for a moment, not comprehending. Then his small eyes turned ugly. "You *what?*"

"I think you've had enough," Zoey said, wishing her voice would quit wobbling all over the place. "If you like, I can call someone—"

Mr. McRoyan's fist slammed down on the bar, causing glassware to ring. Zoey flinched. "I don't take orders from young snot-nosed brats who aren't even old enough to drink themselves," he said. "Now get me a Scotch."

I'll go get Benjamin, Zoey thought. *He'll handle this. I don't know why I didn't think of that before.*

"I don't know why I come here, anyway," Mr. McRoyan grumbled. "It's certainly not to be talked back to by the slut who threw my son over for a killer."

Zoey felt the blood drain from her face, and a pulse pounded heavily in her temples. Mr. McRoyan was referring to the car crash that had killed his son, Wade. Lucas had been in the car crash and had taken the rap for it. When he had come back after two years in Youth Authority, Zoey had fallen in love with him and ended her longtime relationship with Jake.

Now she wondered: How *dare* he? How dare Mr. McRoyan call Lucas a killer? Lucas wasn't a killer. He was the kindest, gentlest person Zoey knew. Lucas made Wade McRoyan look like a—

"Mr. McRoyan," Zoey said in a cool, clear voice she had trouble recognizing as her own. "I'm going to give you the benefit of the doubt and believe that you only said that because you've had too much scotch. I don't see any reason why I should repeat it to Jake." She saw a small flame of apprehension dawn in Mr. McRoyan's eyes and knew her mark had struck home. She smiled. "Now, I believe it's time for you to go home. Shall I call my brother and Christopher Shupe out to escort you?"

This was a bluff. Christopher, for once, had the night off.

Mr. McRoyan rose heavily to his feet. He drained the last of his scotch from his glass and then sent the glass skidding across the bar. Zoey caught it deftly with her left hand.

How did I do that? she marveled. *I can't even catch a Nerf ball without dropping it.*

She heard the door slam and realized Mr. McRoyan had left. She breathed a sigh of relief and held on to the edge of the bar.

"Oh, Zoey," Kendra said, hurrying up to her. "You handled that beautifully."

Zoey laughed shakily. "Thanks, Kendra. Um, could you watch the bar for a second?"

Zoey walked through the swinging doors into the kitchen. "Benjamin? You won't believe—"

She stopped. The kitchen was full of boxes. Literally full. There was only maybe one square foot of free space on the floor, total.

"What is all this?" she asked Benjamin. He was sitting on one of the boxes with his head in his hands.

"Well," he said morosely. "I forgot to mention that the same day I doubled our fall order of beef, I also doubled our fall orders of mustard, ketchup, and straws."

Zoey gasped. "You're kidding."

"And mayonnaise," Benjamin said. "I can't forget the mayonnaise."

Zoey tried not to giggle. "Oh, Benjamin," she said.

"What?" he asked miserably.

"Nothing." She, too, sat down on a box. But she couldn't hold back her giggles anymore. She began laughing and couldn't stop even when Benjamin raised his head and stared at her.

She laughed until her stomach hurt her and her sore heart rose up inside her, as sweet and light as cream.

Claire

Today all the phones were out in the dorm, so I went to use the pay phone, and Paolo, of all people, was on it. He was talking to his grandmother (he told me) in Spanish. For practice in my Spanish class, I wrote down all the words I recognized and looked them up:

<u>Clara</u>	Claire
<u>chica</u>	girl
<u>morena</u>	dark haired
<u>bonita</u>	pretty
<u>pollo</u>	chicken

arroz . . . . rice

tomate . . . . tomatoes

(is he going home for dinner?)

inteligente . . . . . smart

dulce . . . . sweet

inquisitiva . . . . . nosy

(he looked at me here)

?? gustai . . . . . indecipherable

loca por mi   crazy about me

He said that last part twice! Isn't
that irritating? I could kill him
sometimes.

Sixteen

The early morning sunshine put roses in Claire's cheeks as she pedaled her bike out of Cambridge. She wore jeans and an old peach-colored sweatshirt, her thick dark hair pulled back into a ponytail, no makeup. Claire could go without makeup these days. Since the night she had hit Sean with the hammer, the dark circles had vanished from under her eyes and she had put on six pounds, so her cheeks were no longer quite so hollow.

She was on her way to check the student weather station, and she had to be there by eight o'clock. Claire liked checking the station, even though it meant getting up early. She liked the bike ride, she liked taking the readings, cataloging the data, recording her forecast on the answering machine that served as the Weather Hot Line, although since it was run by students, it was notoriously inaccurate and probably no one ever called it. But Claire didn't care. She liked doing it and—

"Ohhhh!" Claire cried out involuntarily as her front tire wobbled. She tilted, regained her balance, and steered the bike off onto the soft shoulder. The front tire was hissing and already as soft as mush.

Oh, great, Claire thought. *How am I going to get to the station in time now?*

She glanced around, hoping to see a gas station, but the road that led to the weather station was a back one, and there was nobody in sight. Fantastic.

She pushed her bike a few feet, but because the tire was flat, she was afraid she might damage the rim. She stopped and scanned the road again. Still nothing in sight. Suddenly Claire felt a prickle of apprehension. There really was literally no one in sight. Not even a farmhouse. No one to help her. No one would hear her if she were in trouble, no matter how loudly she screamed.

Claire's spirits rose a little as a battered blue Datsun came into sight. Suddenly her fears seemed foolish. Maybe it would be some nice, respectable older couple who could give her a lift. The Datsun passed her and then put on its brake lights, pulling onto the shoulder.

The Datsun's door opened, and Paolo stepped out.

Claire groaned. "This is a nightmare," she murmured.

Paolo walked over to her. "What are you, my shadow?"

"Hey, I'm sitting here innocently," Claire protested. "I should be the one who says that to *you*."

"I know," Paolo said. "That's why I said it first. At any rate, I can't resist a damsel in distress. What seems to be the problem?"

Claire gestured to her bicycle. "Flat tire," she said. She checked her watch. "And I'm due at the weather station in fifteen minutes."

"No problem," Paolo said. "Come with me."

He led the way back to his car, with Claire awkwardly pushing her crippled bike.

Paolo opened the trunk. "Here we go," he said, lifting out a toolbox.

"You carry a toolbox in your trunk?" Claire said, surprised.

"Sure," Paolo said. "It's something guys like to do. You should know that from Jake."

Claire was about to say that she had no

idea what Jake had in the trunk of his car, but then she remembered that Jake was supposed to be her boyfriend.

Paolo pointed to a flat blue box in the trunk. "That's a flare gun," he said. "My mom gave it to me, and I didn't really have the heart to ask her how many times she thought my car was going to break down at sea."

He put the toolbox on the ground and began loosening the front tire. "Speaking of Jake . . . ," he said.

"We weren't," Claire said.

"Well, now we are," Paolo said. "One of my students told me something very interesting about him."

"Oh, really?" Claire said.

"Yes, Renee says—"

"Renee?" Claire said. "Are all the students you tutor girls?"

Paolo smiled up at her. "Maybe not all," he said. He was wearing a maroon turtleneck sweater, and his dark hair fell across his forehead. "Anyway, Renee said something very interesting about Jake."

Claire sighed. "What was that?"

"That she was dating him," Paolo said. He had the inner tube out now and was feeling it for punctures. "So," he continued when she didn't say anything, "this leads me to believe that Jake is not, in fact, your boyfriend, and that you were driven to lie by your overwhelming attraction to me."

Claire's lips twisted. "I wouldn't go that far," she said.

Paolo held the inner tube close to his eyes. "Come on, little one, come on," he said softly to the tube. "Where are you?"

Claire felt a strange pang in her chest. For the tiniest of moments she wondered what it would be like to have Paolo hold her and call her "little one" in that gentle voice.

Oh, God, she thought in annoyance. *You want him to talk to you the same way he talks to a tire? That's really romantic.*

She was suddenly glad that Paolo was absorbed in putting a patch over the puncture and couldn't see her face. He held the patch in place for a few seconds. "Okay," he said. "There we go." He rummaged in his trunk and came out with a foot pump.

"God, you really do travel prepared, don't you?" Claire said.

Paolo laughed. He was already tightening the wheel bolts. "Good as new," he pronounced.

"Oh, thank you," Claire said gratefully.

She still had ten minutes to get to the station.

Paolo shrugged, smiling. "You can make it up to me tonight."

Claire paused with her leg over the bike. "Tonight?" she asked.

"Yes," Paolo said, slamming the trunk. "I fixed your bike, you go out with me."

"What are you talking about?"

"Just what I said," Paolo answered matter-of-factly. "I fixed your bike, so now you have to go out with me."

"That's ridiculous," Claire said. "If some hairy old goat had stopped to help me, would I be obligated to go out with *him*?"

Paolo laughed. "Lucky for you it was me," he said, and walked jauntily around to his car door, singing "Better Be Ready 'Bout Half-Past Eight."

"I'd like to see Darla Passmore," Benjamin said to the nurse at the reception desk.

"Visiting hours are from seven to nine," she said.

Benjamin cleared his throat. "I know," he said apologetically. "But I'd really like to see her. She's my mom."

The nurse looked at him for a long moment, then consulted her notes. "She's a burn patient," she said. "Do you know where the changing room is?"

Benjamin nodded.

"Okay," she said. "Gown up, and you can have fifteen minutes."

"Thanks," Benjamin said.

He found the changing room and put on a gown, mask, and cap. He expected to find a nurse waiting for him, but the hallway was empty. He started off in the direction of his mother's room, panic starting to form a small hard lump in his chest.

No, he told himself firmly. *You will not freak out. You won't. You won't.*

The door to his mother's room was open. Benjamin paused outside, listening to the whistling noise of her breathing. Zoey had warned him about that. *Ignore it,* he thought. *Tune it out like background noise.*

He took a deep breath and went into the room.

His mother was asleep, her face pale and drawn against the pillow. Benjamin took another deep breath. *See?* he said to himself. *You've been in here for a full second without screaming.*

He sat down shakily in the chair by the bed and looked around the room. It was just a plain, square, white, sterile room. Not a torture chamber. Nothing to be afraid of.

A pile of magazines was stacked on his mother's nightstand. Tabloids. I Saw Elvis Working in a Convenience Store! screamed the headline on the top. Benjamin smiled faintly. He wondered if the hospital had just delivered the magazines at random, or if his mother had some secret fascination with scandal sheets that he knew nothing about. He picked up the pile.

A moment later he was happily ensconced with an article called "I Was Liz Taylor's Love Baby!" when a change in his mother's breathing caught his attention and he glanced up.

She was awake. Her blue eyes fixed on him eagerly, if a little puzzled.

"Hi, Ma," he said awkwardly. "I thought I'd surprise you with a visit." He rattled the newspaper in his hands. "Shall I read to you? Did you know that there are aliens running a nudist colony in New Mexico?"

She smiled and shook her head.

Benjamin leaned forward and touched the side of her oxygen tent with his index finger. "Did you ever see *The Boy in the Plastic Bubble*?" he asked.

His mother put her finger against his on

the other side of the material. She shook her head.

"Well, neither did I because you wouldn't let me stay up late enough," Benjamin said, laying his hand flat. His mother laid her hand flat, too. He smiled at her. "I forget what my point was, but I'm sure it was something profound."

He heard footsteps in the doorway. "Benjamin?" said a nurse. "I'm afraid your time is up."

"Already?" Benjamin asked, disappointed. "Can't I stay a little longer?"

With a start he realized he meant it.

Seventeen

Claire raised her hand, and the statistics professor called on her. "Yes, Miss Geiger?"

"I need a fresh copy of the test, please," Claire said.

"Why is that?"

Claire smiled coolly. "Because I've changed my answer so many times, there's a hole in the paper."

Aisha walked into her organic chem class, feeling good about the studying she'd done the night before for Shakespeare. *Too bad I had to blow off the reading for this class to do it,* she thought.

The professor walked in briskly, a pile of papers in her arms. "I hope you all did last night's reading," she said. "Because today we're having a pop quiz."

Jake walked into his econ class, and a girl in the front row screamed, "Ah, wolf man!—Oh, hi, Jake."

That does it, Jake thought. *I'm shaving this thing off.*

Lucas was on the fishing boat, reading comic books with deep contentment.

"That's the end of my report," Nina said. "Are there any questions?"

"Yes," the teacher said. "That was a very interesting interview you played, but I was wondering if you could explain how nuclear power works in your own words."

"No, I can't," Nina said. "Next question, please?"

Nina

Things Benjamin Has Done Lately That May or May Not Mean Anything

1. He called to ask me what to wear to the benefit.
2. He got a haircut.
3. He noticed my haircut (it's hard not to, though).
4. He said, "Remember the time we went to that Bach concert?" in a wistful way.
5. He said that he thought Zoey was being too hard on me.

6. He said I did a good job of waitressing (clearly a lie).
7. He told Christopher that he doesn't like girls who are "too skinny" (no problem here).
8. He came to the office to get his transcripts.
9. When he knew I'd be working.
10. He could have called.
11. Most people would have called.
12. All people would have called.
13. Wouldn't they?

"Nina," The Buzzard said ominously, examining the list. "This is written *on school stationery*."

Eighteen

Nina stood in front of her mirror, still unsure about her clothes. She was wearing an avocado green velvet skirt, green tights, a full white satin blouse, and silver earrings that dangled nearly to her shoulders.

She surveyed herself critically. *Well, I either look great or like an overgrown Peter Pan,* she decided. *There's just not much of a middle ground.*

She carefully reddened her lips with her new lipstick and ran her fingers through her hair until it looked comfortably messy. As she slipped the concert tickets into her purse she caught herself humming.

I'm acting like I'm going on a date, she thought suddenly. *I feel like I'm going on a date. I even went out and spent my minuscule paycheck on a skirt the color of a vegetable! That's all very typical dating behavior.*

She sighed and put an unlit Lucky Strike between her lips. She knew she wasn't going on a date. She and Benjamin were going out as friends. As less than friends, practically. Former friends. Benjamin was probably only going with her because it was better than working in his parents' restaurant.

Nina's mind clicked rapidly for a second, trying to calculate the sheer number of things that were more appealing than working in your parents' restaurant. She gave up, overwhelmed.

Anyway, Benjamin was certainly only going with her because *(a)* it was better than working in his parents' restaurant and *(b)* he probably wanted to see this violin thingie.

Nina snapped her fingers suddenly. What was the word her dad had used? She'd better look that up. She reached for the dictionary on her bookcase just as the doorbell ran downstairs.

"Nina!" Janelle called up the stairs. "Benjamin's here."

"Just a minute!" Nina called back, quickly flipping through the *P* pages. *Protagonist . . . protean . . . protégé!* That was it!

She scanned the definition: *a person under the protection of someone influential who intends to further his or her career.*

She slammed the dictionary shut and

scampered quickly down the stairs. Benjamin was standing in the marble hallway, wearing a dark suit and chatting comfortably with Janelle, just like the old days.

He glanced up when he heard Nina's footsteps and his dark eyes swept over her figure in a long, lingering look and then met her own gaze. "You look fantastic," he said sincerely.

Nina took a deep breath. She tried not to read anything into that remark. She tried to take it as a simple compliment. But despite herself the aroma of floor wax and Janelle's bread rolls and the bowl of potpourri by the front door all smelled suddenly fresh and crisp, like a new beginning.

Claire walked languidly down the hall to her room, thinking about how much she hated aerobics. All that mindless flopping around while some sadist shouted at you. Still, it was an easy way to stay in shape, and Claire liked to wear her rose-colored leotard and gray athletic shorts and watch her reflection in the mirror-covered walls. She knew exercise made her look even prettier, adding color to her cheeks and radiance to her skin. She sometimes wished that Paolo could see her in aerobics class.

She opened the door to her room, and for a moment she had the dizzying sensation that thinking about Paolo had caused him to appear. He was sitting on one of the beds, chatting with Jake.

"Hello, Claire," he said, rising. "Are you ready?"

Claire patted her cheeks with a towel. "Ready for what?"

"For our date."

"We don't have a date," she said. "And don't give me that nonsense about fixing my bike, either."

Paolo gave her a mock-heartsick look. "Claire, please, look at me—I'm all dressed up, and I've even brought you a wrist corsage."

Good God, Claire thought, startled. *I didn't know they still made wrist corsages.*

But Paolo was indeed holding a small plastic florist box. And he was "dressed up": khaki pants and a white cotton shirt.

Claire pursed her lips. She knew that if she said no, Paolo would accept her decision with the same maddening calm as always. Paolo sensed her hesitation, and his eyes danced mischievously.

Looking into his eyes, Claire felt the faint

stirrings of something she thought had been snuffed out forever by Aaron's faithlessness and Sean's threats: She wanted to let down her guard. She wanted to get to know this guy.

"Okay," she said finally. "But I draw the line at the wrist corsage."

"No problem," Paolo said, tossing the florist box to Jake. "They were giving them away free in the lobby for Parents' Day, anyway."

The restaurant was closed on Tuesdays, and Zoey barely spared it a glance as she passed. This was the first night she hadn't worked there since her return.

She walked determinedly, her hands thrust deep in the pockets of an old pea green cardigan. Her face was resolute. She was going somewhere she'd been avoiding. She was going to her house. What used to be her house.

She walked slowly up Camden Street, thinking how it had always pleased her that her house stood at the very end of Camden. Even now it was hard to believe that she wouldn't see it as she drew closer, wouldn't see its familiar gray walls gleaming softly in the dusk.

Zoey walked faster. She could see Lucas's house, a light shining in the kitchen, but no sign of her own home. *Come on,* she thought. *Did you really think it would still be here?*

No, she hadn't really thought that, but even so, she was surprised by the emotion that swept through her when she did reach the ground where her house had stood. Nothing was left. Nothing. Just a vague rectangular shape, blackened, charred, scorched.

Zoey took a deep breath and stepped over the remains of one wall and stood where the living room had previously been. Ankle-deep debris and ashes covered the floor.

Here and there Zoey spotted bits of color and wondered what they were. Glasses? Pottery? What material survived a fire best?

Human teeth, her mind supplied her. *Although teeth are the first things to rot in life, they are often the last thing to go in death. Probably any little souvenir you pick up here will be one of Lara's teeth.*

Zoey swept this grim piece of information out of her mind. She picked her way through the rubble until she stood in the corner of the house her bedroom had been in and knelt among the ashes.

Her fingers picked through sooty residue but

encountered nothing substantial. *How could that be?* Zoey thought. *How can there be nothing left of all my journals, all my notebooks, all my letters?*

But that was a dumb question. Everyone knew how quickly paper burned, how dry and brittle it was, how fast flames licked over it and devoured it.

Zoey closed her eyes. All those journals. All her hard work, her thoughts, her dreams. She had planned to turn those journals into novels someday. She would take the emotions she had so diligently recorded and make them into best-sellers, spin her heartache into gold.

It doesn't matter, she told herself firmly. *I'll write a story about this moment, about what it feels like to sift through the ruins of your house.*

But it did no good to tell herself this. Zoey's heart cried out for the lost journals, and she felt tears gather in her eyes. *I won't cry,* she thought. *I've done so much of that already.*

She opened her eyes and blinked, trying to clear the teardrops from her lashes, and that's when she saw Lucas watching her.

Nineteen

When Nina saw the little boy in the tiny tuxedo pick up the violin, she was amazed. "He's just a little kid," she whispered to Benjamin beside her.

He gave her a sideways look. "Yes, of course," he whispered back.

Of course? Nina thought, surprised. *He's acting like it's the most natural thing in the world for this toddler to be up there playing away.*

But when she glanced around, nobody else looked particularly surprised, and after a moment Nina stopped thinking about it and lost herself in the music. It was Beethoven's Spring Sonata, one of the first CDs Benjamin had given her, and she wondered if he would remember that. Nina had played the CD hundreds of times in a kind of dreamy, lovelorn way until finally Burke said he felt like he was living on the set of *Masterpiece Theater* and asked her to please give it a rest. But

Nina still knew the music well, and she still loved every note.

She was so caught up that intermission came as a surprise. "Already?" she asked as Benjamin stood up.

"He's been playing for half an hour," Benjamin said.

"Yeah, I suppose he needs a glass of milk and some graham crackers," Nina said, standing also.

Benjamin looked amused. "Why are you so surprised about how young he is?"

"Because he's about four years old!" Nina said.

"I think he's actually seven," Benjamin said. "But that's what *prodigy* means," he said, gesturing to the concert program.

"It does not," Nina said indignantly. "It means a person under the protection of an influential individual."

Benjamin's lips twisted into a smile. "I think you mean *protégé*. *Prodigy* means child genius."

"It *does?*" Nina said, amazed. She shrugged. "I guess that explains why there was no biographical note in the program. Can you imagine? *Noel is enrolled in Weymouth kindergarten, where he enjoys finger painting and playing in the sandbox."*

Benjamin laughed and steered her toward the terrace, his hand on the small of her back, where, it seemed to Nina, it still fit perfectly.

Lucas had promised himself that he wouldn't try to hold Zoey again. After the night when he'd asked her if they could try again, he'd sworn he wouldn't pressure her anymore. It was too painful to be pushed away by someone you loved as much as Lucas loved Zoey.

But it was hard to keep from going to her when he saw her kneeling among the rubble of her burned house, her blue eyes brimming with unshed tears. Almost involuntarily he took a step toward her.

She rose instantly, brushing the ashes from the knees of her jeans.

"I was looking for you," Lucas said awkwardly.

She raised her eyebrows indifferently, wiping her eyes with the sleeve of her sweater. "What did you want?" she asked.

He held up an envelope. "To give you this."

He expected her to say she didn't want anything from him or to tell him to mail it to her, but to his surprise she walked over and took it from his hand.

And then suddenly he got it: She was showing him. She was saying, *Look how little you mean to me. I can stand right next to you as though you were a tree.*

Zoey opened the large manila envelope and pulled out the letter. Lucas knew the letter by heart:

220 Bluebird Lane
Presque Isle, ME

Mr. Lucas Cabral
27 Climbing Way
North Harbor, ME

Dear Mr. Cabral,

Enclosed please find the original blueprints for One Camden Street. I found your ideas very intriguing and would be interested to know how the construction goes.

My home phone number is 555-9332. Please call me if you run into any difficulties.

Sincerely,
Eric Skaa

Zoey finished reading and handed it back to him. She didn't say anything.

Lucas cleared his throat. "Um, you know that the construction crews are coming next week to clear away the debris and start rebuilding?" he said.

"Of course I know that," Zoey said. "It's my house."

"Well, I volunteered to work as part of the crew in my spare time," he said. "And I tracked down these blueprints, and I thought of some things—"

"Your *ideas*?" Zoey interrupted coolly.

He nodded. "I made some drawings and sent them to Mr. Skaa. Some things I thought you'd like." He felt like he was floundering and hurried on. "That way you could have your old familiar house but with improvements. Like the way you always said your room was too hot? Well, we could put a sunroof and . . ."

Zoey was staring at him impassively. "I don't want a new improved house, Lucas," she said. "I want what I had before. I want what I used to have, what made me happy once. But I can't have that back, and you know it."

Lucas guessed they weren't talking about

houses anymore. He didn't know quite what to say.

Zoey looked at him for a long time, one slim finger against her lips, and then she turned and walked away.

Paolo held Claire's hands across the restaurant table. She permitted this until his thumb stroked a sensitive spot on her wrist, and then she pulled away.

She drew her sweater closed. Paolo hadn't let her change clothes, insisting she looked perfect, and now she was cold in the air-conditioning. "So what are the other types of people?" she asked him.

Paolo reached for her hands again. "What other types of people?"

"You know," Claire said, trying unsuccessfully to pull away. "The first night I met you, you asked me if I liked *The Brady Bunch* or *The Partridge Family.*"

"Oh, yeah," Paolo said, stroking her fingers. "You want to know if I'm really the perfect mate for you? Okay, I'll give you the questionnaire."

Claire rolled her eyes.

Paolo ignored her. "What do you like better, *This Old House* or *The New Yankee Workshop?*"

"I wouldn't watch either of those shows in a million years."

"*Romper Room* or *Sesame Street*?"

"*Sesame Street.*"

"Bert or Ernie?"

"Bert."

"Rudolph or Frosty?"

"Frosty."

"The Beatles or the Monkees?"

"The Beatles, definitely."

"Who was your favorite character on *Gilligan's Island*?"

"The Professor."

"What's your favorite kind of cookie?"

"Fig Newtons."

"Favorite form of potatoes?"

"Mashed."

"Are you really into rooster worship?"

Claire froze. She pulled away her hands. "How did you know I wrote that on my application?" she said in a low, furious voice.

Paolo looked sheepish. "Everyone's roommate applications are on file in the dorm," he said. "I have access because I'm a security monitor." He reached across the table. "Claire—"

"Don't touch me."

"I was just curious about you," he said. "Claire, look at me."

A wave of nausea hit Claire's stomach like a rolling pin. Paolo had invaded her privacy. He had read something never intended for his eyes, and he had done it without her permission. Suddenly she remembered how he had shown up two seconds after she got a flat tire. What was that all about? Had he just happened to be driving along—or had he been following her?

Her gorge rose. He was just like Sean. Slicker, sure, and more handsome, more charming, but just the same.

"Claire?"

She couldn't look at him. She pushed back her chair unsteadily, panic making her hands shake.

"Wait," Paolo said frantically. "What is it? I'm sorry; I—"

But she didn't hear the rest. She was walking quickly across the restaurant and through the door, her napkin pressed against her mouth to keep herself from crying.

The terrace was beautiful, Nina thought. Beautiful and romantic, with green shrubs and white stone benches and the ocean rumbling distantly off across the lawn.

Unfortunately it was also freezing. The wind

from the sea cut right through her silky blouse, and the white bench felt frozen beneath her. She shivered slightly.

Benjamin smiled. "Cold?" he asked.

"A little," Nina said, trying not to let her teeth chatter.

Benjamin shrugged off his jacket and put it over her shoulders. "Better?"

She nodded.

"Then let's stay out here a minute," he said.

Nina was surprised he wanted to stay. She could hear the music starting again inside, and everyone had already gone back to their seats. She and Benjamin were alone on the terrace.

Maybe—maybe he likes being out here alone with me, she thought, and immediately tried to push the thought away.

"Do you mind?" Benjamin said.

Nina shook her head. "Not at all," she said lightly. She hesitated. "There's something a little too perfectionistic about that kid," she added. "Whenever he looked at his mother, his left eyelid started twitching. He's probably going to have an ulcer by the time he's eight."

Benjamin laughed. He relaxed and laid

his arm casually along the back of the bench. "We can hear just as well out here," he said. "I've been cooped up in that restaurant every night."

Nina let herself lean back very gradually against his arm. "Do you know how long you and Zoey are going to have to work there?"

He shrugged. "At least another couple of months, I think."

"And when will you go back to school?"

"I don't know," Benjamin said quietly. "When I do, it probably won't be Columbia."

Nina was having trouble concentrating; she was too aware of his arm around her. "Why not?"

He smiled faintly. "Because it's a very expensive school, and I doubt we'll be able to afford it."

"Oh," Nina said. "Did you like Columbia a lot?"

"Sure," Benjamin said. "But I think I mostly liked living in a big city. I can probably find a cheaper place to go. And a cheaper city to live in than New York." He shifted slightly but kept his arm around her. "What about you? Do you know where you want to go next year?"

She shook her head. "Not a clue. I might go visit Claire and see how much I like Cambridge."

"Oh, well, and I could take you down to New York and show you around," Benjamin said. He smiled again. "Someday way in the future when I have free time again."

"I'd like that," Nina said simply, and they both fell silent, listening to the music in the dark.

Nina stared at the lighted windows of the conservatory and let the music wash over her. The violinist was playing her favorite part of the sonata, and suddenly it seemed to Nina that it was the sweetest piece of music she had ever heard. The notes hovered in the air like silver bubbles, rising and floating away, taking Nina's heart with them.

She heard a sigh catch in Benjamin's throat and thought, *He remembers. He remembers that he gave me this CD*. His arm tightened against her shoulders.

Nina turned toward him. In the light from the windows she could see tears gleaming on his cheeks. *Oh, Benjamin*, she thought in a rush of tenderness. *I still love you.*

"Benjamin?" she asked gently. "Benjamin, what is it?"

Benjamin brought his free hand up to cover his eyes. "I miss Lara," he said.

Aisha walked slowly through the lobby of her dorm, convinced she was thinking in iambic pentameter.

The Shakespeare exam had been brutal. Felicia, apparently forgetting all about their conversation last night, had breezed in at the last minute and sat with her usual friends in front. Aisha had actually saved her a seat, and she felt foolish and rejected. Her only consolation was that Felicia had still been laboring over the test when Aisha finished and left. She had spared Aisha a quick, conspiratorial smile.

Thinking of it now, Aisha frowned. *One may smile, and smile, and be a villain,* she recited silently, and then abruptly rolled her eyes. God, now she was quoting Shakespeare automatically. What next?

All the Shakespeare reading still filled her head like a heavy damp towel. She wanted to clear her mind and do something frivolous, like go out to dinner.

But who could she go with? Her good old buddy Felicia would doubtless go out with her own crowd after class.

Aisha sighed and collected the mail from the mailbox. Maybe she would reward herself and call Christopher, she thought as she trudged to her room.

Aisha unlocked the door and dumped the mail on her desk. The room smelled stale and stuffy from their all-nighter. She opened a window and lifted her face to the breeze.

After a minute she picked up the phone and called Christopher. She got the answering machine. "Christopher?" she said, and waited. "I guess you're not home. Just wanted to chat. I love you. Bye."

She glanced at her watch. Where was Christopher? It was almost seven. Shouldn't he be home? *Oh, for heaven's sake,* she thought. *Stop being so suspicious. Give the guy a little space.*

But a small voice spoke up in her mind:

*When my love swears that she is made of truth,
I do believe her, though I know she lies.*

Enough! she thought. *I do not need Shakespeare talking in my head.*

She began flipping through the mail. Two letters for Felicia, Aisha's bank statement, a Victoria's Secret catalog, and the phone bill, which came in Aisha's name.

Aisha slit open the envelope with a letter opener and scanned the pages casually. She and Felicia were both big talkers, and their bills were usually horrendous. Sure enough, there were dozens of calls to the Chatham Island area code. Aisha sighed and skimmed the columns, hoping that at least no calls were in the double digits.

Suddenly she frowned. There were—she counted quickly—eleven calls to Christopher in a row. Short calls, less than thirty seconds each, as though she'd gotten the answering machine and then hung up. *Boy, I must have been in a hurry to talk to him about something,* she thought. She glanced at the date: September 12. All on the afternoon of the twelfth.

She stuffed the bill back in its envelope and dropped it back on her desk. She decided to take a shower and then try Christopher again. She had just taken off her T-shirt when a thought occurred to her, making her skin feel cold. September 12? Aisha wadded up the T-shirt and threw it on the floor. She stood frowning for a second and then crossed the room to check the calendar.

For no reason at all she remembered Felicia saying, *Maybe I'll have to call Christopher for help.*

October, September—her finger trembled as she turned the slick page. She scanned the white squares. There it was. September 12: Muscular Dystrophy Walk.

Aisha had walked twenty miles and made three hundred dollars for charity. It had taken her six hours. It had taken *all afternoon*.

Aisha hadn't made a single one of those calls to Christopher.

*The twenty-seventh title in the fabulous
MAKING OUT series:*

Falling for Claire. That's what Paolo's doing,
and Claire can't cope with it. She's used to
fighting everyone – especially herself – and she
can't believe that anyone could love her for
who she is. Has Claire met her match at last?

Falling
for
Claire

'Morris and I are going to live here,' Holly said proudly. 'It's all planned.' Her eyes were wide and dark, the irises mere rims of grey around the black pupils. 'He wouldn't deceive me like that,' she said positively, needing nevertheless to hear a firm voice making the statement. 'He loves me.'

'Does he? And do you love him?' Adam Wilde's voice was relentless, probing her mind, searching out secrets she was keeping even from herself. 'Do you, Holly? Or is there some other reason why you've agreed to marry him—something you're half ashamed of and can't admit? Something you need and only he can give?'

'Isn't that usually the reason for wanting to marry someone?' she flashed, twisting away so that he couldn't meet her troubled eyes with his searing glance.

'Usually, yes. But what two people need from each other, that only they can give, is usually love. Real love, a burning consuming passion that gives them no relief, no respite from its demands. A fire that burns night and day, so that you can't think of anyone or anything but the beloved . . . Is that what you feel for Morris Crawley, Holly? Is that what he feels for you? Has he ever said as much?'

Another book you will enjoy
by NICOLA WEST

HIDDEN DEPTHS

The Grand Canyon in Arizona was a long way from home, but Tessa was going for a purpose—to make up the twenty-five-year-old quarrel between her mother and her grandfather. She was already doubtful whether she could do it—so she certainly didn't need her arrogant cousin, Crane, obstructing her at every move . . .

ANOTHER EDEN

BY

NICOLA WEST

MILLS & BOON LIMITED
ETON HOUSE   18-24 PARADISE ROAD
RICHMOND   SURREY   TW9 1SR

First published in Great Britain 1988 by Mills & Boon Limited

© Nicola West 1988

Australian copyright 1988 Philippine copyright 1988 This edition 1988

ISBN 0 263 75935 0

Set in Baskerville 10 on 11 pt. 01–0388-54324

Typeset in Great Britain by JCL Graphics, Bristol

Printed and bound in Great Britain by Collins, Glasgow

CHAPTER ONE

'THERE you are. That's it. Sleadale Head. Your future home.'

'*Our* future home,' Holly Douglas said softly, gazing along the track that wound deep into the valley ahead of them. 'Morris—it's beautiful!'

Morris Crawley smiled complacently. 'Glad you like it, darling. I just hope you won't find it too lonely, that's all. Three miles from the road, and the last two along a very rough track—that's a long way from civilisation.'

Holly's grey eyes laughed at him. 'Not to me—don't forget I'm a farmer's daughter, brought up in the wilds of Herefordshire. And my grandparents' farm in Wales was just as remote as this. No——' she turned away from him, gazing again along the silent valley, her ebony hair feathered by the breeze '—I'm going to love it. And so are you.' Impulsively, she turned and kissed him. 'After a few weeks here, you'll wonder how you ever managed to live in London.'

'Well, I've always intended to come into farming.' Morris shrugged more deeply into the sheepskin jacket that covered his suit. 'And when one of the best sheep-farms in the Lake District comes under the hammer—well, you don't pass up an opportunity like that. Especially when you're looking for a place to settle down and raise a family!'

Holly moved close into the circle of his arms. 'Morris, you're the sweetest man I know. I still can't believe my luck! I mean—why me? Why should a man like you—a

5

successful businessman, travelling all over the world, meeting glamorous women everywhere you go—pick on an ordinary girl like me? It doesn't make sense.'

'It makes every kind of sense,' Morris told her, drawing her close and dropping a kiss on the top of her windblown head. 'All right, so I meet a lot of glamorous women—but none of them can hold a candle to you for freshness and simplicity. And I mean that in the nicest possible way! There's nothing ordinary about you, Holly—you're like a breath of fresh air to me. Something that's been missing from my life for years.'

'Well, you'll get plenty of it here!' Holly laughed as a gust of wind blew the unlatched gate wide open. 'Three miles between us and the road, and a whole valley all to ourselves. Where *is* the nearest house?'

'In the next valley.' Morris unfolded a map and laid it on the bonnet of the car. 'Hold that end down . . . yes, there it is. Brackenfold. About half a mile away as the crow flies, but a good deal longer in road terms—six miles, at least.'

'You could walk it in about an hour, though, crossing the ridge,' Holly observed. 'And it looks as if there are several buildings there—quite a little hamlet. I wonder if they're all occupied.'

'Probably holiday cottages. That's what seems to happen to most of these outlying places nowadays.' Morris began to fold up the map again. 'Well, let's go on along this murderous track and see what lies at the other end. They say the house has been modernised, but that could mean anything.'

'Yes . . .' Holly climbed into the Range Rover beside him, her small, triangular face sober. 'Morris , you don't think we're taking all this rather for granted? It isn't ours yet, after all—suppose there are other people after it? I'd hate to get all excited about it and then lose it.'

'Don't worry.' Her fiancé's hand patted her knee comfortingly. 'There won't be anyone else after it—apart from one or two locals, possibly. And I can match any price *they* can afford.'

'Mm.' Holly bit her lip, staring anxiously out through the windscreen. 'I suppose so. All the same, I shan't feel really happy until the auction's over. And—well, you'll think I'm being silly, I know, but——'

'But what?'

'I can't help feeling a bit sorry for any locals who *do* want to buy it. I know how Dad would have felt, back in Herefordshire, if he'd wanted to buy some more land and some tycoon had stepped in from London with more money than he could afford.' She gave the man beside her an apologetic glance. 'I told you you'd think I was being silly.'

Morris smiled fondly. 'Not silly at all. Just my darling Holly being her sweet self, that's all. Thinking of everyone else first. It's one of the things I love about you, my pet—but all the same, I'm afraid it's something you're going to have to learn to control. Because, unfortunately, it just isn't the way to get on!'

He turned away, concentrating on the track ahead of them. As he'd said, it was extremely rough, degenerating rapidly into little more than a stony mass of rocks and pot-holes. Holly clung to the door of the car, understanding now why her fiancé had refused to bring his sleek Jaguar along here, insisting on using the Range Rover he'd bought since coming to the Lake District. No normal car would be able to withstand this punishment day after day.

But the beauty of the valley, with the farm standing isolated and alone at its head, more than compensated for the difficulty of reaching it. As they jolted slowly along, pausing occasionally to allow Holly to jump out and open a gate, the serenity of the calm hills rising on either side seemed to absorb itself into her heart and mind, stilling any doubts she might have had about this new life into which she was rushing so headlong. The tinkling chatter of the stream that accompanied them for most of the way, growing wilder as they climbed, the tender clarity of the blue October sky, the occasional querulous bleat from one of the sheep who raised their heads to watch the strangers approach—all these added to the peace of the atmosphere. This, she thought, leaning for a moment on the last of the gates and gazing at the curve of the hillside that must, surely, soon reveal the house itself, was her kind of country.Wild, remote, isolated—but close to all the things she loved, the life in which she knew she could blossom.

A brief peep of the horn brought her to herself, and she climbed back beside Morris, laughing.

'Sorry! I was just overwhelmed by it all. It's so lovely, Morris—I can't think of anywhere I'd rather settle down.'

'Well, you may feel differently when the rain's lashing down and there's a high wind, and you're driving back alone and have to keep getting out to open and close all these gates. Or when the snow's three feet deep round the house and the only way out is on skis.' Morris manoeuvred the Range Rover around a particular large rock. 'Or when you've cracked your sump on one of these boulders and can't go forward or back and the car's full of shopping and——'

'Screaming kids,' Holly finished with a grin. 'Yes, I know, you're right—all those things could rather take the shine off! But not for me, Morris. I'll love it even in those conditions. Because the house will always be there at the end, waiting. And not just a house. Our home. That's what will make it special.'

Morris didn't answer. They had rounded the last bend in the track and at last the house was in view, a square, solid, grey building that looked as if it had grown from the valley, thrust into shape by the relentless action of wind and weather. A boulder of a house that had taken everything that the elements could hurl at it and had withstood it all, reaching this final perfect shape, never again to change.

A house you could rely on, Holly thought, her heart going out to it. An uncompromising house; but a safe one.

Morris drove along the last, roughly cobbled stretch of track and brought the vehicle to a halt in the yard, between the house itself and a large barn.

'Well, there it is. Not exactly a thing of beauty, but——'

'Oh, but it is!' Holly was still gazing at the grey stone walls of the house, the deep, sturdy porch that sheltered the door. 'Not in the modern sense, perhaps—it doesn't have clean white walls or huge plate-glass picture windows. But for what it is—where it is—it's perfect. So square and solid—so *determined*. It *is* beautiful, Morris. Can't you see it?'

He smiled. 'Or course, if *you* can. And it's certainly solid. I don't imagine we'll find much wrong with it—as I said, the previous owners have done quite a lot to it, though I don't know what—it may be that we think their alterations and ''improvements'' would have been better not done! Anyway—let's have a look. I've got the key.'

With each step they took around the old house, Holly felt more and more at home. She wanted to stroke the thick walls, lay her hands on the broad windowsills, embrace the great beams that spanned the ceilings. When they had finished their tour and were standing once more in the big living-room, she spread her arms wide and gave Morris a happy grin.

'It's wonderful! Everything is so exactly right. They

must have been very clever, whoever lived here before.'
Arms still outstretched, she indicated the spaciousness of
the room they were in. 'Look at this! Obviously it was two
smaller rooms originally and they've knocked it into
one—but it's been done so sensitively, with this end
raised up just a little to separate it from the other part and
make a cosy sitting area. And that lovely woodstove at the
far end, with the open fire at this—it must be beautifully
snug in winter, when your snowstorms are raging round
outside or all that wind and rain are lashing the walls.'
She twinkled mischievously at the man who watched her.
'And the kitchen's gorgeous, with those open beams and
all that wood, and that superb Aga . . . I just wish we
could move in straight away!'

'Well, you'll have to wait a little while, I'm afraid.
There's just a small matter of an auction, and a wedding.'
Morris kissed her lightly. 'Anyway, I'm glad you like it.
Now . . . I want to take a look at the outbuildings and the
generator—there's no mains electricity laid on and I want
to make sure it's in good working order. Coming with
me?'

Holly shook her head. 'I'll go over the house again. I
just can't believe it's all going to be ours—our own home.
Oh, I *hope* no one outbids us at the auction! I couldn't
bear to lose it now I've seen it.'

Left alone, she began to prowl around the rooms like a
cat assessing its new territory. She rather hoped that
Morris wouldn't come back too soon—without him, she
felt able to savour the delight of knowing that it was going
to be hers, planning the furniture she would need, the few
small changes she would make. She paused at each
window, gazing out at the sloping fellsides, burnished
with the autumn russet of dying bracken, watching the
glittering stream as it leaped down the hill beside the
track, delighting in the glowing red of rowan berries

against the clear blue sky.

She was upstairs in the bathroom when she heard the sound of someone coming in at the back door, and ran to the top of the curving stone staircase.

'Morris? Come and have another look at this enormous bath! It'll take us both, I'm sure, and——' She stopped abruptly. 'Oh!'

The tall man at the foot of the stairs said nothing. He stood quite still, his eyes glinting up at her, a deep and startling blue in the rich tan of his face. Hair as dark as her own sprang in tousled disorder from his well shaped head, and his fingers, resting on the wall beside him, were long and slender without being over-delicate—hands, Holly thought in the daze of that first moment of shock, that would be strong as well as sensitive, as powerful as they could be passionate . . .

Hastily, Holly jerked her mind away from the thoughts that had so incredibly forced their way into her mind. She swallowed, bit her lip and finally found her voice.

'I'm sorry—I didn't know there was anyone else here—I didn't hear your car . . . Is there anything I can do for you?'

There was a flicker in the man's eyes at that, but his voice gave nothing away. He spoke coolly, calmly, as if there were nothing at all unusual in finding a strange girl in an empty house, burbling away about the bathroom . . . Holly's cheeks flamed as she remembered the words she'd been calling out as he'd come in. What on earth must he be thinking of her?

'I can't think of anything just at the moment, but I'll let you know if I do.' Was he making fun of her? Well, perhaps she deserved it. She grinned weakly at him and wondered where Morris had got to. And—more immediately important—who this man was and what he wanted.

A sudden fear came to her. Perhaps he had come for the same purpose as she and Morris—to look over the house. Perhaps he, too, was a prospective buyer. As soon as the thought came into her mind, she knew it must be true. When she spoke again, there was an edge of hostility in her voice and she took a step down towards him.

'Who were you looking for? There's nobody living here at present. The house is for sale—my fiancé and I are buying it.'

One of the dark eyebrows lifted. 'Indeed?' The deep voice was sardonic. 'I understood it was being auctioned.'

'Yes—that's right, but——' Holly floundered helplessly. 'We're going to buy it, anyway,' she went on defiantly. 'So if you were thinking of it too, you might as well save your time. My fiancé is a very determined man,' she finished with a lift of her chin.

'And so am I.' The man was lounging easily against the wall now, effectively blocking her way down the stairs. 'I'll look forward to meeting him at the auction. Or is he here now?'

'Yes, he is.' Holly found herself absurdly thankful to be able to say this. The stranger lacked Morris's sturdiness, yet had a loose-limbed grace that seemed to imply powerful reserves of catlike agility and strength. He emanated danger. I wouldn't like to be really alone with him, in this isolated spot, Holly thought, and jumped as her heart gave a sudden quiver. 'He's outside somewhere—he'll be back at any moment.'

'Then we might as well introduce ourselves. I like to know whom I'm fighting.' The firm mouth widened in an undeniably attractive grin. 'Adam Wilde—not at your service, I'm afraid. But enchanted to meet you, all the same. Why don't you come down those stairs? I'm getting quite a crick in my neck, looking up at you.'

Reluctantly, Holly came down the remaining steps,

feeling that by doing so she was losing some kind of advantage over this self-possessed man. And feeling, too, that Adam Wilde was all too well aware of it. She looked up at him, realising the difference in their heights—he must be several inches over six feet, she thought, a good deal taller than Morris. Unwillingly, she held out her hand.

'My name's Holly Douglas,' she said, and repressed a gasp as he took her hand in his, curling his fingers around hers almost caressingly, pulsing into her palm a warmth that was totally unexpected and extremely disturbing. As soon as she could, she pulled it away again. 'My fiancé's Morris Crawley.' Her voice shook slightly.

'Crawley?' The dark blue eyes widened slightly and Holly wondered for a brief moment whether he already knew who Morris was. It wasn't impossible—as Morris himself was fond of pointing out, he was well known in business circles. 'And what do you intend to do with this property, once it becomes yours? Farm it?'

'Of course—what else?'

He shrugged. 'Who knows? People have strange ideas these days. And there are a lot of speculators about—developers.'

'I don't see how you could develop a place like this,' Holly said. 'It's within the Lake District National Park. There are too many restrictions. Nobody would be allowed to build——'

'Who said anything about building?'

Holly stared at him. 'What other kind of development is there? Anyway, the whole thing's academic—we don't intend to do anything that would spoil the valley. We're just going to live here and farm the land and bring up a family.' She turned away from him and wandered back into the living-room, gazing out of the window that looked back down the track. The dale stretched before

her, a vista of wild loneliness, sweeping fells and empty
sky. There was barely another man-made object in sight.
No house; no telephone wires; no pylons. Only the rough
stone walls that crossed every part of the Lake District,
built a century or more ago. It was a scene that would
have intimidated many young women, but in that
moment Holly knew that it was the only place she ever
wanted to live.

With a quick movement, she turned to the man who
watched her from the door.

'Please,' she said, and her voice was tense, 'there must
be other places you could buy. Places that would be just as
good as this. Places that could mean just as much to you.
But for me—there just isn't anywhere else. I don't know
why—I don't know what it is—but I *belong* here. Please
don't take it away from me.'

Adam Wilde stared at her. Her figure was taut and slim
against the window, her face shadowed as she turned
away from the light. Dark hair formed an aureole around
her small head, lifted in urgent supplication. Breasts that
were small but undeniably feminine jutted against her
thin sweater, and the narrow-cut trousers she wore did
nothing to conceal the slender curves of her legs.

'Please,' she repeated, a tiny catch in her breath as he
took a step towards her. And as their glances locked, and
the atmosphere in the room took on a quality that had
Holly's heart kicking against her ribs, they heard a sound
from outside. And then a voice.

'Holly? Darling, where are you? Still mooning over the
view?' Morris came into the room, looking almost stocky
beside Adam Wilde, his words an intrusion that Holly
found herself on the verge of resenting before
thankfulness flooded in. 'I've been looking at that
generator, and do you know, it's——' He became aware
of the stranger and stopped. 'Hello. Who's this?'

Holly hurried forward, relieved to find that the strange spell, which had rooted her to the spot only moments before, had been broken. 'It's Adam Wilde, Morris. He's come to look at the house, too.' She linked her arm through Morris's, turning to the stranger as if she were proving something to him. 'This is my fiancé, Mr Wilde. Morris Crawley. As I told you, we intend to buy Sleadale Head Farm. So you really are wasting your time, you know.'

She let her eyes meet his: dove-grey, deceptively soft, challenging the dark blue of Arctic seas. And, although their glances met with a clash so violent she felt sure it must be audible, she didn't waver.

Adam Wilde might be determined to become the master of Sleadale. But she was equally determined to be its mistress. And if there was one thing certain, it was that there wasn't room for the two of them in this isolated valley.

In the comfortable lounge of the Crookbarn Hotel, Holly stared at Morris and repeated the words he had just spoken.

'You want me to go to the auction alone? Bid for the farm without you? But why?'

Morris shrugged and reached for his whisky. Here in the civilised surroundings of the hotel, he looked urbanely at home. He lifted his glass to her and smiled.

'It's simple enough, my dear. Obviously there are more people interested in the place than we thought. We've already met one of them—and, as I explained to you, he and I have crossed swords before. It's not beyond him to force the price up just for the pleasure of making me pay through the nose. Well, that's something I'll have to cope with in my own way—and I don't imagine that he's really much threat. But at least I can prevent the same thing happening with other old rivals, by simply not being there.' He sipped again, his eyes narrowed as if he were facing his adversaries at that very moment. 'There could be others there who'd like to outbid me.'

Holly stared at him. Until now, the whole thing had seemed so simple, a matter of going along, bidding higher than anyone else and securing possession of the valley she already loved. Morris's words sent a chill through her—as if she were wading into waters that were too deep.

'But why should they?' she asked. 'What have you ever done to make enemies like that?'

Morris laughed easily.

'Now, who mentioned enemies? Rivals, I said—no businessman gets through life without a few of those, Holly. And—yes, I suppose some of them might be said to be enemies, in that they'd always be pleased to put a spoke in another man's wheel simply because he's more successful. I'm afraid our friend Wilde comes into that category.'

'Adam Wilde?' Holly recalled the dark, lean face, the direct blue gaze. 'Really?'

'Very much so. Don't let that charming smile of his fool you, Holly. Remember, confidence tricksters have one vital attribute—they can all inspire confidence. It doesn't do to be led astray by a pair of bright blue eyes. Behind that handsome face there's a very devious mind. And a very spiteful one.'

'You speak as if you know a lot about him,' Holly said.

'I told you,' Morris answered grimly, 'we've crossed swords before.'

That was, in fact, all he had told her. But Holly had known, from the moment when she'd made her over-bright and shaky introduction in the old farmhouse, that there had to be more to it than that. The atmosphere between the two men, as soon as they'd recognised each other, had been as charged as the last moment before a thunderstorm broke the heavens. She had almost expected a crash, a blinding light. There hadn't been any such thing, of course—but Adam Wilde's searing and comprehensive glance, in the instant before he turned on his heel and strode out of the farmhouse, had been very nearly as explosive.

'But what could he do to you now?' she asked timidly. 'Put up the price?'

'That, certainly, though it's not what's primarily bothering me.' Morris leaned forward. 'No, Holly, it's rather more complicated than that. I've got a lot of interests, money tied up in all kinds of ventures—it would take me too long to list them all now. But if word got around that I was thinking of retiring—leaving all that to settle on a remote Lake District farm—well, it could do a great deal of harm, one way and another. To other people as well as myself. Shareholders, you understand.'

Holly nodded. In fact, she had only a hazy idea of what Morris was talking about. High finance had never been something she had even bothered to try to understand. But, since knowing Morris and becoming engaged to him, she'd made up her mind to learn.

'Can't you tell me——' she began, but he shook his head and leaned back.

'Take too long, my dear. One day, I promise you, we'll sit down and go through the whole thing—that's if you're still interested.' He smiled, showing his white teeth. 'Meanwhile, all you have to do is go along to that auction and bid for Sleadale Head. Your doing that should convince Wilde that it's not really that important to me. And it should be quite exciting for you—especially when the auctioneer knocks it down to you and you know it's really yours.'

'Ours,' Holly corrected him with a smile, but to her

surprise he shook his head again.

'No, my dear. Yours. Sleadale Head is to be put in your name, not mine.'

'Mine?' Holly frowned. 'But why? Why not in your name, too? I don't understand——'

'As I said just now, it's really too complicated to explain.'

Morris finished his whisky and stretched his arms above his head. 'We've had a long day and a lot of fresh air,' he said easily. 'Let's go to bed now—talk about it some more in the morning, hm?' Rising to his feet, he took both her hands and pulled her up against him. 'Let's just call it my wedding present to you,' he murmured against her hair. 'And before you say it's too much—it's not. You know I'd give you the earth if I could—but since even I'm not *that* rich, I'll just give you a bit of it. The bit that I think you like the best—am I right?'

'Oh, yes—yes,' Holly breathed, her mind far away from the comfortable lounge, somewhere out on the wild Cumbrian fells with the nearest neighbour an hour's walk away over the hill. 'And—thank you, Morris, darling.'

'Thank me on Thursday—when you've been to that auction and bought it,' he said, and kissed her lightly. 'And now—bed. I'll see you down here for breakfast at eight sharp.'

'Eight sharp,' Holly agreed with a smile, and went up the stairs to her room.

Morris was the sweetest, most generous man on earth, she thought, pausing at the top to give him a last loving smile. She still couldn't believe her luck in meeting him.

So why, just at that moment, did the picture of another man come unbidden into her mind? A tall man, lean yet strong, with disturbingly blue eyes and a mouth that was mobile enough to quirk with humour at one moment and harden with anger at the next. A man whose deep voice sent shockwaves through her body, whose touch was like handling bare electricity.

What did Adam Wilde have to do with her? Except for the fact that he, too, wanted Sleadale Head?

The auction rooms were full, more crowded than Holly had expected. She hesitated at the door, wondering if she were even going to find a seat. A woman in a blue hat, seeing her indecision, waved a hand and pointed to a vacant chair in the back row.

'Oh—thank you.' Hurriedly, Holly made her way along the row apologising as she went to the people she disturbed. She sat down, still breathless, and loosened her collar thankfully. The room, apparently fully heated, was unbearably hot with so many people crammed into it.

'No fiancé?'

Startled, Holly turned and found that she was sitting next to the one man she would have liked to avoid—Adam Wilde, smiling a smile that managed somehow to be as devilish as it was composed. 'You seem a little flustered,' he continued smoothly.

Holly gave him an exasperated look. 'I couldn't find the place. Is it hidden deliberately?'

'The locals know it well enough,' he said blandly.

'Really? And you're a local, I take it?'

'As near as makes no difference,' he agreed. 'Anyway, you're here now. A few minutes more and you'd have missed it altogether.'

'Which would have pleased you very much, I've no doubt.' Holly was aware of a part of her mind that stood back, astonished by the way she was sparring with this man. But she seemed unable to stop. She went on coolly, 'But, as you say, I'm here now. And, as I told you the other day, I intend to buy Sleadale Head.'

'You—or your fiancé?'

'Both of us, of course.' Why should she tell this stranger that Morris was giving her the farm as her wedding present? 'Is that so very strange?'

'I'm not sure.' The dark eyes, Mediterranean-blue this afternoon, rested on her thoughtfully. 'I just don't see Crawley as a farmer. Especially *that* sort of farmer. But perhaps you know him better than I do.'

'I should imagine I do,' Holly said tightly, her eyes on the brochure on her lap.

'Well, you certainly should. You've known each other a long time, no doubt.'

'Long enough.'

'Several years? Months?' A slight pause then, with an inflection of mock surprise, 'Weeks?'

Holly turned on him. 'And what if I have? Is it any of your business? Stop questioning me like this!'

'My apologies, I'm sure. Just making conversation, you know.' Adam Wilde gave her a level look, then glanced down at his own brochure. 'It just seems a little surprising, that's all.'

'What does?' Holly asked sarcastically. 'The fact that a man like Morris Crawley could meet a girl like me, fall in love and decide to marry her, all in a matter of weeks?'

Adam raised his eyes and the expression in them caught her up short. There was something there she hadn't expected to see—something apart from the curiosity, irritation and downright hostility that their arguing had led her to expect.

Something she couldn't quite analyse.

'No,' he said slowly, 'that isn't what seems surprising. Quite the reverse.' His sapphire-dark glance moved over her face, as if seeking something hidden. 'What seems surprising to me is the fact that a girl like you could meet a man like Morris Crawley and decide to marry him—all in a few weeks.' He paused, then added deliberately, 'We'll leave out the falling-in-love bit, I think.'

Holly gasped. Her lips parted, but for once she had no ready retort. Speechlessly, she stared at Adam Wilde, who smiled pleasantly back at her before turning again to his brochure.

And at that moment, the auctioneer mounted the rostrum and tapped lightly but firmly with his gavel.

The auction had begun.

CHAPTER TWO

'YOU did it! Well *done*!' Morris hugged Holly to him and gave her an enthusiastic kiss. 'You know, you're a real wonder—you can be my bidder at every auction from now on.'

'And how many of those are there going to be?' Holly teased him. 'I understood that you were retiring from business and settling down as a nice, quiet, Lakeland sheep-farmer.'

Morris looked confused for a moment, then laughed and shook her gently by the shoulders.

'Of course I am! Just a figure of speech, that's all. I've been sitting here and biting my nails ever since you went out. Had a sudden nasty fear that you might find yourself up against someone really determined to have the place—that character we met out at the house, for instance.'

'Well, he was there.' For some reason, she didn't tell Morris that they'd sat next to each other. 'And you were right—he did want it. It was he who pushed the bidding up so high.' She thought again of the figure she'd finally paid for Sleadale Head Farm and shook her head, still barely able to believe that a barren, treeless stretch of fellside could command such a price.

'But not too high for us,' Morris said comfortably. 'And he dropped out in the end, which is the main thing. Now all we have to do is decide what to do next.'

'What to do next? But, surely—now you've got it, we can just get married and move in. Wasn't that what we'd

22

planned?'

Morris smiled. 'Of course, darling. But not just like that, I'm afraid. You saw the place—it needs a lot doing to it, whatever the previous owners may have thought. And then there's the management of the land itself to consider—what stock we're to buy in, just how much we're going to farm it for sheep, that kind of thing. Anyway, you needn't worry about all that, it's my problem. You just think about that wedding—get your dress and bridesmaids organised and so on. That's your part!'

Holy looked at him doubtfully. She wanted to tell him that the farming was her part, too—that she intended to work beside him in every part of their new life. Choosing a wedding dress and deciding on bridesmaids—all the trappings and trimmings of a traditional wedding—would be fun, and she was looking forward to it. But it wasn't all there was to getting married, and her dreams of what came after the wedding itself—striding with Morris over the windswept fells, working through the night with him at lambing-times—were by far the most exciting part.

'Now,' Morris said before she could speak, 'you won't mind if I dash off for a bit, will you, darling? Got a few people to see, now that everything's settled. Shan't be long.'

'I'll come with you,' Holly offered, reaching for the jacket she had slipped off when she had come into the room, but Morris shook his head.

'Be too boring for you, my sweet. Anyway, you've more than done your part. No, you stay here and think about those bridesmaids' dresses. There's a lot to be done before a wedding, you know—and I'm afraid I'll be leaving most of it to you, with all the farm business to attend to. Promise I won't be long.' He kissed the tip of her nose, grinned and went swiftly to the door. 'And—just in case I didn't mention it before—congratulations! You're a very clever girl.'

The door closed behind him and Holly, after staring at it for a few seconds, as if she thought he might come back and ask her to go with him after all, went slowly across to the window.

There was something in the little scene that left her feeling vaguely uneasy. A sense of something not quite right. She couldn't put her finger on it, but it was there. She stood at the window, gazing thoughtfully down at the garden behind the hotel.

Perhaps it was because Morris somehow didn't seem to have accepted her as an equal partner in their joint future. His evasion of any discussion with her about the farm's future, his refusal to take her to whatever meeting he was off to at this moment, together with his continual references to bridesmaids and wedding dresses grated slightly. It was almost as though he had given her a little pat and told her not to bother her pretty little head about it. Almost patronising.

Holly have herself a little shake. What nonsense! Hadn't Morris sent her to the auction alone, to bid for the farm? Surely to have done that must mean that he trusted her, had faith in her business abilities. And the fact that she'd succeeded in buying the farm—against some pretty stiff opposition, too—must have confirmed that faith.

Holly sat down on the wide window-seat. From here, she could see a part of the hotel car park. Morris's car, which had been parked within sight of the window, had disappeared, presumably taking him to his meeting—wherever it was. Kendal, the nearest town? Or further afield—Lancaster, or Carlisle? Well, there was no point in sitting here wondering about it. Obviously he would have told her more, if there'd been time. All she had to do was wait until he came back.

Meanwhile, she might as well make use of that luxurious bathroom and wash off the dust of the auction rooms.

Soaking in the scented water, Holly thought again about the auction—and about the man who had sat beside her. Adam Wilde. She felt again the slight tremor as his arm had touched hers, sensed the nearness of him, an aura that was almost tangible, an electric crackling of the air between them. It was a sensation she'd never experienced before, and she didn't like it. If there had been another seat in the rooms, even a space in which to stand, she would have taken it, no matter how many people she might have needed to disturb. But there was nothing. The room was packed.

It occurred to Holly to wonder just why the sale had attracted so much interest. Sleadale was a long, narrow valley and the farmhouse that stood at its head was the only building in the entire three miles of its length. There was, she knew, considerable interest in Lake District houses, even isolated ones, from people who wanted to buy them as holiday homes or for retirement. But Sleadale Head Farm was being sold as a whole, with several hundred acres of land. And there must be few people who would want a house quite so remote as this one, with the nearest neighbour five miles away by road, or over an hour's tough walking across the hill.

Yet the auction room had been full of people. And most of them, she guessed, had been local. Probably farmers.

They might, of course, have been attending the sale out of curiosity—the price that Sleadale Head fetched would have an effect on the valuation of their own properties.

She remembered the silence that had fallen as the auctioneer tapped the bench with his gavel . . .

In that moment, she was more acutely conscious of Adam

Wilde beside her than of anything else. Their hasty argument, conducted almost in whispers, had left her feeling shaken and disturbed. How was it that he ruffled her feathers so easily? She wasn't normally quick to take offence—nor to give it. In ordinary circumstances, she would never have dreamed of speaking to a stranger as she'd spoken to him.

In ordinary circumstances? But what was so extraordinary about these? They had just happened to meet while viewing a house they both wanted to buy and, as might have been expected, they were both attending the auction. What was unusual about that?

Nothing, Holly told herself firmly—and felt another tingling surge of awareness as he moved slightly and his arm brushed against hers.

She moved away sharply and, from the corner of her eye, caught the turn of his head, the flicker of amusement on his face. Her own cheeks burning, she looked resolutely down at her brochure, following its words with her eyes as she listened to the auctioneer's description of the property.

'Sleadale Head Farm . . . seven hundred acres of farmland, four hundred of which are in the fell area . . . ideal for the sheep-farming for which this area is so justifiably well known . . . part of the Lake District National Park, yet away from the normal tourist routes . . . secluded and quiet . . .' It's that all right, Holly thought. 'A rare opportunity to acquire one of Lakeland's wildest and most beautiful valleys.' The auctioneer paused and looked slowly around the room, holding the moment of tension before bidding began. 'What do you say, gentlemen? Do I hear one hundred thousand for this very desirable property?'

He makes it sound like a semi-detached bungalow, Holly thought, looking cautiously around her. No one seemed keen to start, and she felt an almost overwhelming desire to make a bid, just to get things started. But Morris had

warned her about that and had counselled her to have
patience. 'Let someone else lose their nerve,' he'd advised
and Holly bit her lip and waited.

Someone spoke from the back of the room. 'Seventy
thousand.'

The auctioneer looked pained. 'I imagine that's a joke.
But still, to get things started—I have a bid of seventy.
Now, gentlemen, is there any advance on seventy?'

You're going to regret that 'gentlemen', Holly thought
with a twitch of her lips. She felt the man beside her move
and knew that he was looking at her. Look as hard as you
like, she told him mentally, I'm not saying a word. Not
yet . . .

'Seventy-five thousand, I have. Seventy-five. Come
now, gentlemen, we're here to do business this afternoon,
shall we stop playing games? Do I hear eighty? Eighty
thousand pounds. Eighty-five? Ninety? He looked
exasperated, as if he thought the bidding should go up in
tens of thousands rather than fives. 'One hundred
thousand—will anyone give me one hundred thousand?
Thank you, sir. Any advance on one hundred thousand?'

'For a big crowd, there aren't many bidders,' Adam
Wilde murmured in Holly's ear. 'Aren't you going to say
anything?'

'Aren't you?' she countered, and received a glare from
a man in front of them. With a sudden spurt of irritation,
she raised her voice. 'One hundred and ten thousand.'

The auctioneer glanced at her in surprise. 'One
hundred and ten thousand, from the young lady near the
back. Well, gentlemen, a new bidder has entered the
arena—and a much better-looking one than the rest of
you, I may add . . .' This raised a muffled laugh, while
Holly felt her irritation grow. Couldn't men leave sex out
of *anything*? And she hadn't meant to bid quite so early,
either—it was that annoying Adam Wilde, muttering in

her ear . . . She gave him a quick, baleful glance, and was further annoyed to see him grinning at her as if the whole thing were extremely amusing.

All right, then. So he thought it was funny, did he? Well, maybe he'd change his mind when *she* won this ridiculous contest and walked out as the new owner of Sleadale Head—leaving him licking his wounds. Wounds which would, she was sure, be mostly to his ego, badly damaged after being beaten by a mere woman . . . Let's see him smiling and laughing then, she thought, with an unaccustomed viciousness.

'One hundred and twenty thousand,' the auctioneer said, and Holly realised with a shock that she had missed a bid. If she didn't keep her mind on the proceedings, she would lose the farm altogether! She fastened her eyes on the auctioneer's face, determinedly ignoring the man at her side. 'One hundred and twenty-five.' He looked her way and Holly stared blandly back. She had entered the bidding too soon, but she wasn't going to make that mistake again. Competition was still lively. Let the others exhaust themselves—and when there were only one or two contenders left, she would join in again, just as Morris had told her.

The price went steadily up. A hundred and thirty. Forty. Fifty. And then—sure sign that the two bidders left were flagging—a hundred and fifty-five. It was time, Holly decided, her heart thumping suddenly, to make her voice heard again.

'A hundred and sixty,' she said clearly, and heard the rustle that went round the room.

The auctioneer gave her an appreciative glance. 'A hundred and sixty from our lady bidder. Any advance on a hundred and sixty?'

The two previous contenders hesitated, then shook their heads. Clearly, they had gone as far as they'd

intended—perhaps even a little further, for one of them
looked distinctly relieved. Holly waited, her heart thudding
with excitement. Was Sleadale Head hers? Had it really
been as easy as that?

The auctioneer struck once with his gavel, then raised it,
ready to strike again.

'Seventy,' said a laconic voice beside Holly.

The rustle this time was much louder and accompanied by
an intake of breath. Holly herself couldn't prevent a gasp.
But there wasn't time for more. She lifted her head, and this
time, when she spoke, her clear voice was edged with
hardness.

'A hundred and seventy-five.'

'Eighty,' Adam Wilde countered.

'Eighty-five.'

'Ninety.'

Every eye in the room was now on the pair who sat, side
by side, bidding furiously against each other. Holly felt
anger spread like a tide of liquid fire through her body.

'Ninety-five,' she said loudly, as if daring him to go any
higher, yet knowing that he would, and panic-stricken
because she really didn't know how much higher Morris
would want her to go. If only he'd given her a limit, she
thought despairingly, she'd have more confidence in her
bids. But he hadn't—and the cheering thought came to her
that perhaps that was because there *was* no limit. Morris was
a rich man and he'd already said that——

'Two hundred thousand,' Adam Wilde said without
raising his voice, and settled back in his seat, as if the matter
were settled.

It was probably that which sent Holly's rage soaring
completely out of sight. If he hadn't sat back like that, she
thought afterwards, if he'd made his bid without that degree
of quiet arrogance which was so infuriating—well, things
might have been very different. Her whole life would have

turned out differently. But as it was——

With a sudden, quick movement, Holly turned and dropped her shoulder-bag. It was a large bag, and heavy—Morris had asked, all too often, what on earth she carried in it to make it weigh so much. It was quite enough, as it fell on Adam Wilde's toes, to make him jump and look down quickly as he lifted it from his foot. Quite enough to distract his attention from the auctioneer while Holly nodded her head to indicate another bid.

'Is that your final word, gentlemen—and lady?' The auctioneer gave a final glance around the room. 'Two hundred and ten thousand pounds, I have. Going, then, at two hundred and ten thousand pounds. Going once——' he tapped with his gavel '—going twice——' tap '—gone.' A final quick blow with the gavel and he straightened slightly, nodded round the room and stepped quickly down from the rostrum. 'Thank you, ladies and gentlemen. The rest of the auction will proceed in twenty minutes' time.'

Holly sat quite still, hardly daring to breathe. She couldn't believe it had all been so easy. She dared not look at Adam Wilde—he must be absolutely livid at the trick she'd played on him. Quickly, she got to her feet and went towards the front of the room. Morris had told her the documents would have to be signed right away, and a deposit placed on the property. Presumably the auctioneer's clerk would be the man to——

'Just a moment.'

The voice had iron it it now, and so did the fingers which had closed around her arm. Holly stopped—the way the fingers were holding her, she had little choice. Slowly, she turned.

Adam Wilde was looking like thunder. Thick, dark brows were drawn like a steel bar straight across his smouldering eyes. His mouth was set like a trap, the lips thin and hard. Even his hair looked angry, clenched rather than curled.

'Did you just do what I think you did?' he asked slowly.

Holly attempted flippancy.

'That rather depends on what you think I—ow! Let go of my arm—you're hurting!'

Several people nearby began to look interested, and Adam Wilde loosened his fingers without letting go of her.

'You know damned well what I think,' he growled. 'You just bought Sleadale, didn't you? Over my head—under my nose—by the dirtiest trick I've ever seen! You——'

He can't hurt me here, Holly reasoned with herself. There are too many people about. She lifted her chin and looked directly into his eyes.

'I'm sorry, Mr Wilde. The auctioneer said quite clearly what the last bid was. If you couldn't remember whether or not it was yours, well——' Delicately, she shrugged her slim shoulders. 'You can't really blame me, can you?'

He stared at her, brows knitted together. Then, as if suddenly accepting that argument was useless, he dropped his grip from her arm. Holly backed away a little, rubbing the spot where his fingers had surely left a mark.

'I'm sorry, Mr Wilde,' she said again. 'But I'm sure you'll agree that all's fair in love and—and——' she floundered '—auction rooms.' It would have been better if *love* hadn't come into this, she thought obscurely. 'I'm sorry—I'll have to go now. There are things to do—documents and so on.' She gave him a slightly frightened smile and turned away.

Frightened? she thought now, lying in the steaming bath. What had she been frightened of? Adam Wilde was an intimidating man, but there was no reason to suppose their paths would ever cross again. No reason at all for her to fear him.

All the same, it was difficult to forget that last baleful glower and the words Adam Wilde had flung after her as she'd made her way to the desk where the auctioneer's clerk sat.

'All's fair, is it? We'll see about that. You needn't imagine you've heard the last of this, Miss Douglas—you and that greasy boyfriend of yours!'

Words, she told herself now, that were just bravado. Intended to scare her and, in the case of the epithet according to Morris, to hurt and annoy her. But no more—surely, no more—than that.

And their effect had been more than expunged by the reception Morris had given her when she'd arrived back at the hotel and told him the good news.

Holly squeezed the sponge over her shoulders, luxuriating in the trickle of warm water down her naked back, and then stood up and reached for a large, fluffy towel. It was yellow, the clear lemon that most suited her dark colouring, and she wrapped herself it it and stepped from the bath. Everything that was needed lay ready to hand, provided by the hotel, and she looked appreciatively at the choice of talcs, choosing one that matched the honeysuckle-scented soap she had just used.

She had just finished drying herself and begun to sprinkle the talc over her body when the telephone rang.

Holly wrapped the towel around herself again and padded into the bedroom to answer it. Probably Morris, she thought, making sure she was 'respectable' before coming to her room. Really, he was unusually scrupulous about these things—it went with the touch of male chauvinism that occasionally irritated her, but which she felt sure could be eliminated. Old-fashioned, she acknowledged, but quite endearingly so.

There was a smile in her voice as she gave the room number. But it wasn't Morris—it was the receptionist, sounding slightly harassed.

'Miss Douglas? There was a gentleman here, asking if

you were in—said he wanted to see you. I'm afraid I gave him your room number.'

'Oh, that's all right.' Morris had mentioned that a friend of his might be calling in some time that day. 'Tell him to come up in a few minutes—I've just had a bath but I'll be ready quite quickly.'

'He's already on his way. I'm afraid.' The receptionist sounded anxious, even apologetic. 'I'm sorry—he seemed rather impatient.'

Holly laughed. 'Don't worry—I know who it is. There's no problem.' She replaced the receiver and went to her wardrobe to take out a dress. Morris's friend might be surprised to find her wrapped in a towel, but he could come in and wait while she slipped into the bathroom to dress. Or, if he were as old-fashioned and correct as Morris, he could wait on the landing. It didn't really matter.

There was a tap on the door and Holly pulled the yellow towel more tightly around her and went across to open it, already smiling to think how Morris's friend would react on finding himself faced with a virtually naked woman. Not, she thought hastily, that she was any less respectable than if she was fully dressed—but she could never resist shocking her rather strait-laced fiancé and his equally conventional friends.

'Come in!' she cried, flinging the door wide open. 'Just too late for the bath, I'm afraid, but Morris left a bottle of champagne to celebrate our becoming farmers, and I know he won't mind if we—oh!'

The words died on her lips, leaving them parted. Her eyes widened and she felt the blood rush scarlet to her face.

'Quite a welcome,' Adam Wilde remarked laconically as he leaned casually against the door-jamb. 'And one I don't feel at all disposed to refuse. Even though your . . . fiancé——' he glanced at the towel that was in danger of slithering from Holly's still-damp body '—might conceivably expect me to refuse. Or would he? It didn't seem to be him you were expecting to see just then.'

He was in the room before Holly could move, moving past her with a sensual grace that was almost insolent. Paralysed, she watched as he strolled across to the window and stood looking out.

'I—I wasn't expecting you,' she said at last, aware of how feeble her words sounded. 'I—I thought it might be a friend of Morris's.'

'And any friend of Morris's is a friend of yours, hmm?' Adam Wilde swung round and raked her with his eyes. 'How very sociable of you. You normally entertain in a towel, do you?'

'I'd just had a bath. And if you'd had the decency to wait at reception until it was convenient, instead of just barging your way in as if—as if——'

'As if I were a friend of Morris's,' he supplied helpfully. 'Yes, I'm afraid I was rather impatient to see you—even before I knew what your entertaining arrangements were. You see——' his voice took on an edge, as if beneath the calmness was a smouldering anger '—there were one or two things I wanted to say to you.'

'Oh, yes?' Holly drew the towel more tightly around her, burningly aware of her nakedness. If only she could take her clothes into the bathroom and dress! But all her instincts told her that this man was trouble—and that the sooner she got rid of him, the better. 'I can't imagine what you think we might have to discuss,' she added icily.

'Did I say anything about discussion? I said there were things *I* wanted to say to *you*. Any further talk between us would be pointless, since I don't imagine you're capable of reasonable discussion and I don't intend to get involved in a screaming match.' His eyes were as cold and empty as Arctic wastes as he regarded her, and Holly shivered. 'But I don't see why you should be allowed to get away

with what you've done without at least knowing what I think
of you.'

'Oh, you don't?' Holly cursed the squeak in her voice.

'No.' He came a step nearer and Holly realised once
again just how big he was. His leanness only looked thin
because he was so tall—in fact, she thought numbly, he was
quite as broad as Morris and looked a good deal more
muscular. Morris inclined to—well, a certain *softness*.
Though that would change once he was farming, and . . .
Thoughts tumbled chaotically through her mind as Adam
Wilde came slowly, inexorably nearer and Holly backed
frantically away, clutching at her towel, feeling it tangle
around her legs . . . Oh God, what was he going to do?

He stopped at last, only inches away from her. Holly
found her back pressed against the wall. She gazed up at
him, her eyes wide and frightened.

'No,' he said again, and his voice had dropped a few tones
and was so deep it was almost a caress. 'I don't think you
should get away with it. If I read you right, you've got away
with too much already in your young life. You need teaching
a lesson—and the way I feel right now, I could be the best
teacher you'll ever find.'

'Please . . .' Holly gulped and took in some air. She pulled
herself together—what was she doing, letting this man
intimidate her? 'Please,' she said more strongly, 'go away
and leave me alone. You've no right to come here and
browbeat me. I suppose you're angry because I bought
Sleadale and you wanted it. Well, you were there right
beside me at the auction. You must have heard that there'd
been a bid after your last one, the auctioneer repeated it the
usual number of times. It's hardly my fault you weren't
attending properly—you could easily have bid again. Or
perhaps you couldn't go any higher,' she added deliberately,
and watched the flush of anger spread up from his neck.

Now what would he do? Holly tightened her grip on the

towel and lifted her chin, hoping that he couldn't tell how scared she was inside.

Adam Wilde didn't speak for a moment. He seemed to be struggling with a choice of several replies. Finally he made up his mind.

'You cheeky little hussy,' he said slowly. 'You really do think you've been clever, don't you? Not your fault that I wasn't attending—when you'd just done your level best to break all my toes? What in hell's name do you carry in that bag? Offensive weapons? It's an offensive weapon in itself! You knew damned well that I wouldn't realise you'd put in another bid—you did it so quietly, on top of causing me extreme pain, that I'm surprised the auctioner himself noticed it. But that's what you were banking on, wasn't it? And it worked.'

He paused and Holly knew that his anger, until now damped down like a dormant volcano, was coming close to erupting. His next words came from between his teeth in a gritting undertone.

'You ought to be banned from all auction rooms in the country, you and that slimy boyfriend of yours,' he snarled. 'You're not fit to mix with decent people. And as for Sleadale Head—it breaks my heart to think what you'll be doing to it.' His eyes were like swords, piercing her with his scorn. 'People like you make me sick. And to think that you now own that beautiful wild valley—well, it doesn't *bear* thinking of! I just wish I weren't going to be around to see it.'

He was so close now that Holly could feel his breath on her face like dragon's fire. Fury emanated from him in waves. His words punched into her like the merciless blows rained by a winning boxer on his opponent towards the end of a fight. Wordless, she shook her head and felt the stinging heat of tears in her eyes.

'No,' she whispered, gazing up at him. 'No, it's not

like that—we're not going to spoil Sleadale, we're going to farm it. It's going to be our home.' She was vibrantly aware of his hard, lean body so close to hers. 'I'm sorry about the auction—I had to do it. I—we wanted it so badly, I couldn't think what else to do and——'

'Don't start giving me the helpless little woman stuff!' he broke in. 'Standing there wrapped in that damned towel, all big-eyed, pretending Sleadale Head's the little love-nest you've always dreamed of! It won't work—I happen to know what you *really* want it for. And it won't be any little love-nest when you and Crawley have finished with it—I know that. One of the wildest valleys in the Lake District,' he said bitterly, 'and it has to fall into the hands of swindling, heartless charlatans like you two—and they say there's justice!'

Without giving herself time to think, Holly swung one hand up and brought it in a stinging slap across his face. The sound cracked through the room like a shot. And then there was a brief silence.

For a long, tense moment, Adam Wilde didn't move. Then, slowly, he put up his hand and touched the blood-red marks of Holly's fingers. He looked down at her.

Holly quivered. There was no way she could escape him. His body trapped her against the wall. She was completely at his mercy. And she knew that if he had ever had any so far as she was concerned, that slap would have destroyed its last vestige.

'You little spitfire,' he said quietly, and reached out for her.

Holly's breath thrust its way out of her body as Adam Wilde dragged her hard against him. She had no time to protest, no time to do more than open her mouth, before his lips had fastened on hers. Their angry hardness was a shock that had her whimpering, but the tiny sound only seemed to add fuel to his emotion. She could feel it, hardening his body, thrusting against her softness, so vulnerable with only the soft towel to protect her. And then she realised with horror that the towel was no longer there—it had slipped, either when she'd slapped him or when he'd grasped her into his arms. She stood naked, trembling, helpless; unable either to free herself from his increasing caresses or to turn her face away from his kisses.

Adam Wilde groaned somewhere deep in his throat. His mouth was still on hers, but the harshness had softened. His lips were firm now, but with a gentleness that robbed them of their previous cruelty. They moved over hers, exploring, insisting—and to her amazement Holly found herself responding. With a tiny moan, she let herself relax against him, arching her body against his, twisting sensuously under his hands.

It was over almost before she knew it was happening. With a groan of an entirely different nature, Adam broke away, almost pushing her from him. Without looking at her, he bent and picked up the towel which lay in a heap at their feet. He handed it to her and turned away, striding rapidly across the room, while Holly, with trembling fingers, wrapped it around herself.

'Your boyfriend's arrived,' Adam Wilde said harshly, staring down in the car park. 'He'll be up here in a moment. I don't think we'd better meet, do you? Not just at the moment.' He turned and stared at her, his eyes like flints. 'It's even worse than I thought,' he said slowly. 'You're one of the most dangerous females it's ever been my misfortune to encounter. But I can't leave it there, I'm afraid. We'll have to meet again. There are still a few things I need to say—and a few we need to sort out.' He moved towards her again and Holly stepped quickly aside, but he made no move to touch her. He went to the door and opened it. 'I'll be seeing you. More's the pity.'

He gave her a brief, curt nod and went out.

Holly stood quite still. Her mind was in turmoil. The events of the past half-hour had been so rapid, so confusing, that she could barely sort them out. She needed time—time to get them clear, time to think over what he had said, what had taken place. Time to make sense of it all.

Morris was coming back. He would be here in a moment, expecting to celebrate her success at the auction, ready perhaps to tell her whom he had gone to meet and what had happened. She couldn't face him yet—not with Adam Wilde's kisses still burning her lips, his caresses still warm on her skin.

Making a quick decision, Holly turned and went back into the bathroom. Morris would never intrude on her there. She turned on the taps and hot water gushed out in a cloud of steam.

In any case, she thought bitterly, she needed another bath—to wash off the feeling of those lips and hands that, however unwelcome, had called forth a response from her body that Morris had never managed.

Adam Wilde had said she was dangerous. But she knew he was wrong. Of the two of them, *he* was the one who spelt danger. And she hoped fervently that, in spite of what he had said, they would never have to meet again . . .

CHAPTER THREE

'AND a bottle of your best champagne,' Morris concluded, handing back the menu with an expansive smile. 'Miss Douglas and I have something to celebrate!'

The young waitress took the menu, smiled back and hurried away. Morris lifted his aperitif, sipped it and sat back with an air of satisfaction. He beamed at Holly.

'Well? And how's my clever little girl tonight?'

Holly smiled faintly back at him. Since Adam Wilde had left her shaken and disturbed in her bedroom, she had found herself doing a lot of thinking. And she hadn't been too happy with her thoughts. Particularly, she kept remembering that little scene in the auction room. It *had* been rather a shabby little trick to play, her conscience told her. If Adam Wilde had done it to her, she would have been just as angry. And so, no doubt, would Morris.

But Holly hadn't told Morris what had happened. Lying in that second bath, coming to terms with her own actions, she'd known that she wouldn't—and not because she thought he wouldn't approve but, rather, because she was sure he would.

Holly was already feeling uncomfortably ashamed. But Morris's approbation wouldn't have eased her guilt—it would have made her feel worse. Because, deep down, she had a strong feeling that Adam Wilde would *not* have stooped to such methods to get his own way. And she didn't want the comparison between him and the man she'd promised to marry.

'Pleasant dining-room, this,' Morris remarked approv-

40

ingly. 'In fact, it's a good hotel altogether. You like it, don't you, Holly?'

Holly started a little. 'What? Oh—yes, it's very nice.' She followed his glance round the softly-lit room, the round tables with their pink cloths and dainty lamps, the spacious feel of the large room. 'I like the way they haven't crowded it. You don't feel that the people at the next table can hear every word you say.'

Morris grinned. 'And that would be dreadful for you, wouldn't it?' he teased. 'Holly, I've never known a girl like you for wanting to keep her privacy. You're very nearly secretive, do you know that?'

Holly stared at him, wondering what he would say if she told him that Adam Wilde had visited her room while Morris had been absent, that she'd stood talking to him wrapped in nothing more than a bath-towel, that she'd slapped his face and that they'd ended up . . . Swiftly, she jerked her mind away, dismayed by the sudden tingling response of her body to her thoughts. How could she possibly tell him those things—and yet, wouldn't he be justified in thinking her secretive if she didn't?

'Don't look so hurt,' Morris said, reaching across to take her hand. 'I know you wouldn't keep any secrets from me.' And Holly gazed at his hand, unable to look up and meet his eyes, convinced that her guilt must show in every line of her face.

For the rest of the evening, she felt that she was acting a part. Somehow, she managed to pull herself together, to behave as naturally as she knew how—raising her bubbling glass to Morris's, laughing with him as she took too large a sip and sneezed, smiling, talking, nodding agreement as he outlined his plans for Sleadale Head. But somehow the celebration, looked forward to for so many weeks, seemed to have gone flat—as flat as the champagne would be if they left it standing until morning.

The memory of how she had bought the farm still nagged at her. The dark guilt that she hadn't been able to wash away still dimmed every colour.

'Morris, I'm awfully tired,' she said suddenly, breaking into a long dissertation on modern business methods. 'I think I'll go to bed now—you don't mind, do you?'

He was all concern at once. 'Of course I don't mind, sweetie. You go on. You've had a pretty exciting day, it's no wonder you're tired. I'll see you in the morning, hmm? Don't hurry down—we've got plenty of time.'

Holly nodded. Suddenly, she was too dispirited even to ask what they were doing next day. Probably signing more documents, making more arrangements about the farm, she thought as she made her way up to her room. And for some reason, the thought—which would have been thrilling only a few hours ago—left her feeling quite cold.

It was all Adam Wilde's fault! Nothing had been the same since she'd met him at Sleadale Head the other day—and it was even worse now that the auction was over. Viciously, Holly slammed her bedroom door behind her and kicked off her shoes. She let her eyes roam around the room, remembering how his presence had filled it, how vibratingly aware of him she had been, how the air had crackled between them. Remembering, too, the feel of his lips, harsh at first, then growing oddly gentle against hers. His hands, cruel and uncaring before they became sensuously caressing . . .

Why *should* he have that effect on me? Holly asked herself in desperation. And why does Morris have to be so correct—so proper—so *old-fashioned?* Why wasn't he up here now, kissing her the way Adam Wilde had, holding her the way Adam Wilde had? Making her *feel* the way Adam Wilde had?

With a soft moan of bewildered pain, Holly ran into the bathroom and turned on both taps.

It would be her third bath in less than six hours—but it was the only consolation she could think of.

'I don't think I'll come into Kendal with you, unless you really need me,' she said to Morris next morning as they sat at breakfast. 'I'd like some fresh air—I might go for a walk.'

'Well . . .' Morris pursed his lips, looking doubtful. 'There are still a few formalities to go through—things to sign. And we'll need you for those, since you are the legal owner of Sleadale Head. But I don't think we'll be dealing with those today, so yes, you go off if you want to. D'you want one of the cars? You can use the Jaguar, if you like.'

'No, I'll have the Range Rover.' Suddenly, Holly had made up her mind what she wanted to do, but she didn't want to tell Morris. 'I'll go out on the fells.'

'By yourself? Do you really think that's wise?'

Holly fought down irritation. 'I won't go far. And I'll leave a note at the desk to say where I've gone. I just feel——' She looked helplessly at her fiancé, wishing she could tell him what was really on her mind, and yet uncomfortably aware that he wouldn't understand her. 'I feel a bit tired still,' she finished lamely.

'Yes, you do look rather washed-out.' He looked her over critically. 'Perhaps you ought to try using blusher when your cheeks are so pale . . . I'll tell you what, Holly, when all this is over and we're on an even keel, I'll take you to London for a few days—show you a really good time. You can go to a beauty salon, have a facial, get your hair styled, and we'll buy you a couple of really good outfits and see some shows. How do you like that for an idea?'

He was smiling, his face alight, and Holly gazed at him in dismay. He really thought she'd enjoy that? She, who thought places like Hereford and Kendal were big cities! And he thought she needed 'making over'—a facial, a new hairstyle, some 'really good outfits'. Instinctively, she glanced down at the dove-grey sweater that had been chosen to match the solf colour of her eyes, and the dark blue skirt that fitted so neatly into her slender waist. They were plain, yes—but were they really so drab as all that? And did her clear skin really need blusher?

'I—I don't know,' she said helplessly, and Morris smiled and patted her hand.

'I know—it's all come rather suddenly for you, hasn't it? The past couple of months—meeting me, entering a whole new way of life. And then buying a farm!' He laughed indulgently. 'No wonder you're so confused. Well, don't worry about it. Morris will see that everything's all right. You just go off for your walk and enjoy yourself—and don't forget to leave word of where you're going. I want to know just where to send the Mountain Rescue, don't I?' He laughed heartily and Holly responded with a sickly smile.

I don't know what's wrong with me, she thought dully as she turned the Range Rover out of the car park half an hour later. Morris is no different from what he was yesterday—last week—when we first met. So why is he beginning to grate on me?

She turned out along the Shap road and thrust the big car into top gear. It must be her own fault. She really was tired—overwhelmed by all that had happened. Mentally and emotionally exhausted. The fact that Morris was a good deal older than she was and understood these reactions didn't make him patronising. It simply meant she could, after all, have confided in him. It meant she wasn't being fair to him.

Maybe when she was out at Sleadale Head again, on her own amid all that wild beauty, she would be able to see things in perspective once more.

The track seemed even rougher today, and getting out to open, drive through and then close each gate slowed her progress even further. But at last the square house, so solid against the rocky hills, came into view and Holly stopped the Range Rover and gazed at it.

Sleadale Head. A house that had stood there for—how long? A hundred years? Longer? And even before that, surely, there had been something here, some building that had sheltered generations of farmers and their families, a tiny community living here alone to wrest a living from the brooding fells. Were their spirits still here? Did they watch her driving slowly along this track and wonder what kind of life she and Morris Crawley would make at the end of this remote valley?

Holly drove the last few yards and parked the Range Rover by the door. She scrambled down and stood there, the wind lifting her hair, staring at the blank walls, the sightless windows. Was the house hostile towards her? It has seemed friendly and welcoming the other day—she had had no fears at all. But now . . . inexplicably, she shivered.

Slowly, she went forward, her fingers on the key in her pocket. You're mine now, she told the silent house, willing it to accept her. I bought you yesterday. Do you resent that? Do you resent *me*?

To her surprise, the door was unlocked. Surely Morris had made sure it was fastened after their last visit? But it swung open under her hand and she shrugged and went inside. It didn't really matter, after all. There was nothing here to steal, and it was unlikely that anyone had even been near the place since they'd left it.

Inside, it was cold and dim. The generator had been turned off and there was no electricity. The walls seemed to close around her, almost threateningly.

Holly couldn't understand it at all. Sensitive as she was to atmosphere, she could swear that there was something strange here today—some almost malign influence—that hadn't been present on her previous visit. She tried to shrug it off, but the feeling persisted. The house had changed towards her, and in her already depressed state it made her want to cry.

Perhaps it was simply because she was alone here, without Morris. The house was isolated, watched only by silent fells. Perhaps it would be better when he was here with her again.

But in that case, Holly thought with a cold stab of fear, how am I ever going to be able to live here? Morris can't be with me all the time. And if every time he goes out I feel this—this oppression, this menace—how am I going to be able to stand it?

I love you, she cried silently to the house. Don't you understand? I fell in love with you the moment I saw you. I'll always look after you—I'll never let any harm come to you.

And just why did I think that? What harm could possibly come to Sleadale Head? Who would want to harm it—who *could*?

She was standing at the bathroom door as the last thought crossed her mind, staring once again at that giant corner bath with its wide shelves in the spacious room. Thinking how luxurious it would be with a new fitted carpet, with a couple of huge plants and some pretty glass . . . if the house would let her . . . Telling herself how ridiculous that last thought was, and trying to push it away.

'Well, well—we do seem fated to meet in bathrooms, don't we? Still contemplating the communal——'

The voice came from behind her, totally unexpected,

and Holly jumped and gave a scream of pure fright. She whipped round, backing away as she did so, hands automatically reaching out for protection . . . and saw Adam Wilde standing in the doorway.

Before she could stop screaming, he was coming for her, hands outstretched. Holly thought of the two miles of rough track between her and civilisation, the hill that reared between Sleadale and its nearest neighbour. Panic-stricken, finding no weapon in the bare room, she held up her hands, fingers curled outwards, nails at the ready.

'Don't touch me!' she hissed. 'Don't come near me!'

But Adam Wilde kept on coming, and she was reacting too slowly. He had her wrists in both his hands, holding them firmly, although not cruelly, and as she raised one foot to kick him he side-stepped and, before she could move again, had her fastened tightly in his arms.

'For crying out loud!' he snapped as he pressed her close against him. 'What in hell's name do you think I'm going to do? Strangle you? Heck, I might *feel* like it—but I've got more respect for my own life and liberty to risk it for a silly bit of a kid like you!'

Holly stood in his arms, trembling violently. She knew by the iron strength that enclosed her that struggling would be futile—and there was a perverse kind of comfort on being held there, even though she knew this man had no cause at all to love her. And also, shamingly, she was aware that her heart was still hammering and her knees shaking too much to allow her to stand unaided.

'You scared me,' she accused him, looking up at the dark face. 'Creeping up on me like that . . . I'd no idea anyone else was here.' A thought struck her. 'Were you already here? Was it you who unlocked the door?'

'I've been here for about half an hour. And yes, I do have a key—one the agents gave me. I hadn't taken it back, so I thought I'd come out again for a last look around *I* didn't expect to see *you* here.'

'I can't imagine why not,' Holly snapped. 'After all, I do own the place now. Or had you already forgotten that small fact? And perhaps, since it seems to be too much trouble to go back to the agent's office, you'd like to give the key to me, before you go.'

'Quite the little landowner, aren't we?' he drawled, and removed his arm from her shoulders. 'Well, since it seems that you're now feeling better, we might continue with our conversation of yesterday. I'd intended doing the whole thing properly, of course, and making an appointment as befits your tenant, but since we're here——'

'*What* did you say?' Holly interrupted. 'My tenant? *You?*'

'*Don't tell me you didn't know?*' His tone was amused, but his eyes were hard.

'*Of course I didn't know! I didn't even know I had* any——' Holly broke off, her eyes widening. 'Oh—you mean that tiny cottage at Little Sleadale? You live *there?*'

Adam Wilde inclined his head gravely. 'I do. I pay you rent—or shall do from now on. Didn't Crawley tell you?'

'I knew about the cottage, of course—I knew it was let occasionally—but I didn't know there was anyone in it at the moment, and I certainly didn't know it was *you.*' Holly turned away from him, aware that dismay showed all too plainly on her face.

'And now I suppose you'll want to evict me.' He spoke with mock regret. 'Turn me out of my little home into the cold, cold snow. Oh, Sir Jasper—I mean, Lady Jasper—do not be so cold-hearted. Where else can a poor man go in winter?' He was below her on the stairs now, arms spread wide. 'I appeal to you—as one human being to another, I appeal to you——'

'Oh, no, you don't!' Holly began to laugh in spite of

herself. 'Get up! Of course I'm not going to evict you. I was just surprised. You never mentioned the cottage before.'

'There were more important things for us to talk about.' Adam Wilde scrambled to his feet, towering above her. He reached down and took her hands. 'Let's find somewhere more comfortable to discuss them. It may take some time.'

Uncertainly, Holly followed him down the stairs and into the big living-room. The previous owners had left the fitted carpet, and its rich red lent the room an impression of glowing warmth.

'There are a few sticks and a log or two here,' Adam Wilde said, rooting in a large basket that stood near the fireplace. 'Do I have your permission to light a fire? It won't do the house any harm to have a bit of warmth circulating around it, and it'll be more comfortable for our discussion.'

'Go ahead.' Holly watched as he set expertly to work. She couldn't make him out at all, and she still wasn't at all sure that it was wise to stay here with him—especially when she recalled his behaviour in her hotel bedroom yesterday. That had been a civilised building, when she was within call of other people . . . What might he do here, in this lonely house, with no other person for miles?

But the touch of humour he'd displayed on the stairs had somehow lulled her suspicions. And that, she thought, remembering Morris's remarks about confidence tricksters, was probably just what he'd intended to do. After all, there was no reason at all for him to have any friendly feelings towards her—not after the way she'd beaten him at the auction.

No, Adam Wilde was not to be trusted, and Holly made up her mind to be very wary of him.

'You still haven't told me why you're here,' she said

suddenly as he sat back to watch the yellow flames roaring up the chimney. 'Coming out for a last look round doesn't seem a very plausible reason. Can't you accept that I've bought Sleadale Head and you're not going to get another chance? Or—is there something here you want?'

Adam Wilde burst out laughing. 'Hidden treasure, you mean? A family heirloom? Or maybe a hidden will that leaves the entire property to me, after all? No, Miss Douglas—or may I call you Holly? Pretty name, though a trifle prickly—no, there's nothing romantic like that about Sleadale Head. It's just an ordinary working farm, typical of a good many others in the Lake District. Or it was, until you and Crawley came along and set eyes on it.'

Holly stared at him. 'What do you mean? It's going to continue to be a working farm. We're not going to change anything.'

'Oh, come on now, you don't have to keep the pretence going now it's legally yours.' The deep voice grated with impatience. 'And sit down, for goodness' sake—I'm not used to having to look up at people!'

He patted the carpeted floor and Holly sat down, keeping a safe distance away from him. Unconsciously, she held out her hands to the warmth of the fire. If only Morris could have been here! she thought wistfully. They ought to have shared this—the first fire in their new home. It could have been really romantic . . .

But she wasn't with Morris, the man she planned to marry. She was with Adam Wilde. A stranger who had come into her life only a few days ago. A man whom she had no reason either to like or to trust—and who, she reminded herself ruefully, had no reason either to like or trust her.

She turned her head and saw him watching her, his eyes dark as sapphires now, sparked by tiny points of flame that reflected the fire he had just lit. There was something in his gaze that made her feel distinctly uneasy and, to mask her discomfort, she spoke abruptly.

'Well? Perhaps now you're ready to tell me what it is you want to discuss? And just why you're here this morning—using a key you shouldn't have to wander around a house that doesn't belong to you?'

The sapphire eyes didn't flinch. They held her own with a steadiness that increased her discomfort, making her feel somehow in the wrong. As, presumably, he believed she was. All right, she wanted to cry, so I played a trick on you at the auction—but all the same, I *am* the owner of Sleadale Head and you don't have any right here . . . But she didn't say it. There was something in that steady gaze that prevented her from admitting she'd been wrong, something that made her want to defend herself, even before she'd been accused.

'Let's leave the question of why I'm here,' Adam Wilde said at last. 'In fact, I told you the truth—I just wanted a last look round. But that isn't important. What is important is why *you're* here. And that's something you don't seem at all willing to talk about.'

Holly sighed. 'I've told you. Morris Crawley and I are getting married soon and this is where we're going to live. It's as simple as that. Is there anything else you'd like to know about my private life?'

The question had been asked with some sarcasm, but the dark-haired man sitting on the floor beside her seemed to take it seriously. He considered for a moment, and then said, 'Yes, since you ask, there is. Quite a lot.' He glanced at her, his brows creased thoughtfully. 'First, the one I asked you yesterday—how did you come to agree to marry him in the first place?'

Holly flushed angrily. 'That's my business!'

'So it wasn't love?'

She began to scramble to her feet. 'You've no right to ask that! I thought you wanted a serious disc——'

Adam Wilde stretched out a hand and caught her wrist, pulling her back to the floor. Furiously, Holly subsided, knowing from previous experience that any struggles would be in vain, and determined not to lose her dignity in front of this insufferable man.

'I do want a serious discussion,' he said calmly, 'but you did invite questions.'

'I didn't mean——'

'No, I don't imagine you did. The subject is far too sensitive, isn't it?' Again, the brilliant eyes assessed her. 'I just think it's a pity, that's all . . . You don't look the type to be going along with Crawley's nefarious schemes. But, since you're engaged to him, and certainly involved in this purchase, I suppose you must be.'

'I don't know what you're talking about! What nefarious schemes?'

Adam Wilde snorted with exasperation. 'I've already said, there's no point in your concealing them now! You've bought the place, dammit, and with the law as it stands at present there's precious little anyone can do about it. You're free to go ahead—ruin the whole valley—and neither I nor anyone else can lift a finger to stop you. And all in the name of filthy lucre!' He got to his feet, impatience in every line of him. 'There's no point in talking to you! I thought you might be made to see reason—I even thought you could be an innocent pawn, not even aware of what Crawley had planned. But I can see now that you'll just continue to stonewall me until I give up and go away. Well——' he strode to the door, turning to glare at her across the room '—you needn't bother. I've better things to do. But I haven't given up—and I won't be going away. I've rented that cottage in Little Sleadale for a year, and I intend to stay there, right under your noses, watching every single move you make!'

Holly sat quite still. None of his words had made any sense to her at all. He must be mad, completely out of his mind. Unless—unless there *was* something Morris hadn't told her? Those mysterious meetings—his unexplained trips to Kendal . . . Coming to a sudden decision, she leapt to her feet and ran after Adam Wilde.

He was already in his Land Rover, driving slowly round from the side of the house where he'd parked it. So that was why she hadn't known he was here! Holly ran in front of it, waving her arms, and the vehicle stopped.

'Please,' she said breathlessly, 'please, come back and tell me what you mean. I honestly don't know what you're talking about. As far as I'm aware, Morris *does* intend to farm the land as it always has been—with sheep. But if there's some other rumour going around—well, I think we ought to know about it.'

'Still trying to play the innocent?' he said harshly. 'That's no rumour, and you know it.' He slammed the engine back into gear and revved it.

'*Please!*' Holly begged him, hardly knowing why she did so, knowing only that for some reason it was imperative that she find out what he was talking about. 'Please, Mr Wilde—come back into the house and let's talk. There really is something here I don't understand—and I think you might be able to tell me.'

Adam Wilde gave her a long look. Then he grunted, cut the engine and swung himself out of the driving seat.

'All right, we'll give it another go. But this time, Miss Douglas, I hope you're going to be honest with me. I don't have time to waste playing games.'

They returned to the living-room. The fire had settled down to a steady glow now, and Adam threw on a couple of logs. He settled himself near it and Holly, rather more hesitantly, sat down on the other side.

'Right. Where shall we start?'

Holly shrugged helplessly. 'You tell me. What I told you before was the truth. Morris and I intend to live here and farm sheep. What's so unusual about that?'

'It would be unusual if it were true,' he said grimly. 'Look—those questions I asked about how long you'd known Crawley—they weren't intended to be impertinent. Well——' he grinned disarmingly '—not entirely, anyway. Let me ask them again. How long *have* you known him? And how did you come to agree to marry him? He's a good bit older than you.'

'Eighteen years,' Holly admitted reluctantly. 'But that's not such a lot—he's only forty. And I don't see what it has to do with——'

'No, maybe not. Maybe it doesn't have anything to do with the farm, and if it doesn't, I'll apologise in advance. On the other hand . . .' He regarded her thoughtfully. 'Tell me where you met. You're not a northern girl, are you?'

'No. I come from Hereford. My father farms there—on the edge of the Black Mountains, in country not so very different from this.' Her grey eyes glinted at him. 'So I'm not quite the townie you may have taken me for. I grew up with sheep, Mr Wilde. I've even worked as a shepherdess.'

'Please, call me Adam,' he said absently. 'All right, so you're not an innocent in that respect. That makes it even more likely that . . . So, how did you meet? Crawley's no farmer. Finance is the name of the game.'

Holly remembered that Morris and Adam Wilde had met before—'crossed swords', in Morris's words. But where, when or why, she has no idea. She answered cautiously, not enjoying the conversation at all, but determined to go along with it until Adam Wilde told her just what he'd meant by his earlier accusations.

'That's right,' she said warily. 'He's a financier. He's worked for the past twenty years or more in London—I don't know all the details, but things to do with high finance, stocks and shares, that sort of thing. He's very high-powered.' She spoke proudly. 'But now he wants to get out of the rat-race and live a different sort of life. He bought a small farm near my father's—that's how we met. He hasn't actually done much himself—he put in a manager. But now he's decided that's what he wants to do, and we looked around for something bigger. And found Sleadale.'

'Just like that?' Adam said, and she nodded.

'Yes. It was a real piece of luck. There was nothing suitable at all in Herefordshire or any of the other places we looked, and then this came up and we both knew it was the answer.'

'And what was the question?' Adam Wilde asked softly.

'I'm sorry?' Holly gave him a blank look.

'You said it was the answer. So what was the question? More precisely, the questions. Yours, if I understand you, was the search for the ideal farm on which to settle down and found a dynasty. And Crawley's?'

Holly flushed at his use of the word 'dynasty' —couldn't the man say *anything* without being sarcastic?—but she kept her tone even as she answered him. 'Exactly the same, of course. What else?'

'What else, indeed?' said Adam. 'Perhaps you should be asking *him* that, Holly. In fact, I think that would be a good idea.' He rose to his feet and paced across to the window, staring out at the swooping fells, tawny with dead bracken. 'Ask him just what plans he does have for Sleadale. Ask how many of the eight hundred acres you've just bought he intends to graze with sheep. Ask what he intends to do with the rest. And——' he wheeled round so suddenly that Holly flinched '—ask just why he wanted *you* to go to the auction. Why it has to be *your* name on the deeds.' He stopped and there was a silence, broken only by the crackling of the fire. Softly, almost as if his voice hurt to use it, he went on. 'Ask him if it isn't true that within two years he will have completely changed the appearance of this valley—that within ten years the land, the wildlife and the character will have been ruined, lost beyond redemption.' His eyes, stormy as a driven ocean, seared her face. 'Ask him those things, Holly Douglas, and then tell me what the answers are. I'll be very interested to know.'

CHAPTER FOUR

HOLLY'S grey eyes widened, pools of bewilderment and dismay in her pale face.

'You don't mean that,' she whispered. 'You can't mean it. Change the valley completely—ruin the land and the wildlife? It's crazy. What do you think Morris is going to do, for heaven's sake? Turn it into a nuclear dump?'

'No. Even he might not go quite that far—although I wouldn't put it past him, if there were money in it.' Adam shook his head and looked out of the window again. 'Come here, Holly.'

Slowly, Holly came to her feet and crossed the room. With some doubt, she stood beside the tall man and allowed him to take her by the arm, drawing her nearer to the panes. Together, they stood and gazed out at the wheeling clouds, scudding like scared white rabbits across the blue October sky.

'See that?' Adam said quietly, nodding towards the hills that soared from the valley floor, patched with purple heather among the golden brown of the bracken. 'Nothing's touched these fells for centuries. Only sheep have grazed there, keeping the grass short. Sheep, a few cows, maybe, rabbits and foxes have roamed these hills for years. Their very wildness is as valuable as their potential for grazing. There aren't so many places like this left in England now. Places where peregrines, even golden eagles, can hunt without interference, where badgers and foxes can roam unseen, where even a few peace-loving humans can wander without being accosted

by ice-cream vans. Do you understand the value of places
like that, Holly? Do they mean anything to you?'

'Well, of course they do!' Holly felt irritation vying
with the strange sensations that she always experienced
when she got close to this man. 'I told you, I grew up in a
place very similar to this. I'm a farmer's daughter. I love
the countryside and everything in it.'

'I wonder. Farmers aren't usually sentimental about
the land they farm, nor about the animals and birds that
compete for a living from it. What kind of farmer is your
father, Holly? The old-fashioned type who lives in
harmony with nature—or the twentieth-century
businessman who sees the land only as a way of making
money?'

'My father is as wise a countryman as you'll find
anywhere,' Holly told him shortly.

'And Crawley?'

'I told you—Morris hasn't farmed before, but he wants
to start now. He wants to get out of the rat-race.' She
looked up at Adam. 'You think he intends to do
something else, don't you? Build here—make a new
road—set up some kind of industry? But he wouldn't be
allowed to do that—the planning authorities would never
allow it, not to mention the National Park. If that's what
this rumour is all about, you can forget it. It could never
happen.'

'I quite agree. Crawley would never be able to build
here.' The blue eyes went again to the window, to the
bare hillsides. 'But what he could do is something equally
destructive—and yet, something that many people might
even approve.' Adam paused, then turned his gaze back
to Holly's face. 'Can you honestly say that you know
nothing of his plans? Can you honestly tell me that you
don't know he means to plant trees here?

'Trees?'

He nodded. 'That's what I said—trees. All right, so it sounds crazy—but that's because you probably don't understand all the implications.'

'Look,' Holly said, 'I'm a farmer's daughter. I've been to college——'

'Then you should know what trees do to the landscape,' Adam interrupted curtly. 'First of all, let's get it clear that I'm not talking about our own oak and ash and beech trees—nice deciduous hardwoods that support immense ecosystems of their own, with animals, birds and insects all living in their own little world on, in and around them. No, the trees that your precious Morris intends to plant are softwoods. Conifers. Not natives of this country, but fast taking it over. You've only got to look at any wild stretch of countryside to see their march. Great blocks of grim, dark green trees, covering miles of hillside, completely obscuring all its natural features—the tiny pools, the rocky outcrops, all disappearing for ever under the shadow of the invaders.'

'I know what conifers do——'

'And it's not just the look of them that is so objectionable,' he went on, as if she hadn't spoken. 'It's what they do to the land. They exude acid into the soil, virtually sterilising it. Nothing grows under a stand of conifers. The ground is dead. And if there are no plants, there will be no insects—no birds—no animals.' His voice grew softer, deeper, as if sounding the knell of doom, and then stopped.

'Look,' Holly said again. 'I *know* all this. Conifers would be a disaster here—I agree. But there isn't any intention of doing anything like that. Morris has never uttered a word about——'

'And do you believe him?' Adam Wilde asked flatly. He lifted his head and his eyes burned into hers. 'If Crawley does what he intends, this valley is doomed. It will become the same as so many other wild places that have suffered a similar fate, and it will never recover.'

Holly shook her head. The whole thing was fantastic.

'Why would Morris want to do this?' she demanded. 'Is there so much money in wood? Wouldn't he have to wait years before getting anything back from it?

Adam gave a brief, mirthless laugh.

'Certainly he would! And that, my dear Holly, is the whole point.' He leaned forward, his eyes on her face now, intent on making her understand. 'It's also the point of getting *you* to buy the farm. Crawley's a rich man—a financier, well known in the circles that deal in money. You're just a farmer's daughter from Herefordshire—a nobody, if you'll forgive my saying so. Now—you buy the farm and agree to Crawley's suggestion that some of the land be used for planting trees. You trust him because he's your fiancé, so you don't look too closely into it. You accept what he tells you—that the trees will enhance the beauty of the valley, that they'll make another crop for the farm, that the land they're planted on isn't much good for sheep, anyway. All right, with me so far? You then apply to the Forestry Commission for grants.'

'Grants? *Money?*'

'You've got it. Money. The whole thing hinges on money. You see, there are some quite interesting tax loopholes to do with forestry, and this whole scheme exploits them very neatly. It'll cost you around four hundred pounds to plant an acre of trees, right? The Forestry Commission will give you a grant of one hundred pounds—and on the remaining three hundred you can get a high rate of tax relief. What's more, after ten years you can sell the whole thing off without becoming liable to Capital Gains Tax, even though your rapidly maturing woodland could then have doubled in value.'

He gave her a twisted, sardonic smile. 'Not at all bad, as an investment. And the remaining acres, together with this very nice house and the cottage at Little Sleadale, would still be perfectly viable as a farm and accrue just as much value as they would have done with the full acreage. Of course, I doubt if Crawley himself intends to wait the full ten years—he'll sell off to investors who want their own tax loophole. I doubt if he even intends to go so far as moving in here—the entire gambit is solely for profit.'

'You're talking nonsense,' Holly said impatiently. 'Oh, not about the grants and the tax relief and all that—I don't know the details, but I know it's probably just as you say. But I've told you—it's just not like that. You're barking—if I may say so, Mr Wilde—completely up the wrong tree!'

'All right,' Adam said after a pause. 'Treat it as a joke. I've clearly been wasting my time.' He got to his feet. 'I gave you the benefit of the doubt—thought perhaps you were really innocent of his plans. Obviously, I was wrong—you're in it as deeply as he is, and you're every bit as devious.'

Devious! That was what Morris had called Adam Wilde. Holly got to her feet, too.

'*I'm* devious?' she flashed. 'Well, that really is something! And you, of course, are as clear and honest as the day is long. Well, it may interest you to know, Mr Wilde, that I happen to know different. I'm not completely blind, you know. I'm not totally unobservant. It was obvious to *me* the other day that that wasn't the first time you and Morris had met—even though you seemed, for some obscure reason of your own, to want to hide it. So I asked Morris on the way home—and he told me it was true.'

'And?' Adam was watching her closely. 'Just what else did he tell you?'

Holly was tempted to say that Morris had told her all about their previous encounter—that she knew just what a confidence trickster Adam was, knew all about the chicanery of which he was capable. But the blue eyes were watching her with a searing contempt that stopped her with a jolt. There was no way of lying to this man, she thought miserably, and was uncomfortably aware that he knew that she'd intended doing just that.

'He said you'd crossed swords in the past,' she said lamely, and Adam gave a yelp of laughter.

'Crossed swords! Well, that's one way of putting it, though the sword isn't quite the weapon that comes most readily to Crawley's hand, I imagine.' His grin faded, leaving his face grim. 'All right—so you say you're not involved in this plan to violate Sleadale. What are you going to do about it, then?'

'Do about it?'

'You know what'll happen if Crawley goes ahead with his plan. You've told me you understand what conifer-planting means. You've even given me to understand that you are as against it as I am. So—what are you going to do about it?'

Holly shook her head. She felt bewildered. Somehow, she seemed to have got herself on the same side as this man, ranged against Morris. Yet how could she be? She loved Morris—she was engaged to him. They had such plans . . . And all she knew about Adam Wilde was that he had once known Morris in the past and that he wanted Sleadale as badly as they did . . .

She looked at him again, meeting the eyes that challenged her like spears. And the truth flashed into her mind.

'It's not that way at all, is it? she said slowly. 'All you've been saying to me—it's the other way around. You've been tricking me, Adam Wilde—just as Morris

said you would. It's *you* who wants to plant conifers here,
isn't it? You who wants to make money out of Sleadale.
You just want to get my sympathy—get me to sell the
farm to you—and then you can do just as you like. Well,
it's not going to happen!' Convinced now that she had the
truth, she lifted her head. 'Morris and I are going to live
here,' she said proudly. 'It's all planned.' Her eyes were
wide and dark, the irises mere rims of grey around the
black pupils. 'He wouldn't deceive me like that,' she said
positively, needing nevertheless to hear a firm voice
making the statement. 'He loves me.'

'Does he? And do you love him?' Adam Wilde's voice
was relentless, probing her mind, searching out secrets
she was keeping even from herself. 'Do you, Holly? Or is
there some other reason why you've agreed to marry
him—something you're half ashamed of and can't admit?
Something you need and only he can give?'

'Isn't that usually the reason for wanting to marry
someone?' she flashed, twisting away so that he couldn't
meet her troubled eyes with his searing glance.

'Usually, yes. But what two people need from each
other, that only they can give, is usually love. Real love, a
burning, consuming passion that gives them no relief, no
respite from its demands. A fire that burns night and day,
so that you can't think of anyone or anything but the
beloved . . . Is that what you feel for Morris Crawley,
Holly? Is that what he feels for you? Has he ever said as
much?'

'No! I mean—you've no right to ask these questions—
it's nothing to do with you, nothing!' To her dismay,
Holly found she was crying. The conversation had
changed, veering away from the matter of Sleadale Farm
to her own emotions, and she didn't like it. 'Go away!'
she begged, covering her face with her hands. 'I know
why you came—you came just to destroy what Morris

and I have, to destroy my faith in him. All this talk about trees and taxes—it's nonsense, a pack of lies you've invented just to spoil my happiness. Go away, Adam Wilde. I want you out of my house—you're a devil!'

'A devil, am I?' She could feel him moving closer, sense the heat of emotion that rippled from his body, the shocking maleness of him. 'Then you won't be surprised by anything I do, will you?' His voice was rough, harsh with some emotion that was raw and terrifying. Holly shrank away as he reached out for her, but already she knew that escape was hopeless. Out here, in this wild stretch of moorland, with nobody to come to her aid, she was completely at Adam Wilde's mercy. And, as she already knew, that was something he was unlikely to show.

'Please . . .' she whispered imploringly. 'Please . . .'

'Please what? Please don't? Or just "please"?' Adam Wilde put one hand on her shoulder, watching her reaction, giving a little grunt as she closed her eyes. Too weak to resist, she felt his hand slide around her, pulling her against him; felt his other arm encircle her so that she was held firmly against his body; felt one hand tip up her chin, so that her lips parted under the pressure of his fingers; and felt his mouth take possession of hers.

Earth and sky wheeled around her in a dizzying kaleidoscope. The flames of the fire seemed to fill the room, burning into her mind, scorching through her veins, consuming her entire body with a throbbing urgency that she couldn't understand, didn't want to analyse, could only allow to sweep her along. As Adam's hands moved slowly over her slender body, cupping her hips, outlining the curving of each breast, she moaned and trembled, shifting restlessly in his arms. Vaguely, she knew that this was something that shouldn't be happening, but already she had forgotten why. She only knew that it was something that would, unless carried on to its inevitable climax, leave her for ever unfulfilled.

'A devil, am I?' Adam whispered against her ear, and his teeth nipped at the lobe.

'A devil?' he whispered again, and laid his lips in the hollow of her neck.

'A devil?' And somehow he had unbuttoned her sweater, thrust aside the lace of her bra, and buried his face in the softness of her breast.

Holly lay back in his arms, swept by waves of weakness, overcome by a languor that was as sweet as it was dangerous. One hand was around his shoulders, clinging to him, her fingers moving on his spine; the other, without any apparent instructions from her, was sliding up his neck to tangle in his thick, black hair. His groan of passion fuelled her own desire, and as he lifted his face to hers she arched against him, ready to share in the kisses he was demanding, to add her own insistence to the complusion that was driving them both to the edge of a precipice whose peril she only dimly understood.

'My God . . . Holly . . .' They were stretched out on the carpet now, bodies entwined as Adam worked feverishly to release the rest of the buttons on Holly's sweater and fully reveal the swelling breasts within. For a moment he stared at them, drinking in their shapely, untouched beauty; then, with a groan that tore its way from his throat, he flung his face down to their softness, raining kisses on each one, nipping gently at the tautened nipples, while his hands slid under her buttocks to hold her even tighter against him, leaving her in no doubt at all as to what he intended next.

Holly's mind was whirling. She was aware of nothing but this leaping rapture, the soaring certainty that this was all that mattered in a world that had suddenly become irrelevant. Nothing mattered but the emotion that was surging between her and Adam Wilde, the desire that was mounting in her, soon to reach a pitch that would be almost intolerable, before the final cataclysmic explosion. Nothing mattered. Not even the farm. Not even Morris . . .

Even the passion that had taken her so much by surprise couldn't prevent the chill that invaded her body at the thought of Morris.

Adam sensed it at once. He raised his head and looked at her and, as she met his eyes, she knew he understood.

'I'm sorry.' He drew away from her and pulled her sweater across her exposed body. He looked suddenly haggard, the desire draining away to leave a disgust that she cringed from. 'I didn't mean that to happen.'

Holly sat up and buttoned her sweater with trembling fingers. She said nothing; there seemed to be nothing to say.

'I should have remembered, you have a fiancé.' His voice was stiff. 'And, in any case, there could never be anything between us. It was simply a momentary aberration, you understand that? It meant nothing.'

'You're absolutely right, it didn't!' Holly turned away from him, folding her arms across her body to quell the shaking. How dared he touch her in that—that intimate way? How dared he kiss her like that—in a way that even Morris had never even begun . . .! The angry thoughts swept about her mind, fury mingling with something else—a dark excitement that made her even angrier . . . Oh, why *didn't* Morris kiss her like that—wouldn't it have given her some defence against the sensations this man's touch awoke in her? She shook her head helplessly, unable to sort out the feelings that were a tumult inside her.

'It must certainly have confirmed your opinion of me, anyway,' he went on bitterly. 'Evil—you'll always believe that now, won't you? And maybe it's just as well.'

'You haven't done a lot to convince me otherwise,'

Holly agreed with force. 'As a matter of fact, you haven't convinced me of anything very much.'

'No, I don't suppose I have.' He spoke wearily now and got to his feet, almost as if the effort were too much. 'Well, there's nothing else for me here, I can see that. I'll go. Leave you to your new toy, your doll's house. And much joy may it bring you.' He walked to the window and stood looking out, as if for the last time. 'I can only say that, if things work out as I think they will, you'd better make the most of that view now. In a few years' time it will be dark with conifers. But then, you probably won't be here to see it, will you? You'll be soaking up the sun in Bermuda or some other little tax haven. Leaving the Lake District just a little poorer for your having been here.'

He walked to the door and turned to look at her.

'As I said—I wish you joy of it.'

'So is it true?' Holly sat facing Morris, her eyes anxious, her hands tense in her lap. 'Is any of it true? Do you really intend to plant conifers in Sleadale?'

Her fiancé leaned back in his armchair and puffed at his cigar. He looked relaxed, confident, as assured as always—but, as she gazed at him, Holly couldn't help wondering if his eyes didn't look just a little wary. As if she had asked him a question he didn't really want to answer . . . But when he spoke, his tone was easy enough, and she told herself that she must have been mistaken.

'Conifers in Sleadale? Well, now, that's quite a thought . . . What do you feel about it, Holly? Would it be so very terrible?'

'So it *is* true! You *are* going to——'

He lifted a hand. 'Now, I didn't say anything either way. I just asked what you thought about it. This Adam Wilde—he seems to have told you quite a lot. I'd like to know if what you think is just what he's fed into you, or whether it's your own opinion—arrived at after knowing all the aspects of the situation.'

Holly hesitated. The morning's events had left her confused and uncertain. While she had been listening to Adam, everything he'd said had sounded plausible, his indignation real and infectious. Now, back in the warmth of the hotel, she wasn't so sure. Were a few trees really so important?

Even more confusing was what had happened afterwards—the way their bodies had once more come together as irresistibly as if a magnet had drawn them. There was something strange about the way she and Adam Wilde reacted together— something frightening. It was a force that couldn't be denied. Nothing to do with love, she told herself unhappily. But everything to do with lust—a raw, primitive need that she had never suspected in herself and didn't like.

When Adam had walked out the second time, Holly had made no move to stop him. Even the icy chill that had come between them the first time wouldn't have been powerful enough to prevent it starting all over again—she was sharply aware of that. And although her body was still clamouring for the sensations it had been so abruptly denied, her mind had taken control again and was saying a forcible 'no'.

She hadn't dared to move until the sound of Adam's Land Rover, fading as it went away down the track, told her that he was definitely gone.

Then, in an effort to recapture her original feelings for the house, she had explored it again, standing for a long time in each room, trying to imagine herself living here with Morris. She had touched the walls, gazed out of the windows, stroked the wooden beams. And, in the end, returned to the living-room and crouched again before the dying embers of the fire Adam had lit.

There was nothing. None of the hostility which she had felt earlier and which had so disturbed her. But neither was there any of the warmth and welcome that she had known on her first visit. It was as if the house had withdrawn itself completely, turned its back on her. As if it was totally indifferent.

Holly told herself she was being fanciful. But she couldn't shake off the feeling that the house had rejected her, and that there was no longer any place for her here.

She went out and pulled on the boots she had thrown into the Range Rover. A walk would clear her head and dispel these ridiculous notions. And she could explore the valley behind the house, climbing up beside the stream that tumbled down the rocky slopes. She'd wanted to do it the other day, but Morris had said there wasn't time.

Holly made her way through the sheepfolds behind the farm, each small walled compound leading to the next through iron gates. From the last, she came out on to a track which led up the hill behind the farm, beside the leaping stream. Beck, she corrected herself automatically—if she were going to live here, she must learn the right words. Like beck for stream, fells for hills and tarns for mountain pools.

The thought caught her up short. *If* she were going to live here? But of course she was! It was all planned—the London wedding, the honeymoon in Italy, the life that waited for them here in one of the wildest parts of Cumbria. And it was all going as planned—nothing had happened to make any difference.

Except for Adam Wilde.

Holly shrugged impatiently. You've got to forget that man, she told herself. All right, so he wanted the house, too. So badly that he was ready to try anything to get it—and was still trying. All that rubbish about the trees—he must have thought that if she believed him she would be prepared to sell the farm to him without even consulting her fiancé. Some chance! You're trying some very outside shots there, Mr Wilde, she thought grimly, and it simply proves how desperate you are—and how aware you are of the impossibility of getting Sleadale.

Pausing for a moment to gaze at the glittering water as it slid over smooth granite rocks, Holly wondered just why Adam Wilde wanted Sleadale so badly. What was it he'd said—'Hidden treasure? Or maybe a will that leaves the place to me, after all?' What had be meant by that *'after all'?* Was there some reason why the farm *could* have been left to him?

Was Adam Wilde related in some way to the previous owners of Sleadale?

Well, that was something that could surely be found out, and it would certainly help to explain his anxiety to own the property. Yet he hadn't seemed the sentimental type. And he definitely wasn't hard up—he had been prepared to go as high as Morris to buy it.

Holly climbed slowly on. The beck was tumbling beside her, filling the crisp air with its song. A rowan tree, stunted and gnarled by the weather, clung to a rock and leaned over the water, its tawny leaves like flames against the sky, its scarlet berries like clusters of glowing rubies. Below, the farm lay in peaceful slumber, a huddle of buildings and walled enclosures, where both humans and animals must have found shelter for generations.

Holly gazed down at it and thought of the generation to come—her children, and Morris's. She tried to imagine them, living here together as a family. Summer picnics by this cool, green mountain pool beneath a cascading waterfall. Winter, when the snow lay piled deep in the valley and Christmas fires burned brightly indoors.

Cars would be of little use then. They would have to

teach the children to ski, so that they could reach the main road and civilisation. Or perhaps they would forget the outside world altogether—stock up enough food to last them through the bad weather, and stay together in their own tight little cocoon of family love and warmth.

Holly sat down on a rock, staring down, picturing it. She could see the children, dark-haired and laughing as they built a snowman and had a snowball fight. She could see herself, laughing and happy with her own family.

But she couldn't see Morris.

Desperately, she tried to force Morris into the picture, tried to see him in country clothes, thick breeches and a heavy jacket. But she couldn't do it. Stubbornly, he insisted on retaining his city suit and cigar. And when she tried to imagine him with the children, he stood obstinately apart, shaking his head and refusing to join in their games.

The man who did appear with them, she realised with sinking heart, was a different man altogether. Tall. Lean. With hair darker than her own, and sapphire eyes . . .

Furiously, Holly scrambled to her feet and set off again up the hill, climbing as fast as she could go, so that she became breathless and the thundering of her heart could truthfully be ascribed to the exercise. Adam Wilde! she thought angrily. That man—why couldn't he get out of her life, out of her thoughts? She'd known when she had first met him that he was trouble, and he was certainly proving it.

All right, so she'd responded to him down in the farmhouse—and yesterday, in her hotel bedroom—as she'd never expected to respond to any man. She wasn't proud of that; she would far rather it hadn't happened. But for goodness' sake, it didn't *mean* anything.

It was just the automatic response of the female body to an attractive and magnetic man. Exaggerated because, if she were to be honest with herself, Holly wanted badly to be loved in just that way—and because Morris had told her he wanted to wait.

'I'm old-fashioned,' he'd said when he'd asked her to marry him, 'and I don't believe in modern permissiveness. I want our wedding to be a traditional one, Holly, with you in a white dress and a wedding night that brings discovery to us both.'

It was the only romantic speech he had ever made, but Holly had treasured it. And she had been content to wait, sure that Morris would bring romance into their marriage. After all, there really hadn't been much time for it until now, with all the negotiations to be made for the farm.

But she must have been missing it, all the same. Longing for something more than the brief kisses Morris gave her when they parted at night and met in the morning. Yearning for the rougher touch of passion, the urgency of real desire. And so, when Adam Wilde had taken her in his arms, she had responded like a hungry man on being presented with a banquet.

No more than that.

She had been cheating Morris, she thought guiltily. But it wouldn't happen again. She would never let Adam Wilde near her again when she was alone. And as for his story about the trees . . . She lifted her head, gazing at the sloping fells, imagining them darkened with the march of conifers, each rugged contour hidden, the beck no longer gleaming in the sunlight, for light would be unable to penetrate the dim forest.

It couldn't be true! Morris would never do such a thing.

'Well?'

Holly came back with a start to the hotel lounge, blink-

ing as she stared at Morris across the low table. She had
been so immersed in her thoughts that her surroundings
had completely disappeared from her mind, and she had
been back again at the farm, sitting up on the fellside and
gazing at the valley.

'I asked what you thought about this tree idea that
Wilde's put into your head,' Morris repeated. '*Is* it just
his opinion, or your own? It's something you ought to be
very clear about, Holly.'

'Yes . . . yes, you're right, it is.' Holly looked at him,
her grey eyes clear and honest. 'Morris, I don't honestly
know. I've never really thought much about it . . . I know
I don't *like* seeing great solid blocks of conifer
plantation—but I know nothing about the ethics of it.
What they'll do to the land, that sort of thing. And if it's
not true and you don't intend to do it, it doesn't really
matter, does it? You've only got to say it's just another
rumour, and we can forget the whole thing.' Forget
Adam Wilde too, her mind said, but already she knew
that was going to be difficult.

Morris puffed at his cigar and picked up his brandy.
Holly watched anxiously. Wasn't he going to tell her that
it wasn't true—that he wasn't going to plant Sleadale with
conifers? She bit her lip and leaned forward.

'Morris?'

Her fiancé gave her a smile. It was a wide smile,
showing his white teeth, but it made Holly feel cold. It
was, she realised, an empty smile. Meaningless. The kind
of smile he might give to a business rival—just before
beating him in some high-powered venture.

'It is true, isn't it?' she said quietly.

Morris took his cigar from his mouth and waved it at her.

'Now, don't jump to conclusions. There are two ways
of looking at this, you know. That's why I asked what *your*
opinion was—not the one that Wilde fed into you. As it

happens, yes, it is true—up to a point. But it's not nearly so bad as you seem to think.'

'Tell me,' Holly said, still feeling dead inside. 'Tell me what you mean to do, then—and why you never thought fit to mention it before.'

'Now, you don't need to get on your high horse,' Morris said affably. 'All right, so perhaps I should have mentioned it before. I certainly would have done if I'd known that Wilde was going to come sniffing around and putting in the poison. But I really didn't see any need. We agreed that we wanted to buy the farm. How we'd run it was something I thought could be left until later. You've got enough to do, arranging the wedding—I didn't see any need to bother you with details.'

'Details! Is planting the whole of Sleadale with conifers a *detail*?'

'There, you see, you're exaggerating the whole thing. Oh, I don't blame you, Holly. You've only got this chap Wilde's word to go on. But I wish you'd come and asked me before getting yourself upset about it.'

'I'm asking you now. He only told me all this this morning.'

'Yes, well, fair enough. And I'm telling you, aren't I?' An injured note crept into Morris's voice. 'I haven't tried to keep any secrets from you, Holly, you can't think that.'

'No, I don't really,' she said reluctantly. 'I'm sorry. Morris. But you'll tell me the whole thing now, won't you? All of it? Just to put my mind at rest.'

'Well, of course I will.' Morris took another sip of brandy. The lounge was empty, except for two elderly ladies dozing in front of the fire. He settled back into his big leather armchair and smiled at her again. 'I'll tell you exactly what I've got in mind and, when I've finished, I think you'll agree the whole thing is very clever.'

CHAPTER FIVE

HOLLY watched impatiently while Morris called for more coffee and another brandy. It seemed to be for ever before he was ready at last to talk, his cigar smouldering between his lips, brandy glass cradled in his hand.

'Right,' he said. 'Well, it's all quite simple, really. I think you'll understand why I didn't think it worth telling you about. Just a few trees, to give us a second crop—you never know what might happen when you restrict your farming to one thing. And there's not much else you can do on these fells. It's just a longstop, that's all.'

Holly waited. There had to be more to it than that.

'A few trees? How many, exactly? How many acres?' That was what Adam had told her to ask, she remembered with a chill.

'How many acres?' Morris said easily, 'Oh, about four hundred or so.' He tossed the figure off as if it were no more than a square of backyard.

'Four hundred?' Holly stared at him. 'But that's half the entire farm!'

'I suppose it is about that,' he agreed, as if he'd never really measured it. 'But it's the least useful part, Holly. Boggy, marshy land that you can't really graze sheep on. We can run as many animals on what's left as we would if we left it bare. And we'll be putting the ground to good, profitable use at the same time.'

'But *is* it good, profitable use? What about what the trees do to the land? Don't they take all the goodness from it—denude it of nutrients? Don't they stop all other life going on around them—birds, insects, animals?'

'Ah, that's Wilde speaking. It's a myth, Holly. *Anything* growing is going to take nutrients from the soil, it stands to reason. Conifers are no worse than any other kind of tree. And do we really want insects and animals thriving in our crop? Don't you know what animals like squirrels and deer do to trees? The less wildlife the better, take it from me!'

Holly looked at him doubtfully. It sounded plausible enough, but was it true? But surely she could trust Morris? She was engaged to him, they were planning to marry within a few weeks and live together in an isolated farmhouse. She had to be able to trust him.

'Look.' Morris set down his glass and leaned forward. 'This is a sound farming and business project, Holly. That area up there is wild, remote and useless. It's not doing any good to anyone. Even the sheep won't go there—it's too wet for them. We can plant conifers there. That will bring employment to the area—and that *can't* be bad. All right, I know environmentalists will object. Obviously, your Adam Wilde is one of them. But they'll object to anything, any change in the countryside. And, you know, when we come to fell those trees in thirty years' time, there'll be a whole new generation of conservationists who will object to that too! D'you see that?'

'Yes, I suppose so,' Holly said doubtfully. 'But—well, Morris, when I was out there this morning I walked up beside the stream—beck—and it was so beautiful. So wild and lonely and bare. I can't bear to think of it all being hidden under conifers.'

'And it won't be. We'll keep the lower part, down near the house, free. Above that—well, I don't know how far you went, but it really isn't all that wonderful. Just great bleak tracks of moorland, too soggy for comfortable walking except in really dry periods. Honestly, darling, you've nothing at all to worry about. You won't even see the plantation from the house.'

'No.' She thought of the fells, swooping away from the head of the valley, and tried to picture them dark with conifers. 'But won't it look rather oppressive?'

'Do the trees in Switzerland look oppressive? People exclaim over the scenery there. Why can't it be equally beautiful here?'

He had an answer for everything. So why did she still feel uneasy?

'And you're not doing it as a—a sort of tax dodge?'

As soon as she'd said it, she knew she'd made a mistake. Morris's face darkened. He thrust the end of his cigar into the ashtray.

'Tax dodge? Just what are you suggesting, Holly?'

'Nothing—really—it was just something— something——'

'Something Adam Wilde said? Well, out with it, Holly.' His voice was hard. 'I want to know just what this interfering busybody's been filling your head with now.'

'He didn't say it was anything illegal,' Holly said hastily. 'Just that it was a—a loophole you were taking advantage of. He said you could get a grant to develop the plantation, and tax relief off the rest. And then you could sell it at a huge profit without paying any Capital Gains Tax. He said you'd probably sell it off to other investors who wanted to save tax, too.' Her eyes were huge as she considered the possibilities. 'You wouldn't do that, would you, Morris? Sell off our land—our beautiful farm? Have other people coming there, sending in tractors and lorries—filling the air with noise and pollution? Tell me it isn't true, Morris, please!'

Morris sat silent, his broad face suffused with anger. Holly watched him in dismay. This was not the Morris she had known, the man who had asked her to marry him, who had treated her gently and with kindness. This was a stranger—a stranger she didn't like, with a look of ruthlessness about the set of his shoulders and the hard lines of his face.

'Morris?' she whispered.

Morris Crawley moved abruptly. He raised his head, and for the first time she noticed how small his eyes were. And how cold.

'Holly,' he said, and his voice was like that of a tyrannical father, telling his children they should be seen and not heard, 'there are a lot of things you don't understand about business. My kind of business. It's not like running a corner shop. There are a lot of things to take into account. And one thing a good business man has to be doing all the time is looking to the future. Do you understand that?'

He paused, and Holly whispered, 'Yes.'

'That's all I'm doing,' he went on. 'Looking to the future. *Our* future. Covering all contingencies. If I can use the tax and planning laws of our country to help me do that, I see nothing wrong in doing so. That's what they're for. Every man has the right to minimise his tax liability—haven't you ever heard that?'

Holly nodded.

'None of us can tell what may happen in the future,' Morris went on, speaking now as if Holly were a public meeting. 'We simply have to take whatever precautions we can against change. We have to cushion ourselves against possible disaster. That's all I'm doing, Holly, and now I think we've talked enough. I hope you won't think any more of this environmentalist nonsense that Wilde has been filling your head with. And I hope you'll make sure you don't meet him again. I don't like the influence he seems to have over you.'

If only you knew the truth about that influence, Holly thought, and felt her cheeks flush scarlet. But the remark had made her realise that Morris still knew more about Adam Wilde than he was prepared to admit, And until she knew the truth about their previous encounter, she would never be entirely happy.

'Morris,' she said slowly, 'tell me about that other time. The time you and Adam Wilde crossed swords. What really happened between you then?'

Morris sighed. He looked at her, frowned and shook his head.

'It's all in the past, Holly. It's nothing to do with Sleadale. It doesn't affect us now.'

Holly leaned forward. 'But it does, Morris. Don't you see, until I know just what it was all about, I can never be sure——'

'Sure of what?' he said sharply. 'Sure of me?'

'No—no, I don't mean that, of course I'm sure of you.' But even as she said the words, she was aware of a tiny niggle of doubt. Thrusting it away, she went on quickly, confusedly, 'But I need to be sure of—of other things, of——' Just what *did* she mean? 'I think I need to understand why he should seem to—to hate you so much. Or why you should hate him.'

'Hate him!' Morris laughed humourlessly. 'Holly, I don't hate him. He's not worth it. I haven't even thought of him in years.' But there was a shade of expression in his voice which didn't ring quite true.

'So, if it's that unimportant,' she said slowly, 'you won't mind telling me, will you?'

Morris gave her a long look. Then he shrugged, picked up his glass and drank some more brandy.

'You're determined to know all about it, aren't you? Even though I've told you it doesn't matter.'

'I'd like to know, please, Morris,' she agreed quietly.

'After all, you said yourself that you were keeping no secrets from me.'

'I didn't mean business matters—oh well, I can see we'll have no peace until you know all about it.' He spoke as if humouring a child. 'All right, Holly, I'll tell you. Just the once. And then—I'd rather it wasn't referred to again, if it's all the same to you. It's not a matter I particularly enjoy discussing.' His face darkened. 'Adam Wilde did his best to humiliate me—and that's not a thing I easily forgive.'

Holly waited, hardly daring to breathe. Morris, humiliated by Adam Wilde, who must be ten years younger than he! She could well understand how such a thing could rankle with her autocratic fiancé. Morris was the kind of man who needed to be at the top and worked hard to get there. He wouldn't take kindly to humiliation from a younger man—or, indeed, from any man at all.

And wasn't Adam Wilde the same kind of man? she asked herself thoughtfully. Hadn't he, too, struck her as the tough, assertive go-getter who would always need to be at the top of the ladder and would make sure he got there?

Had he and Morris once fought for the top rung—and had Adam won?

'Tell me,' she said softly, feeling a sudden pity for Morris.

Morris sighed again. 'Well, all right. I suppose it will do no harm now for you to know—it was all a long time ago. And if it helps to show you just what kind of man he is . . .' He paused, as if marshalling his thoughts, then said abruptly, 'I told you I spent some time in Canada a few years ago, didn't I?'

'Yes, you did.' He'd told her surprisingly little about it, though, and she'd often wondered why he hadn't stayed there. Canada must have offered tremendous opportunities to a man with Morris's abilities. But she'd assumed that he simply preferred to live in England, and somehow there'd never been a chance to ask him any more about it.

'That was where I met Wilde,' he said, and his face twisted suddenly. 'I was doing well—everything was going just as I wanted. I'd made my way, starting small with one business, diversifying, expanding into others, merging them so that the assets of all could be used in the most profitable way . . . I'd become a big man in the city, and I was going to be bigger. I had it all planned. And then along came Adam Wilde and wrecked it.'

'But how? What did he do?'

Morris didn't seem to hear her. His eyes were abstracted, looking into the past, his face still tight with anger.

'There was a big parcel of land,' he said slowly. 'Useless land—no good for farming. I'd just signed to buy a building firm that was going to the wall. I wanted that land. I was going to develop it—set up a new industrial estate, build houses for the workers to live in. It would have been the prototype for a series of developments that, in the end, would have stretched right across Canada. A show development. I'd sunk a lot of money into the design and planning, employed the best architects, everything. I thought nothing could stop it. And then—then——'

'Adam Wilde stopped you?' As soon as she'd said it, Holly knew her words had been badly chosen. The look Morris darted at her was almost one of dislike. 'I mean——' she floundered, but he cut her short with a bitter laugh.

'You mean just what you said—he stopped me. And yes, you're right. That's what it hurts me to say, and that's why I won't talk about it again. Adam Wilde—not much more than a kid just then, only been in the district five minutes—he heard what I was doing and decided it was his job to stop me. God knows why. He had no reason to hate me—we'd never even met. But he pulled out all the stops, and eventually he got the rest of the city on his side and that was the end of all my plans. The end of my prototype estate. The end—for me—of Canada.'

'But what did he *do?* And why?'

'He got up a petition,' Morris said tonelessly, and Holly stared, hardly able to believe the anticlimax of the words. 'He went round and round until he got everyone to sign. He never stopped. He persuaded them all that the development would be a bad thing. I told you how dangerous he is——' his voice rose on the words, taut with hatred. 'I told you he was a con man. He can persuade anyone of anything, Holly. He persuaded that whole city and the district around that the development that would have brought them all prosperity was a bad thing, and they believed it. They turned against me and I had to get out. There was no future there for me any more. That's why I came back to England, Holly. Canada had gone sour. And, what's more, Adam Wilde was in Canada, and I came to the conclusion that no country in the world is big enough to hold the two of us.'

'And now he's in England,' Holly said quietly. 'And he wants Sleadale.'

'And he's not getting it, is he!' There was a bitter triumph in Morris's voice. 'This time, Mr Wilde is going to find the boot on the other foot. This time he's going to be the one who has to get out.' He looked at her. 'You can see now why I don't want you seeing him, can't you? You can see why I don't want him to get any chance of influencing you.'

There were questions Holly wanted to ask then, but she knew that Morris had told her all he intended. She saw that he was making preparations to stand up, presumably to go to bed. But there was still one thing she had to know.

'Why did you want *me* to buy the farm, Morris?' she asked quickly. 'Why was it so important that it should be my name on the deeds?'

He paused in the act of rising, and looked down at her. And, at the expression in his eyes, she felt herself grow cold.

'Because I don't want Adam Wilde to have any chance of getting his hands on it,' he said slowly. 'I don't know just what influence he has now—but if Sleadale's mine it comes within my business interests, and nobody's totally invulnerable—not even me. If it's yours—well, the situation's different. You don't understand, I know—it's all very complicated. But you can believe me.' He paused, and then spoke in a tone so deadly and vindictive that Holly shrank away from him. 'Adam Wilde is taking nothing more away from me,' he said. 'I mean to have Sleadale—and when I want something I make sure I get it. And I keep it.' His eyes were on her face now, burning with an intensity she had never seen before. 'If he did nothing else for me, Holly, Wilde taught me a lesson. Never to let anything get away. And—since then—I never have.' He leaned forward and gave her a brief peck on the cheek. 'And now, I'm going to bed. I suggest that you do the same.'

He walked to the door and went out, leaving Holly alone. The two old ladies had disappeared some time during their conversation. Slowly, she got up and went across to the fire, kneeling in front of it and holding out her hands to the warmth.

The memory of the morning came back forcibly. She had sat in front of a fire like this with Adam Wilde. With him, also, she had talked about the farm and about the possibility of conifer plantations spreading their dark blanket over the fells. With him, she had——

She tried to blot out the memory, but it was useless. Every moment of their encounter was seared into her mind, burned there as if with a branding iron. She closed her eyes, feeling again the scorching touch of his lips against hers, the tender urgency of his hands on her body, the exquisite agony of his kisses against her breasts.

It was never going to be like that with Morris. She knew that now—had known it all the time, but had refused to face it. And she hid her face in her hands, rocking with the pain of her confusion.

What was it to be—marriage with a man she believed she loved, even though she had only just discovered things about him that worried her, and even though she knew he could never give her the satisfaction her body apparently craved?

Or a brief, passionate affair with a man she disliked intensely, a man whom her fiancé had every reason to hate, yet who could take her to heights of rapture she had never suspected might exist?

It was a choice with no choice.

There was little sleep for Holly that night. Restlessly, she tossed and turned in her bed, unable to halt the procession of thoughts that marched through her mind, unable to sort out the confusion when they merged together in turmoil. Eventually, exhausted by the struggle, she turned on the light and made herself tea, thankful for the kettle provided in each bedroom.

Why, she wondered as she waited for the water to boil, should everything seem so different now—since she had met Adam Wilde? For he was the catalyst, the stone that had been thrown into the quiet pool of her life, causing ripples that were still spreading. But why did he have that effect? Why couldn't she just ignore him—forget the things he'd said and done, continue with her plans as if he had never arrived on the scene?

Because you couldn't go back. That was why. You couldn't turn back the clock and pretend something had never happened. You couldn't pick and choose, remembering only what was convenient.

Adam Wilde had come into her life and she couldn't ignore him. For good or ill, his presence had changed things, and the only course she could take was to think it through, assess just what his effect had been, and act accordingly.

So easy, when you put it like that!

The kettle boiled and Holly made the tea. Opening one of the small tubs of milk, she poured half into the bone-china cup. Then she filled the cup with tea and carried it back to bed.

Perhaps she should start by answering one of the questions Adam had asked her. Just how *had* she come to be engaged to Morris Crawley?

Holly sat in bed, the blankets pulled over her knees, sipping her tea and thinking. Thinking back to that day in Herefordshire when her father had come into the kitchen, his face drawn with worry, and told them the news . . .

'Two of the cows are dead.'

Holly and her mother had turned from their work and stared, shocked by the stark words.

'Dead? *Dead?* You're joking!'

'I'm not, Holly. Go and see for yourself. They're out in the paddock now. In any case——' he was reaching for the phone, dialling '—would I joke about a thing like that?'

Mrs Douglas had laid down her rolling-pin and begun to wipe floury hands in her apron. Her face was white, mouth working. Holly went swiftly across to her.

'Sit down, Mum. Lean on me a minute. You'll feel
better in a minute—it's the shock.' She held her mother's
head against her and watched her father with anxious eyes
as he spoke to the vet. 'Is he coming at once?'

'He'll be here within half an hour. Lucky he was in.'
Jack Douglas passed a shaking hand across his thinning
hair. 'God knows what's wrong with them. They were all
right at milking—and then . . . I'd better get out and look
at the rest.'

'Wait, Dad. You won't be able to do any good until the
vet comes.' Holly indicated her mother, who was still
clearly shocked. Jack hesitated, then came over and put
his arms around his wife.

'Sorry, love. I broke it too sharp. But it was such a
shock—I couldn't think straight for a minute.'

'It's all right, Jack. Don't worry about me—it was just
so unexpected.' Jean Douglas gave a wavering smile and
struggled out of her chair. 'I'll make a cup of tea—it'll do
us all good, and the vet'll be glad of one too, no doubt.'

Holly stepped forward, meaning to push her mother
back into the chair and make the tea herself, but Jack
prevented her. 'Leave her be. She'll feel better for doing
something. I shouldn't have blurted it out like that.'

'We had to know.' Holly studied her father. His face
was grey, and she realised that he was as shaken as his
wife. 'You sit down, Dad. What—what do you think it
is?'

He shrugged. 'God knows. Something pretty bad, to
strike like that.'

He hesitated and Holly saw a shadow cross his face. He
knows, she thought with a sudden cold dread, and it's too
awful to say. She turned as her mother handed her a cup
of tea, made from the kettle that was always simmering on
the Aga. 'Drink that, Dad. It'll help a bit.'

'A bit!' he said, and gave a short laugh. 'That's all

anything'll help us in this lot. I don't reckon anything *can* help us more than a bit. This is the end of our dreams, Jean, you know that?' He seemed to have forgotten his remorse at upsetting his wife, and the bitter words poured out as he looked up at them both. 'A farm of our own—what we've always wanted. And now we've got it and look what happens! A poor year with the sheep—well, we could have got over that. But when it's followed by some sort of plague in the cows—that's our chance at making it gone right down the drain. We should never have tried it.'

'Dad, don't!' Holly was on her knees beside him. 'You've worked so hard—it can't all go for nothing.' She thought of the years her father had spent as a farm manager for one of the big syndicates, the dreams he and his wife had shared of being independent farmers themselves one day, if only in a small way. The excitement when they'd finally made it, buying this small farm, stocking it with their first sheep and cows.

It couldn't all be ruined, in one short year.

'It won't be that bad, you'll see,' she promised, knowing in her heart that it easily could be as bad as he feared. Farmers were so much at the mercy of uncontrollable elements—the weather, pests, disease. She looked down at the rough hands that had worked so hard. It couldn't be happening—it was a bad dream. A nightmare.

But over the next few hours the nightmare became reality. Helpless, Holly had to stand by while the vet arrived, examined the dead animals and told the Douglas'es what he thought was wrong. There would have to be tests, he said, to make sure—but meanwhile, none of the milk could be sold.

'It's over. All over,' Jack Douglas said, standing at the window and looking out at the yard. 'Tomorrow's milk will have to be thrown away. We're going to lose the whole herd—you know that, don't you?'

'Dad, please don't.' Holly ran to him, catching at his arm. 'Don't look on the black side—the vet could be wrong. These are just precautions, just in case. When he gets the results of the tests——'

'We'll know for certain,' her father finished grimly. 'We'll be losing the whole herd, Holly. You know it as well as I do.' He stared out of the window again as a cow lowed from the byre. 'Everything your mother and I have worked for—every penny we've saved has gone into this place. And that's not all.'

'What do you mean?'

'Your job's at risk too, Holly.' Jack turned and looked down at her, his eyes haunted. 'You can't leave this farm and go back to those sheep with—whatever we've got out there—clinging to you.'

Holly was silent. She wanted to comfort her father, tell him again that it couldn't be that bad, that two cows dying together was just a horrible coincidence. But she knew her words would be empty. She was a farmer's daughter; she had worked as a shepherdess ever since leaving agricultural college. She knew as well as he did what the vet feared, and she knew that his fears were well founded.

And so it proved. The disease which had killed Jack Douglas's cows, although not so virulent as anthrax or foot-and-mouth, went through the entire herd. Those cows that survived the illness would never really recover, and had to be destroyed anyway. The Douglas'es were, as Jack had predicted, ruined.

It was just about that time that they had met Morris Crawley.

* * *

Holly would never forget the misery of those months. Her father and mother, grey-faced, moving through the days like automatons, brought to life only by occasional outbursts of bitter anger. The compensation they received for the animals was enough to start again, it was true—but when? And what were they to do in the mean time?

It was Morris Crawley who provided the solution.

Jack Douglas had met him at a farm sale. Jack had attended it more for something to do than for any other reason. Without his stock, he was like a lost soul mooning about the empty yard, staring at his barren fields. At sales, he could meet his old friends and have a few hours' talk, a pint or two at the local inn. He went to at least one every week.

Morris Crawley was introduced to him by a mutual friend, who went on to invite Jack and his wife over to dinner a night or two later.

'It's like being given a new crack at life,' Jack told Holly a few weeks later, his eyes on fire with excitement. 'He's buying that big farm over near Leominster, and he's asked me to manage it while I get back on my feet again. More than that, he's going to help us get established again—go into partnership, if you like. He's getting the papers drawn up now.'

'So you won't be independent any more,' Holly said slowly, and her father flicked his fingers impatiently.

'Independence! I've had my fill of that—no one to turn to when the going gets hard. Independence is just another word for being out on a limb! Anyway, there's no problem, Morris isn't a real farmer and he'll leave it to me. You don't need to look so suspicious, Holly—he won't let us down. Anyway, you'll be able to decide for yourself soon—he's asked us all out to dinner at the Green Dragon.'

But Holly had been suspicious. Until she met Morris Crawley. And then the man's undoubted charm had dispelled all her doubts.

It was odd, she reflected, sipping her tea, how well she and Morris had got on. He'd shown such warmth, such genuine interest in her life. There had been admiration in his eyes too, and the attentions he'd paid her—little things like holding her chair for her at the table, the flowers he had brought her on that first evening—had flattered her. It wasn't long before he was asking her out alone, without her parents. And Holly was accepting.

'You're sweet, Holly,' he told her one evening, filling her glass with wine. 'Why is it such an attractive girl hasn't been snapped up long ago?'

Holly laughed. 'Couldn't tell you! I suppose there aren't many chances for romance on a hill-farm, with only the sheep for company.'

'That's true,' he agreed. 'But don't you feel you're missing out on something?'

'Sometimes. But I love my job. And there's plenty of time yet.'

It wasn't long after that when Morris had told her he intended to leave the business world altogether and go into farming himself.

'I've had enough of the rat-race,' he said, taking her hand and stroking it gently. 'I want some real life before I forget what it's all about. Seeing your father and mother has shown me that. I know they've had a rough time lately—but they've still got something very special. I want a share in that.' He paused. 'I want what they've got, Holly—a happy marriage with a woman who loves the life I'll be offering her. It could be bleak and lonely for some women—a remote sheep-farm, miles from anywhere. There can't be many girls who'd like that kind of life.'

'No, perhaps not,' Holly agreed unsuspectingly. 'Some-

one like me would love it, of course, but——' She broke
off, eyes wide. Morris returned her look.

'Well, Holly?' he asked, smiling gently. 'What about
it? Could you bear to marry me and live on a farm, miles
from anywhere? Could you bear to become Mrs Morris
Crawley?'

Now, sitting in her bed at the hotel, Holly found it
difficult to decide just why she had said yes to Morris.
Had she been—or believed herself to be—genuinely in
love with him? Or had she been relieved to receive a
proposal of marriage and one, moreover, from a man who
was not only wealthy and successful, but who could offer
her just the kind of life she loved?

Or had it just been because she was so grateful for what
he'd done for her father?

Jack Douglas was a new man now, managing the big
farm a few miles from his own, and gradually building up
his own business at the same time. He'd never told Holly
the details of that deal with Morris, and she'd never
asked. It had been enough, just to see how happy he and
her mother had become after their disaster.

Had she mistaken gratitude for love? And if she
had—didn't she still owe Morris the same obligation?

Holly sighed and refilled her cup. None of this really
had anything to do with the problems Adam Wilde had
presented. She still wasn't completely sure that he wasn't
right about Morris's plans for Sleadale; now that she
thought it over, hadn't Morris been curiously evasive
when she'd asked him?

But wasn't it equally likely that Adam Wilde himself
intended to use the farm for conifers, just as she'd accused
him? According to Morris, there was no reason at all to
trust his word. He was a trickster, able to gain people's
confidence and use it to his own ends. Hadn't he—she

faced the unpalatable fact at last—done just that with her?

That, she knew, was the crux of the matter, and it was one that had no answer. Even now, wakeful in the small hours, it was Adam Wilde who dominated her thoughts. Beneath all the confusion, one thing stayed constant—her physical response to him. A response she could neither deny nor forget.

Holly lay down, staring at the ceiling. What was there about him that made her heart pound, her knees weaken? Sensations she'd never experienced before. What did it mean, that she'd never had these feelings with any other man, and yet was overwhelmed by them just at the touch of Adam Wilde's hand?

And why, even knowing what she did about him, feeling revulsion for what he had done to Morris, for the way he had used her only that afternoon, could she still feel a desire that shook her body, that turned it both hot and cold, that tormented her with longing and tortured her with dreams?

You're just a late developer, she told herself cynically, and wondered if it might be true. After all, she'd never had any serious boyfriends. Her time at agricultural college had been too full of hard work to allow much chance of relationships with other students. And, since then, she'd worked mostly alone, with only sheep for company.

Another girl might have realised what she was missing and made sure she had opportunities to meet men. But Holly, absorbed in her work, making use of her time off to visit her parents and help them on their new farm, had barely thought of romance. And when Morris Crawley had paid attention to her, flattered her and eventually proposed to her, she had been too dazzled and bewildered to question her feelings.

Now Adam Wilde had come into her life. And he had

brought a new dimension. He had wakened desire in her heart and longings in her body. There was a spark between them that could explode into flame at any moment—a spark that she couldn't help fanning. It was there now, as she lay thinking about him—smouldering through her body, making her twist yearningly as if she could feel him hard against her, bringing a flush to her cheeks and an ache to her breasts.

Holly lay in her bed and faced the facts. She wanted Adam Wilde. She wanted him to hold her, kiss her, make love to her. It wasn't anything to do with love. It was purely animal need, but it was as urgent as a ten-day thirst. It was a torture such as she had never envisaged.

And it could never happen. Because she was engaged to Morris Crawley, whose motives she was no longer sure of, for whom she felt only gratitude—and even that not on her own account—and to whom she was tied by a farm.

With a bitterness that was like a knife twisting in her heart, she wished that she had never heard of Sleadale Head.

CHAPTER SIX

IT WAS past four in the morning when Holly finally dropped into an uneasy sleep. Consequently, she slept late and found Morris finishing his breakfast when she appeared, still feeling only half-awake, in the dining-room.

Morris, however, barely glanced up as she slipped into the chair opposite. He was frowning over a pile of papers.

'Oh, hello, had a good rest?' He didn't wait for her answer. 'Look, darling, I'm going to have to make a trip to London—got a letter here that's rather disturbing. Nothing dramatic, but it needs my personal attention. You'll be all right here, won't you?'

'Oh, yes.' Holly found herself relieved. After hours of lying awake, her thoughts going round in never-ending circles in her brain, she still hadn't made up her mind just what she was going to do. Marriage to Morris, which had seemed so straightforward, now seemed a path fraught with danger. She still felt grateful for what he had done for her father—but was that really a solid basis for marriage? Would love come afterwards?

On the other hand, were a few acres of land and some trees really worth breaking her engagement for—especially as Morris had put such a reasonable and convincing case for his plans?

Perhaps he was right, and Adam Wilde really was just a fanatical conservationist, automatically against any kind of change, seeing only the disadvantages and refusing to acknowledge that there might be another side to the

argument. And, worse than that, a man consumed with
hatred for Morris, determined to smash any plan he
might have, determined to wrest Sleadale from him, just
because Morris happened to want it . . .

She needed time: time to sort it all out, time to explore
her own feelings. If Morris went to London, she could
come to some conclusion, make the decision she clearly
needed to make. Face the facts of her own life.

'You'll be all right, won't you? If I go down to London
for a day or two?' Morris looked at her more closely.
'Holly, what's the matter? You look like a ghost.'

'I'm fine.' She pinned a smile on her face. 'Just a bit of
a headache. Nothing serious.'

'Good.' He went back to his post. 'It's a nuisance,
having to go down there just now, but I'll use the time to
attend to a few other matters. And you can be on hand
here, if anything crops up—I'll let the solicitor and estate
agent know before I leave. Not that there should be any
snags, but you never know.' He was making notes as he
talked. 'I don't think there's any point in your coming
with me this time, I'll be pretty tied up—might even slip
across to Amsterdam while I'm in town, have a look at
what's happening there . . . Better reckon on my being
away for three or four days, I think. Now, are you sure
you'll be all right? You'll have the Range Rover. Why
don't you have a couple of days exploring the Lake
District?'

'Yes, I probably will.' Holly felt an unaccountable
lightening of her spirit, as if she had just been let out of
school for an unexpected holiday. 'And I hope you have a
successful trip.'

'Oh, yes, it's nothing that can't be sorted out, but you
know what they say—while the cat's away.' Morris gave
her a tolerant smile. 'Some of those bright young whiz-
kids can't wait for me to be gone so that they can step into

my shoes. Well, I'm sorry to rush off like this, my dear, but you know how it is—time's money. And I might be able to turn it to good advantage.' He glanced at the expensive gold watch on his wrist. 'Must go and get my things together—I'll pop my head round the door to say goodbye before I go.' He stood up, gathered his papers together in a neat pile and dropped a kiss on her head before walking purposefully from the room.

Holly watched him go. He was a different man this morning, she thought. Brisk, lively, full of drive at the thought of a trip to London, a few days in his own world of business and high finance. For the first time, she realised how little excitement he had shown at the idea of living at Sleadale Head Farm.

He had shown pleasure, yes—but no more than the pleasure he clearly felt at successfully closing any business deal. Or the pleasure he might feel on giving a favourite child a splendid toy.

Was that all Sleadale was to him? A business deal—and a toy for her?

Holly poured herself some coffee. She had requested only a boiled egg this morning, but she left it untouched and nibbled a piece of toast. She had felt, in these past few days, that she and Morris had been drifting apart, that there were too many secrets between them: his plans for the farm, her own shameful encounters with Adam Wilde. A few days apart would probably do them good—help them get things in perspective.

Perhaps she would do what he had suggested—take the Range Rover and explore some other part of the Lake District. Go to Windermere, perhaps, or Langdale. See Derwentwater or Coniston Water. There was plenty to do, and getting away from Sleadale might do her as much good as getting away from Morris.

Half an hour later, wearing dark red corduroy trousers

and a high-necked white sweater, she was ready to leave. She came downstairs, already feeling as if, with Morris's departure, part of the load had been lifted from her shoulders—and came face to face with Adam Wilde.

He was leaning on the reception desk, and there was no possible way of avoiding him.

Holly stopped short at the foot of the stairs. She half turned, as if to go back, then shrugged and went forward. It was ridiculous to behave as if she were afraid of him.

'Good morning.' The voice was as deep and musical as ever, and she wished it wasn't. It did uncomfortable things to her knees. But she wasn't going to let him know that. She lifted her chin and answered coolly.

'Good morning. Could I just reach past you and leave my key? I'm afraid if it's Morris you want to see, he's not here. He's gone to London on business.'

'Indeed?' Adam Wilde said with interest, and Holly immediately regretted her words. He would soon have found out, of course, if he'd wanted to—the hotel receptionist could easily have told him—but, all the same, she wished she hadn't said it. 'Going to be away for long, is he?'

'I'm afraid I couldn't tell you,' Holly said shortly, and handed her key across the desk. She turned away and Adam Wilde followed her.

'As it happens, it wasn't Crawley I came to see,' he remarked conversationally. 'I wanted a quick word with you. But since you're on your own . . .'

'Yes? Since I'm on my own?' Holly stopped and faced him squarely. 'I can't think of anything you might have to say, Mr Wilde, other than "sorry"— and I'm quite sure you didn't come here to say *that.*'

'Believe it or not, that did just cross my mind,' he returned swiftly. 'I wondered if I'd mistaken you after all—if you really were the sweet little innocent you play so

well, and not the temptress I seemed to find beneath the
façade . . .' His dark eyes moved over her slim body,
outlined by the sweater and trousers, and Holly felt her
colour rise. 'You're an enigma, Holly Douglas,' he said
softly, his deep voice faintly rasping like a cat's tongue on
velvet. 'One I'd very much like to solve . . .'

'Well, you're not going to get the chance!' Holly
snapped. 'After yesterday, I don't intend spending any
time at all with you, Mr Wilde. Not that there was ever
any risk of it, anyway. Our paths have crossed
once—briefly—and that's it. They can now diverge, and
the sooner the better.'

He inclined his head. 'In spite of the fact that we still
have quite a lot to discuss?'

'We have nothing to discuss,' Holly said tersely, and
turned to walk out of the hotel.

Adam Wilde was still beside her. '*You* may have
nothing to say, but I have. A good deal.'

'Speak to my fiancé.'

His lip curled. 'Now I know you're joking. Morris
Crawley wouldn't speak civilly to me if his life depended
on it. I suppose he's told you we'd met before?'

'He has. He's told me all about it. It doesn't make me
feel any more kindly towards you.'

'I wouldn't expect it to.' His voice was grim.
'Crawley's version of what happened——'

'Morris told me the truth.'

'Did he? In detail? A blow-by-blow account? Or just a
glossing-over—a brief précis—told, of course, entirely
from his point of view, with perhaps just the odd little
white lie thrown in to make it look better? Or was it more
like a gallon or two of whitewash?' They stopped in the
little rose garden outside the hotel, and Adam towered
over Holly, his eyes spearing hers, relentless and brilliant.
'Which was it, Holly? Do you know the truth—the real

truth—or aren't you sure? Perhaps,' he said, dropping his voice to a soft insinuation, 'you don't really *want* to be sure . . .'

His words cut into Holly's mind like a knife, opening the way to all the doubt she'd been trying to push out. She stared up at him, wordless, still wanting to defend Morris, because to do anything else would raise such unthinkable questions, yet knowing that her own honesty would not allow her to do so.

At least, not until she'd heard Adam Wilde's version of what had happened in Canada.

'Well?' he persisted. 'Will you listen to me? Will you spend the day with me today, go where I take you, see what I show you and listen to what I tell you?' His eyes challenged her.

He's a confidence trickster, she told herself desperately. He can persuade me that black's white. And, worse than that, he's too damned attractive!

'Or are you afraid?' he murmured, moving a little closer. 'Afraid of the truth? Afraid of me . . . afraid of yourself?'

'Of course I'm not afraid!' To her fury, Holly felt her voice tremble slightly. She was vibrantly aware of his attraction, the magnetism he had for her. Burningly, she remembered the torture of longing that had haunted her dreams when she'd finally fallen asleep the night before. She remembered, too, Morris's warnings—his dictum that she shouldn't see Adam Wilde again, that his influence over her could be too powerful.

Too powerful? Huh! A rush of indignation invaded her body, kicking her into a gasp of exhilaration. So both Adam and Morris thought she was no more than a weak, malleable female, ready to be shaped to whatever mould they wanted, did they? They were both as bad as each other! And it wouldn't do either of them any harm to find out they were wrong.

So she found Adam attractive—so what? It didn't mean she had to succumb, did it? And there was a certain spice in the idea of playing with the fire he lit in her body—playing to win.

It would give her great satisfaction to play him along a little, listen to his version of the truth, and then leave him flat. And surely even Morris would approve of that.

She lowered her lashes, then glanced up through them at Adam Wilde.

'All right,' she said slowly. 'I'll come with you. I'll listen to you. And then, if you don't mind, I'll judge for myself what I think is the truth.'

There was a flicker of surprise in the sapphire eyes, gone as quickly as it had appeared. And then Holly saw that the grim, angry expression she'd almost come to associate with him had disappeared. His eyes were almost friendly, his dark brows quirking with humour, his mobile mouth curving in the smile that could be so devastating. In that instant, she wondered whether he had ever married—or whether he had a steady relationship with any woman. Perhaps he was just a philanderer, taking sex where he could find it. With those looks, and that magnetic presence, he wouldn't have much trouble in finding quite a lot.

Well, he wasn't going to find it with her. Forewarned was forearmed, and Holly would be on her guard every moment they were together. Adam Wilde wanted to gain her confidence—she knew that. And she knew why. Because she had something he wanted.

Sleadale. And there could be only one reason—or maybe two—why he wanted Sleadale so badly.

He wanted to use it for conifer-planting. A tax device that would bring him money and leave the valley desecrated.

And he wanted, once again, to ruin Morris Crawley's plans. Perhaps even, in the end, to ruin Morris Crawley, full stop.

But you won't be using me as your weapon, Holly thought as she followed him to the car park. This time, Mr Wilde, you have overestimated your powers of persuasion. Seriously.

'How well do you know the Lakes?' Adam enquired as he drove along the Shap road towards Penrith.

'Not at all, really.' 'Whatever he wanted to show her, or prove to her, he would arrange to suit himself—just as, she thought cynically, he probably arranged the whole of his life to suit himself. Meanwhile, they were going to have to make conversation. 'This is my first visit. I'm looking forward to a guided tour. At least——' she turned in the comfortable seat of Adam's Porsche, looking at him with curiosity '—I assume you know the area? You've been in Canada—but you're not Canadian, are you? Do you actually come from around here?'

'Not too far away,' he said easily. 'I've been abroad for a long time. I guess it hasn't changed much, though.'

As far as Penrith, the road was good. It was the old main road into Scotland, Adam told her; it had been superseded by the motorway and was now relatively quiet. It ran along the border of the Lake District National Park, with some of the wildest areas in England stretching away towards the fells. 'It can get really bleak up here in winter,' he observed as they ran through the tiny, windswept village of Shap itself. 'The winds can blow up a blizzard while the rest of Cumbria's just having a shower. You quite often hear of lorries getting stranded on the motorway when they've ignored warnings not to use it.'

Nearer Penrith the country grew less rugged, but when

they turned off and headed back towards Ullswater, the
mountains rose up once again before them, wild and
craggy, standing like sentinels on guard over the far end
of the long, twisting lake. Holly gave an exclamation of
delight, and Adam drew the car into a lay-by and
stopped.

'Superb, isn't it?' he said as they watched the little
waves lap the shore. 'It's my favourite of all the lakes.
They each have their own character, but to me Ullswater
seems the most unspoiled, the wildest and most beautiful.
Not that it's to be trifled with. It looks tranquil enough
today, reflecting that blue sky, but when a storm blows up
it can get really rough. And, with the mountains virtually
torturing the wind, if you're out on it in a small boat you
don't know where the next gust might come from.'

Holly gazed at the long stretch of water. There were a
few sails drifting like huge-winged birds on the azure
surface, breaking up the clear reflections of the
mountains, but she guessed that most of the sailing-boats
had been put away for the winter. In summer, it must be
thick with sails.

'Do you sail much?' she asked idly.

'A bit. Not as much as I used to. Been too busy for the
past few years.' His eyes reflected the intense blue of the
lake. 'I'd like to get myself a boat and start again,
though—that's if I stay.'

'If you stay? I thought you'd rented Little Sleadale for
a year?'

'A year, yes. If I can't find a place I want in that
time—well, I suppose I'll have to think again.' His face
was sombre and Holly felt a quick stab of guilt. If she
hadn't cheated him at the auction . . . But she'd wanted
Sleadale just as badly. Surely she was entitled to consider
her own future more than that of a stranger?

The trouble was, Adam Wilde didn't seem like a

stranger. She had the odd feeling that she'd always known him. And that the tingling hostility she felt towards him had once been something very different . . .

They drove on slowly, past the lake. At the southern end, where the mountains stood sentinel, they paused at the villages of Glenridding and Patterdale. Holly looked about her with interest, as they took a short stroll.

'There are still plenty of people about,' she remarked, referring to the holidaymakers who thronged the narrow streets in heavy walking-boots and rucksacks. 'I thought the season would be over now.'

Adam shook his head. 'There are always people up here, walking the fells. School parties, university groups, rambling clubs—and individuals who just like to get away from it all. Have you ever done any real walking? There's nothing like it, you know— setting off on a beautiful crisp morning, doing ten or twelve miles. The views and the variety stop it from ever becoming boring, and you're really not conscious of distance at all. You ought to try it.'

Holly felt herself patronised and knew a stab of resentment. 'I am a shepherdess,' she pointed out. 'I do quite a lot of hill-walking—my last job was in the Welsh mountains. And yes, I quite often do it for pleasure too!'

'Sorry, I'm sure.' The stiffness was back in his voice, destroying the tentative companionship that had begun to form during their drive. 'I'd forgotten for a moment that you——' He stopped abruptly. Holly glanced up and caught his eyes on her face. For a brief second they were quite unguarded, and the expression in them made her turn away quickly, shaken and bewildered, cursing the colour that threatened to sweep into her face.

'How long were you abroad?' she asked at random.

They walked back to the car and Adam held the door while she slid into the seat.

'Oh, quite a few years. I went to learn different

farming methods and stayed. There wasn't much for me
here, anyway—and I wanted to make a fortune.'

'And did you?'

'Yes.' He spoke casually, as if money didn't mean
much—not like Morris, who nearly genuflected. 'But I've
discovered that even a fortune won't buy you what you
really want.'

'Oh.' Holly didn't want to pursue that line. She sat
quietly as Adam negotiated the bends and then began the
steep drive out of the valley, up to Kirkstone Pass. 'Did
you spend all your time in Canada?'

'Most of it. There's a lot of opportunity there for a
young man who wants to get on and is willing to learn. As
I'm sure your fiancé has told you.' There was an edge of
sarcasm in his voice, but Holly kept quiet. Perhaps now
he was going to tell her his version of the clash he and
Morris had had. 'I was both, and I did well. But in the
end——' he swung over to one side of the narrow road
while a coach full of smiling, elderly people passed them
'—I decided that I didn't want to be a colonial boy any
longer. I wanted to come home.'

They arrived at the top of the pass. Adam drove past
the inn that stood at the crest and turned right down a
steep, narrow lane. He put the car into its lowest gear.

'They call this road The Struggle—it's marked at the
bottom, where it reaches Ambleside—and when you try
coming up it, you can see why. It must have been hell for
horses in the old days.'

'I wonder if they had extra ones to help them,' Holly
said. 'I remember a hill in Hereford, where there's a pub
at the top called the Tupsley Cock, after the stallion they
used to keep there to give coach-horses an extra pull up
the hill. And that's nothing like this one!'

She gazed out at the scene before them. Its grandeur
caught at her heart. To their left, they passed a long,

green ridge that swept steeply down into the deep
Troutbeck Valley. Ahead, far below, lay the blue stretch
of Windermere, a steamer making its way slowly past the
wooded islands, and beyond that was the rolling
Grizedale Forest, backed by the looming mountains of
Coniston Old Man and Wetherlam.

Adam pointed out all these features as he guided the car
carefully down the twisting road. 'We're coming into
Ambleside now,' he added. 'Look out for the Bridge
House—a tiny place built right over the beck.' He
brought the Porsche down the last, steep decline and
reached the main road. 'See?'

'Oh, yes!' Holly stared in delight at the tiny house. 'It's
straight out of a nursery rhyme! What is it?'

'It's owned by the National Trust now, but the story is
that it used to be lived in by a family of ten or twelve—I
forget which.' Adam grinned as he turned the car left to
go through the village. 'Probably the parents themselves
lost count at times! Of course, it wouldn't have been quite
so overcrowded as people assume—there wouldn't have
been that amount of children all home together. By the
time the eldest one was ten or twelve, it would be out at
work, and I doubt if they raised that amount of healthy
children without losing a few in between. All the same, it
must have been pretty cosy in there at times!'

'The original woman who lived in a shoe, I should
think,' Holly agreed. Their constraint had gone again,
and she felt relaxed and at ease, yet still cautiously aware
that at any moment the hostility might return. If only it
could be like this all the time, without that danger . . . She
looked around with interest as they passed through
Ambleside. 'What an interesting little place. I'd like to
have a walk around.'

'We'll come back after lunch,' Adam said, glancing at
the car clock.

'Lunch?'

'Of course. You didn't think I intended to starve you, surely? There's a very nice hotel midway between Ambleside and Windermere—I've booked a table overlooking the lake. You'll enjoy it.'

'I see.' He must have done that when they stopped at Glenridding, Holly thought. She sat back as they ran beside the lake, only half seeing the autumn colours of the beech trees that lined the road, wondering about Adam, wondering just what was in his mind.

He had called her an enigma. Yet wasn't he even more puzzling? Even more difficult to understand?

Soberly, Holly counted up what she knew and felt about Adam Wilde. Knowledge first—he was clearly wealthy, possible as wealthy as Morris, and therefore as successful in whatever he did; she realised only now that she didn't know what that was. Farming? Business? He had never told her, and Morris had given no hint.

He'd lived in the Lake District, or somewhere near it—he'd admitted that and he certainly knew the area well. And he'd been in Canada.

That was all she actually knew. Morris had told her more—that they'd met there and that Adam had caused him so much trouble that Morris had left and come back to England. Yet she still knew very little about what had happened. Adam had promised to tell her—but so far he'd said nothing.

As for what she felt—she'd already thought enough about that. He was attractive to a perilous degree—yet, this morning, oddly companionable too. And although much of their conversation had been politely stilted, it had been hard not to relax into enjoyment, to let herself believe that she could really like this man . . . really confide in him . . .

And wasn't that just what Morris had warned her of?

And, however relaxed she might feel, she was still never free of the tingling discomfort his presence always seemed to give her—a tingling that became an electric shock whenever he accidentally touched her. She shifted uncomfortably, wishing that she could brush it away, yet at the same time unable to prevent herself from constantly experimenting to see if it was still there—like probing an aching tooth.

It excited and dismayed her. It reminded her too much of the sensations she'd experienced when she was in his arms—and remembering those moments made it even worse. She wanted to touch him, longed to feel his skin against hers—and knew that she was inviting disaster.

I shouldn't have come, she thought wretchedly, and tried to remember Morris, in London by now. But his face was blurred. And the thought of being in his arms did nothing at all.

'I'd been in Canada for about three years when I first heard of Morris Crawley.'

Holly sat opposite Adam at the window table overlooking Windermere, and slowly brought her eyes back from the magnificent view to rest them on his face. At last he was about to tell her what she wanted to know—what had happened between him and Morris. She wondered how it would compare with the version she had already heard, and whether it would make any difference to her feelings for either of these two strong and dominant men.

'I was making my way pretty well,' he went on slowly. 'I'd gone there to study new farming methods—there wasn't a future for me here, where I'd grown up, and it seemed to me that it was best to break right away, make an entirely new life for myself. Canada struck the right note for me. It's a good place to be if you're prepared to work hard—and, as I said before, I was. I knew the locals and they accepted me. I'd made a niche for myself. I liked it there and I was prepared to stay.'

'So . . . how did Morris affect all this?' Behind Adam's head, the blue waters of the lake stretched away towards the mountains of Langdale. The lumpy silhouettes of the Langdale Pikes reared into the sky—Pike o'Stickle, Pavey Ark, Sergeant Man—she could recall only a few of the names Adam had given her as they ate their meal. Did it remind him of Canada? Had Canada reminded him of the English Lakes?

'Morris came into town looking for more ways to make money.' Adam's voice was edged with dislike. 'His reputation came before him, but there didn't seem to be anything anyone could do to stop him. He had money and he had drive, and he used them both as weapons.'

'But how?'

'He was an asset-stripper,' Adam said flatly. 'Not everyone was prosperous. There are always a few who go to the wall, through reasons of inadequacy, incompetence or plain bad luck. Morris was like a spider, waiting in the centre of his web for the vibrations that would tell him that some business was on the rocks. Then he'd be there, flashing his wallet, offering to buy the poor owner out—never offering help, never investing the necessary cash that could put the business back on its feet and give both him and the owner an income. No, he wanted the lot, and he wanted it cheap. And because people in that situation are desperate, he got it.'

'But if he then built up the business—well, that was to his credit, surely?'

'It might have been, if that had been what he did,' Adam said shortly. 'But he didn't. He just drained the life-blood from whatever company it was—then merged it with something else. Added its assets to his empire and discraded the dead wood. Which invariably included a lot of jobs. A lot of innocent people lost their jobs through your fiancé's ruthlessness, Holly.'

Holly stared at him, uncomfortably remembering the way Morris had told her the same story. Two different points of view . . . Which was the right one?

'Well, then he came to the place where I was living,' Adam went on. 'He was quite a name by then, although people hadn't really woken up to the damage he was doing. And he looked around and saw a parcel of land that he wanted to buy and develop.'

'He told me all about that,' Holly said. 'It's just a matter of viewpoint. You see everything he did as bad. You say he deprived people of jobs. But he was going to use that land to build an industrial estate. He was going to *provide* jobs. And he was going to build houses for the people who worked there. He was going to do the same thing right across Canada.' Her eyes flashed scorn at the man who sat opposite her. 'You wrecked all that. So who was it was really did the damage?'

Adam's eyes were like the blue flames that burned when snow was in the air. He kept them on Holly's face, cold and steady, until the betraying colour once more burned her cheeks, and then he turned away, staring deliberately out of the window at the shining lake, the rearing mountains in their cloak of green and brown.

'Look at that,' he said quietly. 'Look at that and tell me you'd like to see it developed. Tell me you'd like to see an industrial estate out there. Houses, cramped and packed tightly together. Streets, teeming with cars. Noise . . . smoke . . . pollution.'

Holly followed his gaze. It was impossible to imagine the destruction of such serenity.

'But surely that's different. Surely——'

'Different. Yes, I suppose it is. Canada's big, after all. It doesn't matter about its beauty being ruined. There's

always a bit more somewhere else. But is there?'
Suddenly, Adam leaned forward, his eyes burning now
with an intensity that shocked her. 'Canada *isn't* big,
Holly. Nowhere's big. Do you know what's happening in
the Yukon now? In the Amazon rainforests? Beauty—
wilderness—everywhere, it's being destroyed. And all too
seldom for any good reason.'

'And you're saying that Morris had no good reason.
The jobs—the homes——'

'Could have happened equally well on another piece of
land. Not too far away. More convenient, in many
respects. But more expensive, too.' Adam sat back in his
chair and swept his black hair back from his forehead with
long fingers. 'Crawley wasn't prepared to pay—not when
he could con some poor farmer into thinking he could
make a fortune by selling what his fathers had loved and
cherished.'

Con. The same word Morris had used about Adam.
Holly felt her head swim.

'But you stopped him.'

'No. The people stopped him. Once they realised what
was happening—what they were about to lose—they were
up in arms, down to the very last man, woman, child.
They stopped him and they made it clear that his little
gallop was ended. He got out, fast, and that was the wisest
thing he ever did.' Adam regarded her soberly. 'All I did
was tell them—show them—and, once they understood,
my job was over.' He leaned forward again. 'If you want
to blame me, Holly, you'll have to blame a populace of
about fifty thousand, too.'

Holly's eyes dropped. She stared at the white
tablecloth, using her coffee-spoon to push a few small
crumbs into a heap. Adam was certainly very persuasive
. . . but wasn't that just what all con men were? And yet,
sitting here, in this big, panelled room with its spectacular

view over the lake, she wanted to believe him. Her
instincts told her that it was right to believe him. There
was none of the uneasiness she'd felt as she'd listened to
Morris last night.

'Tell me,' she said at last, still not looking at Adam's
face, 'why did you come here? Why did you want to buy
Sleadale? Was it just because you knew Morris wanted it?
Was it just out of . . . spite?'

The word came reluctantly from her lips. It seemed so
entirely wrong. Whatever Adam was, he was surely too
big for such a petty motive. But she could think of no
other word to use.

'Spite? So that's what he thinks!' Adam laughed
shortly. 'Yes, I can imagine Morris Crawley attributing
that to me. I can imagine him, nursing his grudge all
these years, probably not even surprised when I finally
turn up to queer his pitch again. Except that this time,
thanks to you, I didn't.' Holly coloured again, but to her
surprise his voice held a rueful humour rather than
resentment. 'No, Holly, there was no spite involved.
What happened in Canada was a long time ago. Plenty of
water's flowed under plenty of bridges since then—and,
until I met you at the farmhouse, I'd barely given Morris
Crawley a thought. Whereas I've no doubt at all that he's
given me plenty—he's not the kind of man to take a
humiliation like that without wanting revenge. It must
have been quite a moment for him when you pulled that
valley from under my nose—quite a moment . . .'

'You mean, it was just a coincidence?'

'I'm afraid so. On my part, anyway. *He* may have
known, of course . . .' Adam's eyes sharpened. 'That's a
thought! I wonder if he did. Perhaps it's him you should
be asking, Holly, not me. Why did *he* want
Sleadale—why is it so important to him? Oh, I'm sure he
means to make money out of it, the way I've told

you—but even that would be peanuts to him. So does he
want it just because he knew *I'd* be in the running? It's an
interesting point. Very interesting.'

'But why?' Holly's impatience caused her voice to rise
and she was conscious of other diners turning in her
direction. She lowered her tones quickly. 'Adam, why do
you want it so badly? If it's nothing to do with
Morris—why did you decide to come home from Canada
and settle just there? Just what does it mean to you?'

The eyes were darker now, like the night sky when only
the evening star has shown its light. They rested on her
face and she felt a sudden stab of empathy for the
emotions they conveyed. Remembrance . . . love . . . and
a vast, empty loneliness. Almost without knowing what
she did, she reached across the table and laid her hand on
his long, cool fingers.

'Tell me what Sleadale means to you,' she said softly,
and at last he answered.

'It's my home,' he said, and she caught the desolation
of the wanderer in his remote tones. 'I grew up there. I
lived there from the age of six months until my eighteenth
birthday.'

CHAPTER SEVEN

THE silence was broken by the waiter, coming to their table with the bill on a small tray. He placed it beside Adam with a deferential smile and moved quickly away but, unobtrusive though he was, his action had freed them from the spell and time began to move once more.

'You grew up there?' Holly repeated. 'It was your *home*? Oh, Adam . . .'

In that moment, she knew which man she must believe. She knew, without any further thought, that everything Adam had told her was true. And that everything Morris said—while not exactly a lie—was twisted to his own point of view; distorted and deformed. And that she would never be able entirely to trust him again.

She thrust away the implications of that thought and returned her attention to Adam, who was now taking a credit card from his wallet and placing it with the bill.

'You mean your parents lived there?' There was something here she didn't understand. 'But then, why——'

'Why isn't it mine, anyway? It wasn't like that, Holly. Look——' He lifted a hand and the waiter came over to collect the tray. 'Let's get out of here, and go somewhere else where we can talk.' His mouth quirked. 'We seem to be doing a lot of talking, all of a sudden. Maybe it's best to give some of it time to sink in. How about a walk?'

'All right.' Holly watched while the tray was taken away and then brought back for Adam to sign the counterfoil. A thousand questions seethed within her

113

mind. Why hadn't Adam inherited the farm when his
parents had died? Or were they still alive—had they
simply sold the farm and moved somewhere else? And if
they owned the farm anyway, why had he gone to Canada
and stayed there for so long? Had there been a rift
between them? A quarrel, which had ended in his walking
out—on his eighteenth birthday?

A few moments earlier, Holly had felt she knew Adam
as well as she knew herself. Now, he was an enigma all
over again, and one she wondered she would ever solve.

They left the hotel and Adam drove back through
Ambleside. Holly looked out at the narrow streets,
remembering their plan to come back and explore after
lunch. He seemed to have forgotten that now, and she
didn't remind him. She sensed that he wanted to go
somewhere quiet, where they were unlikely to be
interrupted, and she knew she wanted that too.

And as they drove out of the village to Grasmere,
passing the blue mirror of Rydal Water that almost
lapped the road, she wondered just why it was so
important to her that she should know the whole truth
about Adam Wilde. And why it seemed equally important
to him.

Grasmere was, as Wordsworth had called it, a 'jewel of
a place'. Holly looked around as Adam drove slowly, and
tried to imagine what it must have been like when the poet
had lived there. Not, perhaps, so very different from now.
The road rough and dusty—or, more frequently,
muddy!—the signs of modern living such as telegraph
wires and TV aerials missing. But the church was
probably the same, rather stark and bare on the outside,
and the little row of cottages now owned by the National
Trust. And the minute house where the famous Grasmere
Gingerbread was still made to a famous recipe—wasn't
that just where Dorothy and William had bought their

own gingerbread?

Even this late in the year, there were still visitors wandering around the village, some English with boots and rucksacks, some foreign—a few Japanese and a group of Americans. Adam had told her that the Lake District was a favourite spot for Americans, with Grasmere top of the list.

'They have Wordsworth Conventions here,' he said, 'and people come from all over America to attend them and see where he wrote his best poetry. Dove Cottage is one of the most-visited places here—beaten only by Beatrix Potter's house at Sawrey, a few miles away.'

He parked the car at the end of a narrow lane and led Holly across a wooden bridge and into a rough pasture. Ahead, she could see the open fells and, where they rose abruptly to the sky, the white trickle of water cascading down the rocky slope.

'Sour Milk Gill,' Adam told her. 'There's a tarn at the top—Easedale Tarn. We'll walk up there.'

The trickle of water was enough to form a sizeable stream which ran down beside the path. Holly gazed at the clear water. She listened to its chatter and heard the bubbling call of a curlew overhead. The valley had a peaceful beauty that reminded her of Sleadale, and thinking of Sleadale reminded her of Morris. Did he really mean to darken such open beauty with the shadows of conifers? Or were his actions now really no more than a petty revenge on the man who had stopped and humiliated him all those years ago?

She stole a glance at Adam. He was walking beside her, his face sombre, eyes fixed on the head of the valley. She took in the firm lines of his face, the high forehead, the straight black brows, the wide mouth above the square chin. It was the sort of face that met troubles head-on, she thought, the sort that told of an underlying strength, a determination of purpose that would take no denial, yet expect more of its owner than of other people.

Inevitably, she thought of Morris, comparing his features with Adam's. Morris, too, was strong, dominant—but his strength came from aggression. Morris, too, went for what he wanted, but his methods were unsubtle, bulldozing. And he knew the value of delegation—there were men, Holly knew, who worked for Morris in a shadowy way she'd never cared to consider. Morris had told her that she 'didn't understand' big business, but now she felt that she ought to have tried.

Adam Wilde would never delegate the tough, unpleasant jobs. Those, she knew instinctively, would be the ones he would keep for himself. But would he ever *need* to carry out the kind of tasks Morris assigned to his assistants? Holly thought not.

They were close to the foot of the biggest cascade now. It was far larger than it had appeared from the road—a towering mass of white water, foaming over the blackened rocks, sending spray across the grassy banks. Adam chose a dry spot and spread his water-proof jacket on the ground. After a second's hesitation, Holly sat down beside him.

She was acutely aware of his nearness, of the way his shoulder brushed hers, of his cool breath on her cheek when he turned towards her. But Adam seemed unaffected by it. His eyes were distant, as if he were far away, back in the past.

'Adam,' she began tentatively, 'you once said something about a will—about Sleadale being "left to you, after all". I thought it was just a figure of speech at the time—a sort of bitter joke. But if the farm really belonged to your parents——'

He interrupted her, but his voice wasn't harsh. He spoke quietly, almost as if he were alone.

'I told you, it wasn't that way. Think about it, Holly. What was the previous owner's name?'

'Of course, it was Barton. So they'd sold it. But——'

'No,' he said patiently. 'It never belonged to my parents. They never lived there. I don't think they even saw the place more than once or twice in their lives. Look, I'll tell you the whole thing. Though why I should be sitting here telling my life story to Morris Crawley's fiancé, I'm not at all sure.'

Holly bit her lip. She touched his hand and said quietly, 'Forget Morris, Adam. Please tell me—I'd like to hear.'

His eyes held hers, and he nodded. 'Yes, I want to.' A tiny pause, as if taking the last breath before plunging, and then he began. And this time there were no interruptions.

'It was Geoff Barton and his wife who lived at Sleadale then. But I wasn't their son. They never had one. I was Sue Barton's godson—not even related.' Adam gazed unseeingly at the waterfall. 'My parents were both killed in a rail accident when I was six months old,' he said soberly. 'I'd been left at home with friends while they went on a day-trip. They never came home. They were both only children, my father's parents were dead and my mother's father couldn't have taken on a small baby. Sue and Geoff took responsibility for me and brought me up as their own. They had no children of their own, and I lived with them at Sleadale until I was eighteen.'

Holly listened, fascinated, thinking with pity of the baby, orphaned and brought to strangers, of the child growing up in the isolation of Sleadale Head. She could picture Adam as a small boy, thin and black-haired, roaming the fells alone or with his godparents, scrambling up the tumbling beck, making camps among the rocks. A lonely childhood, but one that had given him that self-reliant strength that she sensed was so powerful in him. A strength that a man like Morris, growing up in the city, could never have.

Yet he must have been happy there, or why would he want to come back? And——

'Why did you leave?' she asked at last. 'Didn't they want you to stay—help run the farm?'

Adam shook his head. 'Up to a point, they did. But there wasn't really enough there for me. Geoff never ran the farm as a real business, he simply kept enough stock to make a living. For enough to keep the three of us—and remembering that I might want to bring a wife there and raise my own family—it would have meant too many changes. He and Sue didn't want that—and I didn't want to force it on them. I respected their way of life—but I could see that I couldn't share it with them, not as a man. I needed to get away, to grow in my own way. And I wasn't their son. And there were other members of their family with a greater claim on them and the land. So I went to Canada.'

Something in his voice told Holly that it had been a greater wrench than he admitted. Sleadale had been home to him, Geoff and Sue Barton his family. Leaving them had been an act of will rather than desire, and she guessed that he'd never really stopped wanting to go back.

'Didn't you ever see them again?'

'Oh, yes—I flew over from time to time. I owed them a great deal, and I loved them—they'd been mother and father to me, even though there was never any legal adoption. And I wanted them to know that I was doing well, that they didn't have to worry about my future. I reckoned they'd done enough for me.'

'So when they died——'

''They left the farm to Geoff's nephew. I didn't begrudge it—I knew he needed the money. But it wasn't

until I heard about it that I realised just how much
Sleadale meant to me—and knew that I wanted it to be
my home again. Farmed the way I wanted.'

'Why didn't you approach him, then? The nephew?'

'Because I was too late. I was away when Geoff
died—Sue had died a few years ago and he'd been on his
own for quite a while. By the time I heard about it, the
farm was up for sale. And although I could have made
Bob an offer, I didn't think it would be fair. I thought we
ought to let it go to auction and see just what it would
fetch. I knew I could afford it, after selling up in Canada.'

'You had a farm there? And sold it?' Holly's grey eyes
were wide. 'So now—you haven't got anything?'

'Only a large sum of money,' he told her wryly. 'Of
course, you could do something about that . . .'

'*I* could?' She stared at him uncomprehendingly, and
Adam's eyes sharpened, his voice taking on a new
urgency.

'Think, Holly. Think about what we talked about the
other day—the trees, and the harm they'd do to the
valley. You know you don't want to see that happen. And
you know that Crawley means to do it—whatever he may
have said to you.' His eyes searched her face and Holly
drew back a little, suddenly frightened. *Was* he right? Her
feelings about Morris had taken a severe jolt in the past
few days—but could she really believe that Adam Wilde
was telling the truth, rather than the man who had helped
her parents, who had asked her to marry him? There's a
remedy,' Adam said intensely. 'Something that will save
the valley and keep it wild and beautiful—something that
only you can do.'

'Something I can do? You mean, persuade Morris?'
Holly shook her head. 'Not if he's made up his mind,
Adam. I just don't think he'd listen. He believes he's
right—and he thinks I'm just an empty-headed ''little

woman''.' As she said it, she wondered why she had never fully realised it before—why she'd never put it into quite those words.

'If that's true,' Adam said curtly, 'then I'm sorry for you. In this day and age—to waste youself on a man like that!' His sudden anger shook her. 'But that's your business, Holly, and I hope you'll see sense before it's too late. But that's not what I was going to suggest. I'm not asking you to persuade him of anything—I'm well aware of the fact that it would be an impossible task, especially if he were to suspect it might have anything to do with me. No, what I'm asking you to do is quite simple.' His eyes were urgent again and Holly gazed back helplessly, held in thrall by their brillance. 'Sell Sleadale, Holly. It's in your name—he can't lift a finger to stop you. Sell it, and give him the money, if it eases your conscience. But sell it to someone who will care for it, farm it as it should be farmed—not use it merely as a way of getting round the Inland Revenue.'

His hands were on her shoulders, holding her hard, the strength in his long, supple fingers flowing through her body like a pulsing of electricity. She closed her eyes, wanting him to go on holding her, longing for him to gather her closer. His grip tightened and she opened her eyes again to find his face close, every muscle tense.

'Sell Sleadale to me, Holly,' he breathed. 'I'll give you the price he paid and pay all expenses, too.' He lifted one hand and stroked it gently down her face. 'It's the only solution—and you know it . . .'

There was something else in his words, Holly thought as she half turned her head to follow the warmth of his hand. Some other meaning that she ought to recognise . . . But instinctively she knew that such recognition would be dangerous. She pushed it away, and in the same moment, turned her head sharply in the other direction.

'Don't turn away from me, Holly. Look at me.'

His fingers touched her chin, turned her firmly to face him again, and he looked at her.

Holly felt once again the shock that always hit her when she caught the full force of that deep blue glance. And once again, she felt guilt wash over her—along with the now inevitable longing.

She had barely thought of Morris today, unless it were to compare him with Adam—most of the time, unfavourably. Worse, she had been aware every moment of the magnetic attraction that Adam had for her, an attraction that had filled her with a constant desire to be touched by him, held by him, kissed by him. It had forced itself into every thought, coloured every response. And now, as he spoke of Sleadale, of what he wanted to do there . . . With another twist of her head, Holly refused to face what her heart was telling her. She was engaged to Morris—and all right, they had things to sort out, maybe it wasn't as right for them as she'd thought. But she still wore his ring on her finger and——

Adam had admitted that he wanted Sleadale badly. He'd told her of his childhood there, shown her just why he should feel it ought to be his—why he was prepared to pay the money that Morris had given for it, just to get it back.

He ought to have known that she could never agree. The farm was in her name because Morris had wanted her to have it—as a wedding present. To sell it over his head would be to destroy all their plans for the future together.

Dragging together every shred of will-power she possessed, she gave Adam a level look and shook her head slowly.

'Adam, I'm sorry. I can't do what you want. It wouldn't be right. But—I'll talk to Morris as soon as he

comes back. I'll ask him if he really wants to go ahead
with it. If you're right, and all he really wants is
revenge—well, I'll do my best to talk him out of it.' She
would do more than that, she knew—if Morris were really
that kind of man, she could never agree to marry him.
And, in that case . . .? But she couldn't say this to Adam.
She only shook her head and continued, 'If not—I'll do
my best to see that no conifers are ever planted there.
That's as much as I can say.'

There was a long silence between them. Holly was
acutely aware of the roar of the waterfall, the cool spray
which blew towards them on the breeze. Adam had taken
his hands from her shoulders and turned away, and she
gazed at him, willing him to turn back, to take her in his
arms and assuage the agony in her heart with his kisses . . .
But that would only mean worse agony later, she reminded
herself, and the turmoil in her heart twisted like a knife.
What *was* it about this man that made her want him so
much?

They got up at last, and walked back to Grasmere in
silence. There seemed to be nothing else to do, nothing
left to say. Holly felt sadness settle over her like a dark
cloud as Adam drove back through Ambleside and
Windermere, as if something precious, something she
hadn't even begun to appreciate, was coming to an end.

The atmosphere was heavy with tension and regret. Yet
. . . what *was* there to regret? Somehow, she didn't want
to think about it.

Back at the Crookbarn Hotel, Adam turned in the
driving seat and gave her a long look.

'Dinner tonight?'

Holly prevaricated.

'Adam, I don't know—I think it's best if we just say
goodbye now, don't you?' Something had happened
between them that day, something she could not refuse to

acknowledge, something that could become dangerous. 'Let's just leave it at that,' she whispered, and her words were more of a plea than she'd intended.

For a moment, she thought he was going to acquiesce. And then something hardened in his face and he shook his head.

'No. You owe me this, Holly. You agreed to spend the day with me, and the day isn't over yet. We have dinner together tonight, all right?' His mouth softened. 'We won't talk about Sleadale, if you don't want to.'

'Dinner tonight, then,' she said, making up her mind that this really would be the last time they met. And knowing that, for the rest of her life, she would wonder about what might have been. And always feel this same sadness that oppressed her spirit at the thought of their parting.

It was much later when Adam once again saw Holly to her room. They paused at the door and Holly lifted her face.

'Thank you, Adam,' she said quietly. 'It's been——' She stopped, unable to say the word that came to her lips, the only one that could describe the evening they had just spent together. Perhaps it was knowing it was to be their last meeting that had freed her spirit, perhaps it was a reckless desire to know just once the full delight she could experience in the company of Adam Wilde: the laughter they could share, the glow, the caressing glances, the sudden unplumbed depths of understanding . . . But, as if reading her mind, Adam said it for her.

'Wonderful.' His voice was deep and sensual, like the caress of velvet on her skin, and Holly shivered. As she gazed at him, her lips parted, and Adam bent his head and claimed them with his own.

In that whirling moment, as Holly clung to him, she

knew that she could not let him go. Whatever her life
might be in the future, this was something her body
hungered for, craved, something it could not be denied.
And Adam craved it, too; she knew it by the way his arms
tightened around her, by the tense urgency in his lips as
they moved almost desperately over her face and down
into the hollow of her throat, by the groan that was
wrenched from the depths of his being as he held and
kissed her.

'Come inside,' she breathed, and opened the door.

Still locked together, they moved into the room and
stood just inside, kissing as if they would never stop.
Adam's fingers shook as he unbuttoned the silk blouse
that Holly wore and pulled it from the waistband of her
skirt. She felt their trembling as he pushed the fine
material from her shoulders, and flung back her head as
he cupped her breasts in his hands and bent to tug aside
the flimsy lace with his teeth.

All her doubts, all her scruples were forgotten in this
heady moment of rapture. And, as she tangled her fingers
in his thick hair, she knew that there could be only one
reason. She had never loved Morris—not this way, nor in
any other way. Her feelings for him had been gratitude,
obligation, even liking. But never love.

It was Adam Wilde she loved. And it was to Adam
Wilde that she must give herself.

She felt him lift her into his arms. He carried her across
the room and laid her on the bed, standing to look down
at her as she lay there gazing up at him, the shimmering
turquoise silk of her skirt spread around her like rippling
water. He was breathing heavily, his eyes almost black in
the soft pink light of the room, his expression tortured.

'You're sure about this, Holly?' he murmured,
lowering himself to lean across her, one hand on each side
of her shoulders. 'If we take this any further, there'll be

no turning back. You understand that?'

Mutely, she nodded. She was aware that her desire was so great in that moment, the yearning of her body so vibratingly overpowering, that no consideration on earth could now prevent its fulfilment. Adam Wilde was her man, and she his woman. This might be the only night of their lives that they could spend together—and nothing, *nothing* must be permitted to stand in their way.

'Come to me, Adam,' she whispered through trembling lips. 'Please. I've waited . . . so long.'

And so she had. All her life, it seemed, had been geared to this moment. From the second of her birth, this had been the one point of destiny to which every action had been aimed. Her father's farm, his bad luck with the cows, his meeting with Morris, leading to hers and to their engagement. It had all had to happen, so that she could meet Adam Wilde and be alone with him tonight in this softly shaded room. It had all been inevitable.

Adam reached down and began to undress her. Already, she was naked to the waist, her silk top and bra discarded by the door. Now he slowly unfastened the waistband of her skirt and slid it down to her feet, his sensitive fingers caressing her from hip to ankle, lingering on the soft skin of her inner thigh, the hollow at the back of her knee, the soft curve of her calf.

He spread his palms over her insteps and lifted her feet, kissing each toe, keeping his eyes on her face all the time. Holly knew that he was registering each nuance of her expression, each spasm of delight, of sensuous desire, of eye-closing ecstasy. She cared nothing for the fact that with each tiny gasp, each moan, each convulsive movement, she was telling Adam that she was his, completely at his mercy, to do with as he would. I want him to know it, she thought, and her heart twisted again at the tortured desire that showed so plainly on his own face

Oh, God, how can we hold back? Yet it's important to. It mustn't be rushed. It must be taken slowly, slowly . . . even though every long-drawn-out second brings its own fresh agony . . .

She was naked now, her slender body revealed without shame on the soft coverlet. For a long moment, Adam stood quite still, gazing down with a kind of reverence, his fingertips brushing her skin, moving from her shoulders to her breasts, tracing a faint yet searing trail over each and then down to her navel, the soft hollow of her stomach, the hidden cleft of her thighs. She could feel the tension in his fingers like a lethal energy, barely harnessed, ready to surge forth as soon as he released it. An energy that would be as unstoppable and devouring as the eruption of the volcano with which she had once before compared him.

In that moment, Holly felt a jerk of fear. Would anything at all be the same, once she had allowed Adam Wilde to make love to her? Shouldn't she, even now, try to prevent what could be a cataclysm?

It was already too late—and the brief impulse had already passed. With a rapidity that contrasted brutally with his previous lingering movements, Adam stripped off his clothes and stood before her, muscles taut beneath his tanned skin, his body tapering from broad shoulders to narrow hips, in magnificent proportion to his height. But he gave Holly no time to assess him as he had gazed at her. With a sinuous movement, he was beside her on the bed, drawing her into his arms, and his gasp matched hers as their bodies touched, skin to skin, and they could each feel the pulsating warmth of the other's desire, the urgent beat of the other's heart.

'Holly . . . Holly . . .' Her name was dragged from his throat on a groan as he buried his face in her breasts. For a few moments, it seemed as if he would be unable to wait

any longer to consummate the yearning that had been
wrenching at them both for the past week. He was like a
man gone crazy, she thought, helpless as he raged around
her body. His lips were everywhere—on her breasts, her
throat, her arms, her stomach, her thighs, her ankles, her
toes. He rolled her over and kissed her back, lingering
between her shoulderblades, fiery as he reached the
narrowness of her waist. Then he twisted her back again,
staring down into her eyes as if almost frightened; and in
that moment, Holly's own passion, startled for a few
seconds into submissiveness, rose to match his own and
she arched herself towards him, dragging his body against
hers and returning kiss for kiss.

And now they were equal in their abandonment. Limbs
entwined, mouths seeking, they twisted together. Holly
almost cried out as Adam's fingers sought and found
points of sensation that were exquisite to the point of
agony. She writhed against him, uncaring, frantic for
release from the tension that was gathering inside her,
while at the same time her own hands were exploring, and
discovering an equal sensitivity in him.

Slowly, Adam shifted himself so that he was slightly
apart from her. His hands gentled her, calming the storm
that had threatened to break too soon, and his eyes smiled
into hers.

'What a surprising lady you are, Miss Douglas,' he
murmured against her mouth. 'So cool and self-contained
. . . I might have known that there was fire beneath that
icy exterior.'

'And I always did know you were a volcano,' she
returned, still trembling against him. She moved one
hand, stroked her fingers softly down his cheek. 'Adam,
I . . .'

He caught her fingers, pressing them against her own
mouth. 'Don't say it. Don't say anything—not now.'

Holly gazed at him, bemused. She wanted to tell him she loved him—that she belonged to him. And he knew it. But he didn't want her to say so.

Before she could think any more, he had caught her tightly against him again. Excitement surged through her as their lovemaking began, even more passionately than before, and she knew that this time it must end in fulfilment.

Adam lifted himself away from her, raising his body over hers and looking down with a question in his eyes. Slowly, almost fainting with the desire that pulsed through her like a giant heartbeat, she nodded. She felt him come gently down on her body, felt the first warm thrust of him against her, the first sensation that was so strange, yet so welcome.

And the telephone rang.

They lay quite still. Adam had stopped immediately, frozen above her. She stared up at him, imploringly, but he shook his head and lifted himself away.

'You'll have to answer it, Holly. They know you're here at reception—and they probably know I came up with you. We can't let it ring.'

He reached to the bedside table and lifted the receiver, handing it to her without comment. And Holly, still trembling beneath his naked body, held it against her ear and heard Morris's voice.

'Holly? Is that you, darling? Listen, I managed to get away earlier than I thought—came straight up the motorway. Sorry I didn't let you know before, but I just wanted to get there and tell you the good news . . . Holly? Are you there?'

'Yes,' Holly said faintly, 'I'm here. What do you mean, Morris? You're coming back? Tonight?' She gave Adam an agonised glance.

'Darling, I *am* back!' Morris said, his voice jubilant.

'I'm in my room now. Just going to have a shower and then I'll be right along. You aren't in bed, are you?'

'No,' Holly said, feeling sick. 'No, Morris. I'm not in bed.'

CHAPTER EIGHT

' . . . SO THERE it is.' Morris sat back in the armchair and Holly gazed at him. It was as if she were seeing him for the first time. How, she wondered in amazement, could she ever have believed herself in love with this man? She looked at the short, stocky figure which would soon begin to run to fat; the hair, combed straight back from his fleshy forehead; the small brown eyes and full lips.

He wasn't really unattractive, she thought fairly. Plenty of men weren't particularly tall or slim, and she had always believed that it was a man's character that mattered more than his looks. But the kindness and concern she'd always believed she saw in Morris's face seemed to have faded. Or was it self-interest that she saw there, the concern shown merely for Morris himself and his possessions?

Possessions—of which she was one.

'You don't seem very excited,' Morris remarked petulantly.

'I'm sorry, I expect I'm just too tired to take it all in, and I've never really understood business deals. You mean, you've actually bought this company? It's yours?'

'That's right.' His petulance disappeared as he launched once again into the story. 'It's as sweet a little business as you ever saw, too. Full of potential. Of course, I'll change things quite a lot—cut out a lot of the dead wood, get rid of the unnecessary frills. It's never been run economically. But it's all there—the market, the outlets, everything. It just needs building up and it'll be a real moneyspinner.'

'But why have you bought it? You're getting out of big business—that's why we've bought the farm. I thought you were selling your financial concerns, not buying more.' She thought of Adam's remarks about Morris's activities in Canada—asset-stripping, he'd called it, buying up small businesses, merging them with others, sacking half the workers.

'Oh, well, you know how it is.' He grinned and a flash of his old charm came through. 'Can't keep a good businessman down. And I've been thinking about that, Holly—it wouldn't do to give up everything. Ought to keep a few irons in the fire.'

'But you're buying new irons.'

He shrugged. 'It was too good a chance to miss, sweetheart. I can do things with that business. Incorporate it with one or two of the other small companies I've bought lately, develop, expand. I tell you, there's the basis of a whole empire there. Look, this is what I thought——'

Holly listened to his plans, but she couldn't keep her mind on the ramifications of high finance that Morris was expounding now. Her feelings were mixed—confusion warring with anger and disillusionment. And she couldn't stop her mind going back to that last scene with Adam . . .

When the phone rang and she realised that Morris was not only back but in his room just a few doors away, Holly panicked. She stared at Adam with horror in her eyes, and pushed frantically to get him away from her.

'You'll have to go!' she hissed, feeling shame wash over her. How had she ever alowed herself to go so far? 'Please—Morris is here, he'll be along to see me at any minute, as soon as he's had a shower.'

'So?' Adam stayed where he was, immovable as a rock.

'Does it matter if he finds me here?'

'Of course it does! We're *engaged*. He'd be furious—and he'd have every right to be. Adam, *please* . . .'

The eyes were as dark as the night sky, with only a tiny flicker of stars somewhere in their depths. 'You're going to tell him, though, aren't you? About us? So what odds if he finds me here?'

'Tell him?'

'Well, you surely don't intend to go on with that farce of an engagement now.' Adam watched her narrowly.

'No. I don't know.' Holly rolled her head on the pillow. 'I can't think now. Adam, you can't let him find us here like this—at least let's get dressed. *Please.*'

'Well, I have to admit I would feel a little at a disadvantage,' Adam conceded. 'Although *he* might not look at it that way! All right, Holly, stop panicking. We've got plenty of time, after all—he's having a shower, isn't he? And it's my bet he won't come along without ringing you first, anyway, just in case you're still slightly *déshabillée*. Strikes me as a very proper kind of gentleman, our Morris.'

'Which is more than can be said for you!' Holly flashed, as at last Adam slid away from her. Quickly, she rolled off the bed scrambled into her clothes and brushed her hair. Hastily, she straightened out the bed, smoothing the coverlet, and glanced around for any other signs of Adam's occupation.

'Please go now, Adam,' she said shakily. 'He really will be here soon, and I don't think I could face——'

'All right, I'm on my way.' Adam came over to her and took her by the shoulders, looking intently into her eyes. 'But you are going to tell him, aren't you?'

Holly stared up at him, her eyes grey as pigeons' wings. 'What is there to tell?'

'Why, that you're not marrying him, of course!' Adam

exploded. 'You can't pretend you love him—not after what's happened between us. Or was I mistaken about you? Maybe you've just taken the opportunity to have a little fun on the side? While the cat's away, and all that. Is that what you've been doing, Holly? Was that all it meant to you?'

'No. *No*. But—we haven't talked, we've never even mentioned——'

'Words aren't always the most effective means of communication, Holly. And I thought we were communicating particularly well just then.' Adam shrugged into his jacket. 'All right, then. Have it your way. I'll go and leave you to your reunion. But don't imagine I'm leaving it like that, Holly. I've tried to play the gentleman, kept to your conditions, and it doesn't help. You're my woman—engaged or not. And if *you* won't tell Morris Crawley that, *I* will!'

He strode to the door, opened it and disappeared. Holly closed her eyes, certain that he would meet Morris. But there was no sound other than the soft pad of his footsteps going away down the carpeted corridor. And a few seconds later, just as he'd predicted, the phone rang.

'Well, that's better,' Morris said from three rooms away. 'Nice clean boy again. Ring room service and ask them to send up some drinks, will you, darling? I'll be along directly.'

'All right, Morris,' Holly said dully, and replaced the receiver.

Her mind felt numbed. She could not sort out the meaning of what Adam had said to her. Could not even untangle her own bewildered thoughts.

She could only go along with whatever happened next, and hope for the best.

Morris stopped speaking and eyed her expectantly.

'Don't you think that's really the best plan?'

Holly blinked at him. She had only half heard what he was saying, but it had been enough. A cold lump settled in her stomach.

'You meant to do this all along, didn't you?' she said at last. 'You never did intend to sell everything off and settle down as a sheep-farmer. It was all—all a plot.'

Morris laughed. 'Come, darling, don't dramatise. A plot! One has to think ahead, that's all.'

'And that's what you did.'

'Of course. That's what's got me where I am today.'

'A successful businessman.'

'Naturally.'

'And liar. Equally naturally.'

Morris's eyes hardened. 'Now, look——'

'What do you call it, then? When you proposed to me, you gave me to understand that you wanted out. Out of all the world of wheeling and dealing, buying up companies left and right, selling them next day—all the trappings of high finance. You said you'd had enough. You said you wanted a quiet life miles from anywhere, with only the birds and the sky for company. I believed you. And now you're going back on it all. Buying new companies—talking of amalgamation, expansion, development. So what was all that talk about leaving it, if it wasn't a lie?'

Morris sighed. 'Now look, Holly, you don't under-stand——'

'I understand when a man says one thing and does another. That's lying. I understand that perfectly.'

'I wish you'd stop using that word *lie!*' Morris shouted.

'I wish I could, too,' Holly said sadly, 'but it's the only one I know for what you've done, Morris.'

Morris took a deep breath. His face was red, but with an obvious effort he controlled his anger and said, 'Let's go through it again, Holly. I'm thinking of the future—*our* future. We can't afford to simply sit back and rely on a farm to keep us——'

'Thousands of people do. My father did.'

'And look where it got him! For God's sake, Holly, that experience alone should tell you what a risky business it is. I'm not going to end up like him, I can tell you that—scraping around a few acres of mud to pay the bills, old and grey before my time. I intend to have a comfortable life, with enough money to do whatever I want, when and how I want do it. And that goes for you, too. As my wife, Holly, you'll have a life of luxury. You'll never want for a thing. What in hell's name are you complaining about?'

'I'm complaining because you're not being honest with me. My father may never have given my mother luxury, but at least he never lied to her. She's always known exactly where she was with him, and that's worth a lot.'

'But you know where you are with me! Look, you've got to understand—business isn't *like* ordinary everyday life. There are times when a man *has* to keep his mouth shut, even with his nearest and dearest. I couldn't tell you about this, Holly, because if it had leaked out—and I know you'll say you wouldn't have breathed a word, but it can happen—if it had leaked out at all, the whole deal would have fallen through. And you have to realise that there'll be other deals like it in the future. I can't tell you everything, much as I——'

'But that's just it!' Holly felt sick with weariness, too exhausted to argue, but she knew that this was something that must be hammered out here and now. 'There shouldn't *be* any more deals! You said you wanted to get out—and you're not—and I don't believe you ever intended to. *And that's lying!* You based our whole future on a lie.'

'Are you saying you'll only marry me if I'm a small farmer, like your father?' Morris said quietly. 'Only if I'm struggling and unsuccessful? That's a new twist on an old theme, isn't it, Holly?'

'Oh, I don't know.' Holly pushed back her hair. 'It all sounds different when you say it. No, I don't think I'm saying that. What I'm saying is—I thought you were one kind of man, Morris. I thought you had—integrity, I suppose. That you were honest, certainly with me. And you're not that man at all.'

Morris's sigh was one of pure exasperation. 'My God, this is what you get for trying to ensure a secure future! I don't know about you, Holly, I really don't. Most girls would be over the moon to have a husband who was prepared to work all the hours God sends to keep them in luxury. But you——'

'You keep on about luxury,' Holly interrupted. 'I never asked you for that. And you talk about our future. I thought it was planned. I thought we were going to work the farm together. How often are you going to be there, if you're always going to be in London doing all these deals? How can we farm sheep? They may look as if they're running wild on the fells, but they do need attention. What sort of life are we going to have, Morris?'

'Well, I was coming to that, if you hadn't side-tracked me with all this talk about plots and lies.' Morris sounded injured. 'You're quite right, of course, we couldn't work it in the way we first envisaged. In fact, I'm not at all sure that the land is right for sheep, anyway. No, what I plan to do is this—put the whole lot down to conifers instead of just half, do up the farmhouse and keep it as a weekend place. That way, we'll get a very good return on our money, plus a nice little retreat. Naturally, most of the time we'd need to be nearer London, so we'll look for something around the stockbroker belt. Something big enough for you to keep a few animals, if you're really keen to.'

'The—the stockbroker belt? A *few animals?*' Holly shook her head, almost unable to speak. 'Morris—you can't mean it. You can't really be serious. Plant even more conifers—it would be vandalism! I won't allow it! I won't *let* you!'

'Won't let me?' Morris's face was hard, his eyes like stones. 'And just how do you propose to stop me?'

'I'll fight you every inch of the way!' she declared passionately. 'Don't forget, the farm is in *my* name. You can't do a thing on that land without my say-so—and I won't let you plant one single conifer on any of it.'

'You won't, eh? So much for your famous integrity, my dear. The money to buy that property was provided by *me,* if you remember. It may belong to you legally, but morally it's mine. Or perhaps it doesn't suit you to agree with that?'

'No, I agree with that,' Holly said steadily. 'I don't intend to keep the farm against your will. If you like, I'll pay you for it.'

'*Pay* me for it? You haven't two thousand pounds to rub together, let alone two hundred thousand!'

'No. But I've had an offer. I have a buyer who will give me what you paid for it, plus all legal expenses. I'll hand all the money over to you, Morris, and then we can both forget Sleadale.'

'A buyer? Who? And how did he come to know that——' Morris's eyes narrowed. 'Wait a minute! Wilde. It's him, isn't it? It has to be!' He whistled softly and then smiled. 'So he's still after the place! He must want it pretty badly.' His smiled widened and Holly knew, with a sick feeling, that Adam had been right. He wanted revenge— revenge for something that had happened years ago and thousands of miles away, yet still rankled. She remained silent, but

Morris was too absorbed in his own triumph to notice. 'Well, this is one time Mr Wilde will find he *can't* win,' he was saying gloatingly. 'And if you see him again, you can tell him just that, Holly—Sleadale's mine, and it's staying mine! What would he do with it, anyway? Probably exactly the same as I plan to—plant conifers on every square inch and sell 'em off as tax investments!'

'He won't! Adam loves Sleadale—he wants to farm it as it should be farmed——'

'So! It's *Adam* now, is it?' Morris leaned forward, and Holly wondered why she had never noticed before how like mud his eyes were. 'And he's been making an offer, has he? So you've seen him while I've been in London, in spite of what I said. And what other "offers" did he make? Because a man like Wilde doesn't just talk business with a pretty girl. Not in my experience. Maybe *you've* got a bit of confessing to do, Holly—to preserve that precious integrity of yours?'

Holly felt her face flame. She saw Morris's eyes on her cheeks and knew that she couldn't hide her guilt. And knew also that there was no reason to. Adam had told her to tell him—and she certainly couldn't continue with her engagement to Morris, not after the revelations of the past few hours about them both.

'All right, so I have been seeing Adam,' she said, striving to keep her voice cool. 'And yes, we're attracted to each other. So much so that I—well, I think I ought to break our engagement, Morris.' She took off her ring and held it out to him. 'I'm sorry. I didn't mean it to end like this. I wanted to tell you in a—well, in a more civilised way.'

Morris looked at the ring in her hand. He made no effort to take it.

'Are you telling me that you don't intend to marry me, after all?'

'Yes. I really am sorry, Morris.'

'You're going to marry this Wilde—a man you've known only a week?'

'I don't know. We haven't talked about it.'

'You *haven't talked about it?* What in hell's name *have* you done, then?' Morris studied the colour that rose again into Holly's cheeks. 'I see. Clearly, he's not the gentleman that I've tried to be. Perhaps that was my mistake.'

'It's not that,' Holly said wretchedly. 'I don't think it's going to go like that, Morris. He's never mentioned marriage, or—or love. There hasn't been time. I don't know if he ever will. But, knowing that I *am* attracted to him—well, it's made me realise that I would be wrong to marry you. Because——'

'Because you're not attracted to me.'

'Oh, Morris . . .' Piteously, she gazed at him. 'I really believed I loved you. After all your kindness—what you did for Dad—and then saying you just wanted a quiet country life, with me . . . Well, I was mistaken, I know that now. It would never have worked, Morris.' She held out the ring again. 'Please take it.'

Again, he ignored her outstretched hand. 'And the farm?'

'I really would like to sell it to Adam,' she said quietly. 'He wants it very badly, and I don't believe he'd plant conifers on it. There must be other farms you could buy, if you still want to do it.'

Morris shrugged. 'I'm not that bothered. It's a good business proposition, but there are others. No——' he shook his head as Holly's face lit up '—I'm not going to let Wilde have it, all the same. Why in hell should I let him have my farm, when he already appears to have stolen my fiancée?' His small eyes narrowed again. 'And you can put that ring back on your finger, Holly. When I make plans, I carry them out. And I planned that you should be my wife.' His eyes were cold. 'I told you once, Holly, that when I make up my mind to have something I get it. And once I've got it, I keep it. That goes for businesses, houses, farms—and you. You agreed to be my wife. And you're going to be.'

'But you can't force me!'

'No?' He smiled, and there was no kindness in his smile now. 'What about your father?'

'Dad? What does he have to do with——'

'He's had a pretty rough time, your dad,' Morris said thoughtfully. 'Worked hard all his life—scraped and saved for a place of his own—lost all his stock and had to start again. Yes, a pretty rough time.'

'But——'

'Seems to be getting on his feet now, of course— with a bit of timely help.' Morris had been looking absently at the corner of the room, now he switched his gaze back to Holly's bewildered face. 'But if that help were to be removed—well, he'd be back to square one. Minus square one, even.'

'You wouldn't——'

'Your father doesn't own a stick of that farm now,' Morris said, his voice hard. 'I bought the whole thing from him. He's my tenant. I can evict him at any time. just as I can sack him from the job he's got managing the place at Leominster.'

'No! No,' Holly breathed. 'You wouldn't——'

'I don't mind helping family out,' Morris said calmly. 'But I don't help lame dogs just for the joy of it. And if you didn't marry me—well, your old dad wouldn't *be* family, would he? So . . .'

'You swine,' Holly whispered.

Morris looked unperturbed. 'I've been called worse.'

'You'd force me into marrying you——'

'You're dramatising again. It's not that bad, Holly! For God's sake, you were quite happy with the idea a few days ago! If I hadn't left you alone this would never have happened. You'd never have been at the mercy of that Wilde character, and you'd have married me, accepted what I planned for the farm and everything would have gone along as sweet as a nut. But along comes an attractive man—oh yes, I can see he's just the type women would go for—and you lose your head completely. The mere fact that he's already done me considerable damage seems to mean nothing to you—and you dare to talk to me about such concepts as loyalty and integrity!' Morris's eyes raked her with scorn and he got up from his chair. 'I'm not going to waste any more time tonight, Holly. I've had a long drive. I came here expecting to have a pleasant evening, expecting you to welcome me, listen to what I've been doing, share in the pleasure I felt in bringing good news. But it hasn't been like that, has it?' He stopped at the door and looked at her. 'You may think yourself very lucky I don't take offence easily, Holly. Another man might have taken this ring and finished with you. But I'm prepared to make allowances for the fact that you're still young and impressionable. Now, get a good night's sleep, and it'll all seem quite different in the morning. I promise you, you'll be glad then that I didn't let you go on with this foolishness. And, if you can't get over Wilde's superficial attractions, just think of your parents. They're not getting any younger, after all.'

'Wait!' Holly came to her feet and hurled herself towards him, gripping his arm with both her hands. 'Morris, you can't do that—you wouldn't! Dad trusts you—he looks on you as his saviour. He'll work hard for you, he'll never let you down—how can you be so callous? You don't mean it—you couldn't!'

'Couldn't I?' Morris stared down at her, his eyes cold and hard, his face like a piece of wood. 'My dear, you haven't even begun to understand what life's all about. It's about survival, don't you realise that? And survival these days means keeping your head above water, never mind anyone else's. It means being tough. It means looking out for number one and always being ready to take an opportunity. It means being able to *recognise* an opportunity when it comes your way. None of which, I am afraid, are qualities outstanding in your rather weak and foolish father.'

'How dare you!' Holly panted. 'My father is one of the best men who ever walked this earth! He's never cheated anyone, he's always kept his side of any bargain, he's always been honest and trustworthy in everything he's done——'

'Which is why he's ended up a virtual bankrupt—and would have been, if it hadn't been for me.' Morris eyed her sardonically. 'Have you asked your mother what she thinks of his fine qualities? They don't seem to have brought *her* much comfort.'

Holly took a deep breath. Shouting was going to get her nowhere. She tried again.

'Morris, don't go yet. Please, come back—have another drink.' She looked at the whisky bottle which had been sent up. 'Look, we're both tired, and maybe this isn't the right time to talk—but I can't go to sleep with all this in the air. We've got to sort it out.'

'As far as I'm concerned,' Morris said, speaking with deliberation, 'there's nothing to sort out. All right, so I let you think I intended to retire up here and hide myself away on a bleak and miserable sheep-farm in the middle of nowhere. I had my reasons for that—I wanted you as my wife, and I could see that you weren't going to go for the glossy City-and-Home-Counties life-style—not just at first, anyway. You'd get to like it, Holly—you *will* get to like it—there's no doubt about that. But I knew you'd need time to adjust to the idea. Meanwhile, buying Sleadale suited me too, for the reason which Wilde has so kindly given you—the fact that it can make me a lot of money. And I've no objection at all to keeping the house and a few acres of land as a holiday home. Property's always a good investment, after all. And, to top it all, there was what I could do for your father. That, as much as anything, swung the balance in my favour, didn't it? You were so damned grateful, you really thought you were in love with me.' He shot her a look that made her cringe with self-disgust. 'I knew you weren't, of course. I'm not the kind of man who inspires love—I don't set out to be, as a rule. It's a wasteful emotion, the ruin of many lives. But it's time I had a wife, and you suit the purpose very well. As I've told you before, I don't give up anything I possess—not until I choose to. And I don't intend to lose you over some jumped-up story-book hero who's been filling your head with romance. Wilde's interfered in my life once already— he's not going to do it again.'

'You'd marry me just as a—a puppet?' Holly breathed. 'A doll to show off to your business acquaintances—a hostess for your business-account parties? Nothing else?'

'Well, I'd want a couple of children, of course,' Morris said easily. 'Preferably a son. But, once we'd got that side sorted out, I think you'd find me quite undemanding as a husband. And, as I said, you'd have a life of complete luxury, and never any worries about money.'

Holly gazed at him. Could she really believe the things she'd just heard? Wouldn't she wake up tomorrow and find it was all a dream? That Morris was still the kind-hearted, easy-going—yes, slightly dull, but was that a crime?—man she'd always believed him to be?

With a sinking heart, she knew that she wouldn't. If
Morris never spoke the truth to her again, he was
speaking it now. The future he had planned for her was
exactly what he had just spelled out. A luxury home
somewhere near London, the statutory two children, who
would almost certainly be sent to boarding-schools, and a
wide circle of business acquaintances to entertain and be
entertained by. No friends. No love. Empty.

'Please take your ring, Morris,' she said in a low, dry
voice. 'You must realise I can't marry you. Please—take
it, and then go.'

'That's three times you've offered me that ring,'
Morris said, looking at the diamond that glittered in her
palm. 'Be very careful, Holly. I'm a patient man, but
even I have limits. I might just take it.'

'I want you to,' she said.

Morris sighed. He spoke slowly, wearily, as if repeating
a lesson to a stupid child.

'Have you forgotten already what I said about your
parents, Holly? Or have you decided that even you can be
ruthless sometimes? Let's make everything perfectly
clear. If I take that ring, I also take your father's farm.
And his job.' There was a long, heavy pause. 'It's their
home, Holly, that farm. If they lose that, they'll be on the
streets. They've nothing else. Will *you* be able to help
them—when it's your actions that have put them there?'

Holly looked into his eyes. They were flat, expres-
sionless. She knew in that moment that, as a person, as
herself, he had never really cared deeply for her . She was
no more than any other possession—a girl he'd seen as
pliable enough to be moulded in the cast he thought right
for the wife of Morris Crawley. Just one of the
appendages of a successful businessman.

And he certainly didn't care about her parents. He
would throw them out of their home, leave them penniless

and jobless, and never give them another thought.

Slowly, with an aching heart, she slipped the ring back on her finger.

And felt doomed.

CHAPTER NINE

IT WAS the most painful thing she had ever had to do in her life, Holly thought next morning, as she prepared to meet Adam Wilde.

It was true that he had said nothing about love, had made no suggestion that they should marry. But, as she had told Morris, there had barely been time. They had moved so quickly from antagonism to this violent attraction that had proved too powerful to resist. Even friendship, which had begun to grow so happily and promisingly during the past two days, had come second instead of first.

But Adam had made his feelings quite clear after that phone call last night. 'You'll have to tell him about us,' he'd said forcibly. 'You can't go on with this engagement.' And, words that still thrilled her even though she knew there was no hope, 'You're my woman . . .'

His woman. There was a world of meaning in that phrase, a world of passion, of belonging, of ultimate trust and contentment in one another's company. A world she longed for—had always longed for. And now would never have.

Holly looked forward into her own future and found it bleak. The thought of marrying Morris Crawley now sickened her. The idea of sharing his life, and his bed—and she'd have to do that, for Morris had made it clear that two children were part of the bargain—brought a cold horror creeping across her skin.

Marriage on those terms was surely doomed to disaster.

And she thought of those two children— children not even yet conceived—and pitied them for the life they must have. Wasn't it downright immoral even to think of bringing them into the world?

Yet what other choice had she? Morris was, she knew now, utterly ruthless. There was no doubt in her mind that he would carry out his threat of evicting her parents from their farm, sacking her father from his job. And there was little or no chance of her father finding another job at his age. Without savings or home, the couple would be ruined. They would be lucky to end up in a council flat, living from hand to mouth on Social Security.

She couldn't do that to them.

Restlessly, Holly moved around the room. She had been awake almost all night, worrying the problem over like a terrier, turning it this way and that, looking for a way out of her impossible situation. Suppose she simply disappeared—walked out of all their lives, left Morris without going to Adam, even cut off contact with her parents? Would Morris accept that? She visualised his reaction and shivered. Knowing him as she did now, she had no doubt that he would be vindictively angry, and that he would take out his fury on her father and mother. They would lose their home, just the same. As well as their daughter. And she—she would have nothing.

Suppose she went to Adam, told him the truth. Wouldn't he want her to do that—to share with him this trouble that threatened her parents' future as well as her own? Could he, perhaps, even help?

In her heart, she was sure he would. But could she depend on it? Adam had said nothing about marriage. The implication had been there, but suppose he hadn't meant his words that way? Suppose she went to him with the burden of three people's futures to place in his hands—wasn't that expecting rather too much of what

might turn out to have been no more than a sexual
impulse?

The deep love she felt in her heart for Adam Wilde was
not necessarily reciprocated. And the thought of
apparently forcing his hand with what he might well see as
a kind of moral blackmail was intolerable.

So, what else was left? She could go to her parents, of
course, and tell them everything. And Jack would be
writing out his notice, and Jean upstairs packing, almost
before she'd finished. And they would be back at square
one—jobless and homeless. And just what could Holly,
with no job or home of her own and a broken
engagement, do to help then?

No. There was no way out. Her only course was to do
as Morris had said—marry him. The people who had
given her life, and cared for her all these years, were the
ones who deserved her first loyalty now.

Holly gazed out of the window and wished that she
need never see Adam again. It would be easier simply to
disappear than to face him today. But that was something
else she couldn't do. She owed him an explanation,
however difficult it might be. And she *wanted* to see him,
just one last time. See his lean, craggy face, his dark,
sapphire-blue eyes, those dark brows with their humorous
quirk, the mobile mouth that could look so grim, and
smile with such devastation.

She wanted to hear his voice, like rough-edged velvet,
abrasive yet caressing. She wanted to fix every tiny facet
of his personality, every characteristic, every nuance,
firmly in her mind.

It was going to have to last her for the rest of her life.

Holly went to the mirror to brush her hair. It seemed to
have lost its bounce overnight, lying flat against her head,
whatever she did. Her face was pale and haggard, and she
thought wryly of Morris's advice to use blusher. Yester-

day, coming in from her long walk with Adam, her cheeks
had glowed with exercise, fresh air and happiness. She
wondered if they would ever look like that again.

With a determined movement, she laid down her
brush. Indulging in self-pity was going to help no one.
She had decided on her course of action—or had it forced
upon her—and there was nothing for it but to make the
best of it.

Adam was going to be hurt, she knew that. But which
would hurt him most: to know that 'his woman' was
going to spend the rest of her life in purgatory, or to think
himself spurned for a richer man, left for a life of luxury?

Anger, she thought, is always preferable to pain. And
it's easier to recover from. If Adam thought I were
hankering after him all the time I was married to Morris,
would he be able to resist contacting me—coming after
me? And would I be able to resist him?

The answer was no. As long as Adam Wilde believed
her to be in love with him—as he must believe, now—she
was never going to be safe. And, if Holly wasn't safe,
neither were Jack and Jean Douglas.

So she would let Adam think that she had decided freely
what her new life was to be. And live it as positively—and
as happily—as possible. For her parents' sakes, and for
his.

Pinning a bright smile on her face, she went
downstairs.

Little Sleadale Cottage stood half a mile from the gate
which led to the main track along Sleadale. It was the first
time Holly had been there, and she stopped the Range
Rover, looking yearningly at the small stone building
hidden in the tiny valley, sheltered by rocks and trees. A
narrow beck ran down beside it, making a constant
cheerful song over the smooth boulders, and as she

approached a flock of small birds flew over the wall.

'A visitor! Holly, by all that's wonderful!'

Adam came out of the cottage. He was wearing a checked, open-necked shirt and corduroy slacks. He looked young and alive and vibrant, his hair tousled over his forehead, a smile lighting his face. Holly looked at him and felt pain stab at her heart. How could she leave him to marry the ruthless and now totally unattractive Morris?

'Darling, give me a kiss. How did it go last night, was it awful? I hated leaving you, but I know it was something you wanted to do alone.'

She was in his arms, his mouth on hers, and for a moment she gave herself up to the bliss of having his body against hers again, his warmth flowing into her. She clung to him, wanting never to let him go. If they could only stay like this for the rest of time—it was all she wanted. Nothing else mattered . . . With a sigh, she pulled away.

'Hey! That sounded serious.' Adam caught her shoulders, looking searchingly into her face. 'What is it, Holly? What's happened?'

With a tremendous effort, Holly forced herself to look at him. 'Happened? Nothing. What should have happened?'

Adam's eyes narrowed. 'Why, you should have broken off your engagement to Crawley, that's what should have happened. Didn't he come, after all?' He stared at her averted face, then with a quick movement lifted her left hand. 'Holly, what is this? You're still wearing his ring! What in God's name has happened?'

Holly shook her head wearily.

'Let's go inside, Adam.'

Still staring at her, he stepped aside. The light had died from his face; there was a dawning anger and hostility hardening his eyes. 'Sure. Go right in. You're the owner, after all.'

Holly walked through the cottage door. Even in her unhappy state, she could appreciate the cosiness of the interior, with its open-beamed ceiling, white walls and comfortable furniture. A log fire had been laid in the grate, and she thought briefly of how secluded it would be here at night, just two people on that large sofa in front of the fire . . . With determintion, she pushed the picture out of her mind.

'So, what's happened?' Adam repeated.

Holly walked to the fireplace, turned and faced him.

'I thought I ought to see you,' she said steadily, 'to clear up any misconceptions there may be in your mind.'

'Misconceptions?'

'About us. About what . . . happened last night.' She swallowed. This wasn't being any easier than she'd expected—and Adam, standing by the door, his face shadowed and unreadable, didn't look at all disposed to help her. 'You seemed to think—that it put me under some kind of obligation to you,' she managed to say at last.

'Obligation?'

'Well, what *did* you think?' she asked desperately.

Adam moved quickly. He came across the room to her and reached out. Holly shrank away, but he laid his hands on her shoulders, looking deeply into her eyes. She stood rigid, using every ounce of will-power she had to resist the driving need to fling herself into his arms.

'What did I think?' he said grimly. 'I'll tell you what I thought. I thought we were getting somewhere, you and I. I thought maybe what we had was real—something I could believe in. I thought you understood that.' His fingers tightened cruelly as he lifted her towards him. 'I thought you were going to tell Crawley that it was all off between you, that you were going to marry *me*. Are you telling me now that I was wrong?'

Holly blinked back the tears, forcing herself to continue to meet his eyes.

'Adam, you're hurting me. Please . . . Yes, I'm sorry, that's just what I *am* telling you. You were wrong. You jumped to a lot of conclusions that were—were just not true.'

He let go of her so suddenly that she staggered against him. The contact went through her body like a blow, and again she had to use all her determination to prevent herself from clinging to him. Stiffly, her body crying out in rebellion, she moved away.

'I'm afraid I misjudged you, Adam,' she said lightly. 'I thought you were like me—just enjoying a little fun together. I never dreamed you'd take it seriously.'

Adam moved again, quickly as a jungle cat. She could feel his suppressed violence as something tangible in the little room. Trembling, she faced him and found him once again close to her. He gripped her arms.

'A little fun!' he said harshly. 'I don't believe it—not of you. Hell, I've had enough experience to know when a woman's just out for a bit on the side—it's a game I'm not interested in playing, so I take a lot of care not to get caught up in it. And you tell me that you—no, I don't believe it. There's something else behind all this.'

Holly shrugged. 'I'm afraid you have to believe it. You seem to have got caught this time. I was only sorry we were interrupted—but perhaps it's just as well, since you seem to have the quaint, old-fashioned notion that a few hours in bed entitles you to permanent possession. Anyway, I'll have to be going now—I dropped in to tell you that now Morris is back we won't be able to meet again. Shame, but it can't be helped.'

Hating herself for the look on his face, she made to step past him. But Adam remained still, blocking her way. His face was grimmer than she had ever seen it, and she felt a twinge of real fear.

'You're not going yet, Holly. You're going to stay right here and tell me what all this is about. Because I'll never believe what you've just said to me. Something's happened—something between you and Crawley, and you're going to tell me. My God, Holly——' his voice changed, lost its grim anger to become soft, reasoning with her '—don't you think you can tell me anything, anything at all? If you're in trouble of some kind—if Crawley's got some kind of hold over you—why can't you tell me about it? Surely you can trust me to do what I can to help?'

Holly looked at him. The temptation to do just what he suggested was almost overwhelming. She longed to lay her head against his shoulder and pour out the whole sordid story, tell him everything that Morris had done, said, planned. And if he loved her—if she loved him—wasn't that really the best, the only thing to do?

But there was still Morris's trump card—her parents. If she went to Adam, he would have no hesitation in bringing about their ruin.

'Don't torture yourself, Adam,' she said quietly. 'Please, just accept what I say. I haven't broken off my engagement to Morris and I don't intend to. I came to tell you that I won't be seeing you again. Now let me go.'

Baffled, he stared at her. 'You mean, you're giving up what we could have together—throwing it away for that toad? Do you know what you're doing, Holly? Don't you know even now what kind of man he is?'

'Better than you do, I imagine.'

'I doubt it. Don't forget, I knew Crawley years ago and he hasn't changed. He's utterly ruthless, Holly, he'll trample on anyone to get where he wants to go. And that's the top. Look——' he let go of her again and strode to the window '—look out there. You don't seriously believe he means to give up all his shady City dealings to come and live here, do you? This sheep-farm you seem to think he's going to be happy running —it's just a dream. *Your* dream. He's stringing you along, Holly. It won't ever happen.'

He was so close to the truth that Holly closed her eyes, afraid that he might read it there. Oh God, let me get out of here before I give it all away, she prayed. Again, she forced herself to speak lightly, even managing a little laugh.

'The farm? Oh, that's all off—we're not going to run it with sheep. We've decided it would be more economic to plant the whole valley with conifers—just keep a few acres around the house as a kind of garden, and use it for holidays and weekends. It'll probably be quite useful for business meetings, too—we might even develop it as a small conference centre.' She was warming to her theme now, acting as she'd never believed possible. 'The road would have to be improved, of course—proper mains services put in. But it could be quite an attraction.'

Adam was staring at her as if she were an entirely new species.

'My God!' he breathed at last. 'You really do mean it, don't you? Whatever happened last night, it put you right on the other side. I only wish I knew what the hell it was.'

Holly gave him a bright smile.

'Well, since we've got that straight, I'll be going. You're welcome to stay on in the cottage, of course—you said you'd leased it for a year, didn't you? Well, I don't imagine we'll be doing anything to it just yet.' She walked to the door, still half afraid that he would prevent her from leaving. 'I don't think we need meet again, do you?' she said and, in spite of all her efforts, her voice shook slightly. 'So I'll say goodbye now.'

Adam looked at her. His eyes moved slowly over her face, as if seeking the truth. Then he looked down at her outstretched hand.

'Hell's teeth, Holly!' he exclaimed roughly. 'You can't go like this—you *can't!*'

He grasped her hand and jerked her towards him. Taken off balance, Holly fell against his body, reaching out for something to hold on to as she did so. The something was Adam. And he was holding her, hard. And kissing her.

Holly's protests were faint and quickly stilled. They clung to each other, mouths moving hungrily over each other's faces, each murmuring incoherent words of desperation. The world swung around them. Holly felt her hands, working almost without volition, gripping Adam's shoulders, pressing his neck, her thumbs stroking his ears, fingers twining in his hair. I can't let him go, she thought painfully. He's right, we belong together. I can't throw away the only love I've ever known, ruin both his life and mine . . . I can't . . .

Adam lifted her in his arms. He held her there for a moment, cradling her like a child, looking down into her eyes. His own were almost black, burning with a passion that had her swooning as he laid his mouth again to hers in a kiss that affirmed his love. Holly could not hold back her own response; to have done so would have been a betrayal of everything in her. And when he laid her on the sofa and knelt beside her, she knew that there could be no more denial of her feelings.

'I love you, Holly,' Adam said quietly, his voice vibrant with the passion that was only just below the surface. 'I love you with all my heart—with every cell in my body. Don't think I didn't try to resist it, I did. But after yesterday, spending the day with you, making love to you last night, I knew that every day spent apart would be a day lost.' His lips were close to hers, so close that they brushed her own. 'And I know you love me, too. You can't hide it. So what's all this about?'

'Please,' she whispered brokenly. 'Please, Adam, don't ask me. Just let me go—I——'

'Let you go?' The words tore their way from his throat in an exclamation that was pure pain. 'Holly, how can you say that? What the hell *is* all this?' He gripped her shoulders, his eyes blazing. 'Tell me the truth. You love me, don't you? *Don't you?'*

'Yes—yes.' The words came weakly, with a flood of tears, and Adam's grimness vanished. He held her against his broad chest, rocking her like a baby, murmuring words of comfort.

'Holly, darling, don't cry like that. It's all right. It has to be. We can *make* everything all right. We can't let a man like Crawley come between us. All right, so you promised to marry him—you're wearing his engagement ring. But engagements can be broken, my darling. They're not a legal contract any more. You don't have to go through with it and condemn us both to a life of misery—not now that you know what love is really all about.'

Holly pulled away from him, searching blindly for a handkerchief. Silently, Adam handed her one and she blew her nose and drew a shuddering sigh. She looked at him, a world of sadness in her rain-grey eyes.

'It's just because I know what love's all about that I have to marry him,' she said quietly. 'I can't explain it to you, Adam. It's not been easy for me to come here at all this morning, knowing—knowing how we both felt. But there's nothing else I can do. I have to marry Morris Crawley—and the sooner you can accept that, the better it will be for both of us. So, please—let me go now.'

He stared at her, baffled and angry. 'You mean, you're

going to leave me—without even telling me why?'

Holly nodded.

With a slow, heavy movement, Adam got to his feet. He stared down at her and her heart sank at the expression on his face. It would have been better if she'd never come, she thought unhappily. Better if she'd simply written to him, or even gone off without ever trying to make contact again. Better if he'd been left to conclude for himself that she was nothing but a heartless bitch, playing with him while her fiancé was away, and then leaving him without a second thought.

'I don't know what to think about you, Holly Douglas, I really don't,' he said, and there was a weariness in his tone that caught at her heart. 'You give me every impression that you're not really in love with your fiancé and every impression that you're falling in love with me. You respond to me as if you were starving—as if you'd never been kissed before. You seem happy with me, we get along well together, we share the same taste in music, books, films—almost everything we've discussed.' He paced about the room. 'I'll tell you something, Holly—I'm thirty-five years old and I've never been one for sleeping with every pretty girl I meet. I don't go for that kind of thing. I've had one or two relationships, yes—but only with women I've really felt something for. And none of them have ever come anywhere near giving me the feelings you give me. I really thought I'd got it right, this time.'

Again he paced the room, while Holly lay on the sofa, watching him with frightened eyes. There was a repressed violence in Adam that scared her, yet she couldn't help feeling excited by it, too. Because it wasn't, she sensed, a cruel violence—it was the violence of passion. And she knew that it was something he had never experienced before, something that scared him almost as much as it scared her.

'And now—I just don't know.' He was speaking quietly now, almost to himself. 'You were ready to make love with me last night. If that damned phone hadn't rung, we'd have stayed together all night and you would never have been able to leave me. I know it. And then, this morning, you come to me with some story about just calling in to say goodbye, saying it was no more than a pleasant interlude, that you thought I'd understood that, too. Well, Holly, I *don't* understand it. I never will. You're *my woman*. You can't deny it. You tell me the truth more when your lips are on mine than when you're speaking. Every move you make—every touch—every tiny sound— tells me that you love me, as much as I love you. You *can't* marry Crawley. It's obscene! And I'll never, never allow it.'

He was back at her side, his arms drawing her against him, kissing her with a savagery that she was helpless to resist. All the pent-up violence, the smouldering passion that she had sensed in him, was now coming to the surface, an eruption as tempestuous as that of any of the world's great volcanoes, and as terrifying. Yet fear was only a part of Holly's reaction. Already, her treacherous body, which had given her away so many times before, was responding with a storminess that matched his. She arched her body against him and opened her mouth to his, letting her tongue explore just as his was doing, wanting to reach down into the innermost soul of him, seeking, probing, making every tiny part her own. Moving sensuously against him, she could feel every hardened contour of his body, and she revelled in the contact of his lean muscularity against her own softness.

Adam wrenched open the buttons of her blouse and buried his face in the swelling mounds of her breasts. He groaned, and the sound seemed to vibrate within her, echoing in her own whimpering response. With shaking fingers, she undid his shirt and thrust herself against his skin, gasping at the faint roughness of the hairs on his chest, and moving softly to increase the delicious friction.

'You do love me—you do,' he muttered into her neck, and she tightened her arms around him. 'Tell me you do.'

It was a command, and one she couldn't disobey. 'I love you, Adam. I love you more than I ever dreamed I could love anyone. I want you so much, I want to be with you for the rest of my life—here, if you like, in Little Sleadale. Or anywhere. I wouldn't care where, so long as we were together. But——'

He lifted his head. 'But?'

Holly shook her head, pulling him down to her again, desperate to prolong the moment, knowing that once this last encounter was over she would have to leave him for ever. 'Kiss me again, Adam. Don't stop. Just go on—kissing me, and loving me.'

He stared at her, then took her lips again. And once more their passion broke, like the crashing of a king wave on a lonely beach, and as remorseless. Entwined, they rocked together, lost to the world. Now, Holly thought as the intimacy of Adam's caresses increased, now there will be nothing to stop us. In an hour or two we have to part—but, until then, there will be nothing but our own private world of joy, and nothing can come between us.

She abandoned herself to the rapture of Adam's lovemaking. Before her stretched a lifetime to regret—but at least she would have this one precious experience to remember, to cherish in her heart. And nothing, not even Morris at his most cruel, would be able to take that away from her.

And then, just as she was closing her eyes for the final rapturous consummation, Adam paused.

'Holly,' he said, looking down into her eyes, 'you know

what this means, don't you?'

'It means I love you,' she said, her eyes steady on his. 'It means that, whatever happens in the future, however long we live, we'll have had this one glorious moment. Don't wait, Adam. Come to me now.'

He shook his head, very slightly. 'I can't. Because you've just confirmed what I feared—what I tried to forget.'

To her dismay, he lifted himself away from her and lay down by her side, holding her closely in his arms. The warmth of his body flowed into hers, but it couldn't take away the chill that suddenly surged over her. She moved against him, trying to rouse him again, but knew that it was no use.

'What do you mean?'

'You said "but" just now, and I didn't ask what you meant because I was afraid of the answer. But I knew it all the time, really, though I tried not to face it. You meant that it was never going to come true, didn't you? That even if we made love together now, you would still never marry me. Am I right?'

'Yes,' she whispered. 'I love you, Adam. I want to be with you for ever. But I have to marry Morris.' She paused. 'Maybe it's wrong of me to want to know, just once, what life could be like for us. But I wanted it—I wanted *you*—so much.'

His arms grew tight and hard around her and for a wild, joyful moment, she thought that he was going to begin again and complete the lovemaking that had taken them both almost to the high, remote peak of total ecstasy. But instead he spoke, and at the tone of his voice her heart sank.

'We can't do it, Holly. Oh, I've no scruples about Crawley—as far as I'm concerned, he's not fit to walk the same earth as you—but if we go on to make love now, I know exactly what will happen.' His eyes burned into her face. 'I shall never let you go. I don't care what I do to keep you, but once you become fully mine, you stay mine. So, it's up to you. Do I go on now with what we both want so much—and no "buts"? Or do we stop—for ever?'

He was asking her to make the final decision, and Holly knew what he expected her to say. The desire between them was so strong that normal human strength would be totally unable to resist. Looking into his eyes, she knew that her strength was no more than anyone else's, and that if it were not for that single hold Morris had over her she would not even have wanted to resist.

Even so, she wavered. *Could* Morris be bluffing? Could he really be so hard and cruel as to force her parents from their home? If she went ahead with Adam—returned Morris's ring to him, finally and irrevocably—wouldn't he just accept it and go on with his own life, letting Jack and Jean Douglas go on with theirs?

But it was a risk she couldn't take. And neither could she risk Adam's reaction if she cheated him now—by allowing him to make love to her in the belief that it was for ever.

Slowly, she shook her head, and every movement was an agony. When she spoke, each word seemed a vicious slash in her throat.

'I can't, Adam. I want you. I can't deny that. All I said about my love for you was true. But I have to marry Morris.'

'And you won't tell me why?'

'It would do no good. I don't want to talk about it, Adam. Just—let me go.'

And this time, his face shuttered, he did so. He lifted his body from hers for the last time, without even glancing at her. He turned away and picked up his clothes, taking them to a door which she guessed led to the bedroom.

'I expect you'll be gone when I come out again,' he said without looking at her, and her heart wept at the pain in his voice. 'So I'll say goodbye now.'

'Goodbye, Adam,' she whispered, and watched as he went through the door, longing for one last glance, one tiny gesture.

But there was none. The door closed behind him and there was silence. Outside, a curlew called and she could hear the bubbling song of the beck. But inside the cottage there was nothing, only the harsh noise of her own ragged breathing.

Holly picked up her own tumbled heap of clothes and put them on. She gave one last glance at the closed door and then went outside. She got into the Range Rover and drove away. Away from the cottage, away from Sleadale.

And knew that it was for ever.

CHAPTER TEN

'. . . AND a fitting for my wedding dress. The designer says I'll only need one more and then it'll be finished.'

'That's wonderful!' Morris glanced up from his newspaper to give her a brief smile. 'I can't wait to see it. But, of course, I know I mustn't,' he added hastily, 'not until The Day—brings bad luck, doesn't it?'

Holly looked at him. Bad luck? When the whole thing was doomed from the start? It could hardly get worse . . . Firmly, she took herself in hand. Hadn't she made up her mind to go through with this with a smile on her face?

She moved restlessly around the expensively furnished sitting-room. The tiny flat that Morris had rented for her to use during the few weeks before their wedding, luxurious though it was, would never seem like home. Perhaps because she never actually did anything in it: it was cleaned each day by one of the maids working in the block of service apartments, and even meals could be ordered to be sent up from the restaurant downstairs. It seemed an unnatural way of living to her, poised uneasily between being in a hotel and being at home. For business people, it must be ideal, but for Holly, accustomed to the homeliness of a farm kitchen, it seemed uncomfortable and pointless.

'It'll be nice when I can do some real cooking,' she observed now, and Morris looked amused.

Holly, darling, you still don't seem to realise that those days are over. You know I have Mrs Simmonds in the London flat, and naturally we'll employ a second housekeeper for the country house, once we've settled on which one to buy.' They were still considering where to live, and had looked at several houses in the stockbroker belt—modern palaces of luxury that made Holly ache for the solid warmth of Sleadale. 'You'll have far too much to do to think about cooking,' Morris went on, 'and in any case, it wouldn't be suitable for my wife.'

'Why on earth not? We aren't royalty—and I bet even they like throwing a few things together in a casserole occasionally.'

'So they may. But we're different—we have to work rather harder to maintain our position than princes and princesses. And to have my wife appearing at the door wearing an apron and covered in flour when I bring home an important client, would do nothing at all to improve my image.'

'You mean you want to find me lying back on a chaise-lounge draped in a flowing négligé and eating grapes?' Holly said, and he nodded, completely missing any irony in her tone.

'If that's what you want to do, yes. Why not? As I've told you many times, you'll be living a life of luxury and comfort—and I want you to be *seen* to be living it. Nothing succeeds like success, Holly. If people see you behaving as the wife of a successful man, they'll automatically attribute that success to me—and so it goes on, increasing all the time. And by "people" I mean our neighbours—they'll all be influential in their own way. Your behaviour at home and in the community could have a considerable effect on their reception of us—and thus to my career.'

Holly stared at him, then turned away, sickened. So she was to be Morris's little status symbol! The more expensive she appeared, the better for his position.

And presumably the same thinking would be applied to

their children, when they came along. The son, sent to Harrow or Eton to meet the 'right' people; the daughter, educated at Cheltenham or Roedean and given a brilliant society wedding.

All to enhance Morris Crawley's own image.

I can't do it, Holly thought for the thousandth time, and her mind went back to the lonely valley in the Lake District, to the man who loved it, who had rented a tiny cottage there, just to be near where he had grown up. Oh Adam, Adam, she cried silently, why did it have to happen this way? Why couldn't I have met you first, instead of Morris?

But, as ever, when everything in her rebelled against the future before her, she thought also of her parents. And she steeled herself, not only to stand by her decision, but also to do so with a will—determined that nobody should ever guess at the torment in her heart.

It was, at least, easy enough to keep her days full and busy, blotting out the pain that racked her. Morris had overriden her wish for a quiet wedding, declaring that he wanted all the trimmings, although he was quite amenable to her insistence on a register office rather than a church. 'Plenty of people use them. In fact, they're every bit as fashionable now,' he'd agreed, unaware that all Holly's instincts revolted against the idea of standing beside him in a church to make what seemed such empty vows. 'You go ahead and make all the arrangements, Holly. So long as nothing's left out, you can have whatever you like.'

But something *is* left out, Holly thought sadly as she set out to arrange her own wedding. Love is left out. The sort of love I would have shared with Adam . . . And the longing shook her all over again.

It was just bearable, she found, if she pretended that it was all happening to someone else—that she was just a stand-in. In this way, she chose a wedding dress with all the detached objectivity of a designer working for a wealthy customer. She agreed to have the two daughters of Morris's partner as bridesmaids, and picked out dresses that would complement her own as well as suit their colouring. She interviewed the manager of an expensive hotel, and together they decided on the menu for the wedding breakfast, and the flowers to decorate the room. Even her honeymoon was chosen as if it were to happen to someone else.

'Italy? Yes, fine. Somewhere warm, where we don't have to do too much sightseeing,' Morris said when she asked his opinion. 'Although we ought to see the main places, of course. It helps when you're meeting people socially—gives you something to talk about. Rome, Florence—a day or two in each, I should think.' He was looking through some papers as he talked, breaking off every few minutes to dictate brief notes into the small cassette recorder he carried everywhere. 'Yes, go ahead and book that, Holly. Can't manage longer than a week just at present, I'm afraid—we'll have a longer trip somewhere later on. Bermuda, the Caribbean—somewhere like that.'

Nothing more had been said about Sleadale. Holly doubted now whether they would ever go there again. Morris had clearly never intended to live there, nor even to use the house for holidays; it had been intended only as a bait, to which she had risen.

And in a strange way Holly was thankful that it was not, after all, to be a part of her life. She didn't think she could have borne to go back there and see the long, straight furrows of the young conifer plantation; or, later, to see the splendid isolation ruined by the dense green of the forest, the head of the valley become a gloomy place of shadows, the tumbling beck a forgotten watercourse emerging from the sinister depths.

And she certainly couldn't have borne the pain of being there without Adam.

The day of the wedding drew inexorably nearer. Holly felt as if she were encased in a thick polythene bag, going through the motions of all that was required of her, yet without any real consciousness of it all. Dimly, she knew that this withdrawal was certain to have repercussions later, but there didn't seem to be a thing she could do about it.

Each morning as she woke, and each night as she fell at last into exhausted sleep, she thought of Adam. Where was he now? Had he left the cottage at Little Sleadale, or was he still there, roaming the fells he had known as a boy, saying his last goodbye to the lonely valley? Perhaps he had given up and bought another farm; perhaps he had decided that England held nothing for him after all, and returned to Canada.

More and more, Holly found herself getting up in the night to make tea in the tiny kitchen, wandering around the little flat and staring hopelessly from the windows into the darkness of the park opposite. Time, which she had hoped might gradually dull the sharpness of her agony, had proved to be of no help at all. In fact, it was making things worse.

I must see Adam again, she thought over and over again, knowing that to do so would be intolerable. And then, I must at least see Sleadale. Perhaps now—cold and misty in November—it would look less attractive, perhaps I could then put it out of my mind . . .

But she knew that it wasn't just Sleadale she wanted to see. And she knew that if she did go there, she would be unable to prevent herself from going again to the cottage. And once there . . . anything could happen . . .

The telephone shrilled, jerking her out of her thoughts, and she glanced at her watch in surprise. It was nearly midnight—who could be calling now? Adam, she thought stupidly, knowing that it couldn't be. Her heart thumping suddenly, she picked up the receiver; it shook as she lifted it to her ear.

'Holly?' Her mother's voice sounded as clearly as if she were next door. 'Darling, I'm sorry to ring so late —I hope I didn't wake you.'

'No, I wasn't in bed.' Worn out after a long day around the shops and at the hotel, Holly had gone to bed early, only to get up again to make the inevitable tea. 'Is everything all right, Mum?'

'Yes—oh, yes.' Her mother's voice sounded hurried, as if she didn't want to be questioned too much. 'It's just that—well, I'm afraid I won't be able to come up to see you as we planned on Tuesday. I'll have to put it off until next week—I hope it won't be too much of a nuisance.'

'No, it doesn't matter at all.' Holly was almost relieved. Much as she wanted to see her mother, she'd been dreading this visit, planned to buy Jean's wedding outfit. She wasn't at all sure that she would be able to hide her own unhappiness from eyes that had known her all her life, and she didn't want her parents to have any idea that her wedding to Morris was taking place for any reason other than love.

'But what's happened?' she asked now. 'You and Dad are all right, aren't you? There's nothing wrong on the farm?'

'No, nothing at all and we're fine. I'll explain it all when I see you. Will Monday be all right? Oh, and don't try to ring us before then—we'll be away.' There was an undercurrent in her mother's voice that Holly didn't understand. 'That's why I had to ring you now—we're leaving first thing in the morning. I didn't want to miss you.'

'Away? But where? What about the animals? Mum, what's *happened?*' Holly almost shook the receiver in her agitation. Her parents seldom left the farm, and never without a good deal of planning. What on earth could have made them take a trip at what appeared to be a moment's notice?

'Tell you all about it next week,' Jean Douglas said cheerfully. 'Now, I'll have to go, Holly, we've a lot to do—and don't worry. Everything's going to be all right!'

All right? Holly replaced the receiver and stared at it. What on earth could her mother mean? How could 'everything be all right'? And what was this mysterious trip all about?

It must be something to do with Morris—wasn't he away, too, this week? Another ploy to bind her more tightly to him, she thought with a sinking heart, some other way of holding her parents as unwitting hostages. A blind fury rose in her heart, and she reached for the phone again, intending to ring her parents and warn them against having any further dealings with him. And then, even as she began to press the buttons, she stopped.

If she told her parents about Morris, the whole story would come out. They would know just why she was marrying him—and how desperately she didn't want to. They would never allow it. Her father would, she knew, walk out of his job, his wife firmly beside him, even though it meant their losing their home, livelihood, everything.

She couldn't let it happen.

Slowly, Holly put the receiver back. Whatever Morris's latest scheme was, he hadn't wanted her to know. He'd sworn her parents to secrecy, and gone away without leaving her any means of contacting him.

Whatever it was, there wasn't a thing she could do

about it.

There was fog on the motorway, and the TV weatherman
had covered the north of England with blue zeros and
black clouds exuding snowflakes. Holly, immured in the
battered Metro she still clung to, in spite of Morris's
entreaties to let him buy her something smarter, thought
that it would have needed to be fire-breathing dragons
and volcanic eruptions to have prevented her from
travelling north that morning.

She still wasn't sure what had got into her. And she
knew, quite clearly, that this sudden journey wasn't going
to do any good. How could it? Nothing could change the
situation; she would come back to London still trapped in
her engagement to Morris, still doomed to a future that
seemed blacker every time she thought about it.

But it was as if her body had begun to act
independently of all reason, ignoring the panic-stricken
terror of her mind. So what if she did meet Adam
again—what if they did make love in the small, cosy
sitting-room of Little Sleadale? Didn't she deserve just
one hour of happiness? Even if it did mean an even
greater pain to follow?

And if he wasn't there? Confused, unable now even to
understand her own motives, Holly half hoped that he
wouldn't be. At least she would be spared making any
further decisions.

If he was . . . She refused to think about it.

As she made her way slowly north, Holly found herself
still wondering at the sudden impulse which had driven
her out to the car so early in the morning. The idea of
going back to Sleadale had hit her like a blow, after the
two sleepless nights since her mother's telephone call. She
hadn't paused to think it out, knowing that only in the
solitude of the valley was there any chance of her finding

peace. There was something there that called to her. She
might even—although her still-rational mind told her this
was nonsense—find some solution to the problems that
tortured her mind.

What that solution might be, she had no idea. She only
knew that, with Morris away and her mother not coming
to London after all, she had an opportunity that might
never be repeated—an opportunity, for just one last time,
to do exactly as she wished. To go exactly where she
wanted, to let the wind of life blow her wherever she
should go.

As she drove past Lancaster, the fog lifted. It was late
afternoon by now and dusk was setting in; but it was a
clear, pale dusk, touched with the faint apricot glow of the
setting sun. And, as Holly gazed ahead, she caught the
sharp outline of the first of the Lake District mountains,
and felt her spirits rise.

By the time she reached the track leading into Sleadale,
it was completely dark. At the first gate, Holly
hesitated—was she completely mad? But as she stood
there, gazing ahead into the blackness, she caught sight of
the silvered edge of a full moon, rising above the fells. She
put her hand into her pocket and felt the reassuring
hardness of the key which she still had, and gripped it
tightly.

I've come this far, she thought. And I don't know
why—but I'm damned if I'm going to turn back now.

Driving along the track alone and at night took even
longer than during the day. The ruts and pot-holes
seemed deeper, the rocks larger and sharper. Several
times, the car hit something with a sickening thump and
she clung tensely to the wheel, expecting at any second to
tip over into the ditch that ran beside the track. But the
moon was up now, clear of the hills, filling the valley with
a pale, icy light. She could see the house, its white walls

glimmering against the shadows of the fell; it seemed to be beckoning to her, the call she had felt in London even stronger now that she was so close, and there was never any thought in her mind of turning back.

Holly negotiated the Metro over the last stretch of cobbles, and stopped outside the door. She got out of the car and stood in the middle of the yard, turning slowly to look all around at the shadowy slopes, lightened by the gleam of rock where the moonlight caught the crags. The beck glittered as it tumbled past the house, spray flying like a crystal shower from the boulders scattered in the shallow water.

The glassy tinkling of the water was the only sound to be heard. A soft disturbance in the air made her turn her head, and she saw the broad shape of an owl swoop soundlessly past. Two eyes showed green in the lights of the car, and a sheep blundered by with a rattle of hooves before silence descended again.

Holly drew a deep breath. She knew that there was nobody, no human person, within two miles of her—maybe more. And knew that this was what she needed.

In the crowds and noise of London, pressurised by Morris and the life he had mapped out for her, there had been no room to think, no peace in which to come to terms with what had happened. For that, it had been essential to come back to Sleadale, where it had all begun. To make any sense of it at all, she needed to be alone.

With a little sigh, she opened the door and went inside.

The pale November sun, streaming in at the uncurtained windows, woke Holly next morning, and for a moment she blinked around the room, wondering where she was. The fire she had lit the night before had gone out, one of the cushions she had brought had slipped out from underneath her so that she was half lying on the floor, and her sleeping-bag was twisted around her body.

Slowly, she sat up, remembering the hostility she had once felt in this house. It had disappeared now; the walls seem to gather themselves protectively around her. She looked around the room, sensing its plea for a protection of its own, and her heart yearned towards it. I'd do anything I could, she told it silently, but you're not mine. And you ought to be—I know you ought to be. Mine—and Adam's.

Holly wriggled out of the sleeping-bag and went to the window. The close-cropped turf of the fell was white with frost, the sky still clear. The valley was even more beautiful than she had remembered it, and the ache in her heart grew sharper.

There was a movement somewhere down the track.

Holly watched, a tiny frown between her brows. Someone coming to Sleadale?

Surely it could only be one person?

With a sudden surge of panic, she whipped round, found her clothes and scrambled into them. Desperately though she longed to see Adam Wilde again, she knew that she hadn't the strength to face yet another meeting here, in the isolation of Sleadale Head. This house, and the knowledge they shared that this was where they both belonged, was too strong for them. If he found her here, alone, there would be no holding back.

It was a situation that must not arise. Frantically, Holly thought of Morris, of the smug, orderly life he had planned in the stockbroker belt. Everything about it was totally alien to her—but she dared not risk destroying it. And giving way to the passion that flared between herself and Adam Wilde would do just that, as certainly as lighting a fuse to a time-bomb.

Once she had made love with Adam Wilde, Holly knew

that she would never be able to leave him, whatever the
consequences. And, once again, she heard her mother's
voice over the phone, talking mysteriously about going
away. Once again, she wondered just what new plan
Morris had evolved to bind her to him through her
parents. Through their livelihood, their home, their
entire future.

No, it was a risk that couldn't be taken. Before Adam's
car, now clearly visible as it crept along the track, could
reach the house, she had to be out of the way. And she
would have to stay out of the way until he had gone.

Breathing quickly, Holly slipped out through the door.
Her own car stood there, in full view, and she hesitated,
cursing it, then made up her mind and dashed across to
one of the outbuildings dragging open the door. To her
relief, it was empty. She ran back to the Metro, flung
herself into the driving seat and started it.

With any luck, Adam wouldn't have seen it yet; the
yard was hidden from the track by one of the stone walls
that ranged across the fells and encircled the farm. She
drove into the outbuilding, dragged the door closed again
and stood panting.

But there wasn't time to stop. She had to be out of
sight—away, up the path at the back of the house—before
Adam came into view. Thankful for her boots, Holly
crunched across the frosty grass and through the
sheepfolds to reach the open fellside. The track led away
up the slope, twisting to ease the gradient. Within a few
minutes she was above the house, looking down, and as
she paused the car came round the last bend and stopped,
exactly where her own had been.

Knowing that she ought to get well out of sight, yet
unable to resist a last glimpse of the man she loved so
much, Holly sank down behind a rock and peeped around
it.

Adam's Land Rover stood in the grassy yard. The driver's door opened and he got out and stood for a moment, gazing around. As he lifted his head to look up the fell, Holly dodged back behind her rock.

A moment or two later, she peeped tentatively around again. And saw that he was now on the passenger side, helping someone out of the back seat.

He had someone with him. Two people. People that Holly, unable to believe her eyes, recognised.

Jack and Jean Douglas—her own parents—stood beside Adam Wilde in the yard of Sleadale Head Farm. As Holly watched, too shaken now to think of hiding, they glanced around the yard as if pointing something out to each other. And then, unbelievably, Adam took a step or two towards the fell, lifted his head and called her name.

'Holly! Can you hear me?' He paused. 'Why don't you come down, darling? We've got a lot of things to discuss—you and I.'

CHAPTER ELEVEN

SLOWLY, Holly came out from behind her rock. She felt rather like a naughty child caught hiding after some misdemeanour. But the faces of her parents were far from reproachful as she came down the path and into the yard. They came forward at once and embraced her, holding her tightly, murmuring consolingly, almost as if something disastrous had happened, as if they wanted to give her comfort and reassurance. And perhaps they were right, she thought dismally.

She didn't dare to look at Adam.

'Holly, you silly girl!' Jean Douglas spoke with a fond, half-scolding tone, as if Holly were ten years old again, afraid to own up to something that really wasn't so serious after all. 'Why ever didn't you tell us——'

'Never mind that now.' Jack's voice was gruff. 'She did what she thought was best.'

'Oh, I know. All the same, she should have known——'

Adam interrupted. He came forward and Holly lifted her eyes at last to look at him. Her heart jumped. After the weeks apart, he seemed taller than ever, the dark good looks even more devastating than she remembered. His face was sombre.

'Let's go inside,' he said quietly. 'We've got a lot to talk about—but we can't begin to discuss it now. Someone else is coming, and I think he's almost here.'

'Someone else?' Holly turned and stared down the track. *'Morris?'*

'I thought he ought to be here for the final show-down.' Adam spoke in the same quiet voice. 'There's a lot to sort out, and since it involves him, too . . .'

'But I don't understand.' Holly looked in bewilderment at the three faces. 'What's going on? Why are you here? How did you know I'd be here? And how did you meet Adam?'

'We didn't know you'd be here—not until last night.' Jean took her daughter's arm. 'We were in Adam's cottage at Little Sleadale. We saw the lights of your car going along the track. Not that we knew it was yours then, but Adam and your father walked up to see, and Dad recognised it.'

'We didn't disturb you then,' Adam supplied. 'I reckoned that you probably needed to be alone—I thought you must have come to sort things out for yourself, and I decided that you had the right to your solitude to do just that. As for why *we're* here—well, that's been planned for a few days.'

'So that's why you put off coming to London,' Holly said to her mother. 'But I still don't understand——'

'You will,' Adam said briskly. 'Now, why not go inside? Crawley's not going to be best pleased to find us all here—he only knows he's coming to meet me. Nothing inside to sit on, but we won't bother with getting out the chairs we brought with us. I don't imagine this meeting's going to take too long, anyway.'

As her parents went into the house, he slipped his arm around Holly's shoulders and drew her close. She shook her head. 'I still don't understand how you knew I was here—I put the car away. How did you know I was up on the fell?'

'Footprints,' Adam said succinctly, and Holly looked at the ground and saw her footprints, dark against the frosty

grass, leading out of the yard. She lifted her eyes to his
and saw the softness in their navy-blue depths. 'You see,
you can't escape me. I advise you not to try any more.'

'Oh, Adam,' she said, and misery washed over her. 'I
don't want to—you know I don't want to. But there's
nothing you can do to help. I don't know why you're
here, how you met Mum and Dad, or why you've
brought them here. And I don't see what you hope to
achieve by getting Morris to come. But you can't do
anything to help. Nobody can. I've got to marry him.'

'And that,' Adam said as he bent his head to lay his lips
on hers in a swift, hard kiss, 'is something I refuse to
accept. Trust me, Holly.'

Holly turned to go into the house. She was trembling
with shock, anxiety and the fierce, unassuaged longing
which always rose in her when she was with Adam.

How all this had come about, she had no idea. But
since they were all here—her parents, Adam and herself
and, within a few minutes, Morris—she had no choice
but to go along with whatever the next hour or so might
bring.

Choice? she thought ruefully. Since when *did* I have
any choice? That was a luxury that had disappeared long
ago.

She was in the living-room with her parents when
Morris's Range Rover halted in the yard and they heard
voices outside.

Holly glanced anxiously at her parents. But there was
no time to speak. There was a tramping of footsteps at the
door. The two men were coming through the kitchen.
And, as she turned, they entered the room, Morris in the
lead.

He stopped dead.

'Holly! What in hell's name are you doing here? And
Jack—Jean'—what *is* all this?' He whirled on Adam,

standing in the doorway. 'Some kind of joke?'

'No joke.' Adam came forward and Holly felt a qualm of fear as she looked at his grim face. Did Morris see the menace in those dark eyes? she wondered. 'As it happens, I didn't know when I arranged this meeting that Holly would be here. I wasn't even sure about Jean and Jack. But since we *are* all here—all those whose lives you've done your best to wreck—it's a good opportunity to sort a few things out. For a start——'

'Just a minute!' Morris's face was pale with anger. 'Just what do you mean by that? Whose lives have I wrecked, and how?' He glanced around at the three Douglases, his small eyes snapping. 'I saved Jack here from bankruptcy—gave him a job—even kept his farm for him. How's *that* wrecking his life? And as for Holly, she's going to live a life most girls would give their right arms for. And don't say she doesn't want it! She was prepared to rough it up here with me, living a life that would have made her old before she was forty—instead, she's getting all the luxury she's ever dreamed of. And I haven't heard her complaining! So just who is it whose life I've wrecked?'

Adam gave him a glance of contempt. 'I don't think explanations will mean anything at all to you, Crawley,' he said witheringly. 'But just to give you something to think about—you haven't saved Jack at all. You've put him in a prison—a prison he thought he could never get out of. And the same for Holly. You trapped her into marrying you, holding her father and mother as hostages. You've no idea what kind of life she'd like—no idea at all how to treat her. And you don't even care!' He stepped across the room and placed his arm around Holly's shoulders. 'Given your way, you'd turn her into a puppet, a doll to show off to your business friends. In five years, she would have lost all her freshness, all her originality. Yes, she would have lived in luxury—but at what cost? At the cost of her whole personality, and that's what I mean when I say you'd have wrecked her life.'

Morris took a step forward, but Adam hadn't finished. he turned to Jack Douglas.

'As for Jack, you would have ground him down further and further. Especially as you became more and more dissatisfied with Holly. You'd have blamed them both equally for the empty sham that your own life would have been. You'd have done everything in your power to humiliate a man who was once a fine farmer, whose only crime was bad luck. You would have wrecked his life, as systematically and as cynically as you would have wrecked Holly's and not even known why.'

'Now, look——' Morris began blusteringly, but once again Adam's strong voice overrode him.

'It's not going to happen, Crawley. None of it's going to happen. You've lost control of this particular situation. Just as you lost control back in Canada all those years ago. And do you know why?' His eyes were like polar ice as he surveyed the sullen figure in front of him. 'Because you forget that you're dealing with human beings. You treat people like commodities, and then wonder why they don't like it.' The ice melted as Adam turned to Holly and drew her against him. 'I'm going to marry Holly. I made up my mind to that the first moment I saw her.' He smiled slowly at Holly, who was staring at him, the world singing in her ears. 'I told you once, Holly, that I knew what I wanted but someone else had got there first. You thought I meant Sleadale, didn't you? And I did, a little. But it was you I wanted most. If I'd thought you loved Crawley and that he could have made you happy, I'd have accepted that. But it became more and more clear to me that it just wasn't like that. And I knew, after that last day at the cottage, that he must have some very powerful hold over you.'

'Last day at the cottage?' Morris broke in. 'What does that mean? Holly, what have you——'

'It had to be your parents,' Adam went on, ignoring the interruption. 'I knew where they lived—you told me enough to enable me to find them. I went to see them, introduced myself and told them enough of what I knew to help them to trust me. And between us, we worked out what must be going on.'

'I'd begun to hear a few things about Morris myself,' Jack contributed. 'Things I wasn't at all happy about—like what was happening to some of the other people he employed. Plans he was making for the farm and the estate. And when Adam came to see us——'

'It all fell into place,' Jean finished.

Holly looked from one face to another. They had worked it all out, between them. Between them, they had discussed the whole thing, come to a conclusion that must have been very close to the truth, and decided to face Morris with it.

But what did they intend to do then? And why come here—and ask Morris to meet them?

'I don't understand——' she began, and once again Morris broke in, his voice rigid with barely suppressed fury.

'Neither do I, Holly. And I'm glad to see that you're just as baffled as I am by this whole ridiculous charade.' He glanced at Holly's father. 'I'm afraid you've been brought here on a fool's errand, Jack, and I must say I'm disappointed to see you falling for it. I thought, when I put you in charge of the estate and virtually gave you your farm, that you could be trusted. After today—well, I may have to reconsider that judgement. And Jean—I took you for a sensible woman.' He shook his head sadly. 'I don't know what it is that Wilde has, but I could certainly put it to good use in a sales force. Unfortunately, like a great many salesmen, you'll find he sings a different tune when it comes to delivery. Now, Holly——' he took a step forward and Holly shrank back against Adam's arm '—I think it's time we called a halt to this farce and went back to London. I've wasted enough time here already.'

'Not so fast,' Adam said curtly. 'I haven't said all I want to say yet—in fact, I haven't even started. You and I have a good deal of business to settle, Crawley, and you're not leaving here until we've done so.'

'Oh, no?' Morris's eyes bulged dangerously. 'And just what business might there be between us? I'm not aware of any. And whatever it is, I fail to see how it can concern Holly and her parents.'

'It's of vital concern to them.' Adam's composed voice was in direct contrast with Morris's blustering tones. 'Let's start with Jack, shall we? Don't you have something you'd like to tell Crawley, Jack?'

'I do indeed.' Holly glanced at her father in amazement as he came to stand beside her. 'You stepped into my life at a very crucial time, Morris, and I'm not ungrateful for what you did. Because of you I was able to keep my head above water and continue to earn a living. It's only lately that I began to realise just what I'd got myself into.'

'Now, look here——' Morris cast a quick, nervous glance at Holly as he stepped forward again, but Jack clearly had no intention of stopping.

'I don't like sharp practice, Morris,' he said grimly. 'I don't like animals being treated like a commodity. And I don't like the way some of the men on the estate were being treated. It's no joke losing your job in the country, where they're even fewer and farther between than in towns, as I know to my own cost. And, most of all, I don't like being your fall guy. Those men are my neighbours,

my friends. Being the man to give them the push for no
good reason leaves a sour taste in my mouth.'

'And that's why you're a failure, Jack.' Morris's eyes
hardened as he gave up any pretence of being the kindly
benefactor. 'It's why you failed at running your own
farm, and it's why you're failing at running mine.
Farming's a business, Jack. Animals *are* a commodity.
There's no room for sentiment, either for man or beast. If
you disliked it so much, I'm surprised you didn't hand in
your notice.'

'I would have,' Jack said quietly, 'if it hadn't been for
Holly.'

There was a tiny silence. Holly's mind whirled as she
took in the implications of her father's statement.

'You mean you only stayed with Morris because of
me?' she gasped at length. 'But—but *I*—I only went on
with the engagement because——'

'Because Morris was holding my job over your head. I
know. That's what we worked out between
ourselves—your mother and Adam and I.' Jack Douglas
squeezed his daughter's arm. 'I reckon we've got quite a
lot to thank your Adam for.'

'*My* Adam? But——' Holly got no further. Morris had
come another step closer and was altogether too close for
comfort, his face suffused with rage.

'Oh, yes,' he said nastily, 'you've got a great deal to
thank him for. The loss of your job, for one thing. You
surely don't imagine I'll continue to employ you after
this.'

'I wouldn't want you to,' Jack said calmly. 'I was about
to hand in my resignation, anyway. I've got another job,
you see.'

'Another job?' Holly stared at him in delight. 'But
where? How?'

'On a farm in the Yorkshire Dales. I'll be managing it,

but I'm to be given an entirely free hand. There's a very pleasant farmhouse—and even a cottage for when I retire.' Jack grinned at Holly's stunned expression. 'It looks as if your mother and I are set up for life. And this time, we've got a landlord who I think we can trust.'

'Well, I hope you can,' Adam said solemnly. 'If not, I think my wife will have a good deal to say on the matter.'

'Your——? But I——' Holly's eyes went from one to another of the grinning faces. And then dawn broke. She stared at the gleaming blue eyes, the lean face that twitched with laughter. 'Adam, it's *your* farm?'

'That's right,' he admitted. 'It seemed a good investment. And, since I don't want to live there myself, and knew there was a good farm manager looking for a job——'

'We came up to see it two days ago,' Jean said, her face wreathed in smiles. 'It's absolutely lovely, Holly—a beautiful house and good farming. A new start for us both, and not too far away from you, either.'

'And that's just where you *have* made a mistake,' Morris broke in, his voice now little more than a snarl. 'Because Sleadale isn't Holly's, even if it *is* her name on the deeds. At least, I take it that your precious integrity will work the other way, Holly? I imagine you'll give it back to me, since it was intended as a wedding present, and I assume that you've decided not to marry me although you've not yet had the common decency to inform me of your change of plan.'

Pompous to the last! Holly thought with an inward smile. She looked at him and felt the stirring of a faint pity. Poor Morris, completely nonplussed by the morning's events—well, she could hardly blame him for that, she'd barely begun to take them in herself yet. But one thing was very clear to them both, and she slipped off her ring and held it out to him.

'Yes, Morris, you're right. I'm sorry, but I can't marry you. And you can't be surprised—you've known for a long time that I was only marrying you because of Mum and Dad. If I'd known they wanted out—well——' She glanced at the three faces watching her. 'I agree, we've got a lot to thank Adam for. And of course I won't keep Sleadale—though I'd do almost anything to save it from what you intend to do to it.'

'Oh, you needn't worry about that.' Morris took the ring with an ill grace, thrusting it into his pocket. 'I've given up that idea. It was a bad one right from the start—led to nothing but trouble. No, I'm selling the place—in fact, it's sold, and only wants your signature for the transaction to be completed. And I'll be damned glad to get the place off my back!' He glanced around the empty room with its beamed ceiling and solid stone walls. 'Talk about the peace and quiet of the countryside! This place is *dead*—from the floorboards up. Anyone who wants to live here needs treatment, if you ask me. And hiding the whole dreary valley under conifers is just about the best thing that could happen—but that's only my opinion, of course, and I'm well aware of how much that counts in *these* circles.' He stalked bad-temperedly towards the door and then turned back. 'I'll expect you to be out of that farm by the end of the month, Jack,' he said hectoringly. 'And then, I hope to God I never set eyes on either you—any of you—or the Lake District again!'

The four of them stood quite still, listening as his footsteps crunched out into the yard. They heard the Jaguar start up and begin its roaring progress down the track. This time, it seemed, Morris had stopped caring about what the ruts and pot-holes might do to his vehicle; he was driving it as if he were on an empty motorway.

'Well,' Adam said at last, dusting his hands together, 'that would seem to be that.'

Holly's brow creased. 'But I still don't understand—'

'Adam will explain everything,' her mother said briskly, stepping forward. 'Take her up that path for a walk, Adam—you must have a lot to sort out between you. And Jack and I will get a fire going here and make some coffee. Jack, go and get those folding chairs from the boot, will you, and find some kindling?'

She ushered Holly and Adam out of the door, and almost shooed them up the track beside the beck. Holly, still dazed, allowed herself to be led away, her hand warmly and safely clasped in his. But when they had climbed a short distance and were safely above the house, looking down at the smoke that was already spiralling from the chimney, she stopped.

'Please,' she said, looking up at him with appeal in her wide grey eyes, 'tell me what all this is about. It's all happened too fast. Why did you buy a farm in the Dales? And how did you come to——'

Adam drew her beneath the shelter of a rowan tree and brought her into the circle of his arms.

'I've been longing for this moment,' he said quietly, and laid his mouth on hers. 'Do we have to talk?'

'Oh, Adam,' she murmured weakly, feeling the love flood into her. 'Adam, I thought I was never going to see you again.'

'You did your best to make sure of it,' he reminded her gravely, and she looked down at her feet. 'Another man might have taken that last day as the end. But I couldn't do it, Holly. I *knew* there was too much between us for it to end there. Like I said, you're *my* woman—and I couldn't let you go.'

'So you went to see my parents?'

'It had to be them. I couldn't think of any other hold Crawley could have over you—and there had to be something. You obviously didn't love him, and you're not the girl to marry a man just for luxury. Besides, I knew how you felt about Sleadale. I could see he was stringing you along over that.'

'I realised that, too,' Holly admitted. 'But by then it was too late . . .'

'Once Jack and I got together, it was all plain sailing. He was virtually ready to walk out, anyway—only holding on because of you. And when I told him I was thinking of buying the place in the Dales and needed a manager——'

'That's what I don't understand,' Holly interrupted. 'All right, I can see why you bought the farm in the Dales, knowing that you couldn't have Sleadale—but why do you need a manager? Aren't you going to farm it yourself?'

Adam looked down at her, an odd expression in his eyes. 'How could I?' he said. 'I'll be too busy with my own farm.'

'Your own? But—you mean you've bought *two?*'

'I told you, I came back from Canada with a lot of money. More than enough for two farms. If you want luxury, Holly, you can still have it—with me.'

Holly stared at him. His words about luxury passed her by. She was more interested in the fact that he appeared to have bought two farms.

'But—where's your other farm, then?' she asked, and then remembered a remark her mother had made. 'Is that in the Dales, too?'

'No.' He gazed at her, his face deliberately straight, and then burst out laughing. 'Oh, poor Holly! It's not fair, is it? And I'm not going to keep you guessing any longer. My darling——' he took her hands and drew them around his waist, holding her close against him '—you're standing on the other farm I've bought. It's all come right—we're going to live at Sleadale, just as we should. *This* is going to be our home, Holly—ours and our family's.' He waited for a moment, smiling at her stunned expression. 'Well? Are you pleased?'

'P-pleased?' she stuttered. 'You've bought *Sleadale?*

But—but Morris never said——'

'Morris doesn't know,' Adam said with satisfaction. 'He'd never have sold it to me, out of mere spite. I bought it through an intermediary. Made him, as they say, an offer he couldn't refuse.' He looked down at her with mock severity. 'You cost me quite a lot of money the day you dropped your handbag on my foot,' he told her. 'But it was worth it. Because if you hadn't—well, Crawley might have given up the idea of going into forestry and taken you straight back to London. And we might never have met again.'

Holly turned her head to look around her. She let her eyes move slowly over the swooping fells, dotted with sheep; the noisy, chattering beck throwing its glittering spray into the frosty air; the house, standing below in its sheltered bowl, as solid as the rocks that grew from the rugged hills.

'No,' she said softly. 'It wouldn't have happened like that. We were meant to meet, Adam. We were meant to live here together. It's our destiny.'

'Our own little bit of heaven,' he agreed, his lips in her hair. 'You ought to be called Eve. It's a little paradise.'

'Another Eden,' Holly said.

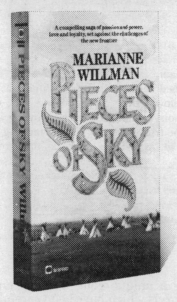

ACCEPT 4
MILLS & BOON
ROMANCES
ABSOLUTELY FREE

...after all, what better way to continue your enjoyment of the finest stories from the world's foremost romantic authors? This is a very special introductory offer designed for regular readers. Once you've read your four **free** books you can take out a subscription (although there's no obligation at all). Subscribers enjoy many special benefits and all these are described overleaf. ►►►

As a regular subscriber you'll enjoy

★ **SIX OF OUR NEWEST ROMANCES** – every month reserved at the printers and delivered direct to your door by Mills & Boon.

★ **NO COMMITMENT** – you are under no obligation and may cancel your subscription at any time.

★ **FREE POSTAGE AND PACKING** – unlike many other book clubs we pay all the extras.

★ **FREE REGULAR NEWSLETTER** – packed with exciting competitions, horoscopes, recipes and handicrafts... plus information on top Mills & Boon authors.

★ **SPECIAL OFFERS** – specially selected books and offers, exclusively for Mills & Boon subscribers.

★ **HELPFUL, FRIENDLY SERVICE** – from the ladies at Mills & Boon. You can call us any time on 01- 684 2141.

With personal service like this, and wonderful stories like the one you've just read, is it really any wonder that Mills & Boon is the most popular publisher of romantic fiction in the world?

This attractive white canvas tote bag, emblazoned with the Mills & Boon rose, is yours absolutely **FREE!**

Just fill in the coupon today and post to:
MILLS & BOON READER SERVICE, FREEPOST, PO BOX 236, CROYDON, SURREY CR9 9EL.

FREE BOOKS CERTIFICATE

SEND NO MONEY NOW – TAKE NO RISKS

EP32R